A
NASTIA
GAME

Best Wishes

RWKay

A
NASTIA
GAME

R.W.KAY

Matador
9 Priory Business Park,
Wistow Road, Kibworth Beauchamp,
Leicestershire. LE8 0RX
Tel: (+44) 116 279 2299
Fax: (+44) 116 279 2277
Email: books@troubador.co.uk
Web: www.troubador.co.uk/matador

ISBN 978 1783060 764

British Library Cataloguing in Publication Data.
A catalogue record for this book is available from the British Library.

Typeset in 12pt Minion Pro by Troubador Publishing Ltd, Leicester, UK
Printed and bound in the UK by TJ International, Padstow, Cornwall

Matador is an imprint of Troubador Publishing Ltd

The book is dedicated to the countless tens of thousands of innocent Iraqi women, men and children who died as a result of the illegal invasion of their country by the American and British troops in 2003.

Author's Acknowledgement

My thanks to the following for their help with my early drafts: Jean Barlow, Alan Powell, Ray Keene, Angela Salt and, especially, Paul Watson.

Author's Note – 'The Iraq Trilogy'

A Nastia Game is the first book in a trilogy of stories. The genesis of the first novel is based on the author's personal experiences when he was posted to the RAF Staff College in Bracknell in 1974 to be the College's first computer systems analyst. There, he and a colleague designed and built a computer war game to be used to help train the students attending the one-year long *Advanced Staff Course* in the art of air warfare. Of the seventy-two students on the course, one third were always from overseas. The software was subsequently sold to the Iraq Air Force by the Ministry of Defence with International Computers Limited acting as agents. The simulations in the game were modified and enhanced by ICL so that the game could be used to test plans for the invasion of Iran, rather than train officers.

In the second book, *Bin Laden's Nemesis,* the main character is Juan Quayle. He is based on a gifted linguist the author met when visiting St Bees School in Cumbria. The plot centres around a rumour picked up when the author was serving at MoD; namely, the IRA were reducing their stock of weapons before having to decommission them as part of the Northern Ireland Peace Process by selling them to a fledgling terrorist organisation called Al-Qaeda.

In the final novel, *Iraq's Retribution,* the heroes from *A Nastia Game* and *Bin Laden's Nemesis* meet up for an apocalyptic conclusion.

The common thread of all three stories is based around the *so-called missing weapons of mass destruction* made famous by Tony Blair and George W Bush who claimed they posed a threat to the West. The three novels have been written so they can be read independently; this, however, necessitates some duplication by way of explanation from time to time in the second and third books.

The real names of politicians and some other characters have been used to add credibility and believability to the stories. Please remember, however, these three books are works of fiction.

R W Kay
Cheshire
March 2013

PROLOGUE

'Didn't you know? He's dead. The IRA shot him. His body was never found.'

The small group of officers were visibly shocked. Wing Commander Tony Horner, an operations officer in the Ministry of Defence, had made the comment that caused the reaction. An RAF navigator and the senior officer present in the bar, he had formerly commanded the Operations Wing at RAF Kinloss in northern Scotland – in charge of the tactical operations of the three Nimrod squadrons based there. An intelligent and thoughtful man, he had been Chairman of the RAF Chess Association for several years.

The first to react was Squadron Leader Phil Watson, a senior administrative officer based at RAF Leuchars, an air defence station near St Andrews.

'But Jim Douglas was just another education officer. How on earth did he get himself involved with the IRA?'

The annual Combined Services Chess Championships were being held at HMS Collingwood, a Royal Navy shore-based training establishment near Fareham in Hampshire. Some of the commissioned officers who were competing had gathered in the bar after dinner to play skittle chess and have a chinwag over a beer. The topic of absent missing friends had arisen. The name of a former champion, Squadron Leader James Douglas, had been mentioned when Tony Horner dropped the bombshell.

Everyone was eyeing Tony for an explanation to Phil's question.

He thought for a few moments, before replying. 'I don't know the full story because much of it was kept under wraps. I do know that James was something of an oddball. He certainly wasn't an ordinary run-of-the-mill education officer. He had become a computer specialist after attending a pre-employment course in software design at, I think, Glasgow University in the early seventies. As such, he was only one of a handful of serving officers at that time with a higher degree in computer science. After several years in the computer department at the RAF College at Cranwell he became one of our top men in digitised aircraft simulators. When I was OC Ops Wing at RAF Kinloss in 1978, he came up to see our Nimrod simulator with a small party. One of them was from the Defence Operational Analysis Establishment at West Byfleet and another from International Computers Limited. With them were two officers from the Iraqi Air Force who, surprisingly, had been given total security clearance. The Iraqis were especially interested in the role Nimrods could play in anti-shipping operations. One was a major, a bit of a sourpuss, but the Iraqi lieutenant was an exceptionally attractive woman who reminded me of Queen Soraya. Do you remember her, the former Queen of Persia?'

He paused, but only Phil nodded positively, the others were probably too young to remember the Shah of Persia's former wife.

Tony continued. 'That night in the bar the lads were round her like the proverbial bees around a honey pot. James told me that after three years at Cranwell he had been posted to the RAF Staff College at Bracknell where he had developed a computerised war game. He had been detached to work with ICL to improve it further and was researching moving map displays with them. The Iraqi Air Force was buying the whole package with MoD's consent and he was looking forward to going to Baghdad with the ICL team to install the game at their Staff College. Apparently, the Army boffins at West Byfleet and Fort Halstead were developing a moving map display on a handheld computer. Army patrols would then be able to communicate via an encrypted communications link with their Operational HQ. It would show them exactly where they were, especially useful in Northern Ireland where the border can be pretty obscure. As far as I know, James returned from Iraq and was seconded to the Royal Signals, who had begun undertaking trials with the kit. In late 1978 he was involved in trials near Castleblayney on the Irish border when the IRA ambushed him together with a Royal Signals major. The IRA, or to be more correct the IIRA, a splinter group calling itself the Independent IRA, claimed James and the major had invaded Eire. After an exchange of gunfire they were killed and their bodies buried in a bog.'

'I remember that incident.' It was Alan Craine, a captain in the Royal Logistics Corps, who chipped in. 'I was on my first tour, as a second lieutenant, based in County Tyrone. It was October. Believe it or not, Project Ptolemy, the name of the moving map comms link, is only just coming into service. The major with Squadron Leader Douglas that day was Bill Norvic. Despite what the Independent IRA claimed, there couldn't have been much of a gun battle as, except for their personal sidearm, neither was armed. There are many bogs on the border and dozens of people are believed to have disappeared the same way.'

'That would explain why I didn't know,' remarked Phil solemnly. 'In October 1978, I was based in Germany.'

There was a moment of silence before Phil continued. 'I can't get over the fact that Jim is dead. I knew him quite well in the early seventies. He was a good egg who always came to the championships with his squash racket and golf clubs. We had some good games of squash, invariably followed by a few beers and a visit to the nearest curry house. I can remember him once telling me that he had been selected to do a post-graduate degree in computer systems design at Strathclyde University. Only two or three officers a year are sent on such courses. So, he was chuffed with himself. His posting to the Staff College at Bracknell came with promotion to Acting Squadron Leader. He was a good chess player and I will always remember one year he played an unusual variation of the Spanish Opening against me. It virtually guarantees Black a draw; unless White knows the refutation. I've used it myself several times since, and whenever White has tried to find a refutation at the board, I've won. I might get the chance to try it out later this week.'

CHAPTER 1

July 1974

'Welcome to Bracknell Staff College.'

'Thank you, sir,' replied Squadron Leader James Douglas, newly promoted and posted from the Department of Engineering at the RAF College Cranwell to the more prestigious RAF Staff College.

'You've come here on the recommendation of your former commandant. He tells us you've built up quite a reputation teaching the capabilities and possibilities of computers in aircraft systems to senior officers at Cranwell. As a specialist in simulation techniques, he tells us you're the best man for the job.'

James smiled, but said nothing. He felt uncomfortable with the praise being heaped upon him by his new boss, Group Captain Brian Ford. He had been at the College for less than an hour, yet already James had formed the impression that Bracknell considered itself one step up from Cranwell. It was much smaller and had a more intimate feeling. There were fewer than thirty staff, all senior in rank to himself. He felt like a fish out of water after having been one of many hundreds of junior officers at Cranwell, where one end of the campus was over a mile from the other.

Group Captain Ford looked at his new member of staff and saw a thirty-three year old in his newly re-ranked uniform, who was both nervous and tense. However, first impressions were good. He was smartly presented, athletically built, a fraction less than six feet tall. He had light brown hair, blue eyes that kept good contact when he spoke in a clear voice with a hint of an unusual regional accent. Ford tried to put him at ease.

'Where are you from originally?' he asked.

'The Isle of Man, sir,' James replied.

His boss looked puzzled. 'Is Douglas a Manx name, then?'

'No, it is Scottish, but I was born in Douglas and went to school there.'

'So, you're Douglas from Douglas.' The Group Captain chuckled, and James smiled at the feeble joke that he'd heard so often. 'I've never been to the Isle of Man, although I've seen it when walking in the Lake District. Is there such a thing as a Manx accent?'

'There is, but I have mostly lost mine over the years, having lived in Nottingham and Leicester while at University. Then I worked for a while in Blackpool before joining the RAF. Since then I have had three years at RAF Cosford teaching electronics, a year in Glasgow doing a postgraduate software engineering course and three years at Cranwell.'

Brian could see something of himself in his fit-looking member of staff and asked, 'How do you keep fit?'

'I play as much golf as I can, which hasn't been much lately. I play squash at station level. You probably know I was RAF Chess Champion in 1969 and 1972.'

'Yes, I had heard.' Then returning to work topics, James' director continued. 'Do you know what the job here entails?'

'Not really, sir. I was given an inkling before I left Cranwell, but would be grateful if you could explain where I am to fit in.'

'We want you to teach our year-long Advanced Staff Course, the ASC, the capabilities of computers, of course, but your main task will be to introduce the use of computers into the exercises we play here,' continued the suave-looking Group Captain.

James looked blank.

'The ASC has many lectures from external specialists, at all levels, on various subjects. The Minister of Defence himself, for example, gives a lecture on the Government's Defence Policy. The First Sea Lord, the Chief of the General Staff, the Head of the Confederation of British Industry, Trade Union Leaders and many other prestigious people come to give lectures. The course also goes away on visits. They have a week in Germany visiting the British Army of the Rhine and a week with the Navy at Portsmouth as well as travelling to see RAF operational and training units. We try to teach them social niceties by taking them to see the Derby at Epsom and visit Ascot during Royal Week. These students are our future station commanders and they will have to learn to mix with local dignitaries and politicians. However, the main thread throughout the course is the use of air power. The culmination of their year comes in the final term with two week-long exercises that are then played out as a war game lasting three weeks. The first is an air defence exercise where they have to plan the defence of a mythical country, Damghut, against the threat of an invasion. The second is the opposite: planning an attack on the enemy country, Nastia. Finally, the climax of their year here, they play a war game between the two countries. Your prime task will be to automate the three exercises as much as possible. Currently, students have to do all their sums with handheld calculators and the number of variations they can try when calculating weapon probabilities is limited. It is also easy to make mistakes.' He paused.

James was thinking, *they don't want much from me.*

As if reading James' mind, the Group Captain continued. 'To be honest, James, you are something of an oddball as far as the staff are concerned. We were not too sure how you should operate, as none of us has anything approaching your computer knowledge and expertise. I will be your line manager, but I have asked Wing Commander Tony Woods to be your point of contact on a daily basis. Any problems you may have on the way things are done, ask him. He was responsible for getting your post established and acquiring the hardware terminals that are linked to a time-sharing computer in Slough. In the longer term, we have money in estimates to have our own computer installed at the College. I believe Tony has already written some programs to help students plan mission sorties and I will introduce you to him at morning coffee break.'

***

'My boss thinks I'm an oddball,' laughed James to his wife, Emma, that evening. 'Wing Commander Tony Woods seems to be the only one who understands why the College needs a computer. He's considered to be one of the bright sparks on the staff. He's a Vulcan pilot by background and was made the youngest flight commander in the V-force at RAF Waddington about five years ago. He's younger than us, but seems a nice chap. Everyone I met was very friendly; although how my job will pan out, I don't know.'

'I wouldn't worry, if I were you,' assured his wife. 'Things will settle quickly once you get your feet under the table and you have shown them what you can do.'

Emma, James and their son, Stuart, had moved into their married quarter on the base four days previously. Emma had already made contact with several of her relatives living in the Guildford area and appeared to be rapidly settling into life at Bracknell.

The family move from Cranwell was their third move in six years of marriage. Emma, having been brought up in an RAF family, was used to regular upheavals. The Bracknell College and married quarters were situated in a beautiful one hundred acre park that was surrounded by a secure perimeter fence, allowing the officers' children plenty of freedom to play in safety. It was ideal for Stuart, aged three and a half. The next-door neighbours had three daughters, their youngest being the same age as Stuart. They could play safely in the woods at the bottom of the road and would become the best of pals.

The College was less than a mile from the centre of Bracknell and was convenient for all the usual needs of everyday life. At Cranwell the nearest supermarket had been many miles away and, as Emma couldn't drive, James had had to drive for their weekly shop. Now, however, Sainsbury's was only a fifteen-minute walk. Stuart's primary school, which he would be starting in September, was about a mile away. Emma had plans to return to work as a nurse when Stuart started school. The nearest hospital at Ascot was not far.

Emma had been a nurse in the Princess Mary's RAF Nursing Service when James had met her at a St Valentine's dance in the Officers' Mess at RAF Cosford in 1968. A few weeks later they had become engaged on his birthday, April Fools' Day. A further few weeks went by and they were married on FA Cup Final Day, 18th May; West Brom beating Everton by a single goal. By any standards it had been a whirlwind romance. Both were twenty-seven years old and knew their own minds. They saw in each other what they both wanted out of a lifelong partner. What Emma saw in James he wasn't sure, but in her he saw a caring, warm person with a good sense of humour. She was blonde, blue-eyed and had a face that was not classically beautiful, but different, interesting and full of life. He never tired of looking at her.

Life at Bracknell looked as if it would be good domestically; work-wise, James was unsure. He could see the mountain of work ahead of him and suspected that even Tony Woods underestimated the time it would take to successfully automate the exercises.

At Cranwell, James had been one of eight flight lieutenants in Computer Squadron working within the Department of Engineering. All his colleagues had various higher degrees in computer science and advice had been freely available whenever a software problem arose. Now, however, he had been promoted to squadron leader and found himself alone as the Staff College's Systems Analyst. He remembered his former wing commander's words, *'In the land of the blind, the one-eyed man is king.'* It had been a bizarre thing to say to his departing member of staff, particularly as he had been largely responsible for selecting James for his promotion and posting to Bracknell.

As the first week at Bracknell progressed, James could see how Tony Woods had been made, at thirty-one, the youngest wing commander in the Royal Air Force. Tall, slim, athletic, handsome and articulate, he had recently completed an Open University degree in mathematics. He had an attractive wife and three young children. However, James suspected that underneath his smooth makeup lay a rebellious streak. His students worshipped him; some of the older staff saw him as too radical. However, it had been his lead that had persuaded the Staff College to get computer terminals. He seemed to be the only member of the senior staff happy to get *hands on*.

James realised his teaching load would present few problems as he could easily adapt one of Cranwell's courses to meet the slightly different aims at Bracknell. Each ASC ran for a full calendar year. The students were squadron leaders, mostly pilots and navigators, who were being promoted to the rank of wing commander at the end of the course. The students had been chosen as having the potential to reach the highest ranks in the Service. Each course had seventy-two students, of whom twenty-four were always from overseas – mostly from either NATO countries or the Commonwealth. The ASC in residence, No 64, was halfway through the year and would not receive his computer training. No 65 Course, due to start in January 1975, would be the first to be taught by James.

Computerising the air power exercises would be his biggest challenge. He began reading the exercises' scenarios. The region of the world used for the exercises was mythical, but based in the Middle East. An unfriendly neighbour, Nastia, was threatening a friendly, oil-rich state, Damghut. The Damghutian's equipment was British and they had accepted the support of a small British presence. The Nastians used Soviet weapons and had much larger forces: 650,000 as opposed to a total Damghutian strength of 80,000. The students worked in syndicates of six and had to calculate probable outcomes of their plans as well as prepare operational orders and write ministers' briefing papers. Using the weapons performance data sheets, pages and pages of apparently meaningless figures, was complex, slow, tedious and prone to error.

The three exercises badly needed to be computerised and James could see why he had been appointed. However, he was certain that complete automation of all three exercises could not be achieved in time for No 65 Course in fifteen months' time. He persuaded Tony Woods to call a meeting with the two wing commanders responsible for the air defence and ground attack exercises. The outcome was an agreed target that was more realistic – the war game would not be ready for play until No 66 course in November 1976, almost two and a half years away.

James also discovered there was a third task that had been briefly mentioned at his arrival interview. He was to prepare the case to replace the time-share terminals with the College's own computer system. The ASC was organised into two groups, each headed by a group captain. Each group had six syndicates, each led by a wing commander in charge of six students – hence seventy-two students. Of the twenty-four from overseas, apart from the NATO states, India, Pakistan, Jordan, and Saudi Arabia regularly sent a student. Other countries were represented less frequently; these officers in general would fill embassy posts at the end of the course. The future computer system would require at least twelve on-line terminals, one for each syndicate.

***

War gaming had originated in Prussia in 1811 using model soldiers and artillery to represent forces that moved according to a set of rules. Decisions were made based on the throw of a dice. By 1824 war games were being used to train the German General Staff. The successful Prussian campaigns against the Austrians in 1866 and the French in 1870 proved gaming's usefulness.

By WW2, a new profession had developed called Operational Research. It applied mathematical and scientific techniques to the solution of military problems. The Japanese attacks on Pearl Harbour and their runaway victories in Southeast Asia, particularly the simultaneous strikes at the Philippines and Malaya, were all gamed at their *Total War Research Institute* well before the event. In March and April 1944, Operation Overlord was gamed at the Supreme Headquarters Allied Expeditionary Force in St Paul's School, London, on a huge map filling the school hall and resulted in the reinforcement of Field Marshal Montgomery's Twenty-First Army with General Bradley's Twelfth Army Group to help in the post-Ardennes offensive. Simulation was providing a means of identifying errors and improving plans without paying the penalties of the real world.

As part of his background research, James made contact with various operational research specialists in the Ministry of Defence. Surprisingly, there didn't seem to be one overall centre of expertise. Gaming, whilst everyone conceded was important for developing strategy and tactics, was managed piecemeal. The Army had two sites, one at the Royal Armament Research and Development Establishment, or RARDE, at Fort Halstead in Kent and the other at the Defence Operational Analysis Establishment, or DOAE, at West Byfleet in Surrey. Visits to both revealed small groups of intelligent scientific civil servants, sometimes aided by senior officers, simulating scenarios on different scales. However, they were purely solving Army problems; neither establishment was considering the possible influence of air power. At *HMS Dryad*, near Portsmouth, the Navy were simulating tactics for the fleet, but, once again, there seemed to be little interest in the contribution the RAF could make to any outcome.

***

James watched Nastia Game played manually by No 64 ASC during November and December of 1974. Three students were pitted against three from another syndicate for a game that lasted three weeks, despite being played late into the evening. Each game required two members of staff and six students to control it. No one disputed the lessons learned from playing the game were worthwhile, but automation was long overdue.

The idea that computer programs and data files could replace the six students in the control team was feasible, but designing and writing the software was not going to be straightforward. Fortunately, help was at hand. Part of Bracknell's contract with the terminal providers included software support. James' contact with the company, John Richards, was to become an enthusiastic ally who saw the challenge of developing a computerised war game as something out of the ordinary.

'Far more interesting than my usual customers with their payroll problems,' said John. He was able to persuade his manager to turn a blind eye to the disproportionate amount of time he was to spend at the Staff College over the next eighteen months. By early 1975, ideas for developing an automated Nastia Game were beginning to firm up.

The most difficult aspect of programming the air defence of Damghut proved to be the use of Combat Air Patrols, or CAPs. These are the defending aircraft that search for intruder aircraft. The Phantom aircraft worked in pairs; one would always be looking in the direction of the expected attack. As their radar profile was shaped like a cone, the enemy aircraft could pass through the area of detection in a few seconds. To prevent the computer becoming blocked with too many calculations, it was decided the software would update the position of the aircraft only every minute. Successful testing during the early summer proved the air defence exercise was ready for use by No 65 ASC in the autumn.

The ground attack exercise against Nastia was more difficult to program, largely because Nastia was geographically much bigger than Damghut and the targets more diverse. Damghut was a small Arabian state with a population of just one and a half million. Nastia, with nine million people to feed, disputed the oil rich border with Damghut; hence the reason for the potentially explosive situation. The object of the ground attack exercise was for the students to devise a retaliatory strike against the advancing Nastian forces to prevent them from occupying the oil fields. By August, it was clear this exercise would not be ready for play by No 65 ASC. Fortunately, the member of staff in charge of the exercise could see the scale of the problems and was not too upset with the slower than anticipated progress.

The design principle followed for the exercises was flexibility. If at some future date the geography or the weapon systems were to change, then incorporating the modifications would be straightforward. By now, the way in which the new war game would be played had been decided. Two games would take place simultaneously. In each game, three students, having previously designed a method of defending Damghut, would try out their solution against the Nastians, played by three other students who would use an initial standard plan. As the games progressed, subsequent moves and strategies would depend on their judgement. At the post-game wash-up, the Allies would have to explain how far they were able to execute their original plan and what forced them to change it. To do this, two members of staff would operate the computer terminal in the control room. A comparison with the second game being played would be made to see whose defending plan had worked best.

The critical success of the software depended on it being able to forecast events in chronological order. For example, a mission to attack a Nastian railway marshalling yard might consist of six Vulcans, each armed with ten 1,000 lb bombs. The students would submit a flight plan detailing factors such as take-off time, route, altitude and turning points. The computer would check the validity of the flight. If approved, the software would forecast, using random numbers, such factors as the number of aircraft that went unserviceable, the time when and position where the Vulcans would be seen by Nastian radars and the expected time on target. The programs would show the umpire what events were about to happen. He could then advance the game time in irregular periods, deciding what information to pass to the players. If nothing was due to occur in the next hour, the umpire would advance the game time. Informing the Nastians that one of their air defence radars had seen four or five large unidentified aircraft approaching would probably lead to the scrambling of interceptors. The simulation of the air interception of the Vulcans by the Nastian Migs would create further future events. The attack on the marshalling yards might result in their closure for hours or days. In this way a single game move could create dozens of events spread over a long timescale and a complex scenario would ensue. The most important lesson of war gaming, the so-called *fog of war*, would soon become apparent. Only the umpires could see the total picture.

The security of the software was paramount. Access passwords were required to play the game, but only the designers of the game could change the software and data files. John devised a unique system. Initially, a chess position was entered into the computer. An algorithm then interpreted the position to create random numbers that were used to encrypt the programs and files. Subsequently, to gain access and get a decrypted listing, the user had to answer a series of questions concerning the chess position.

'Did you know there are more positions on a chess board than there are atoms in the universe?' John had asked Douglas when he initially proposed the system.

'No, I didn't,' replied Douglas. 'It seems unbelievable.'

'It's true. It means hacking into the program by the students will be impossible.'

By Christmas of 1975, the ground attack exercise was finished. Unfortunately, the helpful and supportive Tony Woods had been posted to be Officer Commanding a Vulcan squadron at RAF Waddington. A jolly Welshman, Wing Commander Bryn Jones, who was full of enthusiasm for the project, replaced him.

CHAPTER 2

Apart from the usual NATO and Commonwealth students on No 66 ASC that began in January 1976, there were two Saudis, an Iraqi, an Iranian, an Israeli, a Chilean, a Brazilian and a Sudanese. All were married, typically in their early-thirties. They all lived in married quarters within the College campus. Each syndicate of six students contained two overseas officers; most were destined to fill embassy posts in London at the end of their course. The first highlight in the College's social calendar was the *International Night*. Overseas officers' wives would decorate a stall to display their countries' cultures and traditions. It was an excellent way of encouraging integration among the families and was always fully attended by both staff and students.

Emma and James were talking with the Danish student and his wife at their stall when James saw a familiar face accompanying the Commandant across the hall.

That's Captain Johnson.

He recognised at once the senior naval officer who had attended one of the computer courses he had taught at Cranwell. Briefly, he wondered whether he should cross the hall and introduce himself. Leaving Emma with the Danes, he hesitatingly walked over.

'Hello, sir. Do you remember me? James Douglas.'

'Yes, of course. The Commandant told me you were here. Congratulations on your promotion. The Air Marshal tells me they are keeping you busy building a computer war game. Any chance I could see it?'

'No problem. I could give you a demonstration tomorrow morning, if you like?' He paused, thinking if he should ask why the captain was there.

However, Captain Johnson continued. 'I'm a friend of your Commandant. My wife and I are staying at Air Marshal Williams' residence for a few days prior to my taking up a new appointment as Deputy Director of the Joint Military Intelligence Committee.'

After exchanging a few pleasantries James excused himself, having arranged to meet Commodore Johnson in the morning.

The evening continued with Emma and James circulating around the hall. Emma knew most of the overseas wives as she helped to run the crèche; nearly all the foreign students had children under school age. Consequently, James had spoken to most of the non-RAF students by the end of the evening. More importantly the overseas students had discovered who he was and what he did at the College.

James was in the office the following morning in plenty of time to prepare a demonstration of Nastia Game. Not all the features of the war game were complete, but James encouraged observers to plan their own Damghut missions and attack whatever targets they wished. He would then place Nastian Combat Air Patrols, typically Mig-21s, in positions to demonstrate air interception. The programs were sufficiently rigorous to withstand such tests and the results usually impressed everyone.

A fortnight previously he had given a demonstration of the software to the Reading Branch of the British Computer Society. Included in the audience were several academics from the University as well as research workers from some of the blue chip companies located along the M4 corridor. The Branch Chairman was sufficiently impressed to invite James to repeat the talk to the Central Branch of the BCS in London later in the year. It was, therefore, no surprise that Commodore Johnson was excited by what he saw.

'I like the way you can easily change the geography, the weapons and the targets. However, I'm intrigued about the security system.'

James explained how he was receiving help designing the game from

John Richards whose idea it had been to protect the programs and data files by using a chess key. As only John and James knew the chess position, a hacker could not break into the software.

'It's an excellent idea. I will have to look into this concept with my staff. No one could ever guess the correct position. How did you choose a position that you could both remember?'

'We chose a position from one of Bobby Fischer's games against Spassky at Reykjavik. The computer asks for the position of five pieces before allowing the user access to the software. For example, the computer might ask, *"What is on the square a8?"* and the user must give the answer.'

'How is the case going for the College to get its own system?'

'I expect ICL will win the contract with a 2900 computer. We are stipulating that software conversion costs must be part of the contract. With ICL's software division, Dataskil, located at Reading, we won't have far to go if things go wrong.'

'Why is the game set in the Middle East?'

'I don't think anyone knows how the scenario was originally chosen. Nastia is a large peninsula crudely stuck onto the south-east corner of Oman. It vaguely resembles Korea. The game brings the course to a successful finale and is the academic highlight of the year's study.'

'What strikes me is that with only minor modifications to the map, you could be gaming a war between countries that have students here at the moment. Obvious possibilities are Egypt against Israel, or Iraq against Iran. Don't be surprised if some of your students don't try to get a listing of the programs.'

'They can try, but they won't be able to get past the security system. One other thing you might be interested in?'

The Commodore nodded for him to continue.

'At present, we can only show the total picture of what is happening in the game by using a printed matrix of missions. However, with the right equipment we could have a map display. A graph plotter, using a pre-printed map, would allow us to plot the movement of Damghut and

Nastian forces over the terrain. The umpire could see at a glance what was going on. In a few years' time, VDUs will be available that should be able to show the movement of missions in real time, in other words – a moving map display. I have decided to use this idea as the basis of an application for a Defence Fellowship.'

Each year the MoD offers between six and eight fellowships to staff, both civilian and service, to undertake research on a relevant topic at a university of their choice. The award is considered extremely prestigious, and competition is fierce.

'I wish you well. Does the Commandant know?'

'Not yet. The application is still with my first reporting officer.'

'I'll put in a good word for you. His support will be critical.'

By March, Wing Commander Bryn Jones had persuaded six of the directing staff to play Nastia Game over a three-day period, giving sufficient time for the war to advance by six or seven days. Played just before the Easter holiday, it went better than either James or John could have expected. There were some software bugs. The biggest problem was response times. In demonstrations, such as that given to Commodore Johnson, the programs had validated a single flight plan in a few seconds. However, when playing the game for real, the teams were entering dozens of simultaneous missions. In consequence, the computer slowed down dramatically to the point of staff grumbling. Rewriting some of the disc software helped. Computer response times were reduced, but it took most of the summer to achieve.

***

James had his interview for his Defence Fellowship a week after the Easter break. The Chairman of the selection panel was the Government's Chief Scientific Officer. Other members included the Assistant Chief of the Defence Staff and an Undersecretary of State for Defence. For a boy from a small comprehensive school in the Isle of Man, it was a world away from being interviewed by such a high-powered committee. He didn't make a good account of himself. His choice of university for the year's study, Glasgow, was one obvious weakness that the committee pounced on. Other more suitable universities were surely available, they suggested. James' defence of his choice lacked conviction as he had chosen it for domestic reasons; he was on a slippery slope. Coming out from the interview, which had lasted for about forty minutes, he knew his chance had gone. It was no surprise when he received a letter a few days later that began with the well-hackneyed phrase: 'We regret to inform you…' A month later the four or five successful candidates were promulgated in Defence Council Instructions. One was to *Study the possible use of Air Balloons for Army Logistical Transport,* and the other three or four subjects seemed equally fatuous. Three of the fellowships had been won by *pongos* – officers from high-powered regiments, two with double-barrelled surnames. A seed of resentment, unknowingly perhaps, was sowed in the back of James' mind, *someday I'll show them.*

A few days after receiving the letter, Emma remarked, 'I think I'm pregnant again and we'll need a bigger car.' The good news cheered James up and helped him to get over his disappointment. A month later, Emma's suspicions were confirmed and their second child was due to be born in early December.

***

The Air Defence and Ground Attack exercises were played on the computer terminals in October 1976 without any hitches. The students found the programs easy to use and the staff agreed that more plans and ideas could be tested than previously.

As the weeks of playing Nastia Game on the computer approached, two syndicates were chosen. The other ten syndicates would have to play the game manually using charts and china-graph pencils. Needless to say, Bryn Jones chose his syndicate as one of the guinea pigs.

John Richards moved into the Officers' Mess for the first week of play so that he would be available around the clock in case a software problem arose. James told Emma not to expect him home until late evening as any problems would have to be resolved immediately. Both games went remarkably well. The computer response times were still disappointing, particularly in the early part of the game when both sides were mounting dozens of Combat Air Patrols. Millions of calculations were positioning the aircraft for every minute of their sorties.

In the two computerised games, the game time advanced much more rapidly than those being played manually by the other syndicates. At the end of the first week, the two computerised games were both in day four of the battle, but in the manual games some were still in the first day of fighting. At the end of the third week of gaming, the computer syndicates had almost played a month of fighting whereas some of the manual games were still in week one. Bryn's syndicate included an Iraqi officer, Major Azi Tumbrah, nicknamed 'Tumbler'. He came out of his way to express his thanks to James and John for the way the game had gone. James thought no more about his unusual gesture. He couldn't have known that Azi's enthusiasm was to dramatically change his life.

***

Emma began labour on 8th December and went to the delivery ward at Heatherwood Hospital in Ascot. She struggled for twenty-four hours. Her mother, Pat, had come from Ilford, where James' in-laws lived, to help look after Stuart. When nothing happened and Emma's contractions stopped, she was discharged and returned home. Pat reluctantly went back to Ilford. Two days later, Emma was back in hospital. Pat arrived again, this time declaring she wasn't going back 'until it's all over.' Jennifer Helen was born the next day, three days before her brother's sixth birthday. Stuart was not impressed when his sister arrived home with Emma to spoil his party.

***

By early 1977, as a result of the success of Nastia Game, the Systems Analyst had become an accepted member of the directing staff at Bracknell. Senior staff were beginning to accept that computers were the way forward. James was no longer seen as a boffin who didn't have a place in the College. The news that the College was going to get its own computer began to excite one or two of the younger members of staff. The presentations given by the computer companies vying for the contract were usually attended by the Commandant or his deputy. Other staff would attend to be seen as being interested. The activity created a buzz around the College with James in the thick of it.

By April 1977, ICL had won the contract to install the College's first dedicated computer. The resources they poured into the project were much greater than the other companies, possibly because they realised it was a prestigious site and hoped it could lead to similar contracts with other air forces. ICL's software division, Dataskil, agreed to convert all the College's software free of charge and were expressing interest in buying the copyright of the programs.

Interest was heightened in May when the Head of MoD's Defence Sales, a dapper undersecretary, Hugh Noel-Barker, came to the College. He explained that several Middle Eastern air forces wanted to buy the College's computer programs, particularly Nastia Game. As this would be the first time that software would be sold by the MoD, he asked, 'How does one assess its value?' None of his staff had any experience. 'Furthermore,' he added, 'the legal boys and the security wallahs will have to be involved.'

A meeting between the interested parties was held in early June. The College assessed the software production time as six man-years. This formed the basis for its valuation. ICL, acting as agents for the sale, accepted the charge without a quibble. However, the thorny question of the intellectual copyright was not resolved. ICL wanted to have the right to make future changes or enhancements to the programs without reference to the MoD. This was unacceptable to Rear Admiral Johnson, who had been promoted to become the Head of the Joint Military

Intelligence Committee. His representative at the meeting, Colonel Mike Mitchell, was adamant that the MoD must keep control of the software and any future enhancements to it.

Eventually the contract stipulated that the copyright of the software remained with the MoD and that ICL could only sell the programs to a third party after getting MoD's agreement. Furthermore, if the third party wished to enhance or change the programs then an MoD official would be appointed to work with the software team and vet the changes. The security chess system to protect unauthorised access would be rewritten by Dataskil. ICL agreed to install the ICL 2900 computer at the College during the August 1977 break.

***

A day or two after the meeting, the phone rang. It was James' desk officer, the officer responsible for his career interests including selecting his next tour. Squadron Leader Alison Humphries had been in touch with James before Easter about suitable future appointments and the best timescales for a move. Although he knew his nominal three year *tour-ex* point was July, he had tried to defer his move until nearer the end of the year to see the ICL system installed.

However, Alison sounded enthusiastic. 'The right job has come up for you due to someone taking early retirement,' she said. 'How do you fancy Officer Commanding Computer Squadron at RAF Locking?' The RAF's biggest computer training squadron at Locking was near Weston-super-Mare. A new airman trade, *Computer Maintenance Technician*, was being created. The RAF needed its own technicians to maintain the mushrooming number of aircraft simulators coming on-stream as well as the new air defence radar systems driven by digital computers. A real-time programming course was also due to start. It was a plum posting, but for James it wasn't what he wanted.

'You will be responsible for a staff of over thirty instructors in a purpose-built building,' she added.

'Couldn't I do something different for a change?' asked James.

'We can't afford to lose your expertise,' Alison retorted. Her tone told him there was no way he would get the tour of his choice. 'You will be boarded for RAF Locking next week.' He sighed, and knew there was no point in wasting breath on something that had been done and dusted.

CHAPTER 3

James had been at RAF Locking for seven months. With his family, he had settled in to their own bungalow in Kewstoke, a quiet village to the north of Weston-super-Mare. Emma had passed her driving test and become a district nurse. Her use of the family car gave James an excuse to resume his long-lost interest in motorcycling, inborn in most Manxmen. He had bought a Honda CX-500 for travelling the four miles to work. Emma's parents had retired from London and had bought a house in Kewstoke to see their grandchildren whenever they wished. Stuart started at the village school. Domestically everything was very comfortable. Emma was on the Parish Church Council. Bill, Emma's father, became the school's Lollipop Man and Pat was secretary of the village allotment association.

James found managing Computer Squadron at RAF Locking undemanding. His staff were first-class: the NCO instructors were experienced and had all volunteered for teaching duties, his five education officers had relevant higher degrees and his software manager had a PhD from Edinburgh University.

The station commander, Group Captain Mike Wallace, had known James briefly at Bracknell and had pulled strings at the RAF's Personnel Management Centre to have James posted to Locking to run the station's most prestigious squadron. The winter of 1977 was the first in fifteen years to have snow on the ground at Weston. By mid-February the weather had begun to improve and the early signs of spring were promising better days ahead, when one day the station commander's PA rang, asking James to come up to see the CO.

As James entered the inner office, Mike Wallace stood up from behind his large oak desk. In the corner of his eye he caught sight of an Army officer to his right. His face looked familiar, but James couldn't remember where he had seen him.

The CO spoke first. 'I gather you've met Brigadier Morrison before?'

Looking at the Brigadier's rugged face, it dawned on James where he had seen him. 'Weren't you on a computer course at Cranwell some years ago, sir?'

'Yes,' beamed the Brigadier. 'I was on the same course as Rear Admiral Johnson. I'm his number two on the Military Intelligence Committee. He asks to be remembered to you.'

Group Captain Wallace explained. 'The Brigadier has come to talk about Nastia Game.'

'Please, both of you, call me Ian.'

It was always a nice gesture when senior officers asked juniors to call them by their first names, but James noticed that even his boss had difficulty in using the informal form of address. They sat down and the PA brought in a tray of coffee with biscuits.

Brigadier Morrison described, largely for the Station Commander's benefit, how the reputation of Bracknell's computerised exercises had grown and several Middle Eastern countries were vying to buy the Bracknell set-up. ICL, acting as agents, still wanted the MoD to release the software copyright in order to tailor the programs to meet individual countries' parameters. James knew this background, but Group Captain Wallace had to clarify several points.

'The problem,' the Brigadier continued, 'is that the whole thing has become political. ICL realise that if they can get sales with the Gulf States, before the Americans and IBM get their feet under the table, then they will make a lot of money. Once ICL can show the Arabs their computers are reliable and up to speed, they think other governments over there will buy ICL. Their sales could mushroom and be worth many millions.'

'Yes, but I am not sure where we fit in,' queried the Station Commander.

The Brigadier resumed. 'I'm coming to that. In short, Rear Admiral Johnson has agreed for the first sale of the war game software to go ahead and wants James to become the MoD's project officer. He knows the design of the programs better than anyone else. Although ICL Dataskil has since converted them to run on ICL computers, James is the best-placed person to oversee the first sale to the Iraqi Military College in Baghdad. We, and by we, I mean the Military Intelligence Committee, are not prepared to release the software copyright. That has been made very clear to MoD Sales. We are happy for ICL to modify the programs to meet any individual countries' requirements, changing the scenario, the weapon performance parameters and so on, but, and it is a big but, they can only make the changes with our agreement. James will, as project officer, have a triple role: firstly, to help Dataskil with documenting changes; secondly, help with training the Iraqis; and thirdly, refer any problems to me or Admiral Johnson whenever in doubt.'

'What you're saying is you want James to be posted to your department,' Group Captain Wallace said.

'Not necessarily,' replied Ian. 'We think there are about four months work involved. We would like him to be detached to ICL Dataskil at Reading for the duration. Dataskil are putting in a team of three full-time programmers, some part-timers, plus their senior systems analyst who led the original software conversion. James would keep an eye on their work, ensuring we are kept in the picture. Although our Government is currently trying to be seen as neutral in the rift between Iraq and Iran over the Shatt al-Arab waterway affair, MI6 are not so sure that Iraq's de facto leader, Saddam Hussein, can be trusted in the longer term. He is openly hostile to the Kurds in the north of his country and seems to be almost as determined to ride roughshod over the Shia tribes in the south. Meanwhile, the Shah of Iran has his own problems with the Islamic fundamentalists. There are strong rumours that both countries are trying to develop nuclear, biological and chemical weapons. We believe they will be at war with each other within five years.'

'Surely, neither side has got nuclear weapons?' asked Mike.

'No, we think not. However, the French are helping the Iraqis build a nuclear reactor for so-called peaceful purposes. Iran – we're not so sure about. Biological and chemical weapons, of course, are relatively simple to produce.'

James had been sitting quietly listening to the conversation, thinking that he rather fancied the idea of working with Dataskil. He was already making up reasons to persuade his boss to allow him to travel each day to Reading on the train, rather than having to stay in a hotel. An HS125 left Weston each morning for Paddington at 0715 hours, stopping only at Yatton, Bristol Temple Meads, Bath Spa and Chippenham before Reading. The idea of travelling first class and having one of British Rail's breakfasts every morning was appealing.

'Suppose the Iraqis do want to incorporate NBC weapons into the game?' asked James. 'What am I expected to do?'

'Contact us for advice whenever you have a problem like that. As I understand, there will be two Iraqi Air Force officers working at Reading with the ICL team. One you may remember from Bracknell. He was on No 66 ASC – a Major Azi somebody, I believe?'

'Yes, I remember Azi well. His surname was Tumbrah, everyone called him Tumbler. His wife used to bring their two toddlers down to the crèche that my wife helped run. She was very pleasant. He was OK, but the sort of fellow who you could never be sure what he was thinking.'

'The other officer is, I gather, the intellectual. She has just completed a PhD at the University of Cambridge. I can't remember her name.'

'When do you want James to start?' asked the Station Commander.

'On 6th March, if that's alright with you.'

Group Captain Wallace looked at James and raised an eyebrow, as if asking the question. A nod from James was sufficient for Mike to agree.

✳✳✳

The daily journey proved to be most pleasant as senior officers were entitled to travel first class. The HS125 service was relatively new and, consequently, luxurious; British Rail's breakfast set up the day nicely. The walk from Reading railway station to Dataskil was less than 400 yards. Each day James felt a spring in his step as he looked forward to the stimulation of another software problem to be solved.

The Dataskil team was impressive. Their leader was a charismatic, red-haired Scot, Hamish Hamilton. The three programmers were in their mid-twenties; two of them, Don Henry and John Bryan, had worked with Hamish when converting the original Bracknell programs. Don and John had been normally vetted by the Government Security Services to work on the project. Hamish, because of his access to the chess security system, had been positively vetted, a much higher classification, giving him clearance to access top secret material. The third programmer, Ben Green, was new to ICL and had only been with the company for a few weeks. Hamish assured James that Ben had come to Dataskil with impeccable references from an American bank. His vetting clearance hadn't come through, but it was assumed to be a formality.

Hamish had drawn up a programme of tasks to be undertaken, the first of which was to redraw the map on which the game was to be played. The new map suggested Iraqi officers would plan war with Iran. The Iraqi embassy had sent ICL a wish list of the changes to be implemented ahead of the arrival of their two project officers. Changing the map would be straightforward. Much more challenging would be simulating the ground battle. In Nastia Game, Damghut was deemed to have lost the war if the Nastian tanks reached the oil fields in overwhelming numbers. The simulation of tank movements and battles had been crude. More sophistication was required to account for mountainous terrain and the positioning of artillery, previously ignored in the Bracknell game. Hamish gave the development of these programs to Ben. 'It'll give him a challenge, and we'll see if he is up to it,' he remarked.

Two other major improvements were discussed. Firstly, James explained his ideas for a moving map display that would considerably help the umpires to see the overall state of the war. A flatbed plotter using different coloured pens was required to show the position of the forces on a pre-printed map. The geographic features would be printed in faint background colours. Getting the plotter was easy and Don was tasked to begin software design. 'There are some new VDUs coming on to the market, which may be able to show the moving map in real time,' Hamish had said. 'But let's take it one step at a time.'

Secondly, James discussed improving the chess key. The current system protected both the data files and the source code. 'What about having two rings of protection?' James had suggested. 'One to allow access to the data files for changing weapon parameters and an inner ring to gain access to the software for program changes.'

Fortunately, Hamish had been a strong chess player, having played for Edinburgh University as a student. He agreed enthusiastically to the idea and John was given the job of its implementation.

On Monday, 13th March, the morning of the second week, the two Iraqi officers arrived, both wearing uniforms, and accompanied by ICL's Senior Project Manager, Jonathon Smith. Azi and James instantly recognised each other from their Bracknell days.

However, when James saw Azi's colleague, his heart missed a beat; butterflies filled his stomach and his pulse began racing. Standing a few steps behind Azi, Lieutenant Kathab al Jised became his sole focus. Even as he was making small talk to Azi, James' mind was elsewhere, *God, what a beautiful, attractive woman.*

After a few minutes, Azi said, 'Let me introduce you to Kathab.' He turned to her. 'This is James Douglas who wrote the software at Bracknell.' Then returning to James, he said, 'Kathab is an air force reserve officer and has just spent four years at Cambridge University.'

She held out her hand, giving James a reserved, shy smile. As he shook her hand, he shivered involuntarily. Something had run down his spine. He wondered if she had noticed his reaction. He felt he was falling into her dark, bottomless, olive-green eyes.

'I've heard a lot about you,' she said in perfect English. There was no trace of an accent. James remained lost for words. Transfixed, he continued smiling, totally spellbound, still falling into her fathomless eyes that were hypnotising him.

James had always been attracted to blonde Nordic types, like Emma: blue eyes and fair skin. His feminine preference had been founded when, like thousands of other lads of his generation, he fell for Marilyn Monroe. By total contrast, Kathab had jet-black, shoulder-length hair and smooth, swarthy skin. Her large, almond-shaped eyes, together with her high, broad cheekbones and wide lips, were magnetic. Five feet eight inches tall, slim, and with legs to her shoulders, she held herself upright, suggesting she may have been taught ballet. She continued smiling at James with a twinkle in her eyes that suggested mischievous excitement.

Having her around is going to be a distraction that will make concentrating on the software conversion difficult over the next three months. Perhaps it's just as well that I'm going home to my family every night.

Spellbound, he heard her say, 'At Cambridge my friends called me Kate.' She was probably amused that he had not uttered a word.

Still bewitched and, without thinking through the possible consequences of an off-the-cuff, jocular remark, James found himself replying. 'Ava would have been more appropriate.'

She looked puzzled and frowned. 'Pardon?'

'You know, Ava. As in Ava Gardner and *On The Beach.*'

The frown deepened suggesting that she had never seen the film of Neville Shute's masterpiece, nor heard of one of Hollywood's great all-time stars.

Perhaps her sense of humour is not like mine. He instantly regretted being too forward. *Mind you, she does look like Ava Gardner,* he thought, justifying the remark to himself.

As she moved along the line to be introduced to the other members of the ICL team, it was clear they were as entranced with Lieutenant Kathab al Jised as James.

The weeks went past swiftly at Dataskil. The July deadline was tight. Everyone pulled their weight.

Jonathon Smith, 'popping in to see how things were coming along', had explained to James that ICL's Middle East HQ was based in Riyadh, Saudi Arabia. From Riyadh other branches in the region, such as ICL Bahrain and ICL Jordan, were administered. A new branch, ICL Iraq, was being set up to handle future trade. The current manager of ICL Oman had been seconded to Baghdad until a suitable Iraqi could be appointed to manage the new branch. Iraqi systems analysts, programmers and computer operators were already being trained at the Middle East HQ. However, they wouldn't complete their training until September. For three months, there would be a transitional stage when Omanis would be manning the Iraqi College site.

Modifications to the game that Azi and Kathab required gave James the opportunity to get to know the two Iraqis well. An amiable relationship developed. Kate was the brains of the pair. She could see how something could be done, as opposed to simply saying what was to be done. She threw herself into the project more than Azi, who at times appeared laid back. However, he held the purse strings. His attitude often came across: *I'm paying your wages, so get on with it.*

Mostly, the changes were not controversial. The majority of the Iraqi weapons originated from the Soviet Bloc, whereas, ironically, the Iranian equipment, now the *Red* forces, was predominantly American. The greater detail and complications of the ground battle necessitated far more computer power than that required for the Bracknell game. The cost implications of this didn't seem to worry Azi, as he appeared to have an unlimited budget for the project. It didn't worry ICL either who could see the dollars rolling into the till.

At one point, James had asked why the new game was so obviously preparing for a war with Iran when, as a result of the Algiers Accord three years previously, the Shah was supposed to have a working relationship with Saddam. 'After all, didn't Saddam expel Ayatollah Khomeini from Iraq to please the Shah?' he had asked.

Both Azi and Kate suspected the days of the Shah were coming to an end. It would only be a matter of months before he would be overthrown by an Islamic revolution that would bring back Khomeini to run Iran. 'We must be prepared for the worst when that happens,' Azi had said with feeling.

The detailed design of the game's improvements was supervised by Hamish. He impressed James with his rapid understanding of the complexities of weapon simulation. Nevertheless, in order to help him comprehend the tactical use of weapons, visits to operational and research sites were organised, under the auspices of Brigadier Morrison. A visit to the nearby Defence Operational Analysis Establishment cleared up the finer points of tank warfare tactics, such as the defending side drawing in the enemy's approaching tanks to a concentrated killing zone. The Brigadier's patronage ensured there were no security problems with Azi and Kathab. Other visits included RAF Kinloss, involving an overnight stay in the Officers' Mess. It became clear that the Iraqis were planning to interrupt Iranian shipping supplies and were interested in the efficacy of air power on shipping.

Hamish's flowcharts were coded by the programmers and, thanks to the original software design being modular, the new enhancements could be tested individually. Only when totally satisfied with the new programs, always under the watchful eyes of Kathab, were they incorporated into the war game. Their inclusion was, however, somewhat complicated, as only James and Hamish knew the chess positions that could unlock the data files and the encrypted source code.

Progress meetings were held every Friday afternoon with Hamish as chairman. Mostly the topics discussed were a summary of the achievements of the past week and a list of targets for the following week. By the time the meeting was concluded, usually between 3 and 3.30 pm, it became standard practice *to stack* and for the team to go for a drink in the nearby *Kings Arms*. Both Azi and Kate enjoyed the social. Everyone got on well, although James instinctively felt that Azi and Kate appeared to distance themselves from Ben more than from Don or Jim. He couldn't fathom why. Despite being Muslims, neither Azi nor Kate had a problem having an alcoholic drink; both seemed fully westernised. It was an excellent way to finish the week and for the team to gel. Azi spent most weekends with friends in London and keeping his Air Attaché in the picture. Kate usually went to Cambridge where she still had a circle of friends.

All four of the Dataskil team were bachelors and had their own apartments in Reading. Amazingly, none seemed to show much romantic interest in Kate. James had remarked on this to Hamish on one occasion and been told, 'She seems more interested in you.' The remark surprised but excited him.

Occasionally, while Hamish and Azi talked shop and the three programmers huddled together drinking, it had been left to James to chat socially with Kate. Week by week, he began to know her better. Her parents and two younger sisters were from a town north of Baghdad called Samarra. They were Sunni Muslims, the smaller of the two Muslim groups in Iraq. Iraq was the only Arab-speaking country where the majority of the population were Shias. When James had asked her about the rules for drinking alcohol she had explained Sunnis were relatively liberal. In Samarra the two groups tolerated each other very well, but in other places, she added, there was considerable tension as the Shias were often segregated from the better jobs. In the Iraqi Army, for example, she explained that the officers tended to be Sunni whereas the NCOs and other ranks were Shia. Her father was some sort of local politician and a member of the Ba'ath party. He had considerable local influence. Kathab had been encouraged and given every opportunity to follow an academic career. 'Education is very important in Iraq. There are more PhDs per head of population than any other country in the world,' she said. Kate had obtained a BSc degree at Baghdad University in botany and had then continued with an MSc in microbiology. She had researched plant toxins for her PhD at Cambridge University.

'Why come to England?' he had asked one afternoon.

'I won a military scholarship when I joined the Iraqi Air Force as a reservist at university. I got a first in my bachelor's degree and decided to apply to Cambridge; after all, it is the best. When they offered me a place at Newnham College, I jumped at the chance. What is your academic background?' she asked.

'Not as distinguished as yours. I did my Bachelor or Science degree at Nottingham University in physics, and then did a PGCE at Leicester University.'

'Did you teach before joining the RAF?'

'Yes, for three years, but joining the Royal Air Force was the best thing I ever did. After my first RAF tour teaching electronics, I was sent to Strathclyde University to take a Diploma in Computer Design Techniques. I'm currently writing up an unrestricted version of Nastia Game for an external degree in Operational Research at Lancaster University.'

On Friday afternoon, 5ᵗʰ May, Kate had surprised James by calling him Captain Towers. She was grinning all over her face and laughed at his reaction when a puzzled James queried, 'Who?'

'Dwight Towers, you know, he was played by Gregory Peck.' She laughed more loudly.

'Touché,' laughed James, who knew he had set himself up for the joke. He continued. 'You have done some research about *On The Beach*?'

'Yes, but I am not sure I see myself as Moira Davidson.'

'True, she was something of an alcoholic, good-time girl, if I remember rightly. But you don't half look like Ava Gardner.'

'And you're not that dissimilar to Gregory Peck,' she joked. They both laughed loudly. The others, with Azi frowning as if he didn't approve of their fraternisation, turned around from their conversation to see the cause of the commotion.

Having thought about it that weekend and after discussing the idea with his wife, the following Friday he invited Kate home for a weekend to meet his family. 'If you would like a change some weekend, perhaps you might like to come home with me to Weston-super-Mare and meet my family,' he had said. 'We have a spare bedroom.'

'I would like that very much,' she had replied. They agreed the following Friday would be suitable. James travelled home later, wondering whether Emma would be jealous when she saw how attractive Kate was. He had fallen for her charms from the first moment he had set eyes on her and had, with difficulty, convinced himself nothing could, nor should, come of it. He would explain to Emma that evening what to expect.

Emma's reaction was typical of her. She trusted her husband totally and couldn't understand that there might be even a smidgeon of a chance of anything untoward behind James' invitation. Nevertheless, James lay in bed that night worrying. With Emma already fast asleep after a hard day with Jennifer, who was now teething badly, he began to think of Hamish's remarks. They had re-kindled his libido and he wondered whether inviting Kate to come for a weekend could be the first step on a slippery slope.

CHAPTER 4

Emma's warm, gregarious personality came to the fore that weekend as she looked forward to meeting Kate. She excitedly had begun planning their weekend: a shopping trip to Bristol or Bath on Saturday, followed by a meal at their favourite Spanish restaurant at the end of the Kewstoke tollroad. A visit to Cheddar Gorge or Wells Cathedral would take up Sunday. 'There won't be time for everything,' James had protested, but it fell on deaf ears.

Kate looked more attractive than ever when she boarded the HS125 on Friday evening. Wearing a smart, classic navy blue suit, with a Kashmiri collar trimmed in red and matching court shoes, James noticed the way other men were looking at her. They were as spellbound as him. As they walked to the station, she must have read his mind about the impracticality of her dress.

'I've brought a pair of walking shoes and outdoor clothes. You mentioned we might go to Wookey Hole, I'd like to see that.' During coffee breaks, James had mentioned some of the places where Emma was planning to take Kate. Excited at going somewhere different, Kate had been asking questions to help make the right choice of what to wear. Judging by the weight of her suitcase, which James was carrying, she had come fully prepared for all eventualities.

'The weather is looking good, so we should be able to get outside a fair bit,' he commented.

Emma met them from the train and took to Kate at once. James need not have worried. Their animated conversation suggested they had known each other all their lives. They chatted on the way back to Kewstoke with James sitting quietly in the back of the car, not getting a word in edgeways.

Stuart fell for Kate's charms too, as did Kate for Stuart. His yellow, curly hair, light blue eyes and fair skin were the antithesis of what she would have seen at home. They formed a bond instantly. While Emma prepared supper, she played with him and his train set, permanently set out in the boarded loft. Afterwards, when James was putting the children to bed, Kate helped Emma tidy up in the kitchen. The rest of the evening was spent chatting as Kate reminisced about her own family in Iraq.

Kate opted for Bath rather than Bristol the following day. The children stayed with their grandparents. Whilst Emma took Kate around the Roman baths and did some shopping afterwards, James went off to see Bath's last rugby match of the season against Saracens; the latter losing heavily to the strongest team in England. An evening meal at the small Spanish restaurant overlooking the Severn estuary, with the sun setting over the Welsh mountains, completed a highly successful day.

Wookey Hole proved to be as popular with Kate as it was for Stuart. A packed lunch taken in Cheddar Gorge, followed by a whistle stop trip to see the magnificent façade of Wells Cathedral and an ice cream on the promenade at Weston rounded off the afternoon. 'The weekend is over too soon,' Kate sighed, as they returned to Kewstoke.

'While I am preparing this evening's meal,' Emma suggested to James, 'why don't you take Kate for a walk up Sand Point? Stuart will come with you and you can show her the Bristol Channel. You should be able to see as far as the Severn Bridge. While you're away, I'll get Jennifer bathed and put to bed. The meal should be ready when you return.'

Five minutes later, the three of them were driving along the front to the end of Sand Bay. They parked the car and walked up the hill to the end of the point. It was a magnificent evening, the sun still high in the sky. The three held hands, Stuart in the middle using the adults to give him a swing. They had a panoramic view: the north Somerset coast towards Minehead, across to Cardiff, and north up the channel. The M4 road bridge was clearly visible, as were several large container ships heading for Avonmouth.

'Can you do a roly-poly?' Stuart asked Kate.

She turned to James, clearly not knowing what a roly-poly was.

'Let me show you,' shouted Stuart excitedly. He lay down on the soft turf, put his arms across his chest and rolled down the gentle slope beneath where they were standing. He stopped some ten yards away, laughing. 'Now, come on, Kate,' he yelled. 'It's your turn.'

She obeyed and at the bottom of the slope was laughing as loud as Stuart.

'Come on, Dad,' Stuart urged.

'Yes, come on, Dad,' repeated Kate.

Soon the three of them were repeating the rolls. They laughed all the way back to the car, feeling giddy.

**

On the train, speeding back to Reading next morning, Kate and James sat opposite each other having breakfast. Kate said little initially, but as they slowed to stop at Bristol Temple Meads, she asked, 'I'd like to go over a few points with you about the game, if I may?'

'Sure.'

'There are going to be developments from time to time in Iraq's weapons capability. How are we ever going to be able to incorporate such developments into the game, if no one is there to do it?'

'Well, I guess you will have to submit your proposals to the MoD Change Committee. They will vet your request and, if they approve, the changes will be incorporated as you want.'

'But that could take months. It could also compromise Iraq's security.'

'Yes, I can see that, but there is not much I can do about it. Is there something you have in mind? Perhaps, we could introduce it before you go back to Iraq.'

Looking him straight in the eyes, she said coldly, 'I'm thinking of nuclear, biological and chemical weapons.'

'Why? Has Iraq got an NBC programme?' He pretended he didn't know, but failed to convince.

'You know it has.'

'If you want to introduce NBC weapons into the war game, then I will have to take advice from the MoD. Do you want me to do that?'

'Yes,' she said. 'Precise details will have to wait until we get back to Iraq. Even I don't know the locations of some of our research establishments, even less where Iran's are.'

'I can't see that as a problem, providing I have the all-clear from the MoD on the general principle. I could update the files during the two weeks that I will be in Iraq on my own after the ICL team have returned to the UK.'

'That would probably be the best; the fewer who know where these things are the better.'

The train sped on and they ate in silence for several minutes. Then, the steely Iraqi Lieutenant, who had been so serious about weapon deployments a short time previously, changed. She smiled and her warmth returned. An amiable Kate was beaming at him. 'On another topic completely, thank you for such an enjoyable time. I am envious of you and your family.'

'I'm sure one day you will be just as lucky yourself.' However, her reaction to his innocent remark was unexpected; a veil of melancholy descended over her face.

'Unfortunately, I fear not,' she replied and turned her head to look out of the window. A hint of a tear appeared in her eyes. Not knowing what he'd done to upset her, he put his hand across the breakfast table. She took hold of it. It was icy cold. 'Someday, maybe, you will understand that what you have suggested is impossible.' James knew not to press her any further. He no longer wanted any more breakfast.

***

The following Wednesday James met Rear Admiral Johnson in his office in Northumberland Avenue. Brigadier Morrison was present. 'I gather the Iraqis want to play with NBC weapons and you want some guidance on what to do. Is that right?' asked the Admiral.

'Yes, sir. Do we put in a facility to allow them to game the effects of NBC? If so, how sophisticated do we make it?'

Admiral Johnson didn't reply, but cast a glance towards his number two.

'If you give them a simple simulation of NBC weapons, what have you in mind?' asked the Brigadier.

'Well, as I see it, the main differences between the three types of weapons are their range of effectiveness, the type of damage they create, the amount of control you can exert on their fallout and the length of its duration. Then, there are the delivery systems to consider and the defences' preparation for the attack.'

'Has there been any demand so far from the Iraqis to incorporate surface-to-surface missiles?'

'Yes, but their range is limited to two hundred miles.'

'No requirement for inter-continental ballistic missiles then?' interrupted the Rear Admiral.

'No, sir.'

The Brigadier continued. 'How sophisticated could the simulation of NBC weapons go?'

'To be honest, I don't know,' replied James. 'I would think that anything approaching the sophistication of Porton Down's simulations for biological and chemical, or Harwell's for nuclear would be too difficult to put into the game. Presumably, we wouldn't want that anyway?'

'Definitely not,' asserted Admiral Johnson. 'If we let them have an NBC facility it must be kept simple.'

'But will that satisfy them?' asked the Brigadier.

'I think it might,' said James. 'I've been talking to Lieutenant al Jised who, I think, is returning to head up some sort of Biological and

Chemical Weapons research team. She tells me things over there are pretty basic and their interest is purely defensive in case the Iranians use NBCs against them.'

'What about Nuclear Weapons research?' asked the Admiral.

'Lieutenant al Jised tells me that there is no research going on in that area, but I only have her word on that.'

'Our information is sketchy at the best, I'm afraid,' said Brigadier Morrison, talking more to his boss than James. 'However, we do know that Yugoslavs are in Iraq building huge underground bunkers beneath so-called palaces and other public buildings. Rumour has it that some of the bunkers are protected by as much as one hundred feet of reinforced concrete. They're up to something. Furthermore, we know the French are helping them to build a nuclear power station south of Baghdad at a place called Osirak. I find it hard to believe its purpose is to produce electricity when they're swimming in oil.'

'I gather from Jonathon Smith that ICL are going out to Baghdad next week to begin installing the computer hardware. Is that right?' asked Admiral Johnson.

'Yes. The head of ICL Oman will manage the Baghdad branch initially. For about three months the operators running the site will also be Omanis. After that, Iraqi staff should be capable of taking over completely. We think there is about another three weeks of programming to be done at Reading, which will take us to 16th June. The following week is for tidying up. The team will fly out to begin installing the software on Sunday, 25th June. I understand that Hamish Hamilton will go out with Don Henry and John Bryan. Ben Green is being assigned to a different project. The testing in Iraq should last no more than two weeks. I will join them on Sunday, 2nd July, for their last week. I will then stay on for a further two weeks on my own to teach their staff how to run the game. I have just about completed writing the User Manual and have prepared most of my lecture notes.'

'I shall be signalling the Air Attaché in Baghdad, Wing Commander Platini, to expect you and to give you all possible assistance. He speaks

Arabic fluently and I would like him to accompany you whenever possible. However, the Iraqis will prevent him from being with you all the time. There are some places where embassy staff are forbidden. You, in order to do your job, will be given escorted access. At all times, James, for heaven's sake keep your eyes open and your ears peeled. Above all else, be on your guard. If they tempt you, don't get ensnared. It could prove to be embarrassing for all concerned.' He added, 'I suppose I'm saying be cautious with al Jised. She could be working for the Iraqi Secret Service. Understand?'

'Yes, sir.' *The old boy is seeing spooks everywhere.* 'So I am to go ahead with designing them a crude NBC facility?'

'Yes,' replied the Admiral.

'One last question, what about logistics and weather?' asked James.

'What about them?'

'It either hasn't dawned on the Iraqis, or else they're not bothered, that the game doesn't calculate the consumption of materials. At Bracknell it was assumed there was an unlimited supply of everything – fuel, weapons and aircraft parts. Now that the game has become so much more realistic, it is a glaring weakness of the simulation. Also, it has always been assumed that the weather for the game would be blue skies with unlimited visibility. Should I draw their attention to this?'

The two senior officers looked at each other with blank expressions. It was obvious that they hadn't thought of it either.

'I think you should keep that one under your belt,' said the Rear Admiral with a wry smile on his face. 'I have told Jonathon Smith that Hamilton is to bring back the latest version of the scenario on a magnetic tape when he leaves Baghdad. When you come back, you are to do likewise. However, it may be prudent in your case to give the tape to Wing Commander Platini for the diplomatic bag. Understood?' He didn't wait for an answer, but continued. 'Also, after ICL have come home and you are out there on your own, I suggest you change the chess key so that you are the only one who knows it. Give a sealed copy of the position immediately to Platini. He will return it in the diplomatic bag as well.'

'I ought to put you in the picture,' replied James. 'There are now two chess positions protecting Nastia Game.'

The Admiral raised an eyebrow, waiting for an explanation. 'Hamish and I decided it would be a good idea to have two rings, an outer one to protect the data files and an inner one to guard the programs themselves. To get to the software, it is necessary to know both positions.'

'Excellent!' exclaimed the Admiral. 'In that case change both positions as soon as you are on your own out there. Who else knows?'

'No one, sir.'

'Good. Let's keep it that way. And while on the subject of security, how are you currently handling the physical security of the programs and data at Reading?'

'At the moment, the most up to date version is on a magnetic disc in the computer operating room in the basement of Dataskil House. At the end of the working day, after the game has been tested, updated or modified, the latest version gets transferred to a magnetic tape. This back-up tape is kept under lock and key in a secure building about one hundred yards away. Each day when the back-up tape is taken to the secure depository, the previous one is brought back to Dataskil House and destroyed. Hamish supervises the process and keeps a logbook. When we are finished completely with the development at Reading and have the final programs that are to go to Iraq with Hamish, the final tapes will be transferred to the MoD.'

'That's fine. It just leaves me to wish you bon voyage.'

CHAPTER 5

The last three weeks at Dataskil were hectic. Kate was especially interested in the design of the NBC simulations and helped to incorporate them into the game. The proposed delivery systems for the biological and chemical weapons were crude but effective: crop sprayer helicopters or suitable mortar and artillery shells filled with the appropriate materials. However, the delivery of nuclear weapons, even small tactical ones of 5,000 lbs TNT equivalent, required suitable missiles, which Azi seemed to think they would have at some future date. Consequently, the simulations had to be flexible.

Simulating the fallout of biological weapons, which could spread widely if the agent was virulent, was difficult to calculate accurately whereas data on the effect of chemical weapons was available from America's use of substances such as Agent Orange in Vietnam. Statistics on the fallout from nuclear weapons was also freely available.

Azi asked that the range of their surface-to-surface missiles be extended to 600 miles. He gave no reason. Such missiles could pose a threat to countries other than Iran so James left a message for Brigadier Morrison informing him of this development. He never received a reply.

The entire program suite was tested by playing a full war game over a three-day period beginning on the final Monday. Azi and Kathab were due to fly out on the Saturday. James was to be the umpire and booked into a local hotel so that the game could be played into the evenings. There were a few minor hiccups that were quickly sorted. Every part of the software suite was tested, so some of the moves made by the sides were artificial. The ground battle needed no modifications – a great relief to all the team. After three long days, the game showed that a stalemate was inevitable between the two sides. Azi was happy to accept the programs and ICL management arranged a small formal farewell lunch to hand over the encrypted programs on the final Friday.

James sat next to Kate. He gained the impression that she was not looking forward to returning to Iraq.

'You must be getting excited about seeing your family again after such a long time,' he enquired.

'Yes, but apart from that, I'm not so sure,' she replied. She wanted to change the subject and asked him if he was looking forward to visiting her country.

'Yes. I don't know if I will get much spare time at weekends or not, but if I can, I would like to go and see Ur.'

She looked surprised. 'Why Ur?'

'At school I was taught that modern civilisation began there. Ur was the world's first city. The land between the Tigris and the Euphrates was the site of the Garden of Eden.'

'Unfortunately, Ur is in the south, a long way from my home town. I've never been there, but would be happy to take you if we get the chance. There is an air base very close to it and I could probably arrange overnight accommodation in the Officers' Club.'

'That would be fantastic.'

'I would also like to take you to my home town. Samarra is a very special place and only about two hours from Baghdad. My parents would be delighted to meet you and I am sure my father would want to introduce you to some of his friends.'

The lunch ended all too soon and it was time to depart. Rightly or wrongly, not seeing Kate daily would be a wrench. As they split up, he felt an uneasy emptiness. He knew it was wrong and that he should grow up, but her presence for the past three months had been exhilarating. His small and innocent flirtations with her had made him feel ten years younger. Withdrawal symptoms were setting in. He was already looking forward to seeing her again in three weeks' time.

The arrangements for the ICL team to travel to Iraq had been finalised. Hamish, with Don and John, would fly together to Baghdad on Sunday, 25th June. Accommodation had been arranged for them to stay in the *Ishtar Sheraton Hotel*. The hardware installation engineers were already in Baghdad. Jonathon Smith had mentioned that the work was on schedule and would be finished by the time Hamish and his two programmers arrived. The final week at Reading saw the team preparing materials to take to Iraq, completing presentation slides, finalising the user manuals and producing sufficient handouts. It was dull work, but essential. Full use was made of Ben's presence as it was to be his final week on the project.

***

GCHQ, the Government's Communications Headquarters at Cheltenham, is the nerve centre of all government telecommunications traffic in the UK. Some fifteen different departments are housed in separate buildings. One of the most secret of these is the CITC, the Counter Intelligence Telecommunications Centre, originally set up at Bletchley Park in WW2. A team of over one hundred specialists, trained in decryption techniques as well as most languages, routinely eavesdrop on suspicious terrorist agencies. Listening to both radio transmissions and telephone conversations is a round-the-clock operation. At any one time there would always be a minimum of twenty-five staff on duty. The work is mostly monotonous, boring and often reveals little. However, just over a month previously a random dip had made a fascinating hit. For the past four weeks, duty staff had been monitoring a call made on Friday evenings at eight o'clock from a public telephone box in the Reading area, but never the same one. It was always made to another public telephone box, also consistently different, in the West End of London. The duty CITC staff had instantly realised the language being spoken was an Arabic dialect. By the third week, when a pattern was being established, the senior head of section ensured one of his specialist Arabic linguists was always available on Friday evenings. The two speakers appeared to use code words that hindered comprehension. The duty officer, in making her report on Friday, 16th June, commented that although the two speakers were fluent, it sounded as if Arabic was not their mother tongue. The dialect could be Syrian; her own Arabic having been learned in Egypt. Her report also noted that one of the topics discussed was the range of surface-to-surface missiles. It seemed to cause some concern with the London listener. At one point the term *XNE* had been used.

***

James spent the week prior to departing for Baghdad at home with his family. He made a visit to RAF Locking to pick up his tropical uniform, which would be worn daily in Iraq. Stuart didn't seem to worry about losing his father for nearly a month, but the strain was becoming more apparent on Emma. She became tetchy at the least little thing. No amount of reassurance or taking her out on several evenings seemed to help. The fact that she couldn't articulate her feelings only made her more frustrated. James was glad that her parents were only two minutes away, around the corner. Joking that she wouldn't have to change a fuse, as she could always get her father to do it, only made her worse.

'Are you worried about me being over there with Kate?' he had asked at one point.

'Of course not,' she replied indignantly. 'I'm glad you brought her home for that weekend. If I hadn't met her then it might be more difficult. She is the sort of person I can completely trust.'

James hoped she was right, but he wasn't so sure about himself.

***

The CITC staff were on duty on Friday, 23rd June. That evening they were scanning the public phone boxes in the Reading area expecting to pick up further information from the mysterious Arabic speakers. Two weeks earlier, the Thames Valley Police had been asked to keep a sharp eye open for any Middle Eastern-looking men in phone boxes at 2000 hours on Fridays. The request had caused considerable mirth with the senior officers at their weekly meeting with the Chief Constable. So far, there had been no sightings. That Friday evening, James' penultimate in the UK for almost a month, nothing was seen nor heard. No phone call was made, unless the Reading caller had changed his modus operandi. The Duty Officer duly made a note in the file and arranged for a memo to be sent to the Head of Section. The following week, he would receive the reply that surveillance would continue for a further four weeks, 'just in case.'

***

The British Airways flights to Baghdad on Sunday mornings left Heathrow at 0500 hours, too early for James to catch an early train to London or for him to expect Military Transport to drive him to the airport from Kewstoke. Consequently, he said his farewells on the Saturday afternoon after a family lunch at Emma's parents' house.

Bill, Emma's father, was one of the old-school and didn't make the departure any easier when he told his daughter, 'When I was in India I didn't see your mother for four years.'

MT drove James to RAF West Drayton where he spent Saturday night in the Officers' Mess. Despite knowing that the time would come to say adieu weeks previously, it was a tearful parting when the MT driver had turned up. It was a relief, to some extent, to get into the back of the car and for it to disappear around the corner. On the one hand, he felt at an all-time low leaving his family, but on the other, thrilled at the prospect of being in Baghdad and seeing Kate.

The flight to Baghdad was uneventful and arrived twenty minutes early. James was met by Azi who had fixed rapid transit through Customs and the immigration authorities. Sitting together in the back of an air-conditioned Mercedes, a hike-up from the Austin 1800 of the previous day, they were driven towards the city centre by an armed chauffeur. The usual pleasantries about each other's families were exchanged before Azi outlined the daily routine.

'As you know, you are in the same hotel as the other ICL staff. Each day you will be driven by an MT minibus to the Staff College at Al-Rashid, which is about five miles to the north of the city. You will be picked up from outside the hotel at 0630 hours.' On seeing James' surprised look, he added, 'We start at 0700 hours at this time of the year, but finish by 1600 hours.' As they entered the city centre, James was struck by the cleanliness, the relative lack of traffic, the standard of the roads and the number of new buildings. 'I am going to drop you off soon, but Hamish is waiting for you at the *Sheraton Hotel*. However, let me explain security arrangements. Essentially, you have the freedom to wander around our beautiful capital wherever and whenever you like, but you must carry this pass with you at all times. If you are stopped by the police, it will explain who you are.'

At the hotel, the Corporal driver, who had neither smiled nor spoken a word, helped James carry his bags into the foyer whilst Azi remained in the car. His departing words were, 'I might see you at the College later this afternoon.'

Hamish was waiting for him in the lounge. 'I expect you would like a beer.' Although drinking in the middle of the day was not one of his habits, James was more than happy to accept the offer, once he had found his room, deposited his kit and had a quick wash. Fortunately, the hotel was fully air-conditioned, but between stepping out of the car and entering the foyer, he had noted the intense heat of the early afternoon.

'I waited for you to arrive because I thought that rather than you kicking your heels around here this afternoon, you might like to come up to the College with me for a quick look around. Wing Commander Platini was here earlier and had hoped to catch you, but he had to go to a meeting. He asked me to give you his compliments and will meet you this evening in the bar at 1930 hours prior to dinner. Don and John are up at the College. If we get a quick snack, then the College's MT will take us there and you can meet the Commandant before you start work tomorrow.'

The Iraqi Military Staff College was situated on the northern edge of an operational air base in its own park. It made Bracknell look minute. It had its own security perimeter and guardhouse where the armed guards scrutinised James' pass closely and looked at him carefully, as if to memorise his face for the future. Between gaps in rows of palm trees, James could see parked Mig-21s and hear the roar as a pair took off. The sports fields in the College grounds were impressive. *On a similar scale to Cranwell,* he thought as he looked out from the staff car window. As the car continued slowly up the driveway, lined with date trees and manicured flowerbeds, he could see a small golf course. Not only were the greens being sprinkled, but the fairways also. Sweeping around a bend, the College came into view. It was as big as the RAF College at Cranwell. Constructed of white marble, it was dominated by an onion-shaped, golden dome and a one hundred feet tall minaret. The front portico was columned with impressive steps leading to a large polished, gilded double-door. It was opulence on a grand scale; clearly money was no object to the Iraqi military.

James had changed into his uniform before leaving the hotel. As he and Hamish climbed the steps, the doors were opened to reveal a large rotunda decked with military banners around its balcony. In the centre, the carpet was a woven image of an Iraqi flag. Two guards held the doors open and saluted James as he entered. He returned their greeting, but secretly wondered if he had done the right thing when one of the guards raised an eyebrow, as if surprised that a senior officer should return their salute.

Azi was waiting in the middle of the concourse.

'The Commandant has asked me to take you up to his office. He's looking forward to meeting you.' Hamish nodded to James and indicated that he would see him later. They climbed the circular marble stairs around the rotunda and went along a wide corridor covered with a plush black, red and white carpet. Knocking before entering, Azi led James into a large outer office where a female major stood up from behind her desk.

'James,' said Azi, 'this is Major Roya Talfah, the Commandant's personal staff officer.'

She came around from her desk, smiled broadly and greeted James in accented English. 'Welcome to Iraq, I hope you will enjoy your visit here.' A well-built, broad girl, perhaps 5 feet 9 inches tall and in her early thirties stood in front of James. With a handshake like a vice, she was what one member of his staff back at Locking would have described as a *bruiser.*

Not the type to meddle with.

'Please, go straight in,' she said to Azi.

Azi led the way in to the Commandant's office, stood to one side to let James enter and smartly saluted the rather round faced, balding man sitting behind a huge oak desk. 'Relax, gentlemen, please take a seat,' he said indicating to chairs that had been arranged in front of his desk. Standing up, he came around his desk to shake hands. He was taller than the impression gained seconds earlier. By no means slim, he had a fine military bearing and was immaculately presented. 'Welcome to Iraq,' he said. A distinguished man, in his mid-fifties, his dark hair was turning grey around his temples. 'You must excuse my English,' he said, 'but I learned my English when I attended the Indian Staff Course many years ago.' He beamed, as if to indicate this was some sort of a joke.

'In my experience, sir, most Indians speak better English than the English,' replied James, hoping this would be construed as a compliment.

Brigadier Ahmed Murtha broadened his smile and chuckled. 'You know, on the Staff Course in India there was a British Army Officer – on an exchange tour, I think you call it?' James nodded to indicate his correct terminology. 'He was from a Scottish Regiment, the Cameronians, and no one could understand him. He failed the English exam during the course because he insisted the plural of sheep was not sheeps.' This time the Commandant roared, whilst Azi and James politely smiled.

He continued. 'When Azi returned to Iraq, after completing the Staff Course at Bracknell, he showed us the documentation of the exercises he had played. We were most impressed with the computerisation of Nastia Game and we realised its potential for training our staff officers here at the College. Perhaps I should explain why we wanted the location to change. Iraq faces two military threats, although they are linked. Internally, we have the Kurdish problem. They want independence. If granted, it would be the beginning of the break-up of Iraq. Externally, we have the threat from Iran. When they illegally took over the Shatt al-Arab waterway from us with help from the Americans three years ago, we were forced to accommodate their claim on the waterway in exchange for their stopping to help the Kurds. Soon we will have a new president, a strong leader. When Iran ousts their Shah, their country will be in turmoil and we will reclaim what is rightfully ours. Azi speaks highly of you. We are hoping that your game will help us with our preparations. Now, what are your plans for the next three weeks?'

CHAPTER 6

By the time James had outlined his plans to Brigadier Murthah, it was time to return to the hotel with Hamish, Don and John. Progress with embedding the software, they explained, had been trouble free. The three Omani computer operators were proving to be first class and were one hundred per cent reliable.

A full test of the war game was scheduled to begin on Tuesday. Azi had arranged for several of his friends to play the Iranian side with Don and John, whilst he and Hamish would play the Iraqi side. James would umpire and a couple of English-speaking junior officers had been assigned to help as messengers. 'It's become obvious to me,' said Hamish as they were nearing the hotel, 'that Iraq will kick off this war and are expecting Nastia Game to help them with their planning. It's not for training purposes like at Bracknell.'

'The game should help them to see whether advancing on several fronts is a better strategy than a single spearheaded attack. It should show where those pushes would be most effective. However, my suspicions are that they will be disappointed with the results,' replied James. 'The two countries are so evenly matched. The Iraqis will discover there is no quick and easy victory. Ahead of them there is only a long, drawn out conflict; rather like the Western front in World War One. It will take something drastic to upset the status quo.'

'Such as?' asked Don.

'Perhaps a massive chemical attack on Tehran or the Americans intervening when they see oil prices rising.'

'Would the Americans intervene?'

'You can never tell; their foreign policy can be erratic. They overthrew Mossadeq in Iran when he nationalised the Iranian Petroleum Company in 1953.'

After a pause, James continued. 'Kate believes CB weapons will only be used as a defensive option by Iraq, but I think she may be pulling the wool over our eyes. Chemical weapons were used to quell a Kurdish revolt in 1974. I was told Iraqi planes sprayed villages with concentrated sulphuric acid.'

They fell silent, trying to imagine the horror that the acid must have created. When they left the minibus, they agreed to meet in the bar at 7.30 pm.

On entering his room, James could feel someone had been rummaging during his absence. He remembered arranging a pile of Nastia Game documentation immaculately. It was no longer quite straight.

Well, Admiral Johnson did warn me. He checked nothing was missing then began running his bath.

Wing Commander Gerry Platini was already in the bar with a beer in hand talking to Hamish when James arrived downstairs.

Gerry greeted him. 'Would you like one of these?'

James immediately made up his mind that Gerry was his kind of guy. A typical Lightning pilot, he was quite short in stature and full of joie de vivre. Aged about forty-five with thinning hair, he had a bright sparkle in his eyes and was quick to smile and laugh. He was fluent in five languages. His father was Italian and had immigrated to Britain in the thirties to sell ice cream. He had met and married a French woman. Several tours in RAF Germany during the early 1960s had allowed Gerry to become fluent in German. Prior to becoming a Lightning Qualified Flying Instructor at Riyadh in Saudi Arabia, he had completed an eighteen month Arabic course at the Defence School of Languages at Beaconsfield. 'We need to talk alone,' he said at one point in their conversation. 'After dinner I suggest we go for a walk.'

'There's a lot going on here,' began Gerry when they were outside and well away from their hotel. 'I don't know how much you have been told.'

'Not a lot. Admiral Johnson told me to be on my guard. I think someone was rooting around in my room this afternoon.'

'I'm not surprised. Your room will almost certainly be bugged. The minibus and staff cars also have concealed listening devices. Be careful when talking to the ICL boys in the bus; unless you want to be overheard. Did you notice anyone sitting around in the hotel foyer reading a newspaper while we were in dinner?'

Without waiting for an answer, he continued. 'You'll see them frequently. They're members of the Mukhabaret, the Iraqi Intelligence Service, and Saddam's henchmen. One of them is following us now. Just ignore them. You'll get used to them after a while. In fact you're safer when they're near at hand as any criminals in the street will see them a mile away and leave you alone.'

James thought of the conversations he had had with Hamish and the others in the minibus about Kate and realised he would have to be more careful in future.

'Let me give you a brief on what's going on. The Revolutionary Council that runs the country are members of the Ba'ath party. Their leader, Saddam Hussein, is rumoured to be plotting to oust President Bakr and proclaim himself President. He effectively runs the country already. Iraq is broadly split three ways, the smallest group, the Sunnis, have all the power. They ride roughshod over the other two groups: the Shias and the Kurds. Saddam is ruthless and keeps control through fear by every so often slaughtering a few thousand Kurdish villagers with chemical weapons. He sees himself becoming the future leader of a pan-Arabian empire. As you realise by now, he is planning to invade Iran. He will claim that the south-west of Iran was originally part of Mesopotamia and belongs to Iraq. This is where your war game comes in. He also has his eyes on Kuwait, which was once Mesopotamia too. Then, who knows, Saudi Arabia itself, perhaps?'

'But where is all their hardware going to come from?'

'The French are building a nuclear processing plant for Saddam at Osirak, about twenty miles south-west of here, supposedly for peaceful purposes. They have several biological and chemical weapons research centres. Al Jised works in one. All over the country Saddam is building palaces, twenty-six at the last count. They are simply underground command posts. We know for certain that the one in Tikrit has one hundred and twenty feet of solid concrete over it. He gets the Yugoslavs to do most of the building work.'

'I knew that Lieutenant al Jised was coming back to lead a team of some sort, but I had no idea things were on such a scale.'

'She's recently been made the civilian equivalent of a colonel – a principal scientific officer. She's in charge of a two hundred-man team with umpteen laboratories at the Al Muthanna research centre, a few miles up the road from here. Much of it is underground. We think it's where they test protective clothing and try to develop antidotes to biological agents such as anthrax and ricin using dogs. Believe it or not, the raw materials and precursors for these chemical and biological weapons are coming from the West: the US, Germany and ourselves.'

'You must be joking.'

'I wish I was, but oil is a precious commodity. Recently, a British company supplied the Iraqis with thirty tons of a substance used for growing biological cultures – thirty tons of the stuff! God knows what they're growing up there. Oil revenue gives Saddam enormous power. Ninety per cent of his conventional weapons come from the USSR. He's in the middle of getting up to three hundred and fifty Mig-23 fighter-bombers. There are more Russian pilots in this country than there are Iraqi ones.' He chuckled to no one in particular. 'Several of the Mig-21 squadrons are flown exclusively by East Germans. Our security boys in the embassy tell me there are currently sixteen thousand so-called Russian advisers in Iraq training the Army and Air Force.'

'Why are the Russians so keen to support Saddam?'

'They think a strong Iraq will ensure that the Iranians will have to concentrate their forces to look west, rather than north and east. After all, they don't want Iran interfering with their Afghan ambitions. The French are in on it too. As well as the nuclear plant, they are delivering eighteen Mirage F1s soon with air-to-surface missiles.'

'Where will all this madness lead?'

'God only knows. Let's turn round and go back to the *Sheraton* for a nightcap. If we turn around quickly and walk straight back, we'll surprise our follower. Have a good look at him as we pass. You'll notice they all look alike. I think I'll embarrass him and say "good evening" to him in Arabic. Incidentally, next Tuesday is American Independence Day. Traditionally we put on a barbeque for the American charge d'affairs and his small staff in our embassy grounds. The Americans haven't had full diplomatic relations with the Iraqis since 1968, so we let them invite the guests and they provide the beer and burgers. Last year it was a good do. The ICL boys know about it and are coming. I'll send a car around for all of you at seven o'clock. OK?'

As they met the approaching man, wearing an immaculate suit with matching tie and shirt and sporting a thick black moustache, he showed considerable embarrassment as Gerry said loudly, '*Salaam wa'aleikhoom.*'

On Monday morning, before boarding the minibus to Al-Rashid, James mentioned to Hamish, 'Gerry thinks the bus and staff cars are bugged, as well as our rooms.'

'Yes, we've suspected that,' he replied, 'but there's not much we can do about it, except to be careful what we say. The Omani operators have been warned.'

The working conditions at the College were exceptional. New air-conditioned offices and the purpose-built computer suite housing the dual processor ICL 2900s had been built. James set about familiarising himself with the layout of the College and the rooms that would be used to play the war games, as well as the theatre where he would lecture to the Iraqi Staff. One of the junior officers assigned to help run the game accompanied him wherever he went. Lieutenant Jalal Murtad spoke good English, having attended a one-year course at the Royal Electrical and Mechanical Engineers' home base at Arborfield.

'It was easy to go to London for the weekends,' he enthused. 'We had a great time there.' James wasn't sure whether he was talking about London or Arborfield, but thought it would be the former.

Everything that James needed for his presentations was laid on. The theatre had the latest equipment, including an overhead projector with back projection, a 35 mm projector, a large white board, and, most impressive of all, a system that could project the display on the lecturer's VDU to a large 10 ft by 8 ft screen. Demonstrating the finer facilities of the war game to the audience would, therefore, be simple and effective. Although many of the officers in the audience would understand English, their fluency would vary. Consequently, the Iraqis had set up a translating facility that allowed officers to use headphones if they wished. The translator would be Lieutenant Murtad. James gave him a copy of the scripts he would be using, but warned Jalal that there might be times when he would have to digress, depending on the outcome of the simulations. 'When I take questions, your guess will be as good as mine.'

'As long as you don't use any unusual colloquialisms and give me time. Remember, one word in English often requires two or three in Arabic.'

This comment made James think about home and Kewstoke where they received HTV from Wales. 'There's a similar problem with the Welsh language,' he joked, but Jalal clearly missed the point. They tried out the equipment, aided by a Corporal technician. Contented that nothing untoward would go wrong, he returned to the computer room to see how Hamish and the others were getting along. He then prepared the paperwork for the following day, showing Jalal what he wanted him to do.

Tuesday, American Independence Day, would be the first real test of the enhanced Iraq-Iran war game, with no artificial inputs or stoppages. He knew that Azi would probably launch his attack with as many pre-emptive air strikes as he could muster. The offensive strategy taught at Bracknell was firstly, to attack air defence communication radar sites and secondly, to bomb the runways; thereby keeping the enemy aircraft grounded. Gaining maximum air superiority for the ground forces was paramount. Destroying aircraft on the ground, especially if parked in hardened shelters was difficult. It was unnecessary if they couldn't take off from damaged runways.

Before starting the game, James briefed the two teams. It was to be assumed that tension had been brewing up between the two countries for several months, owing to Iran having begun to turn back neutral countries' shipping heading for Iraq in the Strait of Hormuz. An assassination attempt on Iraq's president had put both sets of forces on instant alert the previous day.

Game time was set to 0/0000 hours. James explained the clock system to the new players. Major Boroumand and Lieutenant Khali were playing the Iranian side with Don and John. The first figure represented the day of the war, and the second figure was the hour of that day. So, for example, a game time 2/1430 hours was 1430 hours on day two. Both teams were to go to their own rooms and make whatever preparations they wished. At no time were they to enter the other team's room, nor the umpire's room. When they stopped playing for the evening, they had to agree not to discuss the progress of the game with their opponents. All communications during play had to be made through the two messengers. They had until lunchtime, about five hours, to prepare initial plans for the game. After lunch, the game time would advance to 1/0000, midnight on the first day of the war.

CHAPTER 7

The first moves of the game were made by the Iranian team. Expecting a two pronged attack, a major advance in the south towards Abadan over the Shatt al-Arab waterway and a diversionary advance through the Zagros Mountains on the old Silk Road to Tehran via Kermanshah, they mounted some forty Combat Air Patrols, or CAPs, to cover the border area between Abadan in the south and Orumiyeh in the north. Using their tanker aircraft, the pairs of Phantoms could be kept in the air for long periods, dependent only on pilot fatigue. They dispersed their Tiger and Tomcat fighters to some twelve reserve airfields to the east, near the border with Pakistan. Sixty Cobra attack helicopters were split and repositioned from their usual bases to mobile sites near the expected Iraqi thrusts.

Azi's first aggressive moves were designed to gain air superiority over the border region. A total of fifteen squadrons left seven different airfields to attack defence radar sites and western Iranian airfields. Five of the radar sites to be attacked were relatively close to the border, allowing the bombers to fly to their targets at a low altitude and not be seen by Iranian radars until the last minute.

However, the ten Badger squadrons allocated to attack the airfields had targets too far from their own bases for the low flight profile. Consequently, they had to fly at altitude to conserve fuel, allowing the Iranian ground radars and CAPs to see the Iraqis coming from some distance. Knowing the chances of being intercepted were high, Azi accompanied each Badger squadron with ten Mig-23 fighters to ward off Iranian interceptors.

At 1/0630, Azi began a two-pronged ground advance. He opened up a massive artillery barrage on Iranian defensive positions west of Kermanshah, and moved two divisions of tanks towards a small border town on the Silk Road. To reach Tehran the Iraqi troops would have to cover between 350 and 400 miles over mountainous narrow passes as high as those in the Alps. The plan was hopelessly ambitious and, unbeknown to Azi, he was falling into a prepared trap.

Simultaneously, his main advance began north of Abadan.

The first clash in the air war occurred when an Iranian CAP, flying about 200 miles west of Tehran, saw a large number of approaching aircraft at a range of seventy miles. Game time was stopped and the Iranian team given time to react. One of the keys to the success of war gaming is deciding how long to give teams to react to events. Scrambling interceptors, even those on two minutes stand-by and already armed with the correct defensive weapons can take time. How long to give the Iranian team was a matter of judgement as they had to decide how many aircraft to scramble, and from what base. They then had to file a flight plan based on their hunch of the incoming attack's probable target.

At Bracknell, umpires tended to be generous with time. Brigadier Murthah had said, 'Give them no more than fifteen minutes.' However, only James as umpire could see the computer forecasting five more CAP sightings due in the next seventeen minutes. Eventually it took over an hour to play the first few moves. After that, it wasn't long before the Iranian's Tigers and Tomcats were busy trying to find the Badgers and Blinders, with or without the help from the ground radar stations.

The first ground radar site to be hit was at Paveh, thirty miles north of Kermanshah. Azi's only knowledge of the raid was a message saying that the attack was completed. The message added that a surface-to-air missile had shot down one of his aircraft and a second aircraft had received superficial damage. The squadron was on its way home. The computer simulation, however, had decided Paveh's radar was only partially damaged and would be back on-air within forty-eight hours.

Azi would not know this unless he was prepared to make a reconnaissance flight over the site. The 'fog of war' had started.

Azi's follow-up reconnaissance flights put him in the picture on the outcome of his attacks. They were generally successful. Of the five radar sites attacked, two were completely destroyed and three partially damaged. The ten airfields attacked were closed for various lengths of time, between twelve and forty-eight hours. However, the recce information had come at a cost: six recce Mig-21 aircraft had been shot down.

By then, Azi was also learning that the tank advance along the Silk Road to Kermanshah had run into a heavily defended area eight miles inside the border. Extensive minefields and well dug-in forces, backed by heavy artillery, were proving to be impenetrable.

Iran's first incursion into Iraq was timed to follow soon after the returning Iraqi aircraft had landed at their home bases, but before the Iraqis had time to park their aircraft in hardened shelters. At Al-Rashid, a squadron of Tomcat fighter-bombers using cluster bombs and anti-aircraft rockets destroyed six Mig-23s and temporarily closed one of the two runways. Clearing the unexploded cluster bombs would take eight hours. At Al Habbaniyah, fifty miles west of Baghdad, a squadron of twelve Blinder aircraft had been parked in a straight line instead of being widely dispersed and were mostly destroyed.

By 1/1500, as a result of the rapid retaliation from the east, Azi realised he would have to commit some of his fighters to air defence and mounted a string of CAPs near the border to protect Baghdad, Basra and Kirkuk. Unfortunately, for him, Iraq had no refuelling tanker aircraft, and so his Migs could only stay on-station for two hours before being replaced.

Between 1/1600 and 1/1720, Azi's second wave of Badgers and Blinders took off at various intervals to co-ordinate their time over their targets. By such timing, the attacks were more effective as, all at once, the defenders' workload increased. The targets chosen were again the western Iranian airfields. Compounding the earlier battering, the outcome of the attacks was devastating. Eleven of the airfields became unusable for between fourteen and twenty-eight days.

On the Silk Road, the Iranians had blown up bridges over various rivers. Whenever the Iraqis reached the non-existent bridges, they were met with artillery barrages and squadrons of Cobra helicopters firing air-to-surface missiles. However, as darkness was closing in, there was little Azi could do. The troops were told to hold their positions until morning. There would be no further advance on this front for some considerable time.

By coincidence, at this time in the game, it was approaching the end of the working day at the College. They had been playing the game for almost eleven hours. A halt was called with game time at 1/2100. The four Brits left for their hotel, and no mention of the game was made in the minibus. Everyone was exhausted, but looking forward to the 4th July barbeque.

***

The Americans know how to push the boat out, thought James as he was offered an ice-cold Budweiser and looked around the British Embassy compound decorated with stars and stripes flags. Everything had been flown in from the United States for the event including Texan steaks, Coca-Cola, hot dogs, Big Mac bread rolls and even coleslaw. The hospitality and friendliness of the dozen, or so, hosts was first class.

James was settling into his second beer when Gerry introduced him to a well-oiled Major Keith Richardson, the temporary Air Attaché. He spoke with a deep southern states accent, pronouncing one-syllable words as if they had two. A tall, overweight man with thinning hair, he was sweating profusely and was clearly fond of his Jim Bean bourbon. 'I am standing in until a permanent replacement is found. I am temporarily detached from the Pentagon. However, I wanted to meet you,' he said.

'Really, why?' replied James, trying to be polite, but puzzled how an officer based in Washington should have heard of him.

Unfamiliar with the concept of diplomacy, not to talk *shop* at social functions, he made it clear, in an arrogant way, that he knew what James and the ICL team were doing in Baghdad. He wasn't slow in giving his views about Nastia Game. 'The two USAF officers who attended your Bracknell course last year showed us their documentation of Nastia Game. It is an impressive piece of software, Buddy.'

James didn't ask who 'us' was; he didn't care. *And I'm certainly not your Buddy.*

It's an odd fact of life-compatibility. How often do we meet someone for the first time and either take an instant like or dislike to them for no apparent reason? And so it was for James with Major Richardson.

I don't like this guy. I wouldn't trust him any further than I could throw him.

Unfortunately, Gerry had disappeared, probably deliberately. Left on his own with the inebriated Major, he found himself cornered and wondering how he could escape without causing too much offence. *After all, it's their party.* Incapable of reading James' body language, Major Richardson was persistent. 'We were puzzled by the security of the software. What's its secret?'

Mind your own bloody business.

'If you knew, it wouldn't be a secret, would it?' replied James, smiling as politely as he could.

After further probing questions that received similar rebuffs and detecting the cool reception, he changed tack. 'Have you ever been to the States, James?'

James replied as best as he could. 'No, I've no real interest in going except, possibly, to see Mount Rushmore.'

'Not worth the effort, Buddy,' proclaimed the Major.

If he calls me that again, I'll thump him.

'It's in the middle of nowhere and is much smaller than you might imagine from watching Cary Grant in *North by North West*.' Conversation, mostly one-sided, continued for a little longer. However, it eventually dawned on the Major that he was getting nowhere and wasn't wanted. Grunting an excuse, there was an air of mutual ill-feeling as he made off towards a pretty-looking girl in a sari who looked as if she could be from the Indian embassy.

Thank God he's gone, I wonder how Hamish is getting on?

He stood on his toes to look around for him in the crowd.

'Hello, James,' a familiar voice said from behind. He swung around, knowing immediately it was Kate. His heart stopped for a few seconds before beginning to beat at twice its usual rate.

'What are you doing here?' he asked enthusiastically, giving her a welcoming hug.

'I bribed someone to let me come,' she laughed.

Her unique smell filled his lungs. He shuddered as an elusive ghost walked on his grave. Despite the compound temperature nudging 25 °C, a shiver ran down his spine and he felt cold.

'It's good to see you again. You look great,' he said, standing back to admire her in a black cotton, ankle-length dress with high neckline and long, floppy sleeves.

Amazing how black compliments tanned skin.

'I've been told you have been promoted,' he said.

'I've been made Head of one of our research teams at Al Muthanna, an Army base not far from here. I'm a Principal Scientific Officer.'

She was trying to be modest, but James knew that Principals in the British Scientific Civil Service were powerful people. He managed, 'That's great news. You deserve it.'

They walked towards one of the queues to get food. 'One of the reasons I came this evening, apart from wanting to see you again,' she said smiling, 'was to ask if you would like to come to Samarra for a weekend?'

He nodded.

'Well, how about this Friday?'

'Great, why not?'

'Good, I'll pick you up from your hotel at ten o'clock, which means we will arrive in time for one of my mum's lunch specials,' she grinned as if this was something of a family joke. 'We can stay the night and come back on Saturday afternoon.'

With another early start required the following day, the four had all agreed not to stay too late at the barbeque. Hamish, Don and John had joined Kate and James whilst they were sitting on the grass, a little way from the throng at the edge of the compound. The five reminisced happily about their three and a half months at Dataskil. Hamish said, 'We're in the middle of testing Azi's plan for the invasion of Iran and need to get a good night's sleep before another long day tomorrow.'

'That should be interesting,' she replied, adding, 'If it doesn't go the way he thinks then I bet he will blame the computer.'

They all saw the joke, got up, sought one of the American hosts to thank for their hospitality and left.

'I'll drop you off at your hotel, my staff car is big enough,' said Kate. The four Brits nodded and piled into an air-conditioned Mercedes much to the surprise of Kate's chauffeur.

CHAPTER 8

The next morning, the game resumed at 0700 hours. Brigadier Murthah came into the umpire's room almost immediately after play had restarted. He saw the game time advance rapidly from 1/2100, the overnight position, to 2/0300; neither side had planned any moves during that period.

Major Boroumand and Lieutenant Khali made the initial moves of the second day's play. They moved twelve of their Boeing tanker aircraft to two positions near the Iraqi border. An hour later, at 2/0400, sixty Phantoms took off from their dispersed sites, east of the Zagros Mountains. Forty carried offensive 500lb bombs and Maverick air-to-surface missiles and twenty were armed with Sidewinder air-to-air missiles with Electronic Counter Measures – ECMs. Splitting equally into two wings, they headed for their rendezvous with the tankers to fill with fuel. They then swept to low level for the first major mass attack inside Iraq.

The southern wave flew at 400 ft over the Persian Gulf, descending to 200ft to fly north over the Al Faw peninsula. Keeping 30 miles to the west of Basra, they flew over the unpopulated desert on the western side of the River Euphrates with the ECM Phantoms leading. Finally the Wing broke into two Squadrons, timing their arrival over Al-Rashid and Al-Habbaniyah bases simultaneously at 2/0515. Meanwhile, in a similar manner, the northern group attacked the bases at Kirkuk and Baquba, twenty miles from Baghdad. By entering Iraqi air space at high speed and low level the air defences were taken completely by surprise. It came as a rude shock to Azi when messages told him of the attacks on his four airfields. Worse still, because his Migs and Badgers were in the final throws of preparing for taking off on their own missions, the damage was considerable. In total, some seven Mig-23s were lost at Kirkuk and four Badgers at Al-Habbaniyah.

For the Iraqis it was a bad start to the second day of the war. Brigadier Murthah was clearly frustrated. He remarked, 'Our air defence radar operators need shooting for allowing that to happen. They must have been asleep.'

Prior to learning of the attacks, Azi had submitted his first wave of missions for the day. At 2/0500, from the remoter western airfields, he was planning bombing the more eastern Iranian airfields. The Badgers would have to fly at a high altitude, with reduced weapon loads, in order to have sufficient fuel to return to their bases. The high profile was dangerous as the defending Iranian Tomcats and Tigers would be fully fuelled when engaging in air combat over their own territory, whilst the Badgers and accompanying Mig-23s would not.

Reacting to how the Phantoms had attacked his bases without warning, Azi put up two arcs of Mig-23 CAPs, one south of Basra and the other east of Kirkuk. He sent a squadron of Mig-23s, armed with bombs and rockets, to relieve the tank columns bogged down on the Silk Road. He ordered the ground forces to await reinforcements.

The map display on the plotter allowed James and the Brigadier to see the total picture of the game. 'This is much better than your game of cricket,' he joked. 'I watched that game when I was in India, but could never see the attraction of a game that could be played for days without getting a decisive result.'

'I'm afraid you might find the same problem here, sir,' James replied.

'But at least with this game we can radically change our plans, until we get the result we are seeking.'

'True. However, the computer is already showing how difficult it will be for you to get an army across the Zagros Mountains.' There was no response.

The Iranian team had anticipated Azi's plans to relieve the bogged-down Iraqi ground forces in the mountains. Consequently, they despatched Tomcats to defend the areas and further intensified their harassment of the Iraqi troops with Cobra helicopters.

The repeated bombing of the western Iranian airfields had closed them for weeks. However, this was largely futile because the entire Iranian Air force had re-grouped to its eastern bases where they were relatively safe. From there, they could dominate the skies over much of the battle zone by the judicious use of their tanker aircraft. Additionally, the superiority of their American equipment more than compensated for having fewer aircraft.

The Iraqi attacks on the eastern airfields proved unsuccessful. The Badgers that had got through to Isfahan had closed the airfield for twenty-one days, but elsewhere the damage was minimal. The defences around Tehran and Bandar-e-Abbas on the Persian Gulf had been so effective that the Badgers had to turn around, dropping their bombs harmlessly to conserve their fuel in order to reach home. Overall, a total of eighteen Badgers had been lost on what had been futile missions.

When the Commandant left for lunch, he was mumbling something to himself about Azi needing to sort himself out. Later that evening, James was to learn from Hamish that the Brigadier had called for Azi soon afterwards. He had returned half an hour later looking sheepish which explained the complete change of tack by the Iraqi team that afternoon. Just how much might have been given away to Azi, bearing in mind that the Commandant had seen the total picture of the game, would never be known.

Azi concentrated his efforts on the ground by moving two tank divisions and four armoured brigades to support the advance towards Abadan. They were further supported in the air with Su-17s and Mig-21s. Where there was a problem crossing the rivers, Iraqi engineers built pontoon bridges that typically delayed their advance by two or three hours. They used the time productively to bring up logistical support.

Major Boroumand reacted to the Iraqi advance by moving armoured troops south from Ahvez. He also decided to bring fifteen of his Cobra helicopters back from the impasse on the Silk Road to help defend Abadan. The Cobras arrived at 2/1730, but their support crews were not expected until 3/0400. Game events were played out until 3/0100, when a lull in the game was predicted for several hours. It would be some time before the relieving column would arrive on the north eastern edge of Abadan. It was a good time to call close of play for the day.

***

The final day of playing the game saw Brigadier Murthah in the umpire's room at seven o'clock looking much happier than when he had left for his lunch the previous day. Having given Azi a few tips, he was expecting to see an improvement in the Iraqi state of affairs. He must have realized that James would find out from Hamish about his inputs but made no mention of it.

By first light, the Iranian team had their Phantoms in action again, this time in support of their troops defending the river crossings. Using air-to-surface missiles and 500lb bombs, they pounded the Iraqi positions but not without considerable cost to themselves. The Iraqis had brought mobile air defence cover with them – SAMs and radar-air-defence guns. A total of seven Phantoms were shot down, but the delay to the Iraqi advance was increased by a further five hours.

To defend Abadan, Iranian troops were sent from the east with mobile artillery, armoured personnel carriers and light tanks. However, they were strung-out on the approach road. Sensibly, Azi was using his Migs to strafe the road to good effect: the advancing column's casualties were mounting and progress was getting slower.

At 3/0600, Azi moved his troops forward from their positions to try and capture Abadan. This was to be the first real test of the computer's simulation of street-to-street fighting. It was a new aspect of the game designed at Reading after extensive consultation with the scientists from DOAE at West Byfleet. They had produced models based on urban warfare in Northern Ireland. Abadan's old, narrow streets in the city centre were not going to make for a quick rout, despite the Iraqi troops outnumbering the defenders.

Nevertheless, it came as a surprise to James when the computer forecast that Abadan would not capitulate until 5/1800. If the Iranians could further reinforce the town, this estimate could prove optimistic. The forecast was not made available to the game players. They only received vague reports of heavy fighting with mounting casualties. The Commandant who had been, metaphorically, looking over James' shoulder was fully aware of what was going on. He knew the fighting could take several days and, therefore, if he helped Azi a second time, the outcome of play could be radically different. All James could do was hope that Brigadier Murthah had inherited some sense of fair play from watching cricket in India.

With the Commandant still watching, Azi decided to bomb the oil refineries on the eastern edge of Abadan with air-to-surface missiles armed with nerve agents; presumably his idea was to minimise damage to the processing plants. Simultaneously more troops were moved from Basra to the south. From the puzzled expression on the Brigadier's face, this was not part of his plan.

'What on earth is he doing?' asked the Brigadier to no one in particular. It was the first time that the computer was to simulate a chemical attack in a real game. The commandant's face dropped when he saw that the computer was predicting 2,500 civilian fatalities but little collateral damage to the plant.

'Madness,' he exclaimed. 'The oil workers are largely Sunni. Does he not want the locals to rise up in support of our liberating troops?'

An answer was not expected, but James' thoughts were that no computer model could predict human reactions to war.

'How long are you planning to play this afternoon?' asked the Commandant.

'I thought we should go to about three o'clock and then have a post-mortem which would take about another hour,' replied James.

'I have a better idea. As it's almost lunchtime, why don't we all pack up now, have a drink and then take a light lunch. We can start the wash up at, say, one o'clock. We should be finished by two-thirty for the weekend.'

And so, to the players' surprise, the game was halted at 3/1000. The Brigadier must have already planned the lunch as a table had been laid with waiter service. As well as the nine gamers, the Brigadier's personal staff officer, the well shaped buxom Major Talfah, was present. She was to act as secretary at the wash up. It was noticeable during the pre-lunch drinks that the Iraqi officers bestowed on her undue attention, to the point of obsequiousness. Even the Commandant seemed to show her some degree of subservience.

James found himself sitting next to Roya, wondering about the paradox of the Iraqi officers' attitude towards her. She was relaxed and friendly, displaying a lot of interest in the war game and its background. Towards the end of the meal, she asked, 'What are your plans for the weekend?'

Explaining that he had been invited by Lieutenant al Jised to stay with her parents in Samarra, she looked surprised.

'There's a big government reception there tomorrow evening to celebrate the recent refurbishment of the Caliph's Palace. I would have thought al Jised's parents would have been attending, as her father is the Mayor of Samarra.'

This was news to James, although he knew Kate's father was some sort of local official. He replied. 'Yes, I gather I am going along as her parent's guest.'

A frown suggested that she did not approve. However, she quickly recovered her smile. 'If you meet my uncle, give him my regards. Tell him you have met me.'

When James asked who her uncle was, she looked surprised. 'I thought you knew. It's Saddam Hussein.'

CHAPTER 9

Brigadier Murthah began the meeting by thanking Hamish, Don and John for their hard work developing the war game. He then sprung a surprise by inviting them, along with James, to dinner that evening at Baghdad's best restaurant, the *El Castello*.

'General Ali Youseff, our Assistant Commander for Operations, is accompanying us. We will pick you up at the *Sheraton* at 1930 hours.'

Without waiting for a reply, the Commandant continued. 'I think we should play the wash-up as follows: firstly, if you, Major Boroumand, begin by going through the lessons you think have come out of the game from the Iranian point of view. Secondly, Major Tumbrah tells us what he has learned. Thirdly, I would like your ideas, James. At any time, Hamish, Don or John please chip in. Finally, I will sum up.' He looked at Major Boroumand, nodded and waited.

Major Boroumand began. 'On day one, I thought there were four major lessons learned. Firstly, the dispersal of our aircraft to the most eastern airfields was essential for their later operational use. Secondly, our Phantom CAPs added considerably to the effectiveness of our air defence radars, although diverting them to intercept intruders was not a good idea. Thirdly, and perhaps the most important lesson, was the need for tanker aircraft. Without them, the eastern dispersal would have been pointless and we could not have kept the CAPs on-station for so long. Finally, the Cobra attack helicopters were invaluable.'

'What about your handling of the ground battles?' asked the Commandant.

'Perhaps we should have expected the advance along the Silk Road and brought up more reserves earlier.'

Satisfied, the Brigadier asked him to carry on.

'The big success of day two was the ability of the tankers to extend the range of our Phantoms so that they could attack at two hundred feet, well under the Iraqi air defence radars. The co-ordination of simultaneous attacks on target must have given the enemy less time to take defensive action. We were also learning to blow up our own bridges to slow the Iraqi push into the mountains. We should have foreseen the attack across the southern border and had more troops waiting at Abadan. The troops in the garrisons on the border, such as at Ahvez, will have to be more mobile in future, so they can reinforce where they are needed.' None of the others in his team had anything to add.

'On day three our inputs to the game were largely defensive in nature and fairly obvious. I suspect the loss of seven Phantoms at Abadan was expensive for what it achieved, but it gave us extra time to prepare defences.'

James added, 'It slowed the Iraqi advance by several hours.'

'A fair trade off,' commented the Major. 'To summarise, from the Iranian's point of view, I would say the great surprise to me has been the degree of flexibility that the tankers gave us. Without them we would have lost control of the air when our western airfields were taken out on the first day.'

'Good,' said Brigadier Murthah. 'Now what about your side, Major Tumbrah?'

'The first thing I noticed was the poor serviceability of our aircraft on take-off. If we are to destroy the eastern Iranian airfields and their major cities, such as Tehran, then we must get tanker aircraft and plenty of them. The need for better reconnaissance aircraft to measure the effectiveness of our attacks is essential. For much of the time, I was working in the dark. Our CAPs need tankers and a better search radar than those fitted to our Mig-23s. On the ground, we will have to find a quicker way through their minefields, if we are to take advantage of a surprise attack.'

'What about the safety of returning aircraft?' asked the Brigadier.

'I'm not sure what you mean, sir?'

'Well, you lost a lot of aircraft on the ground when the Iranians, effectively, followed your aircraft home and hit them on the airfields' taxi-ways.'

Somewhat embarrassed, Azi managed, 'In future it will be necessary to have air defenders covering our backsides.'

There was a pause; the Brigadier didn't look too convinced.

Azi continued. 'The second day was a disaster because our ground radar systems didn't see the Phantoms' low level attacks until it was too late. Again, we need better CAP aircraft with tankers to keep them on-station longer. Finally, our raids to the east of the Zagros Mountains were expensive because we had to fly at a high altitude. Yet again, tanker aircraft would have helped. On the ground, there is no point moving troops into the mountains without massive air cover. Sending Mig-23s to help out against the Cobras was too little too late.'

He finished by adding, 'The final day was to have been a major advance into Arabstan. I had planned to take Abadan quickly and move to cut off relieving Iranian troops coming from the east.'

Brigadier Murthah nodded his head slowly, but didn't say a word. After a few moments, he stirred and asked James what he had thought were the principal lessons.

'I think the main lesson is that you must have clear aims that are realistic and obtainable. In this war Iraq must decide what it wants to achieve and go for it with all possible force. If the aim is to control the Shatt al-Arab waterway and liberate Arabstan then it will have to begin with a surprise attack on Abadan. Once started, it must not lose momentum and stop because of a shortage of logistics. The right tools for the job are necessary. Tanks will not win in urban street-to-street fighting. Troops, who have practised and trained in this type of warfare, are needed. Crossing the Shatt al-Arab River will have to be swift and decisive. Attack and transport helicopters will have to be concentrated at the crossing points in large numbers, as you will not be successful without air superiority. The Iranian tankers denied you this, but I saw no attempt being made to search and destroy them. The critical front is Abadan. This is where I would have expected the surprise attack to have begun, not in the north towards Kermanshah.'

The Brigadier sat up in his chair and stretched, expanding his not inconsiderable chest. He thought for a moment to get his ideas together.

'I agree that we must have clear aims that are realistic. Azi, what was your aim in moving troops across the borders in the north?' he asked.

'I was hoping for a swift advance towards Tehran along the silk route through Kermanshah. I now believe that plan is impractical.'

'I would accept that route could be used by our enemy to invade Baghdad, but not the other way around. The Zagros Mountains are virtually impenetrable for us to go east, but the Iranians can come down from them easily. I think, however, that when we attack Arabstan we must always have some units positioned on those borders to protect our backsides,' replied the Brigadier.

It was a fair comment and went some way to excusing Azi's plan. 'Nevertheless, the first principle of war is concentration of force and James is right, we must make our primary aim the liberation of Arabstan and put most of our efforts there. This brings me to another principle of war, the psychological factor. If the Sunnis in Arabstan (James noted they all called the southern Iranian province by its Iraqi name, as opposed to its Iranian name of Kazistan) are to rise up and help us win their liberation, then using chemicals on Abadan oil refineries is fatal to our cause. Had you used nerve agents to slow down the relief column heading towards Abadan then I could have understood your logic.'

He stopped and looked at Azi for an explanation, but there was none.

The Brigadier continued. 'Economy of effort is another principle of war. I felt that your repeated attacks on runways were overdone. I know it kept the Iranian Air Force to the rear, but on the second day it might have been more effective to be more flexible.' Azi nodded. 'Both of you were active, and co-ordinated your ground and air forces quite well, although I think that it is a weakness of the game that you control both.

In the real scenario, there can be conflicts between senior commanders.' He paused and asked if there were any comments. No one offered anything; it had been a hard week.

'Very well then, I would summarise, as follows. Firstly, we must have clear, simple, achievable goals. Secondly, we must concentrate our forces towards achieving the aims and not get diverted when following them through. Thirdly, we must use the surprise element more effectively. Fourthly, to gain complete air superiority Iraq needs tanker aircraft and more helicopters.' He stopped, smiled and added, 'I look forward to seeing you this evening at 1930 hours in the foyer of the *Sheraton*.'

***

The night out with the two Iraqi generals began with the meal at *El Castello*. After starting with a mezze, the main course was mazgouf – a flat fish, native to the Tigris, roasted on an open wooden fire. Finally, the meal was completed with honey yoghurt and nuts. It was an experience never to be forgotten, enhanced as it was by the consumption of many bottles of a two-year old French Sancerre. It was the first wine the lads had tasted since their arrival in Baghdad.

After the meal the generals, who were enjoying their evening on expenses, insisted on visiting a nightclub, *The Thousand and One Nights*. The interior was dimly lit, the walls decked in coloured silks. They were ushered to a reserved table near a small front stage. Several bottles of champagne instantly appeared. Minutes later the floorshow began. Musicians formed a semi-circle around an elderly man squatting in the centre of the stage playing a flute. A spotlight illuminated a reed basket in front of him. As the music built up, everyone's attention was focussed to see what was going to appear.

From the basket a cobra snake slowly rose.

The snake continued to rise to a height of about five feet, remaining eerily motionless. Meanwhile, scantily dressed dancing girls appeared from the rear and proceeded to synchronise their movements to the heady music. At the finale, one of the dancers picked up the snake, which enveloped itself around her and danced suggestively in front of their table. The applause was rapturous, the two generals laughing raucously.

James and his colleagues returned to their hotel in the early hours. They said their farewells. Hamish and his staff were not flying back to London until Saturday morning. However, James would not see them again as he was being picked up by Kate at ten o'clock, long before the ICL trio would fall out of bed.

***

Kate arrived promptly in a chauffeur driven Mercedes; her job obviously carried status. She was dressed traditionally: a loose, jade-green, ankle-length dress tied at the waist. She wore a matching headscarf. She looked as radiant as ever and seeing his admiring look, she posed, asking, 'My mother is rather old-fashioned in matters of dress, do you like it?'

They sat in the back together. The driver wore an Army private's uniform and had given James a smart salute when holding the door open for him to enter the car. 'If we go directly to our house, it will take about one and a half hours. I thought, therefore, we might make a small detour of about twenty miles to see Agargouf. It's the site of one of our finest ziggurats built around 1500 BC.'

Heading out of Baghdad in a north-westerly direction on a good-surfaced road, the twenty miles to Agargouf went quickly. Kate asked how Azi had got on with his war game and was amused to hear that it had not gone as well as he had hoped. She had never met Brigadier Murthah, although she knew he was a friend of her father's. When Major Talfah was mentioned, however, James could tell there was no love lost between herself and Roya. Mentioning that she had dropped into conversation at lunch that Saddam Hussein was her uncle, Kate had retorted, 'Typical! She's only a niece of Saddam's wife.'

Intrigued, James ventured to ask, 'Why don't you like her?'

'When we were at university, we were in the Military Training Corps together. She is a year older than me. I joined in my third year when I won the scholarship to go to Cambridge. She was inordinately jealous and, being a senior cadet, threw her weight around. She's a bully and, like all bullies, has the knack of not getting caught. I stood up to her on one occasion and she's hated me ever since. The feeling is mutual, I'm afraid.'

The ziggurat at Agargouf was impressive. Measuring about one hundred yards long and seventy-five yards wide, it had at one time risen to a height of almost 200 feet. It had been partially restored to a height of about seventy feet. Built of brick, its four corners pointed north, south, east and west. An hour wandering around went by quickly and it was soon time to resume their journey to Samarra.

While cutting across country on a minor road to reach the main Baghdad to Mosul road, Kate outlined the history of Samarra. It had, for a while, been the capital of the Abbasidian Empire until it was destroyed by the Mongols in 1258. Baghdad, by then the capital, fell too and some one hundred thousand books from its library were thrown into the Tigris, its treasures plundered and up to two million people were slaughtered.

Kate clearly knew more of her country's history than James knew of his. 'There are many palaces and mosques in Samarra, but as we go over the river in a few minutes you will see the spiral minaret, called the Malwiya. It stands about one hundred and eighty feet tall and was built in the ninth century. It was one of the few buildings that wasn't destroyed by the Mongols. We will visit it after lunch and climb it. The view from the top is fantastic. My parents' house lies in the north-west of the city. We will be there in about ten minutes.'

Their house was in an expensive-looking district. In common with the neighbouring houses, it was detached, surrounded by walls to give privacy, stood well back from the road and had an ingress and egress with controlled gates. The garden had two crescent-shaped lawns, surrounded by flowerbeds, with a tiled fountain in the centre. Palm trees increased the garden's privacy and gave shade from the overhead midday sun. The exterior of the house was white marble. Steps went up to the front door, where Kate's parents were waiting. After receiving warm hugs from both her parents, Kate introduced them to James. Her mother, an attractive woman called Ala, probably in her mid-fifties, was dressed traditionally. She gave James a welcoming smile and, although unable to speak much English, gave him a friendly embrace. Her father was more formal and somewhat sombre with his hospitality. He shook hands, greeting James in a slow, considered way as if trying to sum him up. His English was about as good as James' French – just passable.

'We're having a light lunch,' explained Kate after all the family had been introduced to James. 'This evening we are going to a banquet to celebrate the recent partial refurbishment of the Caliph's Palace. I believe the smaller of the two underground swimming pools has been updated and modernised.' Kate's younger sisters, Hind, aged twenty-one, and Lina, aged seventeen, were similar in looks to Kate, both pretty with black, shoulder-length hair and dark green eyes. Hind was a final year student at Mosul University where she was studying fine art, while Lina was hoping to become a physician. Both spoke excellent English, though with noticeable accents. James could see why Kate's father, Qassim, was proud of them.

During the meal, conversation tended to be a series of questions from the younger girls about life in England. Qassim would sometimes stop the chatter and get Kate to translate for his and Ala's benefit. The girls were intrigued that we had a queen as the head of state and couldn't understand why Prince Philip wasn't the king. The questions asked and the topics discussed ranged widely. The hardest to answer was, 'What does the sea look like?' It hadn't occurred to James that the girls had never seen the sea. James explained that he was born on a small island where the furthest you can be away from the sea is only five miles. They were mystified with the idea that the sea changes its colour. No two days are ever the same; some days it is blue, some days green and on other days grey. When he told them that it can be flat or it can have ten metre waves, depending on the weather, they didn't believe him.

Ala had prepared a starter that James had never seen before, fried eggplant, coated in yoghurt with spices. Their main course was a chicken casserole in a fig sauce and there were tiny pastries filled with honey and almonds to finish. Mint tea and fruit juices complemented a delightful meal.

Qassim had visibly relaxed towards James by the finish. 'Where are you planning to take James for the rest of the afternoon?' he asked Kate.

'I thought we would start at the Abbasid Mosque and climb the spiral minaret so that James can get a good view of Samarra. Then I thought we should go to see the Al-Askariyah Shrine,' she replied.

'Excellent, I will drive you there. I know the chief guides at both Mosques and will make sure you get VIP treatment.'

Climbing the 180-foot minaret proved to be taxing in the afternoon sun. Qassim had enough sense to stay in his car, yet another air-conditioned Mercedes. However, the view of the city and its relationship to the Tigris was worth the climb. The good visibility allowed them to see the Zagros Mountains shimmering in the haze to the east, one hundred miles away. It reminded James of Azi's ill-fated attempt to cross them in Nastia Game a few days previously. The spiral, built around 850 AD by one of the Caliphs, was in superb condition and had been well maintained. James could see why it was considered to be one of the wonders of the Islamic world. Coming down, Kate took hold of James' hand, smiled and said, 'Wait until you see the Golden Dome of the Al-Askariyah Mosque, it will blow your head away. It's an important shrine to the Shias, as it contains the tombs of the tenth and eleventh Imams.'

Her hand felt firm and cool. It frightened him. Up to now he had considered their friendship to be purely platonic.

Suddenly he wondered, *she can't possibly fancy me?*

She gave a childish, happy skip.

What would Emma think?

It was exciting. It was the first time for ten years that he had held a woman's hand, other than his wife's. His heart was pounding.

Emma will never find out.

He gave her hand a gentle squeeze, she responded.

She must know that a relationship is impossible. Stop being stupid.

She skipped again, beaming at him. Briefly, she let her head touch his shoulder.

She led him around the perimeter of the mosque, a rectangular building with walls thirty feet high. Measuring 250 yards long and 180 yards wide, it is one of the largest mosques in the Islamic world, capable of holding over 80,000 worshippers. She kept a firm grip of his hand; sometimes her hip rubbed against his and she would laugh mischievously. She only let go of his hand as they rounded the corner to Qassim's waiting car.

The Al-Askariyah Mosque was the most dazzling building James had ever seen. The great shining, golden dome, with its accompanying minaret, both entirely covered with gold-leaf, took his breath away as soon as he caught sight of it. Qassim parked the Mercedes in a VIP car park about one hundred yards from the outer courtyard and accompanied Kate and James towards the entrance.

'I will go over to the controller's office and get passes,' he said. 'I will try to get the senior guide to let us in to the mausoleums. There may be a problem with you not being a Muslim; even we Sunnis are treated as intruders.'

As they stood outside waiting for Qassim, James was in awe looking at the tiled mosaics that completely covered the outer walls of the building. The patterns looked like a mix of scenes from a story, coupled with Arabic writing.

Seeing him staring at the mostly blue, white and ochre tiles, Kate explained, 'Scholars claim that the contents of the entire Koran are written on these walls, along with stories from the Prophet Mohammed's life.'

'This is Ali, our guide,' said Qassim, as he came out of the controller's office. He says he will show us inside the mausoleum. Ali spoke English carefully; one word at a time. Consequently, his telling of the stories of al-Hadi, the tenth Imam, and his son, al-Askari, the eleventh Imam, both of whom were buried under the golden dome, was rather dull. After the dazzling splendour of the outside, the inside was somewhat disappointing although the self-supporting dome was impressive. The story of the twelfth Imam, al-Mahdi, disappearing in the mosque was intriguing. The second blue-tiled dome, in some ways more magnificent than the golden one, was built over the spot where he supposedly vanished. It is the central article of the Shia faith that some day al-Mahdi will return to bring universal peace to the world. The ironic similarity with Christians who believe Jesus will also someday return to save the world did not escape him. As they walked around the complex, James thought about the slaughter between Muslims and Christians over the centuries. It left him feeling uncomfortable and more than a little circumspect about the whole concept of religion. He was glad to come out into the hot sunshine even though the air was so humid.

He was, therefore, feeling reflective as Qassim drove them back home.

'We have an hour to freshen up before we must leave for the Caliph's Palace,' Kate said as they arrived. 'You must be looking forward to a shower and a change of clothing after climbing the minaret.'

James retired to his en suite bedroom, showered and lay down on the top of the bed in a thoughtful mood. His mind swung from the paradox of the various religious beliefs to wondering what Emma and the kids would be getting up to in Kewstoke. He had nodded off when there was suddenly a knock on the door. It swung open and Kate stuck her head around. 'Wakey, wakey, we are waiting for you in the foyer.' She grinned, showing no embarrassment at seeing James grabbing a towel to cover himself.

They drove to the Caliph's Palace with Qassim and Ala in the mayor's chauffeur-driven limousine. Kate explained that the Caliph, al-Mutasim, was the founder of the city and had built the palace in 836 AD when Samarra became the capital of the Abbasidian Empire. Importing marble from Egypt and palm trees from Basra, he diverted the Tigris to irrigate its great gardens. The palace had an esplanade along the banks of the river half a mile long. The palace had a polo pitch, a racecourse and swimming pools. It had been getting restored, on and off, since the 1960s and this evening's function was to celebrate the opening of the small swimming pool. The Vice-President, Saddam Hussein, was to open it.

Arriving in plenty of time, Qassim and his wife went straight to a huge marquee, where the reception was to take place. Their duty was to welcome the VIP guests. Meanwhile, Kate showed James some of the site, including the large serdab, a circular sunken basin, perhaps fifty yards in diameter. As they walked slowly around, she again held his hand; her eyes shone brighter than ever. James could feel himself blushing; he didn't know how to react to a situation he had never experienced before.

When they returned to the marquee, they were met by Kate's parents. Inside, circular tables had been set with white tablecloths, each sitting eight or ten people. There were at least forty tables. The marquee's ceiling and walls were decorated with hanging silks, back lit, coloured green, white and black – the national colours. A waiter showed Kate and James to their table, near a small stage. The marquee was three quarters full and James felt as if all eyes were on him. A tray of drinks, either champagne or orange juice, appeared. 'We are sitting with my parents and some of their friends,' whispered Kate.

Before long, some of Qassim's friends arrived, a couple in their mid-fifties with their son and his wife, who was heavily pregnant. Kate introduced them to James. He was to discover that the son was a major in the Iraq Army. He spoke excellent English, having attended a course at the Royal Military College of Science at Shrivenham. He sat on James' right, whilst his wife sat on Kate's left.

A gong banged and the marquee went silent. A military band, which had been playing quietly in one corner, started to play the national anthem. Everyone stood silently to attention. A procession approached toward a table in front of the stage. Saddam Hussein and his wife, the spitting image of her niece, Roya Talfah, led the entourage. Fourth in the line of couples were Kate's parents, who joined Kate and James at their table. No one moved until the Vice-President sat down.

Major Ali Jawaid was easy to talk to. He had joined the Army the same year as James had joined the RAF, 1966. As a second lieutenant he had seen some fighting in the 1967 Israel Six-Day War. By 1973, he was a company commander in the Yom Kippur War. He wouldn't say much about them, other than to blame the Syrians' lack of organisation for their defeat. Shrivenham had been the highlight of his career, he said. 'Wiltshire is a beautiful county with some lovely old villages. My wife and I lived in married quarters on the site and frequently went to Oxford.' His sentimental reminiscences were sincere. 'If I could, I would live there tomorrow.'

The catering staff served the dinner efficiently. Afterwards the Arabic speeches didn't last too long. Everyone remained seated as Saddam's party began circulating around the tables. He looked a big man, although he was neither physically tall nor over-weight. He had presence – that mysterious quality so many leaders possess. James' former commandant at Bracknell had it; you knew he had entered the room even if he was behind your back. Saddam was the same. He looked relaxed as he went from table to table. However, James felt there was an air of tension at some tables.

Finally, he came to Qassim's table to thank him for organising the function. Qassim introduced James to Saddam in Arabic. To his surprise, Saddam greeted James in English. 'Welcome to Iraq. I have heard about your war game from General Youseff. Brigadier Murthah has invited me to see it being played next week. I am hoping I can find the time.' He spoke English in a crisp manner, one word at a time but not ponderously. Replying that he hoped he would be able to come, James had stood to attention, bowing his head when introduced. Saddam smiled, brought himself up to his full height, cracked a joke with the ladies at the table and, accompanied by Qassim, left towards the exit. People began sitting down and resuming pleasantries. Shortly after, Qassim returned, blew a sigh of relief to Ala, and said, 'Let's go home; it's been a long day.'

CHAPTER 10

'I thought we might go for a stroll along the river bank and have a look at the town centre before lunch,' Kate suggested at breakfast the following morning. 'I have asked our driver to come for us at two o'clock. We should get back to Baghdad by four o'clock. Is that OK?'

Too busy munching into Ala's freshly baked breads, taken with lashings of honey, James nodded. He had wanted to buy a present for Ala who had shown him so much kindness. This would be his chance. He had fallen for her almost as much as for her daughter. About twenty-five years older than himself, she had a kindly, lived-in face, with warm, friendly, dark eyes. She had repeatedly tried to speak to him in her broken English and he had much appreciated it.

As James and Kate walked together along the path next to the Tigris, James asked what he should get her mother for a gift. 'Oh, just some flowers would suffice,' she had replied dismissively. However, when they reached the bazaar Kate showed a lot of interest in the gold merchants. Even James, who would not normally give a jewellers shop window the time of day, realised that the prices were cheap. 'You should get something for Emma,' Kate had suggested. In the end, and after considerable bartering, mostly conducted by Kate, James bought Ala a gold necklace chain with small coins attached to the links. Kate thought it was much too expensive.

He noticed Kate admiring a brooch. It was the shape of a scabbard with emeralds in the handle. Despite her initial protests, he bought it. 'I have never bought anything for you. Think of it as a small present to thank you for bringing me to Samarra, which will be the highlight of my visit to your country.' He realised it was not the greatest reason he could have used to buy her a gift. She quickly acceded to his insistence, however. She showed her gratitude by putting her arms around his neck and kissed him on his cheek. As her firm body pressed against him, a shiver passed down his spine. His toes curled and a tingle passed up his legs to his groin.

He saw a delicate gold necklace with a small pendant in the shape of the golden dome of the Al-Askariyah Mosque and he knew Emma would be pleased with it. 'I was thinking of buying her a rug,' he said. However, Kate insisted she would appreciate this much more.

Ala was over the moon when James gave her the chunky necklace, tears welled into her eyes and she gave him an embarrassingly close and long lasting hug. He knew her affection for him was genuine. He could not understand why she showed him so much kindness. He wondered if he had become her surrogate son.

Tears welled again after lunch when time came for the pair to leave. The al Jiseds were a close-knit family. Even Qassim showed some emotion. 'It's been a great weekend,' James said, 'and I can't thank you enough for showing me your beautiful city. Taking me as your guest to last night's function was a great honour.'

'I am sure some day you will find a way of thanking us,' he replied dourly. The remark passed over James' head, but it would come to have significance in the future.

Travelling back to Baghdad, Kate mentioned that Saddam had talked briefly to Qassim. 'Saddam wanted to know what our relationship was. Dad was shocked. He had some difficulty in persuading him it was purely a friendship brought about by the work on the war game.' She spoke quietly about there being much distrust within the Ba'ath party. The party was splitting into two camps, those pro-Saddam and those wishing to keep Bakr in power. She thought her dad was one of the latter group. 'Times are dangerous as Saddam is ruthless. He moves in mysterious ways. Last night, for example, when my father had mentioned that we were thinking of visiting Ur next weekend, Saddam volunteered one of his helicopters to transport us there. It would normally be a six-hour drive, but in a chopper, a mere ninety minutes. He even told my father that we should go via Babylon and could have free rein for an overnight stay in the presidential palace.'

'But that sounds fantastic. It would be wonderful to be able to visit Babylon as well as Ur. Why are you so suspicious?'

'Call me a pessimist, if you like, but I don't believe he is doing this for nothing. There will be a motive. I don't know what it might be, but it must involve Nastia Game or my research work.'

The rest of the journey passed mostly in silence, both thinking over the possible reasons for Saddam's offer. They arrived at the *Sheraton* around 4.30 pm. Kate promised to have dinner with James on Tuesday evening.

When receiving his room key from the receptionist, she handed James a sealed envelope. 'It was left here this morning.'

He took it up to his room and opened it. It was from Gerry and simply read, 'As soon as you get this, ring me on this number... '

'I'll come over this evening. Book a table for dinner, we've got to talk.' Gerry sounded serious and was not prepared to hint at the problem. 'I'll arrive around six-thirty.'

James took a long shower, allowing him to reflect on the events of the weekend. Kate's friendship had begun to worry him. He was overwhelmingly attracted to her; he had been since meeting her at Reading. Up to now, he had managed to keep his testosterone under control, pushing her to the back of his mind for much of the time. However, had she hinted at something more than a platonic friendship or was it wishful thinking? He had approached the edge of a precipice, peered over and liked what he had seen. One more tiny tug from her and he would fall over, hook, line and sinker. He knew that if he bedded her, there would be no going back. He would drown and never re-surface. His marriage would be over and his family gone. There would only be an empty bottle of whisky in a squalid tenement to look forward to in old age. He resolved not to go any further down the slippery slope.

Keep focussed, James, he told himself. *Remember Admiral Johnson's warning. Is she trying to trap you? Do your job; stay professional; be boring and you will be safe.*

He went down to the bar early. The regular barman was on duty and having got to know James, he knew what to serve, a German lager, ice cold. Gerry was punctual.

'This is probably as safe a place to talk as anywhere and I'll come to the point. We received a Flash signal yesterday afternoon from Admiral Johnson. I didn't fully understand its significance, but I was instructed to tell you its contents as soon as possible. However, when I was seeing Hamish and the others off, he told me you had gone to Samarra with Kathab al Jised.'

Thinking his remark needed some clarification, James explained. 'Yes, she invited me to stay with her family. She was returning a favour. When we were at Reading, she came and stayed with my family for a weekend in Weston-super-Mare. What is so urgent?'

'The signal stated that someone called John Richards has gone missing. Furthermore, the Wiltshire Police are treating his disappearance as suspicious. It said you would understand the possible consequences and that you were to be on your guard. I thought that the message was rather obscure, so I contacted MoD. I got hold of a Deputy Director of Intelligence, a Colonel Mike Mitchell. Do you know him?'

'Yes, Mike was big in setting up the security aspects of the Nastia Game contract with ICL.'

Gerry nodded, and continued. 'He told me that Richards has been missing for over a week and that, normally, such a case wouldn't interest MoD. However, when the police did a search of his house to see if there were any clues as to where he may have gone, they found a listing of some computer programs that had 'Copyright of MoD' printed on them. Consequently, the MoD police were contacted. Apparently, he has not cashed any cheques, nor used his bank card since he vanished. His wife is distraught. What Colonel Mitchell didn't tell me was what significance Richards was to you.'

They had both finished their aperitifs and James suggested they should continue their conversation over dinner.

As they ate, James described how John Richards had helped in writing the original programs for Nastia Game and how he had modified one of his company's security routines to the chess key.

'Now that you've explained that, it's beginning to make sense. I think Admiral Johnson's team are worried that Richards has been nobbled so that someone can get into the war game programs. The question is who?'

'Well they won't get very far. Firstly, the programs that were found in John's house would have been the ones written for Bracknell's old time-sharing system. They've since been rewritten in ICL's version of the language and are not compatible. Secondly, and more importantly, even if they discovered the old chess position, it's been changed. As of last Thursday, when we completed the first full game, no one had tried to tamper with the software and gain illegal entry. Thirdly, the programs now have a second ring of defence around them that the original ones did not.'

'How do you know there hasn't been anyone trying to gain entry?'

'The log on the computer in the operating room records all entries to the system. If an attempt is made to gain illegal entry, then the terminal is automatically shut down.'

Gerry nodded. 'But if Richards had told someone how the programs worked, couldn't they then work out how to break into the system?'

'Not really. A locksmith might know how a lock works, but he still can't open it without the key. In this case, there are trillions of legal chess positions to try. John and I used a position from one of Fischer's games against Spassky, but Hamish and I changed it as soon as ICL had rewritten the programs. Tomorrow, I will be changing it again and, as I said, the software is now more secure than ever.'

'How is it that only you and Hamish can change the position?'

'Simple. We both have unique user passwords that the system recognises. It then asks whether we wish to change the chess key. Mostly, the reply is *no*. Other legal users don't get asked the question.'

'So, what you're saying is that if someone thought they could get into the programs at the College, they would first need to know John Richards' password, as well as the Fischer position?'

'Yes. But John's password is no longer accepted and the log would record it as an illegal entry attempt. John's password was an anagram of his name, which we removed at Reading,' remarked James.

'So if someone has nobbled Richards, then it can't be the Iraqis, as, surely, Major Tumbrah and al Jised would know about the latest changes?'

'Yes, of course. It doesn't make any sense.'

There was a pause before Gerry asked, 'What are your plans for this week?'

'Lieutenant al Jised is coming over on Tuesday for dinner. I expect we'll go to one of the restaurants on the river. Work-wise, tomorrow I've a list of additions as long as your arm to make to the data files. Major Tumbrah wants a lot more industrial sites, factories and research facilities to be added to the map, both Iraqi and Iranian. Then on Monday I begin teaching the Iraqi staff. That day will be similar to a package I gave at Bracknell. On Tuesday, I will give a demonstration of the war game to show its facilities. That will take most of the day. On Wednesday, I'll get the Iraqis to begin playing for real. That will continue through to Thursday night. Incidentally, I should mention I met Saddam Hussein last night when I was at an evening function with Kathab's parents in Samarra. He said he might come to see the game being played sometime.'

'James, you're getting into deep and muddy water with al Jised. My worry is you're leaving yourself open to all sorts of blackmail. I know you're going to tell me it's none of my business, but for God's sake be careful. I don't trust any of these Iraqis any further than I can spit.'

'Funny you should say that, but Saddam's offered a military helicopter next weekend to take Kate and me to Babylon and Ur. Even Kate thinks there's a hidden agenda behind his generosity.'

'Have you accepted the offer?'

'Yes, we didn't really have any option.'

'Then I repeat, be careful. Don't get caught in a honey-trap. Changing the subject altogether, how about coming around to my place tomorrow evening for a bite? You can meet my wife, Sally, and some of our friends from the embassy.'

'OK, I'd like that very much.'

'I'll pick you up at seven o'clock.'

***

The next morning, being driven to Al-Rashid on his own for the first time, James felt vulnerable. The Omani staff had arrived and had made James his morning coffee.

'The programs are up and running,' he was told, 'but you'd better look at this.' The operator handed over a roll of paper. James instantly recognised it as the printout of the computer log. One glance and he could see there had been an illegal attempt to gain access.

James looked up from his desk, situated in the small outer office of the computer suite. 'Does anyone else know about this?'

'No, just me and Hassan.' He nodded in the direction of his colleague in the computer room.

'Don't tell anyone about this. Do you understand?'

The Omani nodded and left.

An entry had been made late on Thursday afternoon at 1730 hours.

'Terminal 10 – LOGIN PASSWORD, ************'
'Terminal 10 – Illegal access attempt – Password used, JORDAN HIRSCH'
'Terminal 10 – Date, 06 Jul 78, Time, 1730. Terminal Closed'

JORDAN HIRSCH – the anagram of JOHN RICHARDS! Calm down, James.

He could feel his heart beating against his ribs.

He wished Hamish was with him to discuss the best way forward. He wondered who could have gained access to terminal ten, situated in one of the syndicate rooms. The attempt had been made only a short time after they had left for the weekend. The intruder could have been anyone. His impression was that as soon as everyone had seen the Brigadier leaving, they would not have hung around for long. He didn't know whether he should let the incident go or report it to Brigadier Murthah. He was puzzled as to why an intruder would be stupid enough to think he could have broken into the war game software using John Richards' password. Surely, he would realise that his attempt would fail and be logged. As only he and the Omanis knew of the failed attempt, he decided to keep it that way.

However, two questions kept nagging him: who and why? He thought back to Bracknell, when Nastia Game was played on the computer for the first time. Number 66 ASC had students from Israel, Iran, Turkey and Saudi Arabia as well as Azi. James' prime suspects were, therefore, from one of those countries; his first bet being on someone working undercover for Iran. The rewrite and enhancement of the game by ICL was hardly a secret, so attempting to gain access with the old Bracknell password didn't make any sense.

Next he considered whether he should ring Gerry. However, the telephones were tapped. If he wasn't going to report the incident to the Commandant then there was no point in broadcasting it over the phone. *I'll keep this to myself until this evening.*

His first task for the day was to change the chess position he had used with Hamish. Knowing he would have to do this, he had brought with him his magnetic chess wallet, a flat set that used magnetic discs for the pieces. He had decided to set up a position from an opening trap that he had seen for the first time as a schoolboy. He had played the variation many times, usually successfully. Although it had a fatal flaw, none of James' opponents had ever been able to find the refutation at the board. The variation had been popular early in the 20th century until a future World Champion had demonstrated its flaw. James quickly played through the opening moves and decided to stop after a dozen, or so. He then entered his primary password, hit 'Y' when asked if he wished to alter the chess position, and entered:

'r1bNk2r/1pp2ppp/p7/8/B3p3/8/PPP2PPb/RNB4K'

He checked his typing, satisfied himself it was correct and hit the return key. The computer then asked for a repeat entry. This he did, successfully. He shuffled the magnetic discs on his chess wallet back to their starting positions. Then, taking a blank sheet of paper, wrote:

OK, THE UNLUCKY CAT WAS A VILLIN. (5,6,7,7)

Folding it, he put it inside his chess wallet, just as the phone rang. It was Major Talfah. 'Can you come up and see the Commandant, please? He has the new inputs we wish you to make to the game.' She sounded as distant as if she had been on the moon. He smiled to himself, having noted her use of the word *we*.

I wonder what power she holds over poor old Murthah, he thought to himself, as he left the computer suite to make his way up to the 'Old Man's' office on the top floor.

'The Commandant is waiting for you, go straight through,' Roya Talfah said to him, neither getting up from her chair nor looking him in the face.

By contrast, Brigadier Murthah immediately stood up as James entered his office. He had a warm smile, came round from his desk, shook hands and greeted him as an old friend. 'I hope you had a good weekend. We gave your ICL friends a good send off, don't you think? How did Samarra go? What did you think of the Al-Askariyah Shrine? Did you meet our vice-president?'

All his questions were asked with genuine interest.

James outlined his trip, including visiting the ziggurat at Agargouf as well as the sights of Samarra. He finished by saying that he had met

General Hussein. Frequently the Brigadier had intervened with an enthusiastic comment or question. However, when referring to Saddam as a Lieutenant General, a frown instantly appeared on his face. It became a worried look when James added that he understood he had invited Saddam to see the game being played at the College.

'I never did,' exclaimed the Commandant incredulously. He instantly pressed the button on his intercom. 'Come in at once, Roya,' he said in a vexed tone.

Major Talfah entered, a disdainful look on her face. 'Yes, sir?'

She's been listening to our conversation.

'Squadron Leader Douglas tells me there is a possibility that we may be getting a visit from your aunt's husband later this week. Do you know anything about it?' It was a fascinating way of referring to Saddam Hussein without having to mention his name.

I think the old boy is trying to put her in her place.

She glanced icily at James. 'Nobody has told me,' she replied.

I don't believe you.

'Get on to his outer office. Find out if and when he's coming. We'll have to arrange some sort of lunch if he comes, as well as a guard of honour.' She stretched to her full height, expanding her not inconsiderable chest, inhaling her stomach and swung round on her toes.

A fine pair, James thought as she stormed out.

'Did he give you a clue as to what day he might come?' asked the Brigadier.

'No, sir, but Wednesday or Thursday would be best to get the maximum benefit from the week's programme.'

'Let's hope it's Wednesday then. I've got plans to get away early on Thursday afternoon for a weekend's fishing near Al Amara.'

'I'm hoping to go to Babylon and Ur this weekend.'

'Really, that's quite a lot of driving you'll be doing, then.'

'No, apparently Saddam Hussein has offered us the use of a helicopter from the presidential fleet.'

'Who's "us"?'

'Sorry, I should have said Lieutenant Kathab al Jised and myself.'

'Ah.' He paused for a moment. 'Perhaps I shouldn't say this, but be careful. Everything Saddam does has a sting in the tail.'

'Funnily enough, you're not the first person to say that. Our Air Attaché, Wing Commander Platini, is also suspicious of his motives.'

'I've met Gerry Platini. He was a Lightning flying instructor at Riyadh some seven or eight years ago when I visited the Saudi base for a conference on air power. A nice fellow, I remember.'

James was nodding in agreement when there was a knock on the door. Azi came in accompanied by Major Boroumand. 'I've asked Azi and Abu to come and help with the list of additions we would like to add to the game,' said the Commandant.

The four sat in comfortable chairs in a circle and went through Azi's wish list first. He had arranged the changes in an order of priority. Most were potential targets that the Iranians might attack in future, such as arms factories, munitions dumps, oil refineries, presidential palaces and research centres. He was open and honest about the function of the sites that he thought should be added to the map. He included the atomic research centre and reactor at Osirak, the biological research complex at Al Muthanna and a small chemical weapons production plant at Al Hakam. 'After all, we must assume there are fifth columnists already in our country and they will know where our sites are, even if they don't know what we do in them,' he declared.

You don't know it, but there's already someone in the College who can't be trusted.

Other items on Azi's list were the inclusion of twenty-four tanker aircraft and eighty Mig-25 helicopters. 'I am assuming that we must get some as soon as possible, sir,' he said, looking at the Brigadier.

'Well, when a certain senior officer sees the game's results, I hope so too,' he replied.

Abu's list was not dissimilar. He wanted a lot of extra targets to be included on the map that had, until now, been kept secret. There were also a few additions to the Iranian Order of Battle. After an hour, or so, the meeting finished.

'You've plenty to be getting on with, I think,' said Brigadier Murthah with a smile.

'I think you might be right, sir. This little lot will take the rest of the day to enter.'

'There will probably be even more data for you to enter before we're finished,' added Azi.

For the rest of the day James was kept busy entering new locations to the map. Each target had not only to be identified by its latitude and longitude, but, also, by its descriptor and its ability to withstand bombing – its degree of hardness. Some of the Presidential Palaces and Command and Control Centres had been given the maximum factor by Azi. That meant they could survive a direct hit by an atomic weapon, typically indicating at least one hundred feet of concrete over an underground site. James noted Kate's Al Muthanna site was graded as being able to withstand a direct hit by fifteen 1,000 lb bombs.

Transport back to the hotel was postponed for an hour so that he could get most of the changes incorporated. It was becoming obvious that data had been held back deliberately to avoid Hamish and his team getting to know too much. Single items of information frequently had little significance and could be relatively lowly classified. However, when placed with dozens of other single items of similar information, they could become *Top Secret*. As more and more data was entered into the game, the files were becoming ever more attractive to a potential enemy of the Iraq State.

CHAPTER 11

James didn't arrive back at the *Sheraton* until nearly 1815 hours, giving him just enough time to shower and freshen up before Gerry was due to pick him up. Fortunately, he had asked the hotel receptionist that morning to get him a bouquet of flowers for Sally. She had not let him down.

Gerry was punctual. On the way to his residence in the south of the city, Gerry explained that the other guests were Peter Stacey and his wife, Jennie. 'Peter is officially the embassy's Deputy of Personnel Resources, which is another way of saying he's in MI6.' He chuckled. 'Until I came here I'd never met a spook, or I'd never known if I'd met one.'

'I don't think I've ever met one either, although when we ran computer security courses at Cranwell there were a couple of guys who turned up in mufti on one occasion and we suspected they were from MI5,' James replied.

'I'll be candid with you, James. I've told Peter about how you worked with Kathab al Jised at Reading, went to Samarra with her and met Saddam Hussein. He wants to talk to you about what you may have found out.'

The Staceys hadn't arrived when they reached Gerry's house. Sally was not the sort of woman James had expected to meet.

He's married a sensible type.

She was level-headed, thoughtful, spoke quietly, wore plain clothes and was probably good at keeping Gerry in check. She was delighted with her flowers. 'Gerry never brings me any.' Gerry looked sheepish and shrugged his shoulders, disappearing to the garage whilst mumbling something about getting a decent beer.

While waiting for the Staceys to arrive, James discovered that the Platinis had five children, three in boarding school in England who were coming over to Baghdad for their summer holidays the following week. Their two younger children attended the local International School. James was about to tell Sally about his own family when the doorbell rang. It was Jennie and Peter Stacey.

Jennie was the opposite to Sally. Giggly, joie de vivre, flowery dress, loud plummy accent, she was the type who enhances her husband's career by being the life and soul on the cocktail circuit. They had no children, but had two horses, which they had purchased in Saudi Arabia before coming to Baghdad.

'Do you ride?' Jennie had asked James, soon after they were introduced. Gerry was still pouring the couple two dry sherries. Sally was already looking embarrassed.

Presumably Sally isn't in the horse riding set either.

James didn't know how to reply diplomatically. Having always believed horse riding to be the preserve of the toffs, he settled for a chancy, 'Only motorbikes, I'm afraid.'

However, Peter surprised him. 'Back home, I have a couple of bikes: a Greeves trial bike and a Kawasaki Z305 that I use for commuting.'

He must be OK if he's a biker.

The ice was broken completely when Peter discovered James' Manx roots, as he had been to the Isle of Man to see the TT races several times.

Dinner conversation flowed easily, if a little one sided, owing to Jennie's self-opinionated line of society chat. She was a name dropper; her aunt was a lady-in-waiting to the Queen Mother. However, James remained on his best behaviour; quietly listening and occasionally having asides with Sally to whom he was warming. Gerry kept everything civilised and the wine flowed to accompany an excellent meal. It transpired Peter had been educated at Stoneyhurst College and Cambridge University where he had read engineering before being recruited into the scientific civil service. Jennie's background was a girl's boarding school in Harrogate, a well-to-do Yorkshire family and the eventing circuit. They made an unusual pair.

After coffee, Jennie and Sally disappeared into the kitchen. Gerry had obviously primed his wife that there were some matters to be discussed. Peter was soon asking questions and James outlined the progress with the war game.

'I briefly mentioned to Gerry that an attempt was made on Thursday evening to break into the game. I'm afraid the password used was John Richards' old one, Jordan Hirsch, an anagram of his name.'

'OK,' said Peter. 'I'll signal that off to Brigadier Morrison first thing in the morning. As far as I know, John Richards is still missing. No one knows why.'

'James and I discussed this last evening,' interrupted Gerry. 'We agreed that it can't be the Iraqis.'

'Why not?' asked Peter.

'Because,' said James, 'they know the programs were changed radically at Reading and that Hamish and I re-wrote the software and changed the secure chess key entry.'

'OK. However, what neither of you know is that GCHQ has been monitoring conversations concerning Nastia Game for some time; ever since you began working at Dataskil in fact. Most Friday evenings for several months someone would ring from a payphone in Reading to another public phone box in the West End of London. The conversations were always in an Arabic dialect and used a lot of pre-agreed codes to confuse eavesdroppers. GCHQ experts thought that the Reading speaker was not Arabic fluent, but that his or her natural tongue was either Hebrew, Farsi or a Syrian dialect. Could one of the team you worked with at ICL have been sympathetic to any of those countries?'

'Well, there was a programmer called Ben Green. I used to wonder if he was Jewish because neither Azi nor Kathab were too keen on him. Also, now I come to think about it, I am not sure if his security clearance ever came through. The other programmers were Don Henry, who was from the north-east and an avid Sunderland supporter and Jim Bryan from Somerset who spoke with a real twang. Hamish was about as Scottish as it's possible to get and had been positively vetted.'

'Are you sure there was no one else with access to the game?'

'There were the operators in the computer suite who loaded the magnetic tapes and mounted the discs. Hamish would know more about them than me. You could ask him. Then there was the security site that was used to store the backup tapes each evening. I suppose it's possible someone there could have made illegal copies.'

'How did the backup system work?'

'One of the operators would copy the latest version of the software onto a magnetic tape at the end of the working day. He would then take it across to the secure site. The tape would be logged in and he would bring back the previous day's version, which would be out of date.'

'What would happen to the old tapes?'

'Hamish saw that they were effectively destroyed by overwriting them. I know he kept a logbook.'

'This is all very interesting,' remarked Gerry, 'but none of those people would have known anything about the Bracknell connection with John Richards.'

His remark took a little while to sink in.

'When Nastia Game was played at Bracknell with No 66 ASC, there were students from Iran, Israel, Turkey and Saudi Arabia, as well as Azi Tumbrah. I think you had better warn Hamish to be on his guard. Whoever we are dealing with here will not know that I changed the chess position this morning. They may try to extract the old one from Hamish, hoping to get access to the most up-to-date version of the game. Incidentally, Gerry, the latest position is in this sealed envelope. I have described the position as a word puzzle and then made it into an anagram.' He gave Gerry the envelope.

'I'll arrange for it to go in the diplomatic bag tomorrow.'

'What are you doing at Al-Rashid for back up?' asked Peter.

'Each evening the senior operator copies the contents from the disc drives to a magnetic tape, which is kept in a fire-proof, purpose-built safe in the computer suite. He then overwrites this tape the following evening and so on. Only he knows the combination of the safe.'

'So, if someone could open that safe, they would have access to the war game?'

'No. The software scrambles itself and the data when it is being copied. You would still need the password and chess position to decipher it.'

Peter nodded, but didn't look totally convinced. 'Changing tack,' he asked, 'what do you make of Kathab al Jised?'

'She's very nice, I like her very much.'

'That's not quite what I meant. Let's try a different approach. Has she ever mentioned to you someone called Professor Bucke?'

'No, why?'

'He is a Departmental Head in the Faculty of Pure Science at Cambridge. Amongst other things, he recruits graduates for MI5 and MI6. He recruited me, for example. Overseas students are rather different, but last year he approached Kathab to see if she would be interested in keeping in touch with us when she returned to Iraq. He tends to grade students on a 1 to 5 scale: 1 is "bugger off", 2 is "unlikely", 3 is "possibly", 4 is "probably", and 5 is "definitely interested". He rated her as 2 or 3. I wondered what you thought, now that you are getting to know her.'

'She spent a weekend with my family in Weston-super-Mare and she visited Bath with my wife. We went to Wells Cathedral, Cheddar Gorge and other touristy places. There is no doubt in my mind that she likes England and its freedoms. On the train back to Reading, I remember her slightly misquoting Blake as she gazed out of the window.'

'Blake?'

'Yes, it was somewhere after Chippenham. She was gazing out of the window when she suddenly said,

And did those feet in ancient time
Walk upon England's green and pleasant Land.

I was impressed and asked her how she knew the hymn. She laughed and said something like:

People of quality know everything
Without ever being taught anything.'

'She was quoting Molière at you,' remarked Gerry. '*Les Gens de qualité savent tous sans avoir jamais rien appris.*' For Peter's benefit, he added, 'My mother was French.'

'However,' continued James, 'if you are asking me whether she would spy on her own country, that's a different matter. Are you asking me to try and recruit her in some way?'

'No, not at all. Don't get me wrong. It's just that if she gives you some hint that she might like to keep in touch with us, please let me know. She's obviously a very gifted woman, and would be useful to have on our side.'

'You mentioned the Syrians earlier on as possible suspects who might be after the Nastia Game software. I thought they were now allies of Iraq?' asked James, wanting to change the subject.

'The Iraqis view them almost as suspiciously as the Israelis, ever since the Yom Kippur war,' replied Peter.

James then remembered Major Ali Jawaid's story at the Samarra reception, but let Peter continue.

'Five squadrons of the Iraqi Air Force fought in the 1973 war. Two squadrons of Hunters were based with the Egyptians and campaigned over the Sinai, while three squadrons of Mig-21s were based in Syria and flew over the Golan front. Apparently, they lost more aircraft to Syrian SAMs than to combat with the Israelis. Furthermore, a division of the Iraqi Army was virtually abandoned at one point when the Syrians decided to retreat from advancing Israeli tanks but didn't tell anyone.

Yom Kippur was not the Israel victory we were led to believe. Rather it was a cock-up caused by pathetic Arabic Command and Control. Ever since, Iraq has viewed Syria as something of a liability.'

'I didn't know the Iraqis had Hunters,' said James.

Gerry chipped in quickly. 'We used to train their pilots; they were very good too.'

At this point, the ladies returned, no doubt exhausted from making polite conversation. Jennie announced, 'Peter, it's time we should be going.'

No one was going to argue.

***

On Monday the shortened Bracknell computer course was well received. The demonstration programs kept the audience attentive. There were one or two hiccups in translation, but most seemed to be able to comprehend English without requiring headphones. The questions asked at the breaks displayed enthusiasm and purpose. The course finished at 1600 hours, allowing James to complete the data entry that he had been unable to complete the previous day. It was almost 1830 hours when he arrived back at the *Sheraton Hotel*.

On entering the lobby, he was surprised to see a worried Gerry waiting for him. 'There may be another problem; let's go for a stroll along the riverbank,' he said. Outside the sun was starting to settle in the west and the temperature was slowly becoming bearable.

'It's only about 1530 hours in London, and we may be worrying for nothing, but Hamish hasn't reported for work with ICL this morning. He was supposed to have contacted Colonel Mitchell first thing to arrange giving him last Thursday's magnetic tape. When Hamish hadn't made contact by mid-morning, Mitchell took the precaution of getting one of Thames Valley's special branch officers to go around to Hamish's flat in Reading. The neighbour, who was looking after his apartment, told him that Hamish was still away and hadn't returned. His car was in its parking lot, where he'd left it prior to going to Baghdad. British Airways at Heathrow confirmed that he arrived on Saturday afternoon with Don Henry and Jim Bryan. All three of them caught the shuttle bus to Reading station, where they departed. However, Don told Mike Mitchell that the customs people at Baghdad airport had searched Hamish's suitcase and confiscated the magnetic tape. No explanation was given. When Hamish protested he was given two alternatives – get on the plane or remain in Baghdad. Needless to say he chose the former. Hamish then told Don that he would ring the MoD duty officer and tell him what had happened as soon as he got back to his pad. However, no call was received.'

'So it's reasonable to assume that he was waylaid somewhere between Reading Railway Station and his flat?' asked James.

'It looks like it,' replied Gerry.

'Someone has realised that Hamish's password and knowledge of the chess key are crucial to getting into Nastia Game. However, whereas Hamish's password would gain entry to the version on the magnetic tape confiscated at Baghdad airport, it won't get into the current version at Al-Rashid. I changed the position yesterday morning. Up to when I left an hour ago, no one has attempted access. It's ironical that if Hamish had had the tape on him, then whoever waylaid him would have got something for their efforts. I guess the Iraqis are ruled out again?'

'How do you make that out?' asked Gerry.

'Well, surely, they could have kept him in Baghdad on some trumped up charge if they had wanted access that much?'

'Not necessarily. It would look too bad for international relations to hold someone who has been here helping them build a computer system for the past three weeks.'

'True. There is something not quite right about all this. Nastia Game effectively contains the battle plans for the invasion of Iran. The classified data files are now huge. Only Iran could want to know what the Iraqi plans are, and yet I can't get Israel out of my mind for some reason.'

'Well, legally, Iraq is still officially at war with Israel. Saddam will never forgive Egypt's Sadat for addressing the Israeli Knesset last November and conducting the current peace negotiations to formally end the Yom Kippur war. The Israelis don't trust Saddam any more than we do and are worried about the rumoured nuclear plant at Osirak. If Iraq were to get its hands on a surface-to-surface missile capable of delivering a nuclear warhead to Tel Aviv, then we could expect fireworks.'

'So, what are we going to do?'

'If you find out tomorrow that someone has tried to gain entry to the programs at Al-Rashid, then I want you to ring me at once. This is my direct line number.' He handed James a slip of paper. 'Of course, the call will be monitored, so I suggest we use a code. Perhaps, ring to tell me that you have just remembered you can't make it to dinner because you have another engagement.'

'Actually, I have. Kathab is taking me out for a meal tomorrow night.'

'Good. Don't say why you can't make it. As you are putting the phone down say "Give my love to Sally" if there has been a break-in attempt. If you don't ask for her, then I'll know everything is fine.'

'OK. However, if there has been an attempt to get in with Hamish's password, then that definitely clears the Iraqis.'

'Why?'

'Because they have the magnetic tape that they confiscated at the airport. If they also have Hamish's password, then they can change the game whenever they want. They will have no need to go blundering into the version at the College. The additional targets and weapons that I entered on Sunday they could do for themselves.'

'Without the password the magnetic tape is useless?'

'Yes, it's encrypted. It might as well be in double Dutch.'

'If you tell me the news is bad, then I'll get on the scrambler straight away to Brigadier Morrison's outfit. The shit will then, no doubt, hit the fan. Now, shall we go back to the *Sheraton*? I've asked Sally to come over. I thought we could join you for a meal, rather than you eating alone. Is that OK?'

'Great, but I must get a shower first.'

CHAPTER 12

The following morning James felt apprehensive as he travelled to the College worrying what he might find.

Mohammed, the senior of the three operators came in to his office, looking serious. He handed him the print out of the log, with his coffee. He said nothing. He didn't have to. The log read:

Terminal 10 – Access to Nastia Game – Password used:
***************** / Accepted
Terminal 10 – Date 10 Jul 78, Time 1755
Terminal 10 – CHANGES TO DATA? (Y/N), Y

YOU WILL BE ASKED 5 QUESTIONS ON THE CURRENT POSITION. USE CAPITAL LETTERS TO INDICATE WHITE PIECES, AND small letters for black pieces.

1. WHAT IS ON D7? n
2. WHAT IS ON A5? Q
3. WHAT IS ON C4? P
4. WHAT IS ON E2? N
5. WHERE IS kn? E3

Terminal 10 – Access denied to game, terminal closed, position errors
Terminal 10 – Date 10 Jul 78, Time 1757

Although he hadn't known Hamish's password and, therefore, hadn't been able to remove it from the system, he counted the number of asterisks – seventeen. It was an unusual number. He had known Hamish was a big Heart of Midlothian supporter. He counted the number of letters on his fingers, also seventeen.

I'll give it a try, he thought to himself as he typed in 'heartofmidlothian'. The system accepted the password.

He also recognised the answers to the chess questions; it was the Bobotsov–Tal position he had used with Hamish.

Ah well, here goes.

He picked up the phone and asked for Gerry's number.

'Air Attaché.' It was Gerry's voice.

'Gerry, James here. You remember asking me around this evening for a bite to eat?'

'Yes.'

'Well, I'm afraid I can't make it. I remembered when I got into bed last night that I have made alternative arrangements. Perhaps tomorrow?'

'Sure, that will be OK. I'll pick you up at the same time?'

'Fine. Give my love to Sally.' He put the phone down, hoping the agreed message would work.

Espionage is not my forte.

He picked up his lecture notes and made his way to the lecture theatre to meet Jalal and go over the day's schedule. Azi and Abu had agreed to play against each other, with Ayman acting as messenger. Jalal continued as the interpreter. The large demonstration screen would show the total picture of the game to the audience, including data capture methods. Hopefully, the moves played would excite the audience sufficiently to get an animated question and answer session to clear up queries in the user manual that had been issued the previous week.

'What ifs' from the audience were handled by James with a 'let's see' approach. The suggested moves were entered, after consulting Azi and Abu. Consequently, the game developed somewhat artificially. Nevertheless, it demonstrated the weaknesses of the Iraqi Order of Battle;

they badly needed tanker aircraft and more support helicopters. All day there was a real buzz in the theatre. Lunch was shortened as all were keen to see whether the plan to capture Abadan could be achieved before cease play. James was too busy to reflect on the consequences of the misuse of Hamish's password.

The syndicates for the following day had been drawn up by the Commandant to avoid any arguments. Three separate games involving nine staff in each game, three playing for Iraq, three for Iran, two as messengers and one as umpire, would be played. James, Azi and Abu would be floating consultants. The game's rules were stressed to the audience by Brigadier Murthah, including not discussing their game with anyone. The games would be played until Thursday afternoon and were to be seen as learning games. Next week, he explained, the teams would be changed and would be played for five consecutive days. It was past six o'clock when James fell into the back of the staff car to be driven back to the hotel. He shut his eyes.

'Wake up, you dozy sod.' It was Gerry. He had been waiting at the *Sheraton*. Seeing the staff car arriving, he had come down the steps at the front of the hotel, opened the door and found James fast asleep.

As the car drove away, Gerry began. 'The use of Hamish's password has caused excitement back home. I've been told to tell you that Admiral Johnson has allocated a small SAS team to discreetly guard your family in Kewstoke. He is worried that whoever is after the secrets in Nastia Game may now try to get at you through your family. He says you are not to worry, but he wants you to return as soon as possible next week. I have already arranged for you to fly out next Friday morning. Hamish is still missing and I think they are working on the assumption that both he and John Richards have been abducted.'

'Hello, what are you two talking about?'

They both swung around. Neither had seen Kathab approach. She had arrived to take James out for dinner. Gerry's face was a picture, not because he hadn't seen her before, but because they might have been overheard.

'You look as if you've seen a ghost, Gerry,' she said beaming at him. 'Surely, you remember me from the embassy barbeque?'

'Forgive me,' he replied, quickly regaining his composure. 'You startled me; that's all. It's nice to meet you again. James was just telling me that he had a great time in Samarra.' He was not very convincing. 'We were just about to go into the bar for a drink. Will you join us?'

'Well, it's not often I can have a drink with two good-looking RAF officers,' she joked as the three walked up the steps into the foyer. James ordered two beers and a large orange juice.

'I've just arrived back from the College, Kate. So if you don't mind, after I've finished this I would like to go up and have a quick shower before we go out? I'm sure Gerry will look after you for ten minutes, or so.'

'It will give Gerry an opportunity to practise his Arabic,' she replied, smiling at Gerry.

It was almost 7.30 pm by the time James returned to the bar.

'Feel better?' she asked.

'Yes, thanks. It's been a hard day teaching the capabilities of Nastia Game. Azi and Abu Boroumand played each other and came up trumps. Without them it would have been impossible. Tomorrow and Thursday, the staff have been put into teams and three games are being played simultaneously.'

'So, you'll be late getting back tomorrow as well?' asked Gerry. 'I'll tell Sally that I'll pick you up at eight o'clock, instead of seven-thirty? Incidentally,' looking at Kate, 'I don't suppose you'd like to join us for dinner tomorrow?'

'That's very kind of you, but I don't think I should, do you?'

'Why not?'

'As you know, we're being watched. I think I'd better be careful, just in case... ' She never finished her sentence.

Gerry didn't push the matter any further. 'OK. I'll see you tomorrow, James,' and looking at Kate, 'perhaps, we can persuade you to join us another time? By the way, Kate has given my Arabic a pass.'

They walked to the restaurant in contemplative silence. There was clearly a lot on Kate's mind. Even before they reached the *Abu Samba* restaurant, she said, 'We have much to discuss; I am worried we are falling into a trap.'

'What do you mean?'

She never replied.

The restaurant expected them. The manager obviously knew Kate. He greeted her as if she was a regular customer. They were shown to the best table, near a window overlooking the Tigris. They were well away from the other diners, although the restaurant was but half full.

'What's worrying you?' he asked.

'I was called to see the Head of our research laboratories yesterday.'

'So?'

'A senior member of Saddam's security staff, General Mandhar Tufiq, was there. He made it clear to me that I was expected to get from you the password and chess position to access Nastia Game.'

'He threatened you?'

'Yes, if I don't get what he wants my family could be in danger.'

'You're joking.'

'I wish I was, but that's the way it is in Iraq these days. I was told that there is going to be a change of direction in the Ba'ath Party very shortly. When, not if, Saddam comes to power, there will be a purge. Current supporters of President Bakr will go. By that he meant disappear permanently. He knows my father is a Bakr man. If he is to survive the purge, I was told, "You know what you must do." I asked him how I am supposed to do that. His reply was a shrug and, "Whatever is necessary."'

'Do you think he's serious?'

'I'm certain.'

'So, what you're saying is that if I don't give you the information they want, then your father is as good as dead?'

She nodded, saying nothing; a glaze over her green eyes.

James fell silent in thought; he didn't know what to say.

This is the trap Admiral Johnson and Gerry warned me about. She's flirting with me to get the secret of the key.

His mind was racing.

Bizarrely, he wondered if he could play her along and get away with it.

After a few minutes, he'd made up his mind. He said, 'I want you to promise that what I am going to say, you will never tell anyone.'

'Of course. What?'

'We believe Hamish has been killed.'

'So the killing has started already,' Kate exclaimed.

'We're not sure that it's Saddam's men who are involved,' replied James.

'Why not?' Kate asked.

'Because,' James stopped. He realised that he couldn't explain without telling Kate about the security problems at the College.

'Well?' she insisted.

He hesitated. 'I am not sure I can tell you.'

'Are you trying to tell me there's someone else besides Tufiq trying to get into Nastia Game?'

She's quick; I'll give her that.

'Yes, I suppose I am.'

'Such as who?' He knew he had to tell her the truth; there was no alternative.

'It could be the Iranians or the Israelis,' he suggested quietly.

'What makes you think that?' She was in charge now; her demands overwhelming him.

'Let's just say that our security services don't think it's Saddam's men because there would be easier ways of entering the game. Anyway, Hamish's password no longer gains entry. I changed it on Sunday.' It was a sheepish reply and made him feel distinctly uncomfortable.

Kate gave him one of her hard, steely stares, but said nothing. He remembered the train journey back from Weston-super-Mare when in just a few seconds her personality had also changed.

How can a friendly, warm woman turn so rapidly to be so distant and cold?

They said nothing for a few minutes, both at a loss as to how to continue.

James broke the ice. 'I am worried about the threat to your family. There is no way I can stand back and allow something to happen to Qassim or Ala. There must be something I can do?'

He was fishing for some sort of compromise; wondering whether he was falling into her trap or whether he could keep control.

I can't believe she is flirting with me for an ulterior motive. Surely, she's not some latter day Mata Hari?

'You must give me the chess key before you return to England.' Her words were crisp and menacing. She was demanding, not asking. Her stare went through him like a stiletto; its tip ran down his spine. He was reminded of Snow White's mother: beautiful but pitiless. Her mood swings were unique to him, unlike Emma who was always placid. At Reading, he had seen her friendly nature freeze in seconds with the ICL staff. He didn't know why, but it excited him.

'I'm not sure how I can give you the key to Nastia Game without compromising myself. If I did so, then I would have to come up with a damn good excuse to satisfy London.'

Her head jerked backwards. 'But, don't you see, that's exactly what the bastards want.'

'I'm sorry, but you're getting me confused.' *What the hell is she on about?*

She looked at him pathetically. There was a look of disdain on her face. Her persona had changed again.

You poor man, she must have been thinking, *are you that stupid?*

'Tufiq wants me to seduce you so he can blackmail you. I can't do it. I know I'll probably never meet Emma again, but I couldn't look her in the face if I did. I liked your family as much as you have taken to mine. There is no way I can ruin yours, any more than you can allow mine to be destroyed. Our friendship has trapped us.'

She must be sincere. There's no way she could have come up with that one.

They ate silently; neither enjoying their meal. James had no idea what he was eating, but as he looked at her, he knew he was trapped. He loved his family more than anything. He had never looked at another woman since meeting Emma, yet he knew he had fallen for Kate. Enigmatically, her personality swings made her more attractive, not less. She was the most exciting female he had ever been with. In her presence his heart ran at twice its usual speed. She was fun. She lifted his spirits to a new height. When she stared coldly through him, reaching his very core, the excitement intensified rather than lessened.

'Are we still going to Babylon and Ur this weekend?' he asked after a considerable pause.

'Of course,' she replied. 'I don't think we have a choice. If you were to call it off, then Tufiq would blame me. They have arranged for us to stay in the Presidential Palace in Babylon on the first night and in a VIP suite at the Officers' Club at Ur Air Base on the second.'

He tried to lessen the tension. 'It sounds cosy.'

'Don't get any ideas.' She managed a smile. She was returning to her friendly, girlie-mood. 'The rooms will be bugged.'

'In that case I will make suitable moaning and groaning noises to give them something to think about.' It was a crude effort to suggest he fancied her. As soon as he had said it, he realised what a childish joke it had been.

However, she laughed. She didn't seem to mind his clumsy approach. It had broken the ice. She surprised him by continuing in a similar vein. 'It would be fun to watch you grunting like a pig while some idiot is listening and thinking some bonking was going on.'

They laughed together. Some customers eyed them disapprovingly, probably wondering what an Iraqi woman was doing with a European infidel. Kate and James, seeing their reaction, chuckled quietly.

He put his hands across the table and she allowed him to hold hers. He looked into her jade-green eyes. He whispered, 'We'll work something out.' She smiled, trying to hide the sadness in her eyes. It was the same look she had given him on the Reading train; the moment when he knew he had fallen for her. He was powerless in her grip. They finished the rest of their meal in silence.

'Look,' he said, 'the chess position is less important than your family's safety. If I were to drip-feed the information to you, it would keep the bastards off your back. Each piece of data on its own would be insufficient for them to work out the position, until they had got all the clues. What do you think?'

Her face brightened. 'Could you do that?'

'Yes, but there is a caveat.' She looked at him, nodded, but didn't say a word. 'You must always be totally honest with me. I have to be able to trust you completely no matter what happens.'

It was a desperate attempt to reassure himself. If she gave him her word then he could excuse himself for whatever was coming.

She nodded agreement; the look on her face was honesty personified. At that moment, he convinced himself he could rely on her.

They remained silent, looking at each other. Then she said, 'There is something you should know about me if our friendship is to go any further. What I am about to say, you must never repeat to another living soul. By telling you, I am trying to show you that I will always be open and honest with you. Do you understand what I am saying?'

James couldn't have guessed in a million years what was coming next, but managed, 'I think so.'

'Only my mum and dad know what I am going to tell you, not even my sisters know.' She continued without pausing. 'When I was two years old, I became very ill. The doctors didn't know what was wrong, as the symptoms were vague: terrible bloating, I was not putting on weight and obviously had abdominal pain. I underwent an exploratory operation and was diagnosed as having ovarian cancer.'

James' face dropped.

She stopped, waiting for the news to sink in.

James said nothing, not knowing what to say.

'My father borrowed money for my mother and I to go to Cairo, where I underwent an operation to remove the cysts. In the end the operation amounted to a full hysterectomy. I am, therefore, sterile and will never be able to have a family of my own. That is why I am so envious of you and Emma. Dad had to work eighteen hours a day for two years afterwards to pay the bill. It was early days for that type of operation. The physical scars have all gone, but the emotional ones remain. There are times when my mix of hormones is not right. It was one of the reasons why I became interested in microbiology.'

James' eyes welled up.

God, life is cruel. That seals it. Now I know she is not taking me for a ride.

He squeezed her hands gently, and she held on. The most beautiful woman he had ever known was, after all, not perfect.

'I don't know what to say. You would have made a wonderful mother, like Ala.' It was not the most delicate nor diplomatic thing to have said. He realised at once and tried to correct himself. 'What I am trying to say is that your secret is safe with me and that no one will ever know. I am glad you have been able to tell me, but it doesn't stop me feeling the way I do about you.' He was feeling awkward and he knew it. He couldn't find the right words.

She raised her glazed eyes and looked at him. She said nothing, but her face was asking him to continue.

'I think you know.' He paused for what seemed a long time, and then in a barely audible voice, 'You know I love you.'

She didn't show any reaction for several minutes. Then she whispered, 'I felt you were different from the minute you called me Ava. It was why I researched who Ava Gardner was one weekend when I was in Cambridge. I was flattered that you should think of me in that way. Now you know my secret, you must realise that nothing good can come of our relationship.'

'Not so. There is nothing as wonderful as having a friend in whom you can trust and have faith. I would like to think our friendship will last.'

'I hope so,' she replied softly. And then, looking around the restaurant, she added, 'We're the last ones left. I think the manager would like us to leave.'

The cold night air was a tonic. James felt that a load had been lifted from his shoulders as a result of telling Kate his feelings. As they walked back to the *Sheraton* holding hands, he felt the time was right to mention that he knew she had been asked about becoming an agent. 'I gather you met Professor Bucke at Cambridge?'

She froze and took her hand away. 'How do you know that?'

That instant swing of mood again. Wonderful!

'Someone told me on Sunday evening when I was at Gerry's house for dinner. I want you to know that my giving you the chess key to Nastia Game has nothing to do with Professor Bucke, or what he may have suggested. Indeed, I don't want you to get involved with them. Keeping in touch, as they so euphemistically call it, would be dangerous. I will give you the position in three stages. This weekend I will give you an anagram of a word puzzle that describes the position. It will be too difficult for Tufiq's men. Before I leave Baghdad, I will give you the word puzzle that exactly describes the position. My guess is that it will still be too difficult for them to work out, unless one of them is an exceptionally knowledgeable chess historian. I will give you the final clue to decipher the puzzle when I am safely in England.'

'How will you do that?'

'It will give you an excuse to come to England, or I will send it to you.'

'The first idea is best.'

She had resumed holding his hand and they soon had to depart when they reached the hotel. Her driver was waiting to take her back to Al Muthanna.

***

James tossed and turned all night. His brain switched from one problem to the next without resolving any. What would Emma think if she discovered his feelings for Kate? Did she have to find out? What about the children? Could he let Kate down now that he had promised her the game key? How could he gradually give up the chess secret? Was Kate's family really in danger or was she having him on? Was he being tricked as Admiral Johnson had warned? And so it went on, and on...

The conscience of a lapsed Methodist knows no bounds – worse than a lapsed Catholic, perhaps? He was being torn apart. No matter what he tried, he couldn't fall asleep. He imagined he was biking around the Isle of Man TT course trying to remember all its bends and features. However, his worries soon interrupted his ride and the TT course was forgotten. He tried remembering all his ex-girlfriends; there weren't that many, but it didn't help. Why had his liaisons always ended in torment? Was there something wrong with him?

He got up, made himself a mint tea and looked at his watch, 3.30 am. He was cold. He tried reading a book, but put it down after a few pages. It was no use; tomorrow he would ring Kate and cancel the trip to Babylon and Ur. He would make up some excuse. It wasn't logical, but he didn't care. Would it be better if he left it until the last minute, feigning illness? The decision made, his restlessness cured, he got back into bed and fell into a deep sleep. He was woken by his alarm clock at 5.45 am; it seemed only a few minutes later.

CHAPTER 13

Kate arrived at work as usual by seven o'clock to find her secretary looking worried.

'The director wants to see you in his office at once. He seemed agitated.'

'Did he say what it's about?'

'No.'

Kate nodded and walked up the corridor to her boss' complex. Entering the outer office, the secretary smiled coldly at Kate, telling her to go straight in. She found herself in front of General Tufiq, as well as her boss.

'Well, how did you get on?'

It was the General who, without any informal greeting, had asked the searching but vague question.

'What do you mean?' asked Kate, pretending she didn't know what he was talking about.

'Don't play games, al Jised.' He practically spat the words out. 'Is Douglas going to give you the all-important chess key, or not?'

'Of course,' she smiled at him, but her look was chilly and penetrating. Showing no emotion whatsoever, she continued. 'The infidel thinks he is in love with me. However, he is cautious and has promised to give me the key in stages. This weekend he will give me the first step, an anagram of a word riddle that exactly describes the position.'

'Anagram. Riddle?'

'Yes, a sort of puzzle. Don't worry. I will extract it all from him. It will be like a dentist pulling out a tooth, painful for him but it will give me much pleasure.'

'Excellent.' Tufiq had reverted to a friendlier tone. 'You have done well. The Revolutionary Council will be pleased with you.'

'There is one other thing,' she added, resuming a more feminine posture. 'I think the British want to recruit me as an agent of theirs.' She didn't wait for the General to react, but continued. 'Douglas inadvertently made a big hint of it last night and earlier in the evening Platini invited me to dinner tonight.'

'What did you say?'

'I turned his offer down, of course. It would be wrong of me to have accepted without your permission.'

'Ring up Douglas as soon as you return to your office. Tell him you have changed your mind. After all, it is a woman's prerogative.' He chuckled expecting Kate to smile at his little joke. Instead, she stared at him blankly. He continued. 'It would be wrong for us to turn down this opportunity to plant a double agent in their midst. We are doubly pleased with you.' He chuckled again; again she didn't react to his humour. He gestured for her to leave; their conversation was over. Kate, despite not wearing a uniform, saluted him smartly, and left.

***

James was sitting in his office, grabbing a break in the play of the games that were in full swing. Sipping his coffee, he was thinking of the dilemma over the disclosure of the chess key. The phone rang. To his astonishment it was Kate. She began by buttering him up and thanking him for the wonderful evening they had had together. After some further small talk, she brought the subject skilfully around to Gerry's offer to dinner. She had been thinking that he must have thought her rude to have turned down such a generous invitation. 'Do you think you could ring him and explain to him that I have changed my mind and would love to come?' she asked.

James was somewhat flummoxed, but, not suspecting her of any ulterior motive, was only too happy to oblige. He assured her that all would be well and she should turn up at his hotel at eight o'clock. Excited at the thought of seeing her so soon, he had completely forgotten his plan to cancel the Babylon weekend when he asked the operator for Gerry's number.

***

For the rest of Wednesday he was kept busy sorting out the small snags encountered by the directing staff. There was no time to worry about his problems. The enthusiasm of the Iraqi officers and the speed with which they picked up the game's procedures was impressive. It was embarrassing to compare their energy with that of some of the officers who had been so sceptical at Bracknell. Brigadier Murthah floated around watching the games, giving words of wisdom as he thought fit. The rigorous testing of the software by Dataskil was proving to have been time well spent for no problems arose. Trivial finger keyboard slips lessened as the day wore on. By 1700 hours all the games had been put on hold until the following day and James was able to get back to his hotel relatively early. A shower and a ninety minute snooze set him up for the evening with Kate.

***

Sally was as transfixed with Kate as Emma had been two months previously.

Amazing to see other women's reactions towards her. They don't see her as a threat. Why? I can only assume that when women accept that they have met an exceptionally beautiful woman, they don't need to feel any envy towards her. She's making small talk and flirting with Gerry in Arabic; yet Sally loves her too.

James was reminded of Robbie Burns' *a lass that had acres o' charms.*
Gerry is mesmerised too. It is fascinating to watch.

James felt they were in the presence of someone very special, knowledgeable and gifted.

However, it was Kate who dropped the bombshell. Almost as soon as they were into their main course, she said to Gerry, 'James mentioned Professor Bucke last night. Do you know him?'

Gerry spluttered, put down his fork, looked at James and struggled to reply.

'No, I've never met him. I've heard of him, of course.' Then quickly picking up on the loaded question continued. 'Did you know him at Cambridge, then?'

The ball was now in Kate's court, but she didn't bat an eye lid. 'Yes and I have been thinking about what he suggested ever since.' There was a pause, as if each was waiting for the other to speak.

James blundered in with both feet. 'Kate, there is no need for this, I have promised to help you with... you know what.'

'With what?' Gerry looked James straight in the face and was clearly expecting an answer.

James hesitated, but Kate didn't. 'I have had threats made to my family, specifically my father, but possibly my mother and sisters too.'

'Why?' Gerry asked.

'Some time soon the Ba'ath party leaders are going to stage a coup. They will remove President Bakr from power. Saddam Hussein will become the new leader. There will be a purge on the old guard. My father has been unstinting in his support of President Bakr over the years and it has been made clear to me that his disappearance can only be prevented by my getting the codes to allow us to reprogram Nastia Game.'

The sincerity with which she had answered Gerry's question was not in doubt and when he looked at James again there was some sympathy in his voice. 'So, you have agreed to pass on the codes to Kate?'

'I don't think I have a choice, do you?'

'No, I would do the same.'

James thought he should explain his plan. 'As you know, the description of the current chess position has been passed to London as an anagram of a word puzzle. I have now made some changes to the anagram. I have agreed to give Kate the anagram this weekend. Then, before I leave Baghdad I will give her the word puzzle. My guess is that Tufiq's men will not be able to decipher the codes. They will probably have to send Kate over to London to get the final position. What do you think?'

'I'm not sure. I think we should consult Peter Stacey.' He looked at Kate and for her benefit explained, 'He's our intelligence officer.'

'Yes, I know.' Her remark was something of a showstopper, as Peter's declared post in the embassy was Deputy of Personnel Resources. 'I would like to meet him to discuss Professor Bucke's proposals.' She was totally in control of both men.

'Are you saying you are prepared to become some sort of British agent?' Gerry asked quietly, as if he wasn't hearing her properly.

'Yes.'

Both James and Gerry looked at each other blankly, but said nothing.

'I could be very useful to you – keeping you up to speed on developments in our research with chemical and biological weapons, for example.'

It was James who spoke first. 'You told me that your main area of research was the development of herbicides.'

She paused. 'Yes, but I know what is going on elsewhere in the complex. We all talk to each other. Horticultural research is largely a front for the benefit of the public.'

Gerry coughed to gain attention. 'Look, let's finish our meal and then I will go and get Peter. He lives just across the road.'

They agreed and finished their meal with Sally and Kate engaging in small talk, but with James and Gerry largely silent.

Gerry went to fetch Peter Stacey and was only away a few minutes. Full of alacrity, Peter made a big play when being introduced to Kate. James could see that his boisterous manner was for Kate's benefit, but that it didn't impress her. James knew her better than the others and suspected she might be thinking he was a buffoon.

It's so unnecessary for him to overplay the geniality.

Peter knew she had been to Cambridge University, was intelligent, and must have realised she would see through any artificial bonhomie. James decided to try and dampen Peter's overdone approach. 'Peter, you remember Kate met Professor Bucke when she was completing her PhD at Cambridge. She has been thinking about what he said and has asked Gerry and me whether she and you can be of mutual assistance. Her family are in danger unless she gets the key to Nastia Game. I have committed myself to helping, but we would appreciate your advice on how to proceed. General Tufiq is encouraging Kate to become a double agent. It is a dangerous game and I think we should be serious about this.'

It was a mild rebuke to Peter who got the message.

Speaking to Kate, as if Gerry and James were not present, he said, 'You must realise this is somewhat unorthodox. If you are to become an agent, I will have to get approval at a much higher level. If General Tufiq thinks you are spying for him without also working for us then he's an idiot. He will prime you with material to give to us. That's great, until such time as he suspects you are a two-way conduit. What you will have to give us is your own information, not his. You will then be in great danger. It may become necessary to get you out of Iraq quickly. Have you thought through these possibilities?'

Kate's face displayed her answer.

He continued. 'The other problem will be what can we give you to keep Tufiq happy?'

'Tufiq thinks my contact with you might be used to pull strings. For example, we are currently having problems acquiring chlorine and phenol from your Department of Trade and Industry. We need them for water purification and plant pesticides.'

'That's possible. I see our DTI officer, Phil Lee, every day. We would need assurances. For example, that the chlorine is not being used to make mustard gas.'

'That's where I can be of real value to you. If I saw that going on, then I could warn you.' Kate sounded enthusiastic.

'OK. Tomorrow I'll contact London. Assuming they give the go-ahead, we'll begin to set it up. James has only another week left here so we'll have to get cracking to work out how we communicate with each other after he's gone. Above all else, if it goes pear-shaped at some time in the future, we must have a contingency plan ready that can be implemented immediately.'

'What exactly are you thinking of?' she asked.

'Well, would you want us to evacuate you and your family, or just you?'

'I don't know. If push came to shove, could you get my family out of Iraq?'

'Possibly, but it would be dangerous. We have routes through Kuwait, Jordan and Turkey. But your family would have to be ready to leave at short notice. You would have to keep it secret from them that you work for us.'

'What would happen to my family?' There was an element of doubt in her voice.

'You would be given new identities. You would also receive a pension depending on the value of the information that you had given over the years.'

There followed a silence before Gerry offered Peter and James a nightcap – a large brandy. It was his way of telling everyone that it was time to take James and Kate back to the *Sheraton*.

Gerry dropped them outside the hotel foyer, bid them both good night and left.

'I told my driver not to come until twelve-thirty. I thought we would be later than this.'

James looked at his watch. It was only 11.15 pm.

'Can I come in with you?' she asked.

'Yes, of course.' He led her through the foyer and began to head towards the bar.

'No, I meant could I come up to your room and wait.' James' heart missed a beat. This was the moment he had been both dreading and longing for. He felt totally inadequate. It was like his first date, when he was fifteen. He had taken Anne to the *Picture House* in Port Erin to see *The Dambusters. Do I put my arm around her or not?* Then, later on in the middle of the film, *do I try and kiss her?*

This is ridiculous.

Nevertheless, his knees were weak and a flutter tingled in the bottom of his stomach. He plucked up the courage to hold her hand and she moved closer. He noticed her perfume. A wonderful smell of Arpege; delicate and balmy, he was not to know that its fragrance would become unforgettable. His senses were hyped up; his heart beat faster. He moved his arm around her slim waist and marvelled at her firm body as her hips brushed against his. He knew he had wanted for this moment ever since meeting her at Reading. In the lift, they were alone. He moved his head towards hers and they kissed for the first time. He couldn't believe it as she pushed herself against him, breathing heavily for air. As the lift ascended, their faces were pressed against each other while his fingers combed her thick, lustrous hair. When the lift doors opened, nothing was said. They walked rapidly down the corridor, both knowing the outcome. They entered his suite.

They stood in the middle of the room, the lights low. It was no longer the impersonal room he had been residing in for the past three weeks. It suddenly felt warm and cosy. She pressed her taut body against his and kissed him frenziedly. He fingered the zip at the back of her dress and moments later her dress fell to the floor. She flicked off her shoes, kicking her dress to one side. She pulled at his shirt. He unbuckled his belt.

Together they fell backwards onto the bed and she mounted him. She was in charge. It was wild and wonderful. Murmuring ever more loudly, her movements became increasingly rapid. Her panting grew to a climax. All of a sudden she collapsed on top of him. She was motionless for several minutes, smiling at him – childlike; the cat who had found the cream. They continued to hold each other tightly for a considerable time as their bodies wound down from the frenzy. James' eyes began to feel heavy; the double brandy had caught up with him. It had been a long day. He shut his eyes, slowly and unconsciously releasing his grip on her firm, slim body…

A voice whispered in his ear, 'What is the anagram?'

He couldn't remember replying, 'The lucky villain was Count Ka.'

There was a short pause and the voice asked, 'How do you spell Ka?'

He was falling into a deep sleep. He could see his old Latin master, known as *The Count*, wearing his black, ankle-length gown, a piece of chalk in his hand and a list of words on the blackboard: *insula, insula, insula*… he replied, 'CARR, of course.'

CHAPTER 14

The bedside phone rang. James awoke, startled. It took a moment to realise where he was. He felt he had been drugged.

'Reception here, Squadron Leader. Your driver is waiting to take you to the Military College.' He looked at his alarm clock. It was 6.30 am. He had forgotten to set it. Briefly, he wondered why. Looking around the room, there was no sign of Kate. All his clothes had been neatly folded and put away.

Was she ever here? Have I been dreaming? No, there is a note on the bedside cabinet.

'Tell the driver I'll be down in fifteen minutes.'

'Very good, sir.'

James read the note. It was simple and to the point, *I'll pick you up this evening at 1800 hours. Don't be late; your vitamins were great, Kate X.*

Unsure what she meant by his vitamins, he hurriedly shaved and brushed his teeth. There was neither time for a shower nor breakfast. He noticed her perfume lingered in the room. He could smell her on his chest. Remembering the previous night, goose pimples appeared on his forearms. He splashed on more aftershave, hoping it would drown her perfume.

***

Kate was called to the director's office as soon as she arrived at work. She had been expecting it, so it was no surprise to see General Tufiq sitting in her boss' chair. She stood smartly in front of him.

'Well how did you get on last night?' he demanded gruffly.

'I met the British Embassy's MI6 officer, Stacey. He will set up the arrangement we discussed. However, he seemed too easy to convince.' Her reply was curt, polite and to the point. A shrewd observer would have noticed no sign of warmth in her delivery.

The General ignored her coldness. 'Did he fall for your story about the danger to your family?'

'Yes, I think they were all convinced, the Air Attaché, Platini, too.'

'Don't underestimate Platini. He taught several of our senior air force officers to fly in the late-sixties. They all speak highly of him. What is your problem with Stacey?'

'I don't know. It's just a gut feeling. For example, when we discussed what they could do for us, as opposed to what I could do for them, I mentioned that he might be able to ease the procurement of raw materials for our research, such as chlorine and phenol. As you know, we've been having a lot of hassle with ICI and the British Department of Trade and Industry; yet his reaction was simply, "I'll fix it." It seemed too slick. I don't trust him.'

'In this business, al Jised, you cannot even trust treachery.' He looked right through her, and she wondered if he was saying, I don't trust you either.

Does he know which side I am really on? Do I know myself anymore?

She stood in front of him and felt alone. The greatest fear of all is the fear of being alone. She was vulnerable and she knew it. With too many irons in the fire, it was easy to lose control. She decided to try to regain his confidence.

She smiled, attempting to please him. 'I have the anagram of the chess position. I've written it down for you.' She handed him a sheet of paper.

He took it, saying nothing. He examined it, and then read it aloud. 'The lucky villain was Count Carr.' He paused, putting the paper down in front of him on the empty desk. He looked straight through her again. 'It doesn't make any sense without knowing how many words there are in the answer.'

'I don't follow.' Kate's voice suggested alarm.

'This anagram has twenty-seven letters. Right?'

She nodded, and suddenly knew what was coming next.

'The answer could be nine three-letter words, three nine-letter words, or just about any combination in between. This is almost useless.' He spat the words at her.

She bit her lip. In her hurry to leave James' room neat and tidy after she had gone through all his things, she had forgotten the vital information of the number of words in the anagram. She tried to wriggle out of her dilemma. 'I left him asleep in his room last night and carefully went through all his things.'

'Did you find anything of interest?'

'No, nothing.'

'I could have told you that,' he growled condescendingly. She realised that her efforts to discover something in his room had been wasted. Tufiq's men had already searched it thoroughly.

He continued. 'I am told that to describe a chess position usually requires the names of the players, when and or where the game was played and the number of moves that have been played. Typically that's five words minimum. We'll start to work on your anagram on that assumption and see how it goes. Make sure you get the rest of the information this weekend.'

He stood up, a sign for her to depart. She straightened up preparing to say, 'Yes, sir', but decided to say nothing. She left feeling deflated. Thinking about the safety of her family, she mused to herself, *I don't trust you either, you bastard.*

***

Mohammed, the senior Omani operator, had James' coffee ready for him as he arrived in the computer suite, fifteen minutes later than usual. 'You OK, Boss?' he asked.

'Fine,' he lied. 'The traffic coming out of Baghdad was worse than usual.'

Mohammed must have known this was untrue, but didn't say anything, except to add, 'The three war games have started already.'

'In that case I'd better get up there straight away.' He gulped down his coffee and went up to the syndicate rooms where the games were being played.

Both Azi and Abu greeted him with smiles that suggested, *we know what you've been up to.* Even Brigadier Murthah seemed to smile at him with a bigger grin than usual saying, 'I'd like to wrap up the games at twelve o'clock. I've organised a buffet lunch for everyone. Afterwards I will chair the wash-up. As you are off to Babylon and Ur for the weekend, you will need to get away pronto.'

'Thank you, sir. However, you may remember I told you that we are being taken down there by Presidential helicopter.'

The Brigadier had clearly forgotten. 'Of course, even so it won't hurt if we get away early. I am sure you will enjoy Babylon, but you might be disappointed with Ur. There isn't much there.'

'When I was eleven years old, I remember our history master at school telling us that Ur was the first city of the civilised world and that some 4,500 years ago it had a population of over 60,000 people. I believe it has the best preserved ziggurat in Iraq. The first examples of written communication were discovered there. I felt I should take this opportunity to see the site, as I will never get the chance again.'

'Well, I hope you won't be disappointed,' he repeated pessimistically.

Soon, James and his helpers were busy answering questions from the players, who were now experimenting much more with tactical ploys. Excitement and enthusiasm were high.

It is such a pleasure working with these guys, reflected James as he flitted from one room to another.

There seemed to be a reluctance to stop playing as noon approached, but by 1215 hours everyone was tucking into a finger buffet.

Brigadier Murthah started the wash-up promptly at one o'clock and ran the meeting in similar vein to that of the previous Thursday. The three games played by the College's directing staff bore an uncanny resemblance to Azi's game, but there were some significant differences.

In one, the Iraqi team had decided to attempt an amphibious landing at Bandar-e-Busher, some 120 miles down the Iranian coast. Their aim was to capture the nearby military airfield. Like General MacArthur's landing at Inchon in the Korean War, the surprise pincer movement had been successful. It enabled the Iraqi Air Force to establish air superiority over the road from Shiraz to Abadan and Khorram Shar. The consequent difficulties for the Iranians meant that the team were able to establish a strong bridgehead over the Shatt al-Arab waterway.

'This is an excellent idea,' said the Brigadier, 'although I have my doubts if we could maintain control of Bandar without reinforcements from the sea. However, it illustrates the advantage of having the war game as a planning tool. We shall have to game this plan again to see if it is really viable, or whether this was a one-off.'

In the other games the idea of quick rushes through the Zagros Mountains had hit the same snags as Azi; the Iranians held the high ground and could come down from the mountains, but the Iraqis could not force their way up through the narrow passes. All the staff agreed the need for Tanker aircraft, more tactical helicopters and a better air defence radar system. It was also agreed that without an effective Navy, it was easy for the Iranians to close the Persian Gulf and cut off Iraq's trade.

Towards two o'clock the Brigadier began to sum up. He concluded by thanking Azi, Abu and James for running the games and pointed out that next week's games were for real. Help would be kept to an absolute minimum. He then sprang a surprise, announcing that on Wednesday afternoon Saddam Hussein would be coming to see the games. He would be staying over for a dining-in night that evening. 'I expect you all to be there, as amongst other things, we shall be saying farewell to James that evening as he is flying back to Britain the following Friday.'

After a short pause, there was an outbreak of applause.

'Now enjoy your weekend, gentlemen. Shall we start afresh on Sunday morning at, say,' he paused looking at his watch, 'eleven o'clock?' He then turned to James and added that he had invited the Air Attaché to attend the dinner. Furthermore, Wg Cdr Platini was arranging for James' mess kit to be flown to Baghdad.

***

It was a pleasant afternoon. For once the heat was not too oppressive. With plenty of time to await Kate's arrival, James decided to take a short stroll through the gardens that banked the River Tigris. Reflecting on the previous night with Kate and the possible consequences led, as so often introspection does, to a lowering of spirits. His conscience was like a terrier snapping at his heels; he couldn't kick it off. He began to wonder if he could make some excuse for not going away. Even blaming food poisoning from the College's lunch occurred to him.

However, he knew the minute he looked into Kate's eyes, it would be fatal. Like Newton's falling apple, there was an inevitability about the outcome. The conflict waged inside him, but by the time he returned to the *Sheraton* he knew it was too late. His heart controlled his head; he consoled himself with the excuse that what Emma could not see, she would never know.

***

Kate arrived at the hotel ten minutes early. She was wearing a discreet black dress that covered her ankles but didn't hide her slim figure. Her broad smile and bright eyes instantly removed any lingering doubts James had about the forthcoming weekend. In the foyer she discreetly kissed his cheek.

'The helicopter leaves from the Festival Parade Ground, opposite the Ba'ath Party's headquarters. It may take us a while to get across the Jumhuriya Bridge as traffic is heavy this evening.'

Sitting comfortably in the back of her chauffeured car, James asked, 'Is everything OK? You look worried.'

'Do you remember telling me the anagram last night when you were falling asleep?'

'No, I don't remember very much after… ' He stopped mid-sentence. 'After, you know…'

She blushed. 'You said the anagram was "The lucky villain was Count Carr".'

'Did I?'

'But you didn't tell me how many words there are, or their length.'

'I'm sorry, but I don't remember telling you the anagram at all. However, since you are asking, I might as well tell you now. There are four words,' and counting the letters on his fingers as he went, he said, 'five, six, seven, seven; that's twenty-five letters altogether.'

'But the anagram you gave me last night had twenty-seven letters, not twenty-five.'

'I don't see how it can.'

Spelling each word as she went through the anagram, they counted the letters together until she spelt Ka as Carr.

'But Ka is not spelt Carr,' he remarked. 'What made you think it was?'

'You told me so.'

'Really?'

'Yes. I asked you to spell Ka, and you distinctly said Carr.'

Without realising the significance, he laughed. 'I must have been half asleep. Carr is a very English surname. My old Latin master was Harry Carr, nicknamed Count Carr, for example.'

Leaning towards her, her fragrance filled his lungs, it was heady. He held her hands, gently bringing them to his lips and kissed them. The car was only progressing slowly through the Baghdad traffic. She didn't discourage him, but whispered that they had much to discuss about their future relationship.

He wondered if her conscience was feeling as guilty as his.

The traffic was bad, their progress a trickle. After a while, she said proudly, 'I have some good news, my director is retiring. I am getting his job. It will give me total control of Iraq's research into chemical and biological weapons. I will also have managerial responsibility for transport, concealment and the deployment of the weapons. Think what that means.' Her posture showed she was clearly excited at the prospect. She was expecting James to share her good fortune.

Instead he tried to dampen her overt enthusiasm. 'It's good news about your promotion, but I'm not happy with you working as a dual-agent. I know I can't stop you, but please be careful. I don't trust Stacey any more than you trust Tufiq.'

Kate remembered her meeting earlier that morning. 'No, I don't trust Tufiq either. However, I have been thinking. If you could work out a system to disguise the location of where I conceal the weapons, it would be to our advantage.'

'I'm not sure I follow you.'

'Look. Suppose I have to conceal the location of, say, fifteen gallons of mustard gas. Typically, it would be stored in glass vats, each within a stainless steel barrel. I would decide where they would be hidden. It could be a remote location in the Ar Rihab desert. I would be solely responsible for recording the position of the burial in the archives. In years to come, when the military wish to use the gas, the records would take them to the wrong site.'

'I can see two problems. One, by then, you also will have forgotten where you have put the materials. Two, the military would blame you for the loss. You would be for the chop.'

Kate was not to be put off by James' scepticism. 'I thought about that. If you could design some sort of formula that uses the recorded positions in the files to convert them to the true locations, then, if only I knew the algorithm, only I would know exactly where they were buried. Also, with the more deadly weapons I could dilute their effectiveness. The workers in the munitions factories are low-grade, they wouldn't have a clue what was going on.'

'OK, but what about the workers who dig the holes for the burial? They would know where they had put the stuff.'

'They will always be transient immigrants, frequently from Pakistan. They would be long gone. They come and go all the time.' She remained upbeat.

James, on the other hand, could only see the problems. 'Surely Tufiq's men would eventually realise what you had done?'

'Not if we are clever about it. I would only choose to hide permanently the more dangerous biological materials. I could dish out smaller, less dangerous chemical materials when they are wanted.'

'What do you consider dangerous?'

'Things like anthrax and botulinium toxins.'

'Anthrax?' James sat upright. 'Do you realise that once released, anthrax spores remain toxic for up to fifty years, or more?'

'Yes, of course I do.' Her tone suggested she resented having to be asked such a trivial question.

However, James didn't notice her reaction. 'There's a remote island in Scotland, called Gruinard, where anthrax was released in 1942 to kill a flock of sheep. The island is still a no-go area today, nearly forty years later.'

'Yes, I know. There's evidence to suggest some strains of anthrax spores are virtually indestructible. They can live undisturbed for thousands of years. It's the reason I must take this job. I might not be able to stop what's going on, but I can go a long way towards limiting the damage. You are right, of course. Tufiq may eventually suspect, but as long as Stacey keeps his word and gets me out of Iraq safely, then I'll be alright.' She gave him a smile, a sad smile that was pleading, *please try to understand my motives.*

He was unsure whether to be proud of her courage or cross at her recklessness. He said nothing, but was thinking deeply about her plan to conceal the weapons that could destroy millions of people. When they reached the Festival Parade Ground, James was surprised to see the helicopter was a Wessex, kitted out for VIP transport. They were not the only passengers going to Babylon. Two Frenchmen, accompanied by two females, were waiting for them to arrive.

Kate apologised to the pilot for being late whilst James introduced himself to the Frenchmen. It turned out that they were working on a project to the south-west of Baghdad. They would not elaborate further. Kate later told him that they were probably from the nuclear plant at Osirak. The flight was uneventful. The Frenchmen conversed with their female friends. James and Kate held hands, saying little over the engine noise. An hour after take-off, they landed in a special compound next to the Presidential Palace in Babylon.

They had been allocated separate bedrooms, both beautifully decorated with matching colour fittings but sharing a *Jack and Jill* bathroom. 'There is a champagne reception in half an hour, before dinner at eight o'clock. That doesn't leave us much time to get a shower,' said Kate, a grin on her face, 'unless, of course, we share it.'

She had vanished back into her room, before James could think of a reply.

They shared the shower, the warm water – soft and tingling. Its effect on his senses was dramatic; his nerve endings were hypersensitive to her touching him. It was a totally new experience. She stood on the insteps of his feet with one arm around his neck as she kissed him; it felt as if an electric current was flowing around their circuit.

He felt her slim waist and pulled her closer. The intoxicating thrill increased as he licked the inside of her ear and she groaned, shivering encouragingly. She bent her knees and her body began to convulse. He could feel her firm breasts against his chest. She was self-climaxing. She crossed her legs; her body was in an orgasmic spasm.

As she calmed down, he lifted her off her feet. Her legs instinctively wound themselves around his waist. He carried her into her bedroom. He lowered her gently down onto the base of her bed and whispered, 'The champagne will have to get warm while the bed gets wet.'

They arrived twenty minutes late, but no one seemed to notice. There were about fifteen couples present. The two Frenchmen and their partners were already there. They gave James and Kate a nod by way of a greeting. There was a group of four, speaking German. 'They are East

German pilot instructors,' whispered Kate. The noisiest and biggest group were either Russians or Yugoslavs. Kate didn't know which. At eight o'clock a gong sounded and a tall, portly man, dressed in Arabic clothes and looking not unlike Saddam Hussein, stood on a podium to address the assembly. He was, he said, a minister in the Government Department of Antiquities and Tourism. He welcomed them to Babylon. He outlined the programme for the weekend. After breakfast, served until ten o'clock, there would be a short presentation on Babylon's history. A coach would then take them on a guided tour around the sites of Babylon before a picnic lunch at one of the sites. The afternoon would be free, or they could go to the nearby holy town of Karbala.

'That's when we will depart for Ur,' said Kate.

The lighting in the dining room was subtle and discreet. Perfumed candles created a heady atmosphere. Mostly, couples had their own tables. The distance between tables assured privacy. The meal and wines were a mixture of French and Italian. The Arabian coffee was strong and black. By 10.30 pm couples were drifting away. 'I wasn't expecting it to be like this,' said Kate as they walked back to their rooms. 'I'd heard rumours of wild weekend parties being given for foreign businessmen, but not in Presidential Palaces.'

'Well, we might as well make the most of it,' exclaimed James, laughing as he squeezed her tightly around her waist. All his inhibitions and good intentions had vanished.

By now he was rapidly gaining confidence with Kate. On their first time together, he had been nervous in case he would disappoint her. However, she had taken charge; in so doing it had helped him to relax. The experience in the shower and their follow-up on the edge of the bed had boosted his self-belief. And, so, when Kate came in to his bedroom wearing a flimsy, pale-green nightdress, and looking ravishing, he knew he would not disappoint her. He looked into her face; happiness and expectation were written all over it.

CHAPTER 15

After breakfast, Kate and James attended the half hour presentation on Babylon's history given by the minister who had welcomed them the previous evening. He displayed a considerable knowledge of the Old Testament, claiming how the descendents of Noah, after the flood, came to this part of the world. It was fascinating to be told of the history of what was present day southern Iraq. It was an eye-opener for James to realise that when Babylon was being built the ancient Britons had not completed Stonehenge.

They boarded an air-conditioned coach to drive to the entrance of the Babylon site. 'A reconstructed Babylon is rising from the remains of Nebuchadnezzar's city,' the guide told them. 'It is the most restored site in Iraq. We are going to park here and walk through the new Ishtar gate into the courtyard that leads us down the Processional Way.'

The restored gate was impressive being some sixty feet high and decorated with mosaics of wild animals including bulls, lions and dragons. As they strolled along the Way, they saw the restored remains of the city's original walls, decorated with mythical beasts protecting the ancient city. At the partially restored Palace of Nebuchadnezzar, they stopped. 'It is about here,' the guide shouted to the group, who were already spreading out, 'that the Hanging Gardens were thought to be situated. A canal was built from the nearby Euphrates River and a system of pulley wheels raised water to the level of the elevated gardens.' They continued to the magnificent statue, the Lion of Babylon, carved from basalt. 'You will see markings on its back. It is believed that a saddle was originally there with a statue of the Goddess Ishtar on top.'

Turning back, they visited the site of Alexander the Great's amphitheatre. They were then led to the picnic site. A marquee gave protection from the sun while the tables were arranged to give privacy.

By three o'clock James and Kate were back at the Presidential Palace, a car was waiting to take them to the Wessex. They were the only passengers. It was the same pilot as the previous evening. Kate introduced James as Squadron Leader Douglas.

'Qassim Abdullah, call me Kaz.' He spoke excellent English, telling James that he had trained as a pilot with the RAF after having undertaken a one-year English course at the RAF School of Education at Upwood, near Huntingdon.

'I was there for three months in 1967,' said James.

'Ah, I finished there in December 1966, and then went to RAF South Cerney for basic flying training. Finally, I finished training at RAF Shawbury. I liked Shropshire very much. Shrewsbury is a beautiful town. We often used to go climbing in North Wales at weekends.' He sighed. 'They were happy days.'

Kaz then turned to Kate and enquired, 'I am to take you to the Al Allil Air Base, is that right?'

'Yes, we are staying at the Officers' Club tonight, and tomorrow afternoon you are returning us to Baghdad?' she queried.

'I am to fly you back, but via here. We have to pick up the two froggies, and their tarts.'

This reply surprised James on two counts. Firstly, that he used the slang word for Frenchmen and, secondly, that he expressed such disapproval of their weekend companions in front of Kate, a much senior officer.

'It will take us about two hours to get to Al Allil. I am staying tonight with an old friend who lives on the base,' added Kaz.

They flew down the valley of the Euphrates; the contrast between the east and the west banks was remarkable. The land to the east, towards the Tigris, was relatively green, but to the west the Ar Rihab desert was barren. As they approached Al Allil Air Base, Kaz flew them slowly over the Great Ziggurat of Ur. It was massive. However, it was surrounded by nothing but sandy desert. James wondered if the trip was going to be disappointing, as predicted by Brigadier Murthah.

They were met at the base by a lieutenant who introduced himself as the Duty Officer. He apologised for the base commander being unable to greet them, and took them in a staff car to the Officers' Club. 'This car will be available to you at all times. When you want it, you merely have to ring for Military Transport,' he said as he left them at the front of the building.

There was a feeling of emptiness about the base, reminding James of the exodus at weekends on many RAF stations. The Officers' Club, although quite modern, looked remarkably similar to a standard 1937 RAF Officers' Mess. Entering through a colonnaded door into a large reception area, they were met by a somewhat stiff warrant officer who was waiting for them. He turned out to be the mess manager. He took their bags and led them to a large suite of rooms of the highest quality located at the end of the VIP corridor. He was formal, obviously respectful of Kate when addressing her in Arabic. There was a tension in his demeanour. He knew that Kate had power and James suspected he resented it. When he went, she translated. 'He said that dinner was being served this evening between seven and seven-thirty, and that there would not be many in the dining room as most livers-in have gone away for the weekend.' She looked at her watch. It was already past six o'clock. She grinned. 'That doesn't give us long, does it?'

'If you don't mind, I would like to have a bath to get all this sand off. When we landed I seemed to get covered in the stuff.'

'Good idea,' she enthused, and they found themselves, a few minutes later, sharing a large bath. Although it wasn't what he had had in mind when suggesting he wanted a bath, he soon found himself lying on his back, with Kate again in charge. Covered by the warm, steaming water and copious quantities of soap bubbles, her hands roamed under the water.

The soap bubbles began to multiply.

***

Dinner in an empty room is never enjoyable, even when accompanied by a beautiful partner. Only two large bench tables, normally capable of sitting twenty, had been laid. James and Kate sat alone at one, while at the other, two very junior-looking officers sat in total silence, not saying a word to each other. It was a situation that took him back to his days as a bachelor at RAF Cosford, when the mess would be deserted on Friday and Saturday nights. There were no hot choices on the menu, as the chefs had probably gone and a single steward had been left to hold the fort. However, when they had finished, the evening air was still warm and they were able to take their coffee sitting outside in the club's gardens.

'I have been giving a lot of thought to your dilemma about hiding the biological and chemical weapons,' he said. 'What do you know about chess?'

'My dad taught me the moves, but I wouldn't call myself much more than a novice. Why do you ask?'

'The board is an eight-by-eight matrix. Sixty-four squares in total.' He paused, and she nodded.

'You label the squares from the bottom left to the bottom right *a1* to *h1*. So the white queen's starting square is *d1*, and the white king's is *e1*. OK?'

She nodded again.

'The squares *a1* to *h1* are called the first rank. The white pawns in front of the white pieces are on squares *a2* to *h2*, or the second rank.'

Again she nodded.

'The squares on the third rank are labelled *a3* to *h3*, and so on to the eighth rank *a8* to *h8*.' He stopped to see if she was keeping up.

Looking pleased with herself, she confirmed her understanding. 'So the black queen starts on *d8* and the black king on *e8*?'

He nodded. 'Now suppose you superimpose an eight-by-eight grid on top of a map of where you are proposing to hide the weapons with the ranks lying due west–east. If the squares were one kilometre by one kilometre, then the total area covered by the board would be sixty-four square kilometres, or twenty-five square miles.'

She said nothing, but indicated she was still following his logic.

'If I can teach you a chess position that you cannot forget, then your records could show that weapons were buried at say square *b5*, when in reality they would be elsewhere, say *f1*.'

'I don't follow.'

'OK. Suppose in the position you learn, white king's bishop is on square *b5*. You enter *b5* in your records as the site where the weapons are buried, but, instead, you bury the stuff on the previous square occupied by that piece. In the case of the white king's bishop this could be its starting square *f1*.'

'Mmm,' she pondered. 'Perhaps when we are alone tomorrow in Ur you can show me and explain that bit more slowly. I'm feeling chilly. Let's go inside and have a nightcap.'

Kate got as close as she could to James when they got into bed. She felt cold. She wondered why. His outlining of a clever, seemingly foolproof way to hide Saddam's toxic weapons in the desert had made her realise the dangerous nature of the game she was playing. She was getting out of her depth. Once she started the process of concealment, there would be no way of going back. She shuddered at the thought. She felt even colder.

Can I really be betraying my country for this man? I must be mad. I love being with him; feeling him; smelling him; tasting him. Allah, forgive me.

Her toes and fingers were like ice. She bent her legs and brought her toes upwards, placing them between his warm thighs. 'I need warming up. Hold me tight and let me feel the heat from your body.' He held her firm, but said nothing. She closed her eyes, slowly getting warmer from his radiant heat. He even smelled warm. They lay motionless for some considerable time.

Gradually she forgot about hiding weapons. Her mind went blank; simply enjoying being alone with him. Doing nothing was pleasurable in itself; she felt safe in his arms. As long as he was near her, the rest of the world didn't matter; it could go and hang itself. She lay there for what seemed a long while, saying nothing, enjoying the peace, warmth and cosiness; like a cat curled up in front of a fire.

She continued to dream in a state of utopia. She wondered if he was enjoying the moment like herself, but didn't ask. As long as he was close, that's all that mattered. His warm hands slowly took hold of her cold feet and his head bent towards them. Taking each foot in turn, he placed her toes inside his mouth, kissing them. She could feel his hot breath. Simultaneously, his thumbs gently massaged the soles of her feet. It felt erotic. A tingling sensation that had begun in her toes, started to spread upwards. The warmth of his lips, now kissing the inside of her thighs, increased the sensation. Her eyes were closed tight. She began to gasp for air and breathe heavily. She no longer felt cold.

He whispered, 'Do you love me?'

'Yes, yes. I do. You must know that, ever since you called me Ava.'

'Are you warmer now?' he asked.

She only had the energy to murmur, 'Mmm…'

She knew then, if she didn't know already, that she wanted to live the rest of her life with him – a married man and an infidel. *What a mess I'm in.* James slowly sank into a deep sleep, but she lay awake; her mind was in overdrive. She didn't know what would be worse: dealing with Tufiq, or explaining to her parents about the man she loved. Despite her worries, however, she knew, for the first time, she was truly in love.

***

The dining room was even quieter for breakfast; they were alone except for the duty steward. They both ate heartily; the yoghurt, honey, dates, freshly baked rough bread and copious quantities of black coffee tasted good. As they were finishing, Kate said, 'I'll just go and ring for our car.' She disappeared towards the foyer where she picked up the phone.

'Yes?'

'You told me to let you know when I have the rest of the anagram.'

'Well?' The voice sounded impatient.

'It's four words, five, six, seven, seven.'

There was a short pause. 'That's only twenty-five letters. The anagram you gave me had twenty-seven letters.'

'The count's name is not spelled CARR, but KA. I must go. If I am away too long he might get suspicious.' And before he could reply, she had put the phone down. She dialled for MT to take them to the archaeological site at Ur.

When Kate asked the young airman to leave them at the ziggurat and return at one o'clock, the driver explained he had been given strict instructions to wait until they had finished their sightseeing. He assured Kate that he had brought a book to read, would park in the shade and had sufficient water.

The great ziggurat dominates the flat, sandy desert landscape. Little remains of the rest of the city and its original walls, built some 4,500 years ago. It would then have been located at the mouth of the Tigris and Euphrates rivers on the banks of the Persian Gulf. As such, Ur was ideally placed for sea trade and on the land routes into Arabia. Today, as the result of the flow patterns of the two rivers changing, and the sea receding, Ur lies about one hundred miles from the Gulf.

At about the time the ziggurat was built, the first laws were documented, the plains surrounding the city were irrigated and two harbours were built inside the city walls. According to the Book of Genesis, the prophet Abraham was born in Ur. However, owing to drought, Ur began to decline around 550 BC and by the time of Alexander the Great it had become uninhabited. The desert sands gradually buried the city, including the ziggurat and its location was lost for over 1,000 years.

James and Kate began their visit by climbing to the top of the ziggurat. Standing some sixty-five feet high, it allowed them to survey the whole area. To the south they could see the remains of various royal burial chambers. The whole site seemed to be strewn with broken fragments of pottery and looked sorry for itself. It had been extensively excavated in the early 1930s by archaeologists from the British Museum, one of whom had been his old history teacher. Many valuable artefacts had been removed. As James came down from the ziggurat, he began to feel that the trip had been something of an anticlimax. He had expected to see so much. Instead, apart from the ziggurat, it amounted to little more than a pile of old stones. Walking around the site compounded his disappointment; the graffiti artists had been at work. The royal graves were empty, apart from rubbish. Some small signs in Arabic told the visitors what the tombs were.

They found a shaded spot and sat down. Kate had brought water and they drank together. She seemed disappointed too, but said little.

'Shall I explain further my ideas for hiding your chemical weapons?' he asked.

'Yes, that's a good idea.'

He found a suitable piece of broken pottery and in the sand drew an eight-by-eight matrix. 'Imagine a map, and you superimpose the sixty-four squares on top. The files are pointing north to south, and the ranks are, therefore, east to west.'

She nodded.

'The bottom left-hand corner of each square will have its own unique latitude and longitude. Agree?'

She nodded again.

'Let's say this square, *b2*, is exactly forty-six degrees east, thirty degrees north. That's somewhere south of here in the desert. Now we set up a chess position on the board that only you know.'

'How am I to remember an exact position?'

'The easiest way is probably to remember twenty or twenty-five moves from a game that leads to a position where quite a few of the pieces have left the board. By playing the moves over and over again, you will soon remember them and be able to set up the position whenever you want. Shall I show you?'

'OK.'

'I'll show you one of my better games. The first fifteen moves were a standard line in the Spanish Opening.'

He drew a *P* on the square *e4*, and circled another *P* on *e5*.

'I'll put circles around the black pieces.'

He continued in similar vein, counting the moves as he went along, explaining what he was doing. Whenever a piece that had already been developed moved again, he carefully dusted over the square, removing its traces.

He could see Kate's eyes glazing over and hurriedly played out a further ten moves.

'Now suppose you decide to record something as being buried here at square *b2*; you actually would bury it at *g7*, because the black bishop currently on *b2* was previously on *g7*. As the squares are one square kilometre each, then those particular weapons would be over five kilometres away from where you have recorded them and only you would know that. All that your record would show is location: forty-six degrees east, thirty degrees north. You would also have to hide on the record that it referred to the square *b2*.'

'How could I do that?' she asked.

'Presumably, your record will have details such as, Weapon – Anthrax, Date of Manufacture – 2 Jul 78, Date Stored – 15 Jul 78, Purity Value – 69% and so on?'

'Yes, of course.'

'Then wherever the first letter *b* occurs, put a full stop immediately after it. Similarly, after the first number *2*, again put a dot. Anyone looking at the record will think there has been a typing error.'

'What if there isn't a letter *b* on the record sheet?'

'Devise substitute letters – say for *b*, the letter *p*. Look let me show you.'

He wrote on the sand: Typ.e of weapon – Anthrax

Date of Manufacture – 2. Jul 78

'See? No one would know you have encoded *b2* on the record. To make it more difficult for anyone investigating the record, add some later dots at random. It would help disguise the system.'

She nodded slowly, thinking deeply about the logic. Then proving to

James that she was following him, she said, 'So, if I record weapons at *e4*, I put the exact latitude and longitude of *e4*'s bottom left-hand corner on the file, putting a dot after the first *e* and the first *4*. The weapons I would actually hide at *f6* because this black knight on *e4*,' she pointed to it, 'was previously at *f6*.' She knew she was right, the penny had dropped. She grinned, pleased with herself.

He smiled. 'You've got it.'

They found their driver where they had left him and soon they were being dropped off outside the Officers' Club. Kaz was waiting for them in the club's anteroom. 'Do you mind if I have lunch with you before we go back? How did you find Ur?' he asked, by way of polite conversation.

'Disappointing,' Kate replied, 'although I suppose it would be prohibitively expensive to restore the whole city.' She looked at James to confirm her statement.

He nodded, adding, 'I had hoped for more, but I suspect the close proximity to this Air Base deters tourists.'

'To be honest, visitors are actively discouraged. You were allowed to climb to the top of the ziggurat unhindered. Generally, it is not allowed.' Small talk continued throughout the meal, Kaz making the most of his opportunity to practise his English, asking questions about the RAF and James' postings.

The flight back to Baghdad, via Babylon, was uneventful. James and Kate hardly spoke due to the noise of the Wessex. Even the two Frenchmen and their partners were quiet, although James wondered if some friction had developed between them.

Kate's car was waiting when they arrived. James thanked Kaz for looking after them and they departed for the *Sheraton*.

CHAPTER 16

The receptionist smiled, handing James his keys, a letter and a small suitcase. 'Wing Commander Platini came here earlier and asked for these to be given to you.'

James turned to Kate, who had left her driver outside, asking, 'Are you coming up and staying for dinner? I expect this case contains my mess kit for Wednesday's dining-in night.'

'No. If you don't mind, I have plenty of catching up to do in my apartment. It's been a wonderful weekend, the best in my life. Perhaps, we can dine together tomorrow? Shall I book the same restaurant as last time?'

He was disappointed, but tried not to show it. 'Yes, that would be great. Will you pick me up here?'

'I'll be here for seven-thirty.' He felt alone without her as he went up to his suite carrying his parcel.

Emma had packed his mess kit carefully. Inside there was a note saying how much she and the kids were missing him and how they were looking forward to his return. There was no mention of the SAS minders; clearly she wasn't aware of their presence. He put her note down, feeling guilt ridden. The euphoria of being with Kate was over. The reality of having a loving family back home waiting for him to return hit him. He was torn in two. There was no solution. He'd dug the hole. He could only hope that, somehow, the problem would sort itself out.

He read Gerry's note. It was short. 'If you get back from Babylon before 2100 hours, give me a ring and I will come over to update you on recent events.'

He picked up the receiver, and asked for Gerry's number.

'I'll be across in forty-five minutes. Have you eaten? No? Good, book a table for three.'

James put the phone down and rang reception to book the table, thinking Gerry must be bringing Sally. He took a shower and smartened himself up. As he entered the bar he was surprised to see Peter Stacey with Gerry. The pleasantries over, Peter began. 'I am not sure you're flavour of the month with Admiral Johnson's team.'

'Really, why not?'

'They think you have been set up and that Kathab al Jised is working for Tufiq. What she told us the other evening is just a front. What the Iraqis are after is the chess key and will do anything to get it.'

'Do you believe that too?' asked James.

'I don't know what to believe. She convinced me that she really wanted to help with hiding the chemical weapons. Her story of the danger to her family seemed genuine. You never can tell.'

'Well I believe her. And I'll tell you why.'

'Before you do that,' said Gerry, 'let's go into the dining room.'

They sat down, ordered their meal and James summarised the weekend. He explained the foolproof way of hiding weapons using an eight-by-eight kilometre square and superimposing a chess position. He had shown Kate how to remember a position that she would not forget and had been impressed by the speed with which she picked up the idea. Both Peter and Gerry showed great interest with the plan as James sketched a position on the back of his paper napkin to help explain its simplicity.

'I'm sure once she begins to tell us the locations of the hidden weapons, MoD will be assured she's genuine. In any case, despite their misgivings, I have been instructed to go ahead and recruit her anyway. They see her as a worthwhile risk. You can go ahead and give her the chess key, but only the one that accesses the data. Does that make sense?'

'Yes, it does,' replied James.

'Also, you're not to give it until you are about to leave Baghdad.

Meanwhile, they want me to arrange a way of communicating in future. Perhaps, you can set up a meeting for me?'

James explained to Peter that he had no method of contacting her. 'Fortunately, she is coming here tomorrow evening at seven-thirty to take me to dinner. If you're here then you can do the necessary. What sort of things do you want to arrange with her?'

'Oh, the usual, she'll have to have a code name, an escape route, learn how to keep in touch and so on.'

James didn't enquire any further; he felt the less he knew, the better.

***

The following morning, Sunday, 16th July, saw the College awash with activity. The playing fields were being spruced up, grass cut, road markings being painted, flowerbeds replanted, cleaners everywhere. James had seen a similar level of activity before at Bracknell. There, even the ladies toilet had to have the correct make of cigarettes conveniently waiting for the Queen's sister. Clearly the visit of the future president was being taken seriously.

The war games began on time, with James, Azi and Abu acting as consultants to the umpires. By now the problems being encountered by the Iraqi staff were few. There was relatively little for the three of them to do except socialise and drink coffee. Azi and Abu spoke freely about their hopes and aspirations for the future of Iraq. Both thought Saddam Hussein would be a strong leader who could keep the three factions, Sunni, Shia, and Kurd, under control. Iran was seen as a thorn in their flesh, stirring trouble by encouraging the concept of an independent Kurdistan. A war with them was inevitable. Iran's aspirations had to be curtailed and Iraq had to show the world it couldn't be pushed around. They hoped that Nastia Game was the tool to help them plan a successful campaign.

'You do realise the two major weaknesses with the software are the lack of logistics and no allowances being made for weather?' asked James.

They both nodded. Azi was surprisingly honest when he remarked,

'That's why we need your security key to make the necessary upgrades.'

'I don't think you'll have to wait much longer, Azi.'

He looked puzzled, and asked, 'Why?'

'It'll be the last thing I give Kathab al Jised before I leave on Friday morning.'

His face registered surprise, but he quickly recovered. 'Why Kathab?'

James had to be careful. He knew he mustn't give Kate's position away. 'She is being coerced by General Tufiq.'

'Tufiq? What the hell is she doing with Tufiq?'

'Let's just say Tufiq has put pressure on her.'

'He's a nasty bastard. I hope she doesn't trust him. He'll do anything to get what he wants and then sell her down the river. A man without honour.' He made the gesture of spitting on the ground.

Abu then admitted, 'Perhaps I shouldn't say this, James, but you should know that there is little love lost between the Army hierarchy and the Air Force. The Republican Regiments, in particular, are run by the Ba'ath party clique. They don't care for the less prestigious sections that make up the bulk of the Army. Ba'athists are power crazy and Tufiq is one of the worst.'

'To be honest with both of you, I am not happy with what is going on,' said James. 'It's out of my hands. However, when you have the ability to modify Nastia Game, what ideas have you got for simulating weather and munitions consumption?'

Azi replied. 'The logistic question should be straightforward, it is really just a matter of keeping some sort of tote, but the weather could be trickier?' He was fishing for ideas.

'I have thought that the simplest method would be to break down the weather into such factors as rain, fog, wind, temperature, and so on,' said James. 'Then scale their severity onto the performance of the various weapons being used. For example, tanks might get almost completely bogged down in torrential rain if the roads became flooded. Tanks are possibly one of the worst examples because it would also depend on the type of terrain they were traversing.'

Azi smiled. 'You wouldn't like to stay and build the model for us, by any chance?'

James returned the smile, shook his head and said, 'I think you'll manage pretty well without me, Azi.'

***

Kate had expected it – the phone call to go and see Tufiq. The only surprise was that the call didn't come until early afternoon. As usual, there were no pleasantries when she arrived to see him. 'My men have been working on the riddle all weekend. They claim it can't possibly describe a chess position, as four words are insufficient. They have made dozens of different words to no avail.'

'I'm sorry, sir, but I can only imagine your team are missing something.'

'Such as what?' he snapped. His aggressive manner made Kate shudder. This man was to be feared.

'I don't know. Perhaps some of the words have a double meaning.' She was grasping at straws, and she knew it.

'Go on.'

'Well,' her mind was racing, trying to remember what James had shown her in the sand at Ur; something about a Spanish Opening. 'If the position is from a Spanish Opening, then maybe one of the players is Spanish too?'

Judging from his reaction to her answer, the General knew nothing of chess. He seemed satisfied, at least for the moment. 'I'll put that to my team. When do you see him again?'

'This evening.'

'Get the solution from him tonight and let me have it tomorrow morning.'

'I'll do my best.'

'I don't want your best, al Jised. I want the solution.'

She turned to leave, but he stopped her by asking, 'Why was Douglas with Platini and Stacey last night?'

150

'I didn't know he was.'

'They're hatching something. Find out what it is.'

As she left, she felt frightened. Not for the first time, she felt she was swimming out of her depth.

***

As always, Kate arrived promptly that evening. She was surprised to see Peter waiting with James. 'Peter needs to go over a few things with you and I couldn't think how I could arrange a meeting between the pair of you,' he explained apologetically.

'That's OK, I never gave you my phone number because the lines are so insecure,' she replied. Then turning to Peter, 'Will it take long?'

'Quite a while, I'm afraid. If you wish we can arrange to do it another time.'

'No, we might as well get it over tonight. I think it may be easiest if you come with James and me to our restaurant. There will be fewer prying eyes there.' She looked around the foyer as she spoke. 'I assume that what you want to tell me can be said in front of James?' She was already in charge.

'Yes, of course,' replied Peter.

They left the *Sheraton* and strolled along the bank of the Tigris through the gardens that smelled strongly of the ripe dates hanging on the trees. It was a beautiful summer evening, for once not too hot. The sun was beginning to settle in the west as they entered the *Abu Simba*. The manager had given Kate a discreet table near the back of the restaurant, presumably as she had requested. He must have been somewhat surprised to see her arrive with two escorts. However, unabashed, he rapidly reset the table without asking any questions.

'As this is something of a business dinner, I will claim it on expenses,' said Peter. After they had ordered, Peter explained that, first of all, a code name must be selected that would always be used whenever Kate contacted them.

'That's easy,' she laughed. 'Will Ava do?' She turned to James and he smiled.

'What's the joke?'

'Look closely,' said James.

Peter stared, and began to smile. 'Yes, I see, Kate has an uncanny resemblance to Ava Gardner. Excellent, I like it.'

Throughout the meal, Peter went methodically, detail by detail, over what was required for Kate to keep in regular contact, both when being watched by Tufiq's men or when not. Emergency, if all else fails, procedures were covered.

'Do you remember Jonathon Gleeson?' he had asked early on.

'Yes, of course, he was my PhD tutor at Cambridge. Why?'

'As you know, he's one of the world's leading authorities on plant pathogens and toxic botulisms.'

She nodded, as if unsure where this line of questioning was going.

'He is also fluent in Arabic and comes to this part of the world regularly for academic conferences, lecturing and so on,' Peter added.

Again, she nodded but said nothing.

'You also go to such conferences, yes?'

'Where is this going?' she asked.

'I am coming to that. From now on whenever you meet him, he will be expecting you to brief him on new technical developments in your weapon research programmes. I stress, however, he's your scientific point of contact only. He merely works for us as a consultant.'

She looked surprised, asking, 'Will he be at Amman University next month?'

'Yes, I believe so and will make contact with you,' replied Peter.

'Fine, I've no problem with that as I usually go to such academic conferences on my own.'

'Yes, but be careful, Kate. You never know who may be watching.' It was James who interrupted. 'I am concerned for your safety. Even Azi doesn't trust Tufiq. He told me so only this morning.' He'd let the cat out of the bag.

She glared at James. That steely stare of hers pierced him like a rapier. 'You've not told him anything, have you?'

'No, of course not. Tufiq's name came up in conversation, that's all.' James realised he had made a boob. Despite his fears for her safety, he decided he'd better stay out of the conversation.

Peter continued. 'Whenever you want to see me, for example, to procure basic supplies, such as growth mediums from our Department of Trade, you will do this with Tufiq's agreement, presumably?'

She nodded.

'No doubt he will give you snippets to feed us? And such contacts can be, relatively, above board?'

She nodded again, but looked puzzled.

'Fine. This is our contact telephone number.' He handed her a slip of paper. 'On these occasions use your real name, then we'll know there is no panic on.'

She understood, but said nothing.

'If you want to contact us desperately, and without Tufiq knowing, then it gets trickier. Is there anywhere you go fairly regularly that wouldn't look out of the ordinary to someone keeping tabs on you?' he asked.

She thought for a moment, then began listing her regular haunts, the gymnasium – four or five times a week, the shops – as required, the hairdresser – weekly, the local Chinese takeaway – once or twice a week. 'Living on my own, there's a tendency to be lazy over cooking,' she said, half apologetically.

James butted in, despite his resolution. 'I didn't know you liked Chinese food.'

'One of my little weaknesses.' She smiled.

'Right, let's use the Chinese,' said Peter.

'I don't follow,' she queried.

'Do you ring to make an order before you go to pick up your meal?' Peter asked.

'Yes, of course.'

'Then, if you want to contact us surreptitiously ring this number before you order.' He gave her a second slip of paper, adding that she was to memorise this number and destroy the paper. 'Let it ring four times, then put the phone down as if you'd made an incorrect dial. Wait ten minutes and ring your Chinese order through as usual. Tell them you will pick up your meal in twenty minutes. When you arrive you'll find someone else waiting to pick up his meal also. He will ask you the time and grumble about having to wait for his chicken foo yung to be cooked. He will be your contact. Give him whatever it is that you want us to have. The system will also work in reverse. If we want to get hold of you without anyone knowing, then we will ring you and put the phone down after exactly four rings. That will be insufficient time for anyone to try and trace the call. You then place your Chinese order and go to pick it up. You will meet your contact who will give you the necessary information.'

'I understand, but what if there is a real emergency and my family and I need to get out of Iraq quickly?'

'We talked about this last week. Have you discussed it with your father?'

'No, I haven't had a chance. I thought I should only discuss it face to face.'

'I agree. This is the plan.'

Peter then described to her that a sleeper in Samarra would be used to transport her family across the border into either Jordan or, more likely, Turkey – he didn't know which as much would depend on the security state at the time. To ease her family's get away, her father should start transferring monies to a foreign bank account immediately; in sums small enough not to arouse suspicion. Preferably, she should have joined her family in Samarra when she implements the plan and they must be ready to leave in less than half an hour. Getting her out from Baghdad separately would be more difficult. They must also decide where the family want to settle; perhaps a friendly Arab country, such as Tunisia. Britain would be safer, but, joking as he said it, colder.

'But what do I have to do?' She sounded apprehensive.

'You ring the second number that I gave you. The embassy's duty officer will always pick it up after the fifth ring. All you have to do is say two words, Ava and a keyword that we can choose now. Any ideas?'

Kate looked at James for a suggestion.

'How about *Swordfish*?' he ventured.

'*Swordfish*?' queried Peter.

'Yes,' enthused Kate. 'The name of the submarine in the film *On The Beach*.'

'I thought it was *Scorpion*,' corrected Peter. 'But I've not seen the film, only read the book. However, let's leave it as *Swordfish*.'

'So, to implement our escape all I have to do is ring this number and say "Ava – *Swordfish*"?'

'Yes. If you say anything else, such as "This is Ava, implement Operation *Swordfish*", then we'll know you are being coerced. It will be too late for us to help.'

'Suppose I can't get to Samarra?'

'You implement the plan anyway but you change the code, say "Ava…"' He thought for a moment, looking at James, and continued. 'How about "Gregory"? Not that I think you're as handsome as him.' They all laughed. 'Your family will still be taken out within half an hour and we will pick you up from the Chinese restaurant. Your route from Baghdad will either take you to Kuwait or Saudi Arabia. We would then arrange for you to be reunited with your family at our NATO base in Cyprus.'

'If my family were to flee to Britain, how would they manage to live?'

'They would be granted political asylum, be given British citizenship with new names and receive the usual State benefits. I've no idea how much. Your sisters could continue with their education, should they wish to do so.'

'And me?'

'You would also be given a new identity and probably be offered an appointment in the Foreign Office as an interpreter. Alternatively, you could seek a job in one of our universities. With your qualifications, I should have thought your chances would be very good.'

She seemed satisfied and smiled at James, but with a distant, frightened look in her eyes.

'I think that's just about covered it all. I'll get the bill paid and leave you two to finish your coffee on your own.' Peter stood up, he bent over Kate and kissed her cheek, whispering, 'Good luck', and left.

For some time Kate and James sat silently sipping their coffee, both in a world of their own. The enormity of what she had done worried James. He felt helpless. When he'd undertaken the intellectual challenge to build the software for Nastia Game at Bracknell and had the pleasure of witnessing its successful sale to Iraq, it had gone some way to getting back at the establishment for not awarding him the Defence Fellowship. Being able to help with the game's enhancement at Dataskil had been icing on the cake. He'd no idea how he had come to drift into this mess. The woman he'd fallen in love with had become a spy and two good friends had probably been murdered for a unique password system that he was going to give away anyway.

His mind was in a muddle when Kate spoke. 'James, how did we get into this tangle? Here I am wanting more than anything to spend the rest of my life with you – an infidel. I am agreeing to give away what amounts to State secrets and endanger my family. I am agreeing to stay in Iraq, knowing that when you fly back to England on Friday, I may never see you again. And it's all because of that wretched Nastia Game of yours. Are we both mad?'

He lent across the table, taking hold of her hand. Looking into her jade-coloured eyes, he sighed. 'They say great minds think alike. I was thinking exactly the same thing. God knows where all this will end.'

There was further silence; they were both at a low ebb. Kate sounded depressed when she casually remarked that she had been called in to see General Tufiq that morning.

'I expect he wanted more of the chess anagram?'

'Yes, but he wasn't satisfied that a chess position could be uniquely described in just four words. He got quite nasty.'

'What did you do?'

'I panicked, not knowing what to say, but I remembered you showing me the Spanish Opening, and said that perhaps some words could have a double meaning.'

James raised an eyebrow, and looked at Kate. *God, she's bright!*

'What happened then?' he asked.

'Well,' she replied, 'I said that maybe a Spanish player was playing the Spanish Opening. He seemed satisfied with that and let me go, but told me he wanted the solution to the anagram tomorrow morning.'

'In view of what you have agreed to this evening, I can't see what harm it will do. You might as well know the answer. The solution is WHITE CLOAKS UNLUCKY LATVIAN.'

'Let me write that down.' She checked her spelling, adding up the number of letters to twenty-five.

'If they do work it out, they still won't get into the software without my password. I'll tell you that when the time comes – it will make you smile. If you're under pressure for the answer to the anagram and they won't let you out of the country to get the solution, then I suggest you contact Ray Kane. Tell him I gave you his name. If he doesn't remember me, remind him that I looked after him in the Officers' Mess at RAF Cosford in 1969 when he gave a simultaneous display there. He's a former British champion, a grandmaster and probably the most knowledgeable chess mind in the United Kingdom. If he hesitates to get the position, then tell him what you told Tufiq this morning. I'll bet he then gets it within a few minutes.'

She listened intently, but didn't understand the significance.

They wandered slowly back to the *Sheraton*. It was getting late. Without speaking a word to each other, Kate got into the lift with James. They entered his suite, and both exhausted they fell into bed together. Holding each other loosely, they kissed gently. Kate, feeling his warm body next to hers, knew she was safe with him; he would never let her down. It was an illogical idea, but in some way – reassuring. She was happy to be with him; she'd forgotten Tufiq and the outside world. Here, under the sheets, the two of them were indefatigable. No one could harm them. They continued holding each other. She wanted the slow rhythm of their bodies locked together to last forever, but soon after climaxing, she was fast asleep.

CHAPTER 17

James awoke; Kate wasn't there. Like a spirit, she had slipped away in the night. Only a note remained to prove her former presence: *I'll ring you this evening before you go to Gerry's. Love XX.*

He'd forgotten he'd promised to go to Gerry's that evening for dinner and was certain he hadn't told Kate.

The note was a useful reminder, however, and before leaving for the College he asked the receptionist to order a bouquet of flowers to take to Sally. Her smile, 'No problem and have a nice day', summed up the kindness shown to him by the hotel staff throughout his stay.

The war games were in full swing at the College and James spent most of the day watching the Iraqi staff enthusiastically playing the games. Azi confided he was being promoted to become a permanent member of the College staff; his current attachment had been temporary. His responsibilities would include the computer facilities. Consequently, he was keen to cash in on James' expertise before he left Baghdad. His attitude towards James had changed. From the somewhat distant indifference shown at Reading, there was now an awkward attempt towards being friendly. At one point he managed to bring himself around to thanking James. 'Without you I would never have achieved promotion so soon.'

'How do you work that out?'

'Well, if you had never designed and built Nastia Game at Bracknell Staff College, I would not have been in a position to persuade the powers-that-be to buy the game.'

'I suppose there's some truth in that. However, it was you who showed the initiative and had the energy to drive the purchase through. I just hope that it doesn't backfire.'

'How could it do that?' Azi asked.

'Although the game is already showing up weaknesses in Iraq's Order of Battle and the impracticability of charging through the Zagros Mountains, I wonder if your planners will do anything about it. You badly need tanker aircraft and more helicopters.' James paused before continuing. 'Furthermore, the game cannot delegate decisions to field commanders. Everything in the game is decided at an operations control centre. That's fine, as air force operations are planned centrally to the nth degree. However, Army operations can only be planned in outline. Field commanders have got to be allowed to implement plans as they see fit. It's the reason why Army officers often make better man managers than air force officers; they're used to handling crises and getting the best out of their men from day one.' Adding, 'Of course, that's only my own opinion.'

Azi listened intently, but said nothing. James felt he was getting the message.

'You see, Nastia Game was designed purely as a tool for air warfare. By getting ICL to add a sophisticated ground-war model, you are expecting the game to do something it wasn't meant to do. I am worried it might lead you up the creek.'

Azi looked at James, perhaps not having understood the last simile. He thought for a few moments and then asked, 'Are you telling me the whole thing is useless?'

'No, not a bit of it, but it needs to be treated with caution. If you allow your top brass to think it is the panacea to all their problems for invading Iran then you're heading for big trouble.'

'How do I warn them off?'

'I don't know. My worry is that if you plan the invasion of Iran using Nastia Game then you will make early gains. However, the Iranians are not fools. If they come up with some novel tactic, or a set of circumstances that you have not foreseen, then they could stop you in your tracks. The war would get bogged down. A bit like World War One on the western front, it would become a stalemate.'

***

'Well?' General Tufiq, slouching in his chair with his Buddha-like pouch protruding over the top of his desk, was his usual boorish self. Kate's dislike of him increased each time she met him. She was having great difficulty not showing it. She no longer brought herself to attention in his presence, barely managing to stop herself being overtly insolent. He could destroy her family by simply picking up the phone and so she must make sure she was always one step ahead of him.

'The answer to the puzzle is WHITE CLOAKS UNLUCKY LATVIAN,' she said. There was no feeling in her voice, no pride in having seduced the answer from James, just a tone that reflected, *this is what you wanted, now take it.*

'Are you sure it's just four words?' It was asked as if he didn't believe her.

'Yes, positive.'

'Did he say anything else about it?'

'He doesn't think your team will be able to crack the code.' Kate thoroughly enjoyed saying it, and couldn't resist a small grin. The pleasure was heightened by the look of thunder that appeared across his face. She wasn't going to tell him about Ray Kane, at least not just yet. That could wait for another day.

'When are you seeing Squadron Leader Douglas again?'

'Tomorrow evening. Tonight he is going to his Air Attaché's house. I have not been invited.' After a pause, she added, 'Although I could try to muscle in, if you want me to.'

'No, that won't be necessary. Anyway, my team will have the answer by tonight.'

Kate was dismissed; she left hoping that James would be proved right and Tufiq wrong.

***

James spent the latter part of the afternoon with Brigadier Murthah in his office. Although generally warm towards him, Ahmed Murthah had always kept himself at a certain distance that befitted their difference in rank.

'Azi was telling me at lunch about your concerns on the limitations of Nastia Game. I thought I should hear them from you so that I can gauge for myself how serious they are.'

James repeated his doubts and the Brigadier nodded, mostly in agreement.

'Our problem in Iraq is that our political leaders are also our military leaders, unlike in Britain where elected politicians generally take advice from your professional Chiefs of Staff. Consequently, decisions here are taken centrally and there is very little delegation down the chain of command. The problem is exacerbated in that the middle ranks, say at lieutenant colonel level, do not get into the habit of taking minute-by-minute decisions. They have become mere puppets to their masters. In the end they become afraid of making the wrong choice. We end up in a chicken and egg situation where everything is done from the centre. Perhaps I am mixing my metaphors, but you know what I mean. You are quite right to be concerned, but I fear that there is very little either Azi or I can do. We must hope for the best. I shouldn't say this, but I retire soon and won't be around when the whole thing blows up. I met my wife in India when I was at their Staff College and we plan to go back there to retire. Do you know Uttar Pradesh?'

'No, sir, I've never been to India.'

'My wife, Dacksi, comes from a small village near the Nepal border. Beautiful.' He looked as if his mind was miles away and said nothing for what seemed several minutes. Then changing tack, he asked, 'Do you like curry?'

'Yes. I developed a taste for it while at Leicester University.' Adding, by way of an explanation, 'Leicester has a big Indian population.'

'I have been very remiss these last few weeks in not inviting you to come to my residence for a curry supper. My wife makes the most exquisite meals. Could you come before you leave? Perhaps, tomorrow evening?'

James hesitated, knowing that he was planning to go out with Kate that night for what, almost certainly, would be their penultimate evening together. The Brigadier could see James' doubts, and being no fool, said, 'Bring Kathab al Jised along. I am sure my wife would love to meet her. My wife has cousins who live in England, near Cambridge. She visited them last year and came back full of praise for King's College Chapel and the Fitzwilliam Museum. The women will have plenty to talk about.'

James was embarrassed and surprised that the Brigadier knew so much about Kate. He thanked him and said that they would both love to come, hoping that Kate would not let him down.

***

James arrived back at the *Sheraton* earlier than usual and sat outside in the hotel's shaded rear courtyard sipping a long orange juice and soda. Although he couldn't understand their language, the VIP treatment given to him by the Iraqis had been wonderful. Knowing it was coming to an end made him feel gloomy; the black dog had reappeared. He couldn't imagine life without Kate, but his head told him there could be no future in their relationship.

He was missing his family, particularly Stuart. The thought of playing football with him and seeing Jennifer again relieved some of his depression. He sighed at the thought of going back to the humdrum of changing nappies, washing up dishes, cutting the grass and the dozens of other little chores that are a part of everyday life. He remembered the necklace he had bought in Samarra for Emma when his relationship with Kate had still been innocent.

So much has changed in so little time.

Then he suddenly realised he had nothing for Stuart. There would be little time to get anything before Friday. He looked at his watch – 4.30 pm. He went to the foyer and asked the receptionist where he could go to get a present for his six-year-old son. 'The shops and the major bazaars are closed. It is a public holiday – the Anniversary of the 1968 Revolution.'

'But I have been working at the Military Staff College all day; I didn't know it was a public holiday.'

She shrugged her shoulders apologetically, but added, 'We have some gifts in our display cabinets.' Like all display cabinets in hotels all over the world, the prices are at least treble what you would pay elsewhere. James thanked her and decided to see if he could make time tomorrow to get something for his son. Perhaps Azi might have an idea or two. He went to his room, showered and fell asleep.

He awoke to the phone ringing. He looked at his watch. It was 6.15 pm. 'Reception here. There is a Miss al Jised on the line. Can I patch her through to you?'

'OK.'

'It's me, Kate. Are you all right?' she asked.

'Yes, I am getting ready to go to Gerry's. He's due to meet me in the bar in about quarter of an hour.'

'I told Tufiq the answer to your anagram. The cocky bastard thinks he'll have the answer by tonight.'

'He'll be nowhere near it. Did you tell him about Ray Kane, by the way?'

'No fear! I feel I must keep one step ahead of him. Whilst on that subject, what was it I said to Tufiq the previous day that you thought would help Ray Kane if he was stuck?' she asked.

'You said some things can have double meanings and mentioned the Spanish Opening, didn't you?' he replied.

'Yes.'

'Well you were greener than you thought.' He chuckled.

'Greener?'

'It's a game children play. They chant, "How green you are" when the seeker gets close to what he or she is looking for in hide-and-seek.'

'Are we seeing each other tomorrow?' she asked, hopefully.

'Ah. I was going to mention that. How do you fancy coming with me to Brigadier Murthah's residence for supper? We can come back here afterwards, if you want. Apparently, his wife is Indian and makes fine curries. She wants to meet you, as she was in Cambridge last year.'

To his relief, Kate agreed, sounding enthusiastic.

James continued. 'If you come to the *Sheraton* at about this time, he's going to send his driver here to pick us up.'

'Great. I'll see you then. Love you,' she said.

James found himself saying, 'Love you too', before putting the phone down.

***

Gerry was waiting in the bar. He was his usual cheerful self. 'I thought we should get a secret one in before we go home. Sally will never know.' They chatted about the progress of the war game at the College, then about the decisions made between Kate and Peter the previous evening. Gerry broached the subject of Wednesday's dining-in night. 'I have had a nice letter from Brigadier Murthah. He tells me that we will be sitting together with the two officers who have been helping you with Nastia Game at the end of the top table. He will introduce us to Saddam Hussein before the meal. It should be a good night.'

On their way out, James picked up a huge arrangement of flowers for Sally.

Gerry looked at him. 'I know what she's going to say when she sees those.'

'What?'

'Gerry, you never give me anything like this.'

Gerry, of course, was right. He had been married long enough to know his wife's reactions, although it was James who apologised for their late arrival. 'I am sorry, Sally, but it's my fault that we had a second beer before leaving the hotel.' His grovelling worked, as Sally murmured under her breath something about the meal being nearly ruined. In fact, it wasn't; the chicken casserole was perfect.

It was around ten o'clock when the phone rang in the lounge, where they had adjourned for coffee and a liqueur. 'Who the hell wants me at this hour?' grumbled Gerry as he forced himself out of his favourite Parker-Knoll chair.

'Hello?' he asked. He stood listening. Then he unconscientiously turned his back towards James and Sally, as if not wanting them to hear the person at the other end of the phone. He looked at his wristwatch and, nodding, grunted approval to whatever was being said. The call had lasted several minutes, when James heard him say, 'He's here with me now. I'll tell him and get him to the airport within the hour. I'll see you there.' The last sentence was stated not asked. Again he grunted something and put the phone down, still with his back to them. He didn't move, transfixed to the spot. It was Sally who sensed something was wrong.

'Gerry, what's the matter?'

He turned around, his face white, drained of all colour.

'I'm terribly sorry, James, but there's been an accident this afternoon in England.' He looked at his watch. 'At around four o'clock, that's about six hours ago allowing for the time difference, Emma had a car accident. She's critically injured in hospital in Weston-super-Mare.'

'Critically injured or seriously?' was all James could manage to reply. It was a stupid question, for he knew there was a big difference. His mind was blank, his tongue tied, his throat dry and his hands wet. He didn't know how he should react.

'Critically. That was the embassy's duty officer. He didn't know any details. Apparently she was being followed home by one of the SAS guards after having been shopping in Weston. He briefly lost contact with her on the toll road back to Kewstoke and came across skid marks. He stopped; something had made him look around. He saw that her car had gone over a small hedge, down the rocks and into the sea.'

'Did he mention if the kids were with her?'

'No.'

Sally, looking very pale, ventured, 'Perhaps, they were at school?'

'Stuart could have been, but now you mention it, I think they broke up last Friday for the summer holidays. Jennifer could have been with her grandparents.' He was recovering rapidly from the shock and added, 'I must go home as soon as possible.'

'We're already ahead of you there. The next flight out of Baghdad is an Air France flight coming through from Jakarta. It leaves at 2315 hours and is direct to Paris, Charles De Gaulle. An official from our Paris embassy will meet you and ensure you are put onto the first flight to London. Unfortunately, there is no direct flight from here until tomorrow morning. How quickly can you pack your bags?'

James said his sad farewell to Sally, who was in tears. 'We'll meet again in England, under happier circumstances,' she sobbed, as he climbed into Gerry's car. They weren't to know, but they would never see each other again.

The roads were deserted and it was only a few minutes before they were back at the *Sheraton*. James went straight up to his room and threw everything into his suitcases. Normally he was immaculate with his packing, but his mind was elsewhere. Meanwhile, Gerry was settling his account, explaining to the somewhat flummoxed receptionist that there was an emergency in England that entailed James' immediate departure. 'If there are any repercussions with your manager, give him this number and ask for me at the British Embassy.'

Within twenty minutes of arriving at the hotel, they were leaving.

CHAPTER 18

James and Gerry never spoke in the car. Both were too shocked. Gerry drove rapidly, but safely, and insisted on remaining with James when he parked the car at the front of the terminal building. 'Diplomatic plates have their uses,' he mumbled, getting a smile out of James.

As they entered the airport concourse, a colleague of Gerry's approached and expressed his regrets. He gave James his airline tickets.

He explained, 'Our diplomatic privilege allows us to enter the departure lounge and stay with you until you leave. At Charles De Gaulle airport you will be helped through the French customs quickly and onto the first flight for Heathrow. This Air France flight takes about seven and a half hours. It's due to arrive in Paris at 4.40 am local time and it has already landed here from Jakarta; you will be getting called in about twenty minutes.'

James thanked the stranger and the three of them passed through passport control and customs. Only cursory checks were made.

Night duty staff already bored with their shift, thought James.

As they waited, James began to realise the consequences of leaving in such haste. 'Gerry, I have just remembered that I was supposed to be going to Brigadier Murtha's tomorrow evening with Kate.'

'OK, let's think clearly. I'll make a list of everything you want me to do.' He was in decisive pilot mode and continued. 'First thing in the morning, I'll make contact with the College and go and see the Brigadier to explain what has happened. He will be able to give me a number for Kate, and I'll ring her. If I can see her face to face then so much the better, but I doubt if I'll be able to see her at work. What else is there?'

'There's the dining-in night.'

'Yep, I doubt if they'll want me to attend on my own.'

'I was supposed to give you the latest magnetic tape of the game to send back in the diplomatic bag.'

'Well, that's not going to happen, but I don't think anyone is going to hold that against you. What else?'

'The biggest problem is giving Kate the chess key. I was supposed to give it to her on Friday morning in case General Tufiq's team haven't been able to decipher the code.'

'Do you think they will decrypt it?'

'Not unless one of them is a knowledgeable chess historian.'

'Have you got the key on you?'

'No, but I could work it out. I can see the position in my head. It'll only take a few minutes.'

At that point, a tannoy message announced, 'All passengers travelling to Paris, Charles De Gaulle, on flight AF 587, please proceed to gate three.'

'You haven't got time, James. I'll tell Kate what the problem is and providing you get MoD clearance, you can always telex the position to me. Now you'd better go. I only wish we could have left each other under happier circumstances. I hope everything will be OK and Emma will recover.' There were real tears in his eyes and James knew he was leaving behind a genuine friend.

The jumbo jet took off five minutes early and was only half full. James sat alone in a window seat; his mind blank. The combination of fatigue, shock and fear of what lay ahead had addled his brain. Thoughts were floating around inside his head out of control; nothing linking them together. They came and went at random, one minute worrying about Emma and the children, the next about Kate. It began to dawn on him that he could be about to lose the two most loved people in his life, Emma, his best friend for the past ten years, and Kate whom he knew he would never see again. He felt cold, and lonely.

'I was told not to say anything to the Squadron Leader,' the embassy duty officer said to Gerry as they were leaving the building, 'but Mrs Douglas died in hospital just before I left the embassy. Do you think we were right not telling him?'

'Yes, if that's what you were instructed to do. Someone will, no doubt, give him all the details when he gets back to London. Let the poor bastard travel back in hope. That's the least we can do. He deserves better than this. Tomorrow I am going to have a lot of explaining to do to some very awkward people, but at least James is safely out of Iraq.'

***

'Yes?'

'It's the duty passport and immigration control officer here, sir, at Baghdad airport.'

'Well?'

'My instructions tell me that I must report any unusual occurrences to you on this number as soon as possible.'

'It's ten past eleven,' the recipient grumbled. The phone call had obviously woken him up. 'What do you want to tell me?'

The duty officer had, only a few minutes earlier, been comfortably settling into his reclining chair in the immigration complex at the airport. His catnap had been interrupted when one of his junior staff had excitedly entered his office. 'Two British Diplomats have just accompanied someone onto the Paris flight.' When asked their names, the junior had shown his inexperience by being unable to answer. A verbal bollocking had ensued that lasted several minutes. It was now an embarrassed senior officer who knew he was going to receive the bollocking.

He explained to the unknown voice at the end of the line what had happened. Although the recipient had not announced who he was, the passport controller suspected it was the Duty Officer from the Ba'ath

Party Intelligence and Security Service, Saddam Hussein's henchmen, a group not to upset. Being a Shia himself, he was aware that amongst his own sect they were known as the *Bloody PISS*.

'Are they still there?' he asked after listening without interrupting.

'No, sir. The flight to Paris has just taken off and the two diplomats have left in separate cars, both with CD plates.'

'Will they be on the CCTV system?'

'Yes, they passed through the concourse and the usual check points. Their cars were parked at the front too.'

'Good. Get the tapes and I'll send over an officer in twenty minutes to pick them up. OK?'

'Yes, sir.' He breathed a sigh of relief. He had got away with his junior's inefficiencies lightly, or so he hoped.

***

On the plane, James tried to get to sleep, tossing and turning to get comfortable, but to no avail. Determined, however, he kept his eyes tightly closed. He seemed to be hearing everything going on around him. He badly wanted to fall into a deep sleep, knowing tomorrow would be a long day, but he couldn't. He turned this way and that, but always ended up uncomfortable.

It was a surprise when he felt a hand on his shoulder. It was the chic hostess, who had earlier given him a light supper with a small bottle of Merlot. 'Fasten your seatbelt, Monsieur; we are landing in Paris in fifteen minutes.' He couldn't believe it. He looked at his watch. He had been asleep for almost four hours. His mouth tasted like a sewer. He rubbed his eyes, remembering why he was there.

As he walked into the baggage reclaim area, a tall, distinguished, smartly suited man approached. 'Squadron Leader Douglas?' he asked.

'Yes.'

'Anthony Higgins, Duty Officer, British Embassy, Paris. I have come to ensure you catch the next flight to Heathrow.'

'Have you any news about my wife?'

'Sorry, sir. I was simply signalled by the MoD to meet you. They gave me no information as to why. Is there a problem?'

It wasn't long before James' suitcases came around on the carousel and Anthony helped carry them past customs, showing the officer his diplomatic pass. The *dounanière* nodded, saying nothing.

'You'll catch the first BA flight easily,' remarked Anthony. 'The Air France flight arrived fifteen minutes early.' He led the way to the BA check-in desk.

'What time is it now?' asked James.

'It's just 4.25 am. Why?'

'Well, I left Baghdad at 10.55 pm, only five and a half hours ago.'

Anthony laughed. 'That's the wonders of modern aircraft for you. It's only 3.25 am in London and you'll be there almost before you leave Paris. As soon as you've boarded for London, I have to ring the MoD and let them know. Someone will meet you at Heathrow.'

'Any idea who?'

'No, they didn't say.'

They sat and had coffee while waiting for the flight to be called. Anthony tried hard to make conversation, but not knowing the reasons for James's presence, and James having his mind elsewhere, words were scarce. *Silence is golden*, as his old physics master, Taffy Jones, used to say before making him write it out one hundred times. But silence can be bloody awkward too. After what felt longer than twenty-five minutes, James' flight was called. He was surprised to find the aeroplane full – mostly French businessmen commuting to meetings in the City.

Admiral Johnson was waiting to meet him. 'I'm terribly sorry for what has happened. I have arranged for my driver to pick up your suitcases.' Without saying much else, he led James to the empty VIP lounge. Orange juice, hot coffee and warm, freshly baked croissants had been arranged for them on a low table in front of some easy chairs.

'Please sit down, James. There's no easy way of making this easy, but I am afraid Emma died yesterday, soon after being admitted to hospital.

I feel in some way responsible and wanted to be the person to give you the bad news. What makes matters worse is that Jennifer was in the car with her, strapped in a baby chair in the back seat. I am afraid she drowned.'

James had been expecting bad news, but this came as a double blow. He felt a sledgehammer had whacked him in the ribs. He gasped for breath. No air came into his lungs and he felt faint. His head dropped and he stared blankly at his shoes. Tears welled up. He felt them uncontrollably falling down his cheeks and watched as they fell to the floor. He couldn't bear to look at the Admiral. Instead he continued to gaze inanely at his shoes, his mind elsewhere. After a few minutes he wiped his face, firstly with the back of his hand and then with a handkerchief. He blew his nose. He looked up. Admiral Johnson's eyes had welled up too.

'Is Stuart alright?' he asked.

'Yes, he was playing with a friend at his grandmother's when it happened.'

'You said you felt responsible. Why?'

Admiral Johnson thought for a while before answering. 'Because it was my idea that we should not reveal to anyone the chess key; in case once opened, its secret would be compromised. You see, James, we are adopting your chess password method to many of our most secret computer systems. Our chief senior scientific adviser assures me that your system is only foolproof if no one can get into the programs. Once in, then they could work backwards, as it were, and decrypt the algorithms.'

'But that hardly makes you responsible for Emma's death, even if the advice was accurate, and I'm not convinced it was.'

The Admiral sighed, thinking, *why can't academics ever agree on anything?*

He gestured to James as to whether he would like some orange juice. James nodded and the Admiral said nothing until he had finished pouring.

'There is more to it than that. You know John Richards went missing?'

'Yes. Someone tried to use his password to enter the game a day or two after he vanished.'

'Well, his car was found in a central London multi-storey car park last week. It had been wiped clean, no fingerprints, nothing. There has still been no contact with him. We are assuming he is dead.'

James shook his head, remembering fondly the days spent with John at Bracknell.

'How much did Richards, as opposed to you, have to do with the design of the chess algorithm?'

'To be honest, most of it. He was a first-class maths graduate from Oxford. By comparison to my poor second in physics from Nottingham, I wasn't intellectually in the same street. He would explain his ideas to me and I grasped as much of them as I could. There were some areas where I hadn't much of a clue what was going on. Why do you ask?'

'Well, obviously, he must have revealed his password and the chess position you both used together. Our worry is what else did he give away about the design of the system and would it enable someone to hack into the latest version of the game?'

'The answer to that last one is no. When the Bracknell programs were converted to the ICL machines, I was, effectively, cast in John's role. I translated the programs, explaining as best as I could to Hamish what was going on. Between us, we came up with the idea that we should build two rings of protection. I think I explained this to you before I left for Baghdad. We changed the inner encryption algorithms so that the software is encrypted differently to the data. The outer ring protects the data files, so no one can change the data without knowing the first chess position. The inner ring protects the programs themselves. In other words, to modify the software is impossible unless you know both chess positions. The ICL programs, therefore, are much more secure than the original ones.'

'Ah, that's the next point, Hamish. No one knows where he is either. It can't be a coincidence that two key players connected with Nastia Game go missing like this. Furthermore, that weekend when Hamish came home, a former Iraqi prime minister was shot dead in London. By sheer luck the assassin was caught and we believe he is a member of the Iraqi Intelligence Service.'

'That can't have anything to do with Hamish, surely?'

'Probably not, but it muddies the water. MI5 is seeing Iraqi spooks everywhere.'

'But this still doesn't make you responsible for Emma's accident.'

'Except that it may not have been an accident,' replied the Admiral.

James sat up straight. The fatigue from travelling instantly disappeared. His senses were on alert, even though he was lost for words.

'Let me explain. After Hamish went missing...' the Admiral briefly halted. 'What? Ten days ago now? I decided that if someone had nobbled him to get the chess key then they, whoever they are, might try and squeeze you as well; possibly through your family. I had two SAS men discreetly sent to Kewstoke to watch Emma and your children like hawks.'

'Yes, Gerry Platini told me. Thank you.'

'They stayed in *The Owl's Nest*, ostensibly on a fishing trip. Then last Wednesday, the twelfth, a notice appeared in the personal column of *The Times*. It was addressed to me, although it didn't refer to me by name; only by a vague Head of Joint Services Security. It demanded that the chess key was to be printed in Friday's *Times*, or else.'

'That's interesting because it was on Tuesday, the day before, that someone tried unsuccessfully to enter Nastia Game using Hamish's password.'

'Yes, quite.'

'So what did you do?' asked James.

'I drafted in two more SAS men. They stayed at *The Commodore*, supposedly looking to buy a local property. I also opened your sealed envelope containing the position. I was prepared to print it if necessary.'

James blushed; he knew what was coming next. 'What you had written didn't make any sense. I put our GCHQ boys on to it and they took until Friday to come up with WHITE CLOAKS UNLUCKY LATVIAN as the most likely solution, but couldn't get any further.'

'Why didn't you contact me?'

'Four reasons: one, I know how insecure communications with Iraq are. Two, I didn't want to worry you unnecessarily. Three, I had hoped our cipher experts would have broken the anagram easily. Four, stupid I know, but I felt that Emma's protection team would prevent anything from happening to her, as there had been no sightings of strangers in the village, other than holiday makers.'

'What makes you think Emma's accident was deliberate?'

'At the moment the police are not sure of the cause. I don't know the tollroad, but apparently it is dangerous at the best of times; particularly when travelling from Weston towards Kewstoke. I believe there is virtually nothing on the nearside of the road to prevent a car from going over the edge, down the cliffs and into the sea.'

'That's right. There is a small hedge, but in places it's no more than a few inches high. Furthermore, some of the right-hand bends are tight. But Emma knew that and would have taken due care.'

'The officer following her, at a discreet distance, had been held up at the toll to pay his fees, whereas Emma had passed through quickly because she had a yearly sticker in her windscreen.'

James nodded; he could see how her escort could have lost visible contact.

'Have you heard of a stinger?' asked Admiral Johnson.

James shook his head.

'It's a device used by police to stop a car. It can scissor out across a road in seconds and has spikes that blow out the car's tyres, stopping it in its tracks.'

'So what are you saying?'

'Your wife's car is being examined thoroughly today, but when they dragged it up from the beach yesterday evening, both nearside tyres had shredded.'

'But the car was practically new.'

'Exactly. The offside tyres were perfect, which is why the police think the accident was cleverly engineered and that is why I sent Brigadier

Morrison down to Weston straight away. He is staying at RAF Locking with your station commander. I want him on the spot to make sure the Avon and Somerset Police don't slacken in their efforts to find the reasons for Emma's death. I have made it clear to the Chief Constable when I spoke to him on the phone last night that the accident is to be given top priority.' He tried to smile, but James never noticed. The Admiral continued, after a short pause. 'I've arranged for you to be driven to the hospital at Weston. Ian Morrison will meet you there. I am afraid there are certain formalities to go through.'

He looked at his watch. It was 7 am. They polished off the croissants, had another coffee and left. James thanked the senior officer for meeting him at such an unearthly hour.

'I'll come down and see you later in the week, when we know more. There are a lot of unanswered questions and I intend to get to the bottom of this. All I can say, however, is that it looks as if Hamish didn't give too much away; other than his password and the position you used together.'

'Why do you say that?'

'Because, otherwise, why would they have needed to try to get at you through your family and demand the chess key in *The Times*?'

CHAPTER 19

The journey to Weston in the back of the Admiral's comfortable, warm Jaguar was uneventful. James slept most of the way. He woke as they arrived outside the hospital. He found Brigadier Morrison waiting for him in reception.

'James, I'm sorry about what has happened. No words of mine will lessen the blow.'

'Thank you for being here, but I'm afraid I'm still shell-shocked.'

'Of course, it's perfectly natural. I had the driver bring you here first because I thought you would want to see Emma and Jennifer before there is a post-mortem.'

James nodded, but said nothing. The Brigadier led him, accompanied by a nurse, to the mortuary. Seeing Emma, and especially Jennifer, laid out on a cold slab was eerie. He had expected to break down, but instead felt numb. He was in a macabre dream where everything is black or white and there is total silence; no background noise whatsoever. He sat down on a chair by Emma and held her hand. It was ice cold. Her face was white, her eyes shut as if asleep. He smiled at her as he remembered how often he had pulled her leg about her ability to sleep. 'You could sleep for England', he used to say. 'Now no one will wake you up.' Tears filled his eyes; he remained numb. He went to look at Jenny. The tears flooded uncontrollably. So innocent, so pure, so pale, so cold. He had no idea how long he had sat looking at his daughter, but eventually standing, he looked at the attendant, nodded, and left the room where Ian Morrison was waiting patiently.

'I'd like to go home now and see Stuart.' It was already 10.30 am.

'Of course. The Admiral's car is yours for as long as you want. Shall I arrange for you to meet Lance Corporal Wiles this afternoon? He's the man who found Emma's car. Afterwards we can both go to see the Divisional Police Superintendent who has promised to give me a briefing on their provisional findings on the accident.'

'OK. There are some questions I would like to ask Corporal Wiles.'

'Fine, shall we say two o'clock?'

***

He went straight to his in-laws. Pat opened the door, her eyes red. She opened her arms, said nothing and hugged him. Bill stood behind her, looking helpless. What could either of them say? They had lost their daughter and granddaughter in one afternoon. It was James who broke the silence. 'How's Stuart taking it?'

Pat looked at Bill, who replied. 'I don't think it's quite sunk in. He's gone to his pal's house round the corner to play.'

'Perhaps it's just as well. Pat, could you put the kettle on for a coffee? I think you had better hear what I have got to say.'

His in-laws sat silently as James revealed that Emma's death may not have been an accident.

'Has this got something to do with you going to Iraq?' Bill asked.

'More than likely, although we're not sure why.' They were surprised to hear that professional guards had been in Kewstoke for a week keeping tabs on their movements.

'I've not seen them,' exclaimed Pat.

'Nor I,' added Bill.

'You weren't meant to. They are still in the village. They'll be watching Stuart at this very minute. I'm going to meet the Lance Corporal who discovered Emma's car this afternoon. Maybe I'll get to know a bit more then. In the meantime, Bill, can you start to organise the funeral?'

Corporal Wiles was not anything like what James had expected. Short, stocky, tanned, long hair, bordering on middle age, he could have been a prop-forward. It was easy to see how he could pass unnoticed in the village. Incredibly articulate, he read James a copy of the statement he had given to the police. He described how he had followed Mrs Douglas into Worle where she had done some shopping at Sainsbury's. She had then driven into Weston; he had managed to park nearby and follow her into Marks and Spencer where she had bought some lingerie. He had not lost sight of her until the tollroad. The tollroad attendant had waved her distinctive red Fiat 126 through as it displayed a resident's annual ticket. He had been stopped to pay the fee. It would have taken no more than a minute to slow down, stop, pay, get change and continue. Approaching the right-hand bend, where the accident had occurred, he had noticed tyre marks and soil on the road. Something, he knew not what, made him stop. He had a gut feeling that something was wrong. He parked his car, got out, ran back to where the low hedge had been disturbed, looked over the edge and saw Emma's car partially in the sea, twenty or thirty feet below. A car was passing towards Weston; he waved it down, gave the alarm and told them to ring for an ambulance and the police from the café at the end of the tollroad. He had then scrambled down the bank to help. Mrs Douglas' car was on its side, half submerged. Mrs Douglas was still alive; he pulled her out in case she slipped under the water and then had difficulty getting Jennifer out of her baby chair, as she was completely submerged. He gave the baby mouth-to-mouth, but she was already dead. The rest of his statement was routine, describing how the police arrived, followed shortly by the ambulance.

'There's one thing that puzzles me,' said James. He looked at Brigadier Morrison, as if to ask whether he could proceed. 'When you were stopped by the tollroad attendant was there anything unusual?'

'I don't follow you,' replied the Corporal.

'Well, was there anyone hanging around, or did the attendant seem tardy in any way when giving you your change, as if he was trying to slow you down?'

'No, although the old boy couldn't be quick if he tried.'

'When you left him and before you reached the scene, did a car come from the other direction? I'm wondering if Emma could have been shunted off the road.'

'Now you mention it, a car did approach from the other way. It was going quite quick too, but it didn't look as if it had been in an accident. There were no obvious dents or anything like that.'

'Did the police not ask you that question?'

'No.'

'Can you remember what make of car it was?'

'Yes, it was a maroon Rover 2000, but I didn't catch the registration number.'

Brigadier Morrison interrupted. 'I think the police should follow this up, don't you?'

'Yes, it could be significant,' replied James.

Then he asked Corporal Wiles, 'Did you sense if anyone was following you at any time?'

'No, sir.'

***

When James was interviewing Corporal Wiles, the day was drawing to a close in Baghdad. Gerry had had a busy day. Up at 6.00 am, he hadn't slept much since leaving the airport. The news of Emma's death, even though they had never met her, had greatly upset both him and Sally.

He had decided that his first task should be to contact the Military Staff College. By 0705 hours, he was telephoning from home. A Major Talfah had answered, explaining she was the personal staff officer to the commandant.

'I must see Brigadier Murthah, personally, as soon as possible,' he said, emphasising the words *personally* and *possible*.

He then met the well-known active non co-operation ploy. 'The Brigadier has a busy schedule today. Can I help?'

Gerry knew she was fishing to find out what the problem was. Her tactics didn't fool an old stager. Gerry coldly replied that if he was unable to see the Brigadier early that morning, he would have to escalate the problem to higher authority. She backed off and suddenly was able to arrange for Gerry to see the Commandant at 0900 hours. He smiled to himself.

I've met your type before, young lady.

It would give him time to get to the embassy and brief the military attaché and the ambassador on developments.

***

The Duty Officer at the Ba'ath Party's Intelligence Secret Service headquarters had received the airport CCTV tapes soon after midnight. It hadn't taken him long to identify the two British embassy officials who had bundled the unknown third person onto the Paris flight. Delving in the files, however, soon revealed: *Squadron Leader Douglas, RAF officer, visa/work permit expires 23/24 July. Reason for permit: helping develop military software at Military Staff College. Residence: Sheraton Hotel.* If there was any more information held on him, he couldn't find it. Thinking that the RAF officer must have decided to leave Baghdad early, he decided, therefore, not to disturb any of General Tufiq's staff until seven o'clock, their usual time to start work.

***

Kate had gone to work that morning with a spring in her step. She was looking forward to visiting Brigadier Murthah's residence with James. She had frequently enjoyed having curries when she was a student in Cambridge, but had never found a classy Indian restaurant in Reading.

Tonight is going to be a real treat.

It came as a surprise when, soon after 7.30 am, the phone rang and General Tufiq demanded that she instantly come to see him.

Puzzled, she left the office.

As she entered Tufiq's office, she could see he was seething with anger. 'Your friend Douglas has buggered off back to England,' he roared.

She frowned, her eyes narrowed, a question mark appeared on her face. 'I'm sorry?' she asked, not understanding his remark.

'Last night Squadron Leader Douglas left Baghdad on the 2315 hours flight for Paris.'

She gasped for air; her lungs were empty. She stood frozen for a minute. Words wouldn't come out. Eventually, oxygen had filled the vacuum in her chest and she felt faint. She looked around for a chair and without asking, sat down.

'Well, what have you got to say?' demanded the General.

After several deep breaths, she managed to reply. 'I don't understand.' Tears were welling in her eyes, her feelings aflutter, her legs jelly. She could sense she was shaking. She bit her lip – hard.

Pull yourself together in front of this bastard.

'Excuse me, but this is a shock. I was expecting to see Squadron Leader Douglas this evening. We were due to go to dinner at Brigadier Murthah's house,' adding as an afterthought, 'I think the Brigadier wanted to thank the Squadron Leader for his work with the war game.'

'Yes, I know.' He snapped his words out.

How does he know?

He continued. 'The Air Attaché, Wing Commander Platini, has already made an appointment to see Brigadier Murthah this morning at 0900 hours.'

This confirms Talfah works for Tufiq.

'Did you know anything about this?' he asked.

'No. I swear I didn't.'

Tufiq believed her; she was clearly in shock.

'Make up any excuse you like. Contact Platini. Arrange to meet him as soon as possible. Go to his house, if necessary. Then report back to me. This affects how we are going to get the key to the war game.'

So his team still haven't deciphered the word puzzle. Good!

She knew she was being dismissed and left. She was desolate.

How could James do this to me?

Alone in the corridor, she wiped her eyes.

All men are bastards. James is no better than the rest.

As she walked back to her office in a daze, her mind was trying to fathom out the turn of events.

I can't believe this was planned. James wouldn't have done this without a good reason. Something must have happened back in England. Perhaps one of the children has taken ill.

Kate's mind was in turmoil. She was still suffering from shock as she cleaned herself up in the ladies room near her office. Deep breathing exercises gradually helped her to regain control. She looked at her face in the mirror. *I mustn't let anyone see me looking like this.* Ten minutes later she felt sufficiently composed to return to her office and asked her secretary to get a chauffeured car. 'I am going out for a while. I should be back by lunchtime.'

'Where shall I say you have gone if anyone asks?' asked the secretary. It was a cleverly phrased question, made by a prying secretary who had guessed that something was not quite right.

'Refer them to General Tufiq. He knows where I am going.' The answer was smarter than the question and put paid to any further conversation.

Five minutes later the car was ready. Kate looked to a casual observer as immaculate as ever. She got into the rear seat and instructed her driver where to go. He raised an eyebrow but said nothing.

Morning traffic in Baghdad was bad. It was nearly an hour later when they arrived at Gerry's house in the diplomatic quarter. She rang the doorbell.

Sally answered.

'Kate!' she exclaimed, her face beamed friendship, but only for a second. Rapidly it changed. A look of deep sorrow, sympathy and more than a hint of tears appeared. 'I'm so sorry about what has happened.' The sentence was simple and sincere. As Sally spoke, she opened her arms to embrace Kate. Somewhat bemused, Kate responded. They stood in the doorway for some time hugging each other. When Sally released her, she stood back, the tears were now running down her cheeks, and said, 'It's terrible news, isn't it?'

'Why has James gone away and left me like this?' asked Kate, her voice was quivering; her body shaking.

It dawned on Sally that Kate was in the dark and her expression changed to one of puzzlement. 'You'd better come inside.'

They sat together on the settee in the lounge. Sally gently took hold of both of Kate's hands. Looking at her despondently, she related the events of the previous evening. Kate's face went pale then white. Sally explained that James had left Baghdad hoping that all may be well. However, Gerry had then learned that both Emma and Jennifer were dead.

'They were a lovely family, so kind to me when I stayed with them in Weston-super-Mare,' Kate wept. Sally could not reply, but held her hands more tightly. She looked at Kate and marvelled at her beauty. Her shoulder-length, jet-black hair shone, her large jade-green eyes sparkled brighter because of her tears, her red lips glistened and her slim waist exaggerated her firm breasts and long legs. Although old enough to be her mother, Sally wanted to console her and innocently put her left arm around Kate's shoulder. It seemed the most natural thing to do and without any effort she found Kate's sobbing head gently resting on her bosom. She was reminded of her own children, when they were only days old. No words were spoken. They sat motionless giving each other comfort. Many minutes passed.

Sally could smell Kate's perfume. Different to her own, it was subtle, but it made her feel heady. She couldn't believe it when Kate's left hand began gently feeling her right breast. At first Sally thought, *it must be accidental* and, so, did nothing to stop her. But it continued. She could feel her breasts going firm and her nipples standing proud. Her instinct was to push Kate away, but as Kate's beautiful, tearful face rose to look longingly at her, she wanted instinctively to respond. For the first time in her life Sally found herself kissing another woman.

Kate moved closer. As they continued kissing, their breathing grew ever more heavy and passionate. Sally felt Kate fumbling under her skirt; she was excited and tried to protest, 'No,' she said, but knew it wasn't convincing. It was an altogether new experience, *so different, and yet so natural.* It took less than a minute before they climaxed together. They lay, side by side, exhausted. Not a single word had been spoken.

Sally was the first to move. She straightened her clothes. 'I'll go and make some coffee,' she said, as if nothing had occurred and went into the kitchen. Kate followed moments later.

As they waited for the kettle to boil, Sally explained that Gerry had gone to brief the ambassador and then Brigadier Murthah. 'I know he wanted to tell you the awful news himself, but he didn't know how to contact you. He should be on his way back to the embassy by now. If I ring him, then he could come out here and see you.'

Kate had gathered herself together and was beginning to recover. 'No, if you don't mind, I'd better get back to work. My driver might be wondering what I'm getting up to.'

Kate was blushing and held Sally's hand. Looking her in the eye, she apologised. 'I have never done that before. I am sorry.'

'I've never done it before either. There's nothing to apologise for.' Then, after a moment's pause, she added, 'If you wish to come and see me again, please don't hesitate.'

'I would love to come, but it might be difficult as I suspect my movements are watched carefully.'

'Gerry's successor has been nominated and we will probably be leaving Baghdad in October. If ever you come to England, you will be welcome to visit us. We have a cottage in a village just south of Grantham called Colsterworth. It is called The Old Post Office.'

'That's very kind of you, Sally. I shall remember that. Who knows what lies ahead for me?' And with that, they hugged each other and Kate left.

Watching her enter the staff car, Sally was reminded of Sir Walter Scott:

What shall be the maiden's fate?
Who shall be the maiden's mate?

***

Gerry arrived at the College entrance and was met by Major Talfah, who introduced herself. *A big girl,* thought Gerry, *I wouldn't want to get on the wrong side of her.* She was courteous, called him 'Sir', but was distant.

She accompanied him upstairs, took him through what Gerry assumed was her own outer office, barely noticing a major sitting to one side, knocked on the far door, opened it and announced, 'Wing Commander Platini.' A middle-aged officer rose from his desk and came around, arm outstretched, smiling. 'Gerry, so nice to meet you again after all these years.' Gerry looked at Brigadier Murthah, wondering where they had met. 'We met when you gave a talk on air defence at Riyadh. It must be seven or eight years ago.'

Gerry smiled. 'Yes, it was 1971. I was a Qualified Flying Instructor with the Saudi Lightnings. I hope you are keeping well?'

The Brigadier ignored the question. 'I remember you lecturing to us that successful air defence must be built on three foundations: forward looking radars, secure communications and tanker aircraft. Your Nastia Game is teaching us these lessons.' They shook hands in the middle of the room. Gerry heard the door behind him being closed. Polite small talk continued as the Brigadier invited Gerry to sit down at a small coffee table to one side of his office.

'I assume, by now, you know why I have come to see you?' It was Gerry who felt he had to break up the social niceties.

'No, I don't.' The Commandant's reply surprised Gerry.

'I'm not sure where to start.' Gerry paused, but the Commandant waited for him to continue. 'You know that Squadron Leader Douglas never came to work this morning.'

Before the Brigadier could reply, there was a knock on the door and Major Talfah entered with a silver tray bearing a large coffee pot, some biscuits and three cups and saucers. She put the tray on the table in front of them, smiled and left. Brigadier Murthah could see Gerry wondering why there were three cups.

'To answer your question, Gerry, yes. Major Azi Tumbrah informed me when I arrived this morning that Squadron Leader Douglas' driver had returned from the *Sheraton* without him. The driver had been told that he had left the hotel last night. Other than that I know nothing. I have, of course, guessed that your visit must be something to do with James not arriving. Consequently, I have invited Azi to join us for coffee as he is taking over the running of the war game. Is that OK?'

Gerry nodded.

The Commandant rose, went to his desk and pressed his intercom. 'Roya, send Azi in, please.'

Azi entered the room, closed the door behind him and stood to attention. 'Gerry, meet Azi Tumbrah, a graduate of your Staff College at Bracknell.' They shook hands and the three sat down. While pouring the coffee, the Brigadier, talking to Azi, said, 'Gerry was about to explain James' disappearance. I assume you've not heard anything more than what you've already told me.'

The Major replied, 'No, sir.'

Gerry began. 'Last night James came to my house for a meal. Soon after ten o'clock the phone rang. It was the Duty Officer in the embassy.' He then regaled the story. Both the Iraqi officers listened in silence. Their faces confirmed that neither had known what had happened. When Gerry had finished, there was total silence for several minutes.

Azi spoke first. 'My wife will be greatly upset. Mrs Douglas used to run the crèche at Bracknell and our two toddlers went regularly. She was very popular with all the foreign officers' wives and will be greatly missed. I don't know what to say.'

The Brigadier sat himself upright, expanding his chest in the process. 'You were quite right to send James home. We will miss him, of course. He has done a grand job here, but I am sure we will cope.' He was looking at Azi for confirmation as he said this. 'My wife and I were going to entertain him this evening to a curry supper. He was going to bring Kathab al Jised with him. Does she know?'

'Not as far as I am aware. I was going to ask you how I could get in touch with her, as I wanted to tell her myself rather than her getting the news from some third party.'

'You know her then?' asked the Commandant.

'Yes, he brought her to our house for dinner last week. She is very personable. My wife was much taken by her.'

'You do know that she is about to be put in charge of our chemical and biological weapons research and development facility at Al Muthanna?'

'Yes.'

'Weapons that can cover a vast expanse, killing the masses: poisons, germs and those sorts of things are not my cup of tea, I'm afraid.'

Gerry was unsure how to reply.

Azi said nothing. He knew that James had been having an affair with Kathab who had been under pressure from General Tufiq to get the chess key. *The whole thing has become a bloody mess,* he thought.

'I'll get you her number at Al Muthanna,' said the Brigadier, 'but she may know by now.' He then turned to Azi, asking, 'Is there anything you want to ask Wing Commander Platini about the war game?'

Azi felt he was between a rock and a hard place. He had no idea how much Gerry knew of Kathab's role in getting the chess key. He was certain his Commandant knew nothing. He thought before answering. 'No, sir. I don't think there's anything.'

CHAPTER 20

Kate returned to Al Muthanna sitting in the back of her staff car thinking of the morning's events. Her frisson with Sally had been unexpected. It had been exciting and nerve-racking, but felt perfectly natural. She was still tingling. The new experience, a liaison with another woman, made her wonder at her feeling of contentment; so different from being with James. As the car slowly wound its way through the lunchtime traffic, she re-lived the moment with Sally. She felt relaxed, dreamlike, floating on air. Her frustration and anger over James' sudden disappearance was waning. Perhaps, she had found her true sexuality.

She pondered; *I will start a new life without James. Now Emma is dead, he might come back for me. No, no more wishful thinking. From now on, I'll be the boss and make the decisions. To hell with men. No one will bully me again. Only I will know where our chemical weapons are hidden. The chess formula will give me power over men.*

She resolved to handle whatever Tufiq threw at her. She focussed her mind on the position James had shown her in the sand at Ur; she could recall it perfectly.

Kate had hardly got her foot through the door, when her secretary greeted her. 'You've just missed a phone call from a Wing Commander Platini. He said he was the British Air Attaché and had got your personal number from Brigadier Murthah at the Staff College.'

Kate felt no need to explain the call to her secretary and asked, 'Did he say what he wanted?'

'No, except that it was vital, that's the word he used, that you ring him back as soon as possible. He gave me his extension number at the British Embassy and said he'd be there for the rest of the day.'

'Then you'd better make the call.' She went through to her office, sat down and waited to be patched through.

She heard her secretary say, 'I'm putting you through now.'

'Kate, it's Wing Commander Platini here.' Kate recognised Gerry's accented Arabic and, thinking there might be someone eavesdropping, decided to be formal and speak in English.

'Kathab al Jised here. I understand you wanted to speak to me.'

Gerry, too, realised the conversation should be at arm's length. 'Ah, yes, Miss al Jised. Is there any chance we can meet? I would like to explain Squadron Leader Douglas' sudden departure last night. There were one or two things that need to be cleared up.'

Her heart began pounding. Despite her resolution to try and forget James, she knew that there would always be a part of her that would belong to him. Without thinking she asked, 'Where can we meet?'

'I think the *Sheraton* might be as good a place as any, don't you? What about five o'clock?'

'That's fine. I'll see you there.'

She had hardly put the phone down, when her secretary buzzed through on the intercom. 'While you were on the phone General Tufiq rang, he wants to see you.'

She walked apprehensively across the building and up the stairs to his office. As she approached, she bit her lip.

You can beat this bastard. You're cleverer and can outwit him. Now do it!

She knocked on his door and entered.

'Shut the door. Take a seat,' he grunted. She sat in front of his desk, looking him in the eye.

What an ugly bastard you are. What on earth would any woman see in you?

He stared back, hatred in his face. For a moment, Kate felt uncomfortable. She bit her lip again.

Come on, Kathab, you're winning. He'll look away before you.

And he did. He shuffled some papers on his desk, before asking, 'Well, what did you find out at Platini's house?'

'He wasn't there. I gather he'd gone to the embassy to brief his ambassador and then was going to see Brigadier Murthah at the Staff College.'

'Yes, I know all that. But why were you at Platini's house for over an hour, if that's all you learned?'

The driver must have told Tufiq.

'Mrs Platini asked me in and gave me coffee. She told me all the events of last night, including how Squadron Leader Douglas left thinking his wife and daughter were still alive. Soon afterwards Platini learned that they had both been killed in the car accident. Mrs Platini was upset having to tell me and it took some time. I couldn't be rude and rush away, could I?' She emphasised the last two words. For the first time, she saw Tufiq look slightly uncomfortable.

'Everything you have said confirms what the British Embassy has told our Interior Ministry. However, it leaves us with a problem, the key to the war game.' He stopped, clearly expecting Kate to pick up the thread.

Kate played it cool. She crossed her legs and made no effort to answer. The silence of the pause lasted for what seemed ages.

Tufiq broke it. 'The war game is an essential part of our preparation to invade Iran.'

'When?' Kate tried to look surprised. When at Reading she suspected something was afoot. This was the first time someone had confirmed it.

The General looked embarrassed. He had let something out of the bag. He blustered, 'Oh, it will not be for a year or two yet, but we all know it's going to happen.' Then, changing his posture, he pulled himself together, looked her in the eye, glared and quietly threatened. 'What I have just said is Top Secret. Understand?'

She said nothing.

He repeated, but much more loudly. 'Understand?'

She looked away, replying quietly, 'Yes.'

She was losing confidence again. Despite all her good intentions, he was bullying her.

He pressed his intercom. His PSO entered the room, standing behind Kate.

'Ali, have some tea made and bring in some light snacks. Miss al Jised hasn't had any lunch and we have much to discuss. Cancel any appointments I may have for the next hour or so.'

What's the bastard getting up to now?

'Yes, sir.' Kate heard the door close behind her.

He spoke coldly, slowly and menacingly. 'Now I'll ask you again, what are you going to do to get the chess key?'

She inwardly sighed. The crunch had come; she shuffled uneasily in her chair while her mind raced. 'I think,' she spoke slowly as she tried to put her thoughts together, 'that I will have to go to England and get the key from Squadron Leader Douglas.' She stopped to see his reaction. It was as she had expected.

'And never come back? Do you think I am a fool and don't know what has been going on?' He didn't expand further.

'But it was you who encouraged me to seduce the infidel to get the code. I have done everything you have asked of me,' she protested loudly.

'Except get the damn thing,' he replied sarcastically.

'It's not my fault if your experts can't decipher the anagram.' It was brave of her to reply in such a manner. She expected him to explode, but to her amazement he sat quietly in a trance. He continued to stare at her. Looking into the back of her head, he was trying to read her mind.

He spoke deliberately. 'If I let you go to England...' and stopped.

Kate's heart missed a beat. She straightened up, trying to hide a smile. 'Yes?'

'If you were to go to England...' he paused again and then continued. 'There are two conditions.'

Here we go.

'What?'

He ignored her question, pressed his intercom bell and waited for the PSO to appear. A Corporal brought in a silver tray with some chicken kebabs and slices of pizza. The PSO came in with the mint tea. Tufiq gestured for Kate to help herself. Tradition demanded that she pour the tea for both of them. They ate and drank in silence for several minutes.

He then began. 'Firstly, you will only have two full days there. If you are not on a direct flight back on the fourth day, then expect family reprisals. Do you understand?'

She nodded. She didn't have to ask what he meant.

'Secondly, you will have a chaperone throughout. If you so much as try to get away from her, even to make a phone call, then I will get to hear about it and the first condition will apply.'

'Who will accompany me?'

'Major Roya Talfah.'

Oh God, not her. Anyone but her.

She began to make a protest. 'But she and I…' and stopped. Kate knew it was Tufiq's conditions or not at all.

'Yes?' he asked.

'Nothing. When do you want me to go?'

'I will need to discuss Major Talfah's detachment with Brigadier Murthah. I suggest you both leave on Sunday, which will give you Monday and Tuesday in England. You will return on Wednesday. My staff will make the preparations. You will stay in our embassy for the three nights you are there.'

Kate knew there was nothing she could do or say that would change Tufiq's mind, and nodded agreement.

'There is one other thing. The minute you get the position, you are to give it to Major Talfah. She will get our embassy security officer to transmit it immediately to my HQ.'

A defeated and deflated Kate nodded, and left.

***

Gerry was sitting in the foyer when Kate arrived. He rose from his chair and struggled to smile. It didn't disguise the look of sadness on his face. He spoke first. 'I'm sorry about this, but I wanted to explain it to you myself. James insisted that I see you. It was the last thing he said before boarding the plane to Paris.'

Kate tried to smile, but Gerry could see that she was feeling deeply unhappy. She could barely whisper. 'Thank you for making the effort to see me.'

'Look, shall we get a drink and go and sit on the terrace where it's quiet? What about two large orange juices with soda?'

'That would be nice,' she replied in a quiet voice.

Kate found a secluded spot and Gerry arrived with the drinks.

'Last night came as a dreadful shock,' Gerry began. He looked at Kate, pausing, unsure how to continue. She didn't react. 'I understand from Sally that she told you about the accident and how James had to fly back?' He paused again, this time Kate nodded slowly.

'Then you know that Emma and Jennifer both died from their injuries, but James didn't know that when he flew out last night?'

Again Kate nodded.

'Our embassy has apologised officially to your Interior Ministry for any inconvenience and I have seen Brigadier Murthah who has accepted the inevitability of the situation. He assures me the College will manage. Squadron Leader Douglas' work was all but finished. The Brigadier asked me, by the way, to say how much he regrets not being able to entertain you and James to a curry supper this evening.'

This latter remark made Kate smile; she replied, 'Yes, it's a shame. I had been looking forward to meeting him. He's an old friend of my father's.'

'Now, what I have to say next is to go no further. OK?'

'Of course.'

'I have been speaking to London this afternoon. Apparently, the local police don't think Emma's death was an accident. Somehow it was engineered.' He stopped to let the revelation sink in.

Kate went white. Shaking badly, she stammered, 'Are you saying Emma and Jenny were murdered?'

'At the moment we don't know, but our own security wallahs believe there may be a connection between the disappearance of Richards and Hamilton, this accident, and the key to Nastia Game.'

'I don't believe this. What is so bloody special about Nastia Game?' Her voice didn't disguise her anger and frustration.

Gerry stroked his chin, pondered the question and answered succinctly. 'Possibly, millions of lives?'

Kate sat upright in her chair, radiating presence. Gerry could see the latest news had set her thinking; she was alert. 'There are only two governments that could want the game's secrets this much, Iran and Israel.' She stopped, expecting Gerry to confirm her hypothesis.

'They're the obvious culprits, yes,' Gerry agreed, 'but I think at our end they are working on another theory. It's not the order of battle in your game that someone is after, but the secret of the chess algorithms that make the software impregnable.'

Kate stared at Gerry, her radiant beauty hypnotising him.

Out of the strong came forth the sweetness, he mused. Her pronounced features: the dark green eyes, the jet-black hair, the impossibly high cheekbones, the red bowed lips, the light swarthy skin and the firm chin made him wonder, *was this the face that launched a thousand ships?*

'Gerry,' she spoke his name softly.

He blinked. Coming out of his dream, he apologised.

She laughed. 'You were miles away.'

'Yes, I'm sorry. What was I saying?'

'You were saying that someone wants the key for the key's sake.'

'I think they are working on the assumption that there are not that many countries with the expertise to mount such operations without our intelligence services getting wind of it.'

'Well my money is still on the Iranians.' She paused for a brief moment. 'If I may, I would like to change the subject. I have some news.'

'Go on.'

'Tufiq has agreed I can go to the UK next Sunday to get the answer to the anagram that James left us.'

Gerry said nothing for a while, and then let out a long, 'Mmm…'

'What's that supposed to mean?'

'The last thing James was thinking about, minutes before he left, was getting the answer to you. If he'd had a few minutes longer, I'm sure he would have written the position down for me to give to you. However, the suspicion that Emma's death is linked to Richards and Hamilton may change matters. I have a gut feel that he will be ordered not to give you the solution in case the algorithms are compromised. I may be wrong, but I have a hunch that the MoD intends to use the chess system in future to guard all its top-secret software. Furthermore, either next Monday or Tuesday could be the day of the funeral. If you were to attend and afterwards ask him for the meaning of his anagram, he might take it the wrong way.' Gerry shrugged his shoulders, as if to add, *I don't know*.

'But James knows that my family are at risk if I don't get the position. He wouldn't let me down.'

'I'm not sure that he will have any option. The funeral will almost certainly have heavy security measures in place. You might not even be able to get anywhere near him.'

She breathed in deeply. Projecting her voice, so there was no misunderstanding. 'I am determined to go. I have no option.' She paused before adding as an after-thought, 'In any case, there may be an alternative.' She didn't expand, and Gerry felt there was little point in asking what it was. He knew she wouldn't have told him.

CHAPTER 21

It was past 3.30 pm by the time James and Brigadier Morrison were ushered into the briefing room at Weston-super-Mare's police HQ. The Division's Superintendent, Mark Wilson, the county's senior traffic officer, Chief Inspector Peter Swindlehurst and Detective Chief Inspector Eric Squires introduced themselves. They expressed their regrets and offered their heartfelt sympathy. It was the Brigadier who kicked off the discussion by repeating the story of the speeding Rover to the three police officers.

'If it was involved in some way, then it almost certainly would have been stolen. I'll get on to that as soon as we've finished this meeting,' said the Superintendent.

There was a short pause before Chief Inspector Swindlehurst spoke. 'We have been busy this morning and now have the results of the initial inspection of your wife's car.'

James looked at him. 'Go on.'

He opened his file. 'The two nearside tyres of your wife's car had six or seven puncture holes in each. This morning we experimented at our skidpan on a similar car to Mrs Douglas'. We took a piece of five-ply wood, approximately two feet by one foot, and screwed in twenty screws – each between two and a half and three inches long. This is it.' He pulled out from behind his chair the object he had described. 'We then drove at forty-five miles per hour so that only the nearside wheels of the car went over it. With the offside rear wheel still delivering power, and one of the front steering wheels deflating in seconds, the car swings violently to the left out of control. We firmly believe this is how your wife's accident was engineered. You will see from these photographs that the shredding of the test car's tyres,' he handed James two photos, 'are virtually identical to your wife's tyres.' He handed James a second set. He stopped, looking at his boss for acknowledgement.

The Superintendent thanked his traffic officer, adding, 'Your wife wouldn't have stood a chance of correcting the car before it went over the edge of the road. We believe that the homemade stinger was rapidly removed from the scene before Corporal Wiles arrived.'

James interrupted. 'But that was only a minute later.'

'Yes, that had us puzzled too. At first we thought there must have been someone watching who took the stinger and scarpered up through the woods to the top of Worlebury Hill. However, we have extensively searched for evidence of this, including house-to-house enquiries at the top of the hill, but found nothing. Now we know about the maroon Rover, the stinger could have had a wire attached to it and one of the car's occupants could then have hauled it back into their car as they sped away.'

'But surely my wife would have seen the stinger in the road and taken evasive action?'

It was the traffic inspector who answered. 'As you can see, we have sprayed this one dark grey, similar to the road surface. Stick a few leaves on it and it would be perfectly camouflaged. The shadows of the trees on the road, contrasting with the bright sunlight, would also have helped to hide it.'

There was a lull in the discussion as the awful truth of Emma's accident sunk in. Brigadier Morrison broke the silence. 'Where do we go from here?' he asked no one in particular.

The Superintendent took the lead. 'We will push ahead to try and find the Rover. We are treating the incident as murder. DCI Squires will lead the case at this end; giving it top priority. Admiral Johnson has briefed the Chief Constable on the likelihood that there are political overtones. Consequently, Scotland Yard's Special Branch will be helping us. Rest assured, Squadron Leader, we will do our utmost to apprehend the culprits. As far as your wife and child are concerned, we are now satisfied as to the cause of the accident. We are prepared to release the bodies, so that the coroner's inquest can proceed as soon as possible.' He looked at James. 'We could arrange the inquest for Thursday morning if that's what you want?'

James nodded, saying nothing.

However, the Brigadier responded. 'There may be a problem with that.'

They all looked at him to continue.

'How much does the coroner need to know about the murder investigations?' he asked.

It was Superintendent Wilson who asked the obvious, 'Why?'

'My concern is the press. They could have a field day.'

Mark Wilson looked at his Chief Inspector to give the answer. 'As senior traffic officer for the county, I shall give evidence at the hearing. I will deliberately keep it vague, saying that Mrs Douglas' car swung off the road due to her front nearside tyre bursting, which is the truth. I will say that the cause is under investigation. The press will be more interested in the personal angle. You know the sort of thing, *Sunday School Teacher meets tragic end*.'

The Brigadier seemed satisfied with the answer. DCI Squires, who up to this time had been taking copious notes and had not spoken a word then asked, 'It would help my team to know a little about the background to the case.'

'It's all rather difficult,' began Brigadier Morrison. 'Official Secrets Act and all that. However, in essence it's as follows… ' He then explained the background of how James had written the war game, how it had been sold to the Iraqis and modified by ICL. He went on to outline that it now contained much top-secret material and would be used by Iraq to defend itself against an attack by Iran. James tried to hide a smile at this point. The data contained in the game's files would be invaluable to Iran, possibly Israel.

The DCI stopped him at this point to ask why. The Brigadier explained that Iraq could be trying to develop missiles capable of delivering nuclear weapons to Israel. The location of Iraq's experimental facilities would be vital to Israel if they were to make a pre-emptive strike to destroy them. The three policemen listened intently as he continued to tell them that the software was protected by a novel method that was going to be used in future to protect many of MoD's computer programs.

He told them of the missing duo – John Richards and Hamish Hamilton, and their role in developing the chess protection system. 'So, to sum up, we believe that whoever is after the chess key either wants the war game for the data it contains,' and here he paused for what seemed a while to let the message sink in, 'or, to try and break the chess key so as to be able to access other MoD programs.'

James sat up at this fast-ball. *What is he going to say next?*

'If the first hypothesis is correct, then we are looking at the favourite culprits being Iran and, possibly, Israel. If the second hypothesis is correct, then it could be the Russians or the Americans.'

'You're joking, surely?' asked James instinctively.

'Not really, James. If you think about it, we have possibly three, sorry,' he quickly corrected himself, 'four deaths on our hands. All are connected in some way to Nastia Game. There are no clues. Whoever is responsible is capable of mounting a sophisticated operation. I don't think anyone can be ruled out.'

'Why do you not include the Iraqis in your list of suspects?' asked the DCI, whose notebook, by now, must have been overflowing.

'Can I answer that one, sir?' asked James to the Brigadier.

He nodded.

'The game is protected by two circular walls. The outer wall protects the data files, and a chess key is needed to get access. A second key is required to access the programs themselves.'

The DCI was nodding and following the logic. He'd stopped taking notes.

James continued. 'We are giving the Iraqis the outer chess position so they can, in future, add further data. They don't know at this stage that they will be unable to change the programs. In fact, apart from the five of us in this room, hardly anyone knows about the double ring.'

All nodded, before James continued. 'There is a third aspect to the software – the moving map display.'

He stopped to look at the Brigadier, but there was no reaction. 'The war game displays the state of the forces on a dynamic map display, which is currently printed on a graph plotter. Essentially, the programs print maps so the game umpire can see the total picture. ICL are now taking this a stage further by developing a handheld visual display unit combined with a transmitter/receiver that when linked to the RAF's communications satellite would show the operator his exact position. In other words, troops could see exactly where they are – to within ten yards and receive instructions in real time from their HQ.'

The Brigadier jumped in, realising that James was talking about Project Ptolemy. 'You must realise, gentlemen, that this information is highly confidential. The project is still in its early stages and may take several years to come to fruition. However, its usefulness in situations where boundaries are ill defined, such as Northern Ireland, goes without saying. I suppose it becomes a third *raison d'être* for someone wanting the war game software.'

It was DCI Squires who reacted first. It had struck James that he was the most switched-on of the three senior police officers. 'It's obvious to me that we are dealing with highly trained agents. Someone must have been watching Mrs Douglas all morning without your man knowing.' The DCI was looking directly at the Brigadier and continued, 'He, or she, must have radioed ahead when he, or she, saw Mrs Douglas going to the tollroad and warned the Rover to be ready for her. My guess is that whoever plotted the tollroad assassination was also responsible for the disappearance of the two programmers. By now, I fear that the culprits will have flown the nest and may be out of the country. We will probably find the Rover burnt out somewhere, possibly in the London area. I am afraid the best we may be able to do is to point the finger of suspicion at one particular country more strongly than at present.'

Moments passed as the truth of his remarks sank in.

Superintendent Wilson tried to end the meeting on a high note, 'I can only repeat, Squadron Leader, that this business is getting top priority. We are attempting to source the fragments of five-ply wood left at the scene. We will leave no stone unturned.'

James nodded, expressing his appreciation, turned to Brigadier Morrison and suddenly felt very tired.

**

As the staff car drove back to Kewstoke, the Brigadier began, 'James, I'm not sure if this is the right time, or not. However, Admiral Johnson has asked me to bring up the subject of your future.' He stopped, wondering whether to go on. James looked puzzled, said nothing, but indicated that he was listening. 'The Admiral, as you know, feels responsible for the recent events.'

'He couldn't have foreseen what has happened.'

'No, I agree, but he doesn't want anyone else harmed. In particular, he is concerned for you and your son's safety. He would like to come down here tomorrow and discuss one or two ideas with you. Are you happy with that?'

'Yes, of course. Do you know what he has in mind?'

'Not exactly, but I am sure that whatever you both come up with, it will be for the best. The Admiral is going to stay at the *Grand Atlantic Hotel*. Shall I pick you up tomorrow, say 1230 hours? We can have lunch together and then discuss the future.'

**

When James entered his in-laws' house, Canon Ward, the local vicar, was having tea with Pat and Bill. A pleasant, rotund man in his early sixties with a mop of dark hair, he was be-decked in his cassock and looked the very model of a Church of England clergyman. He offered his sympathy. He was a genuine, amiable man. 'If there's anything I can do…'

They sat down as Pat poured James a cup of tea and cut him a large slice of her homemade Victoria sponge.

'Well, vicar. Would it be possible to have the funeral service for Emma and Jenny as early as Saturday? The police are arranging the inquest for Thursday morning and have officially released the bodies. The manageress of the Co-operative Funeral Services is the wife of one of our flight lieutenants at Locking. She has assured Bill they can handle the funeral.'

'If that's what you want. I don't see why it can't be arranged. Do you want a burial in the churchyard or for us to go to the crematorium? It might be a bit late to get a slot at the crematorium,' said the vicar.

James looked at Pat and asked, 'I think it would be nice for them to share a grave overlooking Sand Bay. Don't you?'

She smiled and nodded.

She has aged ten years this week, thought James.

After the vicar had departed, James told his in-laws of the details he had learned from the police about their daughter's death.

CHAPTER 22

Brigadier Morrison arrived promptly to pick James up. On their way to meet the Admiral at his hotel, they travelled along the tollroad passing the scene of Emma's accident. James asked the driver to stop. He got out. Accompanied by Ian, they looked over the precipice to the base of the cliff. They said nothing. There was an eerie silence, merely the lapping of the waves breaking on the rocks below. Any birds in the trees behind remained silent. Although a lovely morning, the shade of the trees made James feel unusually cold. His eyes welled up as he surveyed the water below. The drop was, perhaps, no more than twenty feet.

Had the tide been out, Jenny may still have been alive. The bastards who did this, if I ever meet them... but he never finished his thoughts.

He began to sob; instinctively he took out his handkerchief and blew his nose. He wiped away the tears as best he could, but remained frozen to the spot. He felt Ian's hand on his shoulder.

'The bastards who did this, James, if we ever meet them...' said the Brigadier.

The remark was uncanny, but James didn't notice. He remained motionless in a world of his own, remembering the good times, Jenny's birth, how she had learnt to sleep through the night very early, would always give him a big smile, giggle and blow bubbles at him. Many minutes passed before he felt ready to return to the car.

James explained to the Brigadier, as they were driven along the promenade passing Birkbeck Pier, that arrangements were being made to hold the funeral on Saturday morning.

'On Monday, we have decided that Stuart and I will go away with my in-laws for a few weeks.'

'A good idea,' agreed the Brigadier, but didn't ask where.

Admiral Johnson met them in the foyer of the hotel. 'Do you feel up to a beer before lunch?' His tone was suitably sympathetic.

James nodded. They sat in the front window of the bar. There was a splendid view of the Bristol Channel, the islands of Steep Holm and Flat Holm on the horizon and Wales beyond. The drinks arrived and Admiral Johnson reiterated his regrets at what had happened.

'Had I known how the selling of the war game would pan out, I would never have agreed to its sale.' He spoke quietly and sincerely; sadness in his eyes. For a man who had only met Emma briefly, at the International Evening at Bracknell, his genuine distress was disturbing.

James couldn't stop his eyes welling up again. His heart fluttered uncontrollably, a ripple ran down his spine. He began to shake; he could hear himself speaking, but didn't recognise his own voice.

'Sir, none of this could have been foreseen three months ago.' He was trying to absolve the Admiral from blame, but knew he wasn't convincing. 'After all, it was me who designed the damn thing in the first place and then helped make its security system impregnable.'

'It's nice of you to say that, James, but I will never forgive myself for under-estimating the danger to you and your family. It's an error that I won't make again. I gather Ian mentioned yesterday that we no longer think the recent events have anything to do with the game. Someone could be after the secrets of the chess key?'

James sighed and took a swig of the cool beer. It tasted good. He realised it was his first drink of draught bitter since leaving for Iraq. The thought made it taste even better.

'Yes. Does this mean you are ruling out Iran and Israel from your list of suspects?'

'Iran – yes; Israel – possibly. Israel's Mossad are highly professional and ruthless. They would be capable of implementing what has happened, but we doubt if Iran's SAVAK could. America's CIA and Russia's KGB are also suspects.'

'When the Brigadier floated that idea yesterday, I must admit I was surprised.'

'Well don't be. If any of these three are involved, then they won't be put off by what has happened. I believe we must keep a very close eye on you and your family for some time to come.'

'What about someone wanting to get the moving map software?'

The Admiral looked to the Brigadier to give an answer.

'Moving map development has been going on apace, James. Our project is called Ptolemy because he thought everything revolved around the Earth. When the system is up and running, everything will revolve around the handheld map display and communications device. However, we believe the Americans and the Russians are ahead of us. We know, for example, the Americans trialled a prototype in Vietnam. Furthermore, the handheld hardware is more likely to have intelligence value than the software.'

James nodded thoughtfully in agreement.

Over lunch the inquest and the funeral arrangements were discussed. Admiral Johnson made it very clear that discreet security arrangements would be in place. The possibility of a threat was being taken seriously.

'It's what is to happen after the funeral that I want to discuss with you this afternoon. Do you feel ready to discuss your future? If not, we fully understand. It can wait until you return from holiday.'

'No, sir; I'm fine. I expect I'll find the funeral nerve-racking, however.'

'Ian and I have one or two ideas that we want to put to you. But first of all, where are you off to next week?'

'Pat's family are originally from the Isle of Skye. Her sister still lives there and we thought we'd go and stay with her. She has plenty of space and her husband has a small boat. I thought Stuart would enjoy fishing with him. Perhaps we'll do some hill walking and play some golf.'

'And afterwards?'

'I expect we'll come back to Kewstoke and I'll carry on at Locking. I have an option to leave the RAF in a couple of years. Had Emma's death been an accident that would have been bad enough. However, this affair has made me realise I've had enough. I'll leave the RAF at my sixteen-year option point.'

'Don't do anything rash, James. You have a fine career ahead of you. I'm going to be blunt. Don't take what I am going to say the wrong way. Just hear me out. OK?'

James looked puzzled.

'We believe you, Stuart and your in-laws should move away from Kewstoke to somewhere safe, at least for a couple of years.'

James frowned. 'I don't follow you.'

The Admiral continued. 'Whoever is behind this is not going to stop. They have committed themselves. We think they will try to get the secrets of the chess key any way they can. You and your family are very, very vulnerable.'

'Surely, nowhere can be a hundred per cent safe?' asked James.

'True, but we have a safety scheme that has been around for a long time. Agents who have had their cover blown and have to be brought back from danger, *in extremis,* can be given new identities and begin a new life in a new location. I believe Peter Stacey from MI6 promised something like this to your friend al Jised.'

He stopped, looking James in the eye. James, for the first time felt uncomfortable in the Admiral's presence. There had been a hint of disapproval in his voice when he described Kate as his friend.

'We don't need to go as far as changing your names, but we could accommodate you in a secure area. It would go a long way to guaranteeing your safety,' he added.

'Isn't that taking things a bit far? After all my in-laws are both over sixty. They won't want all the hassle.'

'We don't believe it is excessive. Your chess system is unique. We now believe impenetrable. Our strongest suspects are the CIA. We believe they are trying to unfathom the secret of the protection system as we speak. Have you ever met anyone from the CIA?'

'No, I don't think so.' James paused, and then added, 'There was a Major Richardson at the 4th July barbeque in Baghdad who seemed unduly interested in the chess key. He was supposed to be the deputy Air Attaché.'

'He could have been an agent for the CIA. Do you want to hear our plan?'

'Of course.'

'Project Ptolemy is being developed at Fort Halstead in Kent. A prototype miniature VDU/transmitter/receiver, I believe it's called a laptop, is being manufactured by Marconi. Ian and I think you should be posted to the software development team where your expertise would be a great asset to help with the moving map displays.'

'That sounds great, but how would that help my family?'

'Fort Halstead is one of the Army's most secure sites. We can arrange for you and Stuart to have an adjacent married quarter to your in-laws. Alternatively, if you prefer, a large quarter for all of you. Inside the base, you will have total safety. We can arrange for both your houses in Kewstoke to be sold at current market prices. Ptolemy should be completed by 1981. By then, all this will have died down and you will be able to resume normality.'

'I'll put the idea to Pat and Bill this afternoon. I think they'll go for it, but both of them are north Londoners; so the idea of living south of the river may go against the grain!'

CHAPTER 23

Bill accompanied James to the Coroner's Inquest the next day. It was run efficiently and took less than half an hour. James gave evidence of identification of both Emma and Jennifer. Corporal Wiles gave his evidence of the discovery of the car, outlining how he scrambled down the cliff, found Emma still alive but Jenny already drowned. Asked why he was on the toll road, he had replied that he was having a short fishing break with a colleague. The policeman who arrived on the scene then gave evidence, followed by the ambulance crew who described the actions they took en route to hospital. The A&E consultant confirmed the times of death. The coroner made it clear his job was not to apportion blame for the apparent accident, but asked the police what investigations they had made as to its cause. Chief Inspector Swindlehurst gave evidence that the cause was a blow-out of the nearside front tyre and that investigations were ongoing with the tyre manufacturer. This seemed to satisfy the coroner who offered his deepest sympathy to the family and then gave his verdict as accidental death.

James felt miserable, somehow cheated. He wanted to stand up and protest, 'No, she was murdered.' He managed to restrain himself. He looked at Bill for support. They held each other's hand and then hugged. It was the first time his father-in-law had ever shown any real emotion at the loss of his daughter. He was weeping – openly. Ironically, Bill's tears made James feel he had to be stronger.

'Come on, Bill, Emma wouldn't want to see you like this,' he said trying to console him. 'I'll buy you a beer at the *New Inn* on the way home.'

He sniffled, wiped his eyes, pulled himself to his full height, and nodded.

***

James was surprised at how full Kewstoke Church was on Saturday. Emma's aunts, uncles and cousins from Berkshire and Surrey had been expected, but the number of village children with their parents was overwhelming. Canon Ward was a sympathetic priest, giving a highly moving and emotional valediction. The choir sang beautifully. There was hardly a dry eye anywhere. James looked to see if he could spot any of Admiral Johnson's men, but saw none. The lone policeman standing at the entrance to the church, helping to direct traffic, was the only sign of a security presence. Stuart sat between his grandmother and father crying quietly, but behaving with great dignity. His father was very proud of him.

Throughout the service James' mind wandered, sometimes thinking of Emma and their years together; frequently thinking of Kate. He knew it was wrong, but he couldn't help himself. He was in a daze. There was no sense in his thoughts, trivial one minute, profound the next. How would he cope having to iron his own shirts and master the washing machine? How had Emma been so good at organising everything when his parents had died? How did she find time to do everything: keep down her job as a district nurse, teach in Sunday school and serve on the Parish Church Council? Above all, she was a loving mother and wife. Would he ever see Kate again? How would Stuart cope without a mother? Would he somehow be able to get Kate to come and share his life? What would his in-laws think, if she came? Would Stuart accept Kate as a surrogate mother?

A happy family destroyed, because I wanted to show the top brass that my war game was something unique and should have won a Defence Fellowship.

After the ceremony in the graveyard, the relatives and close friends went to the wake in the nearby *New Inn*. James tried to circulate and show he was coping with his loss. However, conversation tended to be less than fluent; hardly surprising under the circumstances. He was glad when people began to drift away. That evening, Stuart stayed at his grandparents' house, as he had all week. James chose to stay alone at home. He was wide awake; only the cat for company. It was cold, despite being July. He lit the gas fire, opened a bottle of Scotch, *Islay Mist* – his favourite, and watched it disappear as he slowly slumped into a stupor.

He began thinking of moving to Fort Halstead and working with Marconi's software engineers. He'd enjoyed the challenge with the ICL team at Reading. *This will be something similar.* Then he thought of Kate. His mind was in a muddle.

When we return from our break in Scotland, we will begin our new lives in Kent. I wonder how the pongos will take to having an RAF crab working on their project. Is there any way I can safely contact Kate? God, Kate – I miss you. Why don't I resign my commission, put Stuart into a boarding school, fly to Baghdad and bring Kate back? We could disappear to the Isle of Man; somewhere quiet and out of the way. Port St Mary, perhaps?

His thoughts spun around, out of control. He occasionally came out of his trance; he would stroke the cat, have another tot, and slump back again. He felt wretched; morally he was confused. He knew what he had to do: look after Stuart.

Forget Kate. Admiral Johnson was probably right, she had been nothing more than an Iraqi honey-trap to get the chess key. You've had a bite of the cake, liked it, but now you must give it up – for Stuart's safety, make a success of Fort Halstead.

CHAPTER 24

Kate met Roya at the airport. They were civil towards each other, but only just. Their mutual disregard would have been obvious to any casual observer. But why? Both were Sunni, both in the military, both of a similar age. Albeit, one was slim and feminine, the other large and butch. One despised the other because she was in with the Ba'ath elite; the other because she was intellectually superior. Their mutual antagonism seemed more deep-rooted than simple jealousies. The cause underlying their enmity was deep inside their subconsciousness.

They hardly spoke as the British Airways flight headed west. Kate felt she was handcuffed to a prison warden while her mind wondered about the possible outcomes of her visit to England.

Will I be able to see James? If I can't see him, can I find Ray Kane? Will he be able to solve the riddle?

Something niggled at the back of her mind that even if Ray Kane could solve the puzzle, it might not be enough to break into the war game. Try as she might, she couldn't remember what it was. It was something James had said in passing at either Ur or the Abu Samba restaurant.

From time to time, when Kate thought Roya wouldn't notice, she glanced sideways at her escort. Kate had to admit that Roya looked smart. She was dressed in a grey European-style suit, the jacket close fitting with the skirt length suitably two inches below the knee. She was sitting upright; her muscular legs crossed, just showing her knees. She totally ignored Kate, being engrossed in a book. It occurred to Kate that Roya had a fine figure; it was just that there was plenty of it. She had well-shaped, large, firm breasts – much bigger than her own, which made Kate feel somewhat inadequate. Her calf muscles looked strong above a fine pair of ankles. There was no flab anywhere. She obviously kept herself fit.

Bizarrely, Kate wondered, *is she a handsome man in a woman's body?*

She wasn't pretty. Her eyes were black, suggesting cruelty. Kate remembered seeing *One Hundred and One Dalmatians* as a child; Roya's face had an uncanny resemblance to that of *Cruella de Vil*. The thought made Kate shudder. She was still trying to remember what James had said at Ur or the Abu Samba when she fell asleep.

Roya, too, took the opportunity to observe her charge. With Kate asleep, she ordered a large gin and tonic and began to analyse her feelings towards her fellow passenger. Kate was dressed more traditionally than herself. Roya found that surprising in view of her university education in England. However, even in her loose-fitting dress Kate's figure could not be hidden. Roya looked at her long, sinuous legs, her slim waist and her saucy, pert breasts. Her beautifully cut shoulder-length hair, large almond-shaped eyes, wide mouth and high cheekbones reminded her of the Shah of Persia's second wife. She smelled gorgeous too. Whatever perfume al Jised used, it suited her.

A funny thing about perfumes, they smell differently on different people, she mused. *I must find out what she uses and try it myself. Allah can be unkind. Why is she so beautiful? If I can't be like her, then I must destroy her.*

When Kate came around from her doze, she found Roya smiling at her. It came as a surprise in view of the frosty reception when they had met at the airport.

What has changed?

The stewardesses were serving lunch and asking what they would like to drink. Roya looked at Kate and said, 'I think we should have some wine, don't you?' Kate had not expected this and agreed.

I always assumed Roya was a strict Muslim. How wrong can you be?

They ate their lunch, Roya making some effort to break the ice. Small talk was clearly not her forte. She bluntly asked what type of perfume Kate used.

'*Arpege*, by Lanvin. I first bought it in Antibes, when at a conference in Nice. I've not found it anywhere else and now have it sent by post from France.'

Eventually she broached the subject of what Kate's plans were to see Squadron Leader Douglas. She showed surprise when Kate answered, 'I haven't got any.'

'But I'd assumed you would have made contact with him last week.'

'I don't know how to contact him. I am afraid we're going to have to keep our fingers crossed and hope we will meet him when we go to his house near Weston-super-Mare tomorrow.'

'It's a bit of a long shot. What if we can't find him?' asked Roya.

'Then we will have to implement plan B.'

'Which is?'

'James mentioned that if anything was to happen to him, it was almost as if he had a premonition, then I was to seek out a guy called Ray Kane,' replied Kate.

'Who's he?'

'Apparently, he is a chess grandmaster, has been British Champion and written many books on chess. He's also a world authority on chess history.'

Roya said nothing, continuing to eat her lunch, but the frown on her face suggested that she was worried.

***

They arrived at Heathrow on time, collected their luggage, passed through customs without hassle and were met by the Iraqi Air Attaché. Kate recognised Lieutenant Colonel Yassir Sholah instantly. Tall, slim, handsome with the mandatory moustache, he was dressed in a civilian navy blue suit. His eyes sparkled on seeing Kate. They shook hands warmly. Presently, Kate introduced Roya to him, hoping that Roya would not have taken offence at having to stand sidelined while she and Yassir briefly caught up with the latest gossip. As he led them away to their waiting car, he and Roya chatted amicably. Kate was amused to see that he was carrying Roya's suitcase, while she followed behind dragging her own.

Inside the chauffeur-driven diplomatic car, Yassir explained that he had been told nothing officially about their reason for visiting England. However, he was guessing it had something to do with the war game. His boss, the Military Attaché, Colonel Amer Rashid, had told him to give them all possible assistance. Kate affirmed his assumption about the war game. As they sped down the M4 towards central London, she began to outline the reason for their visit. 'Tomorrow we want to go to Weston-super-Mare to see Squadron Leader Douglas.'

Yassir nodded. 'I met him once when I came to see you and Azi at Reading. I was sorry to see his wife and child had been killed in a car accident.' Kate's mind flashed back. She remembered Yassir's visit well. She had been to Kewstoke the previous weekend. Azi had told Yassir about the visit and he had warned her about getting too friendly.

If only you knew how friendly we became! My God! Babylon and Ur seem such a long time ago. So much has happened.

Her trail of thought was miles away. Yassir had to prod her. 'You were saying you needed to see Squadron Leader Douglas, but what if he isn't there?'

She didn't answer. She hadn't even heard the question. Instead she asked, 'How did you know about his wife's accident?'

'It's been in the papers.'

This seemed to satisfy Kate. Gathering her thoughts and coming out of her trance, she asked, 'I'm sorry, what was the last question?'

'I asked what if Douglas isn't there? The paper said the funeral was to be yesterday. He may have gone away.'

Kate's heart sank. Secretly she had been hoping that the funeral would be either Monday or Tuesday so that she could attend. At that moment she knew traipsing down to Weston was going to be unproductive. She fell back into her own world, replying, 'Then on Tuesday, we must see Ray Kane.'

'Who's he?' asked Yassir.

'We believe he will be able to solve the riddle of the chess position that General Tufiq's men can't. It's because of their inability to decipher the puzzle that we are here in the first place. Tomorrow, when we go to Weston, I would be grateful if you could find Ray Kane's address and telephone number. He is a chess grandmaster, a former British Champion, and has written several chess books. He is, also, the Chess Correspondent of *The Spectator*. That should help. If we don't get what we want in Weston, I will ring him tomorrow evening when we get back. Is that OK?'

'Fine. You can have the unlimited use of this car and driver for your trip.'

They arrived at the embassy in Queen's Gate, Kensington. To both Roya's and Kate's surprise, as the car swung through the gates, they saw several armed policemen standing menacingly across the road. They were clearly making their presence felt. It was Roya who asked, 'What's going on?'

'Two weeks ago General Abdul Razak was assassinated here in London. The British police think we had something to do with it,' replied Yassir.

'What? You mean our former President al Naief?' pressed Roya.

'Yes.'

'Did we have something to do with it?' Kate asked the question in a tone that clearly demanded a truthful answer.

Yassir hesitated. The pause was an admission that all was not well. 'I'll tell you tonight. I thought we could eat out at a lovely Italian taverna my wife and I like. It's just behind the National Portrait Gallery. Rihab and I will pick you up at eight o'clock. Our apartment is just around the corner from the embassy. We'll get a taxi.' Both girls looked at each other, smiled and thanked him.

Their chauffeur carried their bags into the embassy foyer, where a receptionist was waiting. She showed them to their adjacent en suite rooms on the second floor. Both agreed they needed a bath and a rest before dinner.

***

Yassir was right about Val Taro's Taverna; small, secluded and lit to maximise privacy, the food was first class, the service friendly and efficient. The two female officers found Rihab, Yassir's wife, charming. She was well educated and had been a teacher of English before she had met her husband. Their table conversation was largely social, catching up with the news from home. However, Yassir, when pressed, made it apparent, somewhat reluctantly, that al Naief's assassination may have been planned from Baghdad.

'There was a thug called Salam Hassan who arrived at the embassy at the beginning of July. He didn't stay long. I think he was a member of the Mukhabaret General Directorate of Intelligence, or as we call them the Bloody PISS.' He stopped and chuckled. When he saw Roya was not smiling, he realised he may have gaffed. He quickly continued. 'Anyway, to cut a long story short he was caught by the Metropolitan Police and has been charged with General Razak's murder. Ever since, the embassy surrounds have been swarming with police. The ambassador clearly didn't know anything about it, as all the heads of department were called in the following day and given a right telling off. Everyone knew it was directed at our local Head of the ISS, but what could the ambassador do? Now you can't go anywhere without the police following you. They probably followed us here. Tomorrow they will, almost certainly, escort you to Weston-super-Mare at a discreet distance. I suspect they think the embassy may have had something to do with Squadron Leader Douglas' wife's death too.'

'Was her death suspicious then?' asked Kate.

'Not as far as I know. In the papers the coroner's verdict was accidental death.'

'But was it?' Surprisingly, it was Roya who pressed Yassir further.
'Honestly, I don't know. I am certain we had nothing to do with it.'

***

Kate did not sleep well. A combination of tiredness from travelling, the news of the assassination of a former president that had been kept quiet at home, the paradox of the coroner's verdict of Emma's accident with the suspicions of the police, the near certainty that she would not see James again; all swam around in her head as she tossed from one side to the other in a strange bed.

The next morning she dressed smartly, hoping for the impossible. She wore the same navy blue suit that she had worn on her first visit to Kewstoke.

So long ago.

By nine o'clock their car was winding its way out of London down the M4. Roya sat quietly; she had been coolly pleasant at breakfast. The Military Attaché, Colonel Amer Rashid, had appeared and introduced himself. He had taken coffee with them.

It was a social visit, he explained. 'I want you to be able to put a face to my name.' He continued by hoping they would get what they wanted at Weston-super-Mare and reiterated he had instructed Yassir to give them all possible assistance. 'I am very tied up with the fallout from this General al Naief affair, as you can imagine. Perhaps we can get together this evening?' He lifted his eyebrow, as if to expect a positive reply.

Roya took the lead. 'Yes, I am sure we have nothing else on.'

Kate smiled, saying nothing. She could see that the Military Attaché was not flattered by Roya's answer. He struck her as a charming man. Perhaps, ten or twelve years older than herself, he was of average height, well built, with a face that looked as if he had been around a lot. His eyes sparkled at Kate, hinting at mischief. Kate could feel her cheeks blushing.

'I'll see you both this evening then.' He rose swiftly and left. In deference to a senior officer, they both stood up. Roya shimmied her shoulders, expanding her chest. Kate watched.

You fool; it's me he fancies, not you.

In less than two hours, Kate was instructing their chauffeur how to find Kewstoke down the narrow lanes after leaving the M5. They parked in the car park below the *New Inn*. As they walked across the road towards James' house, Kate could see a man erecting a 'For Sale' sign in the front garden. She opened the gate and began to walk to the front door. 'There's no one in, Luv,' the man said. 'They've gone away.'

'Are you sure?' It was a fatuous remark, but Kate was not thinking straight. She knew then that this was the end. James would only ever be a memory – a star that would fade slowly from her horizon. In her innermost soul she had hoped James would be there, waiting for her. He would have put his arms around her, whispered in her ear and she would turn round to Roya and tell her to shove off. They would disappear from the face of the earth. Go somewhere where no one would ever find them.

'The owner's missus and kid were killed last week on the tollroad. Everyone around here knows about it,' the man replied, as he continued to erect his sign.

'What now?' It was Roya who asked the question somewhat triumphantly, as if saying, *I told you so.*

'Perhaps Mrs Norris, the next-door neighbour, knows where they've gone.' And without any further ado, Kate turned round, walked to the house next door and rang the bell.

The door was answered after a short while. A rotund woman, in her mid-fifties, greying, wearing a pinny opened the door.

'Mrs Norris?' Kate asked, and without waiting for a reply continued, 'Do you remember me? We met when I stayed with the Douglas family for the weekend two months ago.'

'Why, yes, my lovely. Kate, isn't it? From Persia?'

'No, from Iraq actually.'

'Oh.' She paused, as if thinking Iraq and Iran were the same place. Then she continued in her West Country brogue. 'Have you heard the awful news? Mrs Douglas and Jenny were killed in a car accident last week.'

'Yes, that's why I am here.' Kate lied, 'We have come over for the funeral.'

'That's awfully good of you, dear, but you're too late. It was on Saturday. A bit quick if you ask me.'

'Mrs Norris, do you know where James and Stuart have gone?'

'They went off with Pat and Bill earlier this morning; about an hour ago. They left me the key to keep an eye on the place. Said they would be away about two weeks. They've gone to Scotland to stay with Pat's sister.'

Kate's heart sank. It was all over. The last glimmer of hope had finally been extinguished. She felt like ice. She wiped traces of tears from her eyes. 'Were Emma and Jenny buried in the church yard?'

'Yes, dear. You'll see the grave behind the church. Covered with flowers it is.'

'I'll go and see them before I return to London. Thanks for your help.' They shook hands and Kate looked at Roya. 'I'd like to visit the grave. It's only one hundred metres around the corner.' They were turning to leave, when Kate swung round. 'One thing, Mrs Norris. When they return, would you please tell James that I came to see him?'

'Of course, dearie. He will be sorry to have missed you.'

They walked up the hill, passing the small general stores. Kate went in and bought the best bunch of flowers available.

Roya said nothing and followed Kate to the church yard. Mrs Norris had been right. The grave was a mass of flowers. Evidently, Emma and Jenny had been very popular. She kneeled down and placed her inadequate bouquet next to the large wreath of red roses in the centre of the display. She read the wreath's inscription.

To Jenny and Emma. We'll always miss you, love Stuart and James xxxx.

It was simple and to the point. She wept; tears flooded down her face. All her hopes were gone. She was alone. She wiped her face, slowly standing up. She looked to the north, across Sand Bay. She saw three ghosts playing roly-poly on Sand Point. She could hear Stuart's laughter and feel his weight as he swung on her arm. It had been just over two months ago. The spectres were real. She blinked and rubbed her wet eyes. They had gone and would never return.

They walked back down the hill to the waiting car. Not a word was spoken.

He knew I would have come and stayed with him forever. I would have given up everything for him and he deserts me like this. Why?

Roya followed a yard or two behind, thinking of other things.

They climbed into the back of the car. It was Kate who ordered, 'Driver, we'll go straight back to London. We will stop at the Gordano services and get some lunch.'

'Very good, Ma'am.'

CHAPTER 25

Kate and Roya arrived back in the capital by three o'clock. They agreed to go shopping in Oxford Street. They logged into the embassy, changed into casual dress and minutes later booked out again. They saw no one tailing them; no one stopped them. It was a joy to see full shops. Their Iraqi dinars, worth about $3 US each, went a long way as they bought presents for their families and tried on dresses for themselves. Tea in *Fortnum and Mason's* rounded off a successful and enjoyable afternoon. Surprisingly, Roya had been pleasantness personified. However, Kate had an uneasy feeling that an ulterior motive was behind her behaviour.

They returned to the embassy just before six o'clock. Yassir greeted them. 'I have Ray Kane's telephone number and address.' He gave Kate a slip of paper. 'I gather the Colonel is dining with you this evening. Behave yourselves. He's a bit of a lad with the girls.' He chuckled, leaving Kate and Roya looking bemused at each other.

Roya went to her room. Kate picked up the phone in reception and dialled the number on Yassir's slip of paper.

A female voice answered. 'Hello?'

'Can I speak to Mr Ray Kane, please?' asked Kate.

'Yes, who shall I say is calling?'

'My name is Kathab al Jised. I'm speaking to you from the Iraq Embassy in Kensington. Would you tell him I'm a friend of Squadron Leader James Douglas of the RAF Chess Association.'

There was a pause and then Kate heard the voice call, 'Ray, someone from the RAF wants you.'

A few moments went by and then, 'Hello, Ray Kane.'

'You don't know me, but my name is Kathab al Jised. I'm a friend of Squadron Leader James Douglas.' She paused; there was no reaction at the other end. She continued quickly. 'You know, he has been RAF chess champion.' Again there seemed to be no reaction. 'He told me you first met when you gave a simultaneous display some years ago at RAF Cosford.'

She thought she could hear the penny drop. 'Ah, yes. I remember James. He looked after me in the Officers' Mess the night before the simultaneous display. How can I help you?'

'Well, it's a long story, I'm afraid. In essence, he has left me in a dilemma with a chess puzzle, which I must solve. It's not an exaggeration to say it's a matter of life or death. I know that sounds rather melodramatic, but when I tell you the full story, you will understand why. I came over from Iraq yesterday hoping to see James today, when he had promised to give me the answer. Unfortunately, his wife was killed last week in an accident and James has gone away. There is no way I can contact him.' She paused to get breath.

'I'm sorry to hear about his wife, but what has this got to do with me?'

'James told me that if ever anything was to happen to him, then I was to contact you as you would be able to solve the problem. He said your knowledge of the game and its history is second to none and that you would be able to solve the puzzle.'

'I'm intrigued, but I am not a chess problemist.'

'It's not a chess problem in the normal sense. It's a word puzzle that describes a position. The position is then used as a password into a computer program. Could I see you tomorrow to explain how important it is to our national security? I'll meet you wherever you like.'

'I have a meeting in town at two o'clock. How about meeting me in *The Sherlock Holmes* at twelve noon? It's usually quiet upstairs. We can discuss your problem over a bite of lunch.'

'*The Sherlock Holmes?*'

'Yes, it's a pub in Northumberland Avenue, just down from Trafalgar Square.'

'That's fine. I'll see you tomorrow, then. Thank you for being so accommodating in helping me.'

***

Dinner that evening with Col Rashid was interesting. Roya had made an effort to present herself as glamorously as possible while Kate felt embarrassed wearing her loose traditional dress. Perhaps as much as fifteen years older than Kate, his jet-black hair showed no sign of greying. Unusually for an Iraqi, he was clean shaven. His eyes were mischievous. He was slim and looked fit. They talked seriously about the changes taking place at home. The assassination was not mentioned, nor the reason for their visit. It transpired he was a widower – this seemed to make Roya excited. He was returning to Baghdad on promotion to Brigadier in two weeks' time, which made Roya even more excited. Kate could sense Roya was getting the hots for him; she could understand why. He explained that his new job was within the procurement executive, with special responsibility for weapons and munitions.

'Ah, in that case we could be coming into contact with each other frequently,' said Kate. 'I'm about to become the Head of research, development and storage of chemical and biological weapons.'

As they discussed their possible future working relationship, Roya felt she was being pushed out of the picture.

That damned bitch is flirting with him, she thought, *as soon as we get what we've come here for, I'll show her who is boss.*

After dinner, they adjourned to the lounge for coffee and Roya realised she had no chance with him.

***

Kate and Roya arrived at *The Sherlock Holmes* promptly, noticing several Japanese tourists taking pictures outside the pub. The interior was dimly lit. More Japanese were inside, excitedly chattering away over their steak and kidney pie, with chips washed down with warm beer. Kate looked for a way to go upstairs, but couldn't see one.

'Is there an upstairs?' Kate asked a barman. He didn't answer, merely pointing with his hand and then twisting it to the left, as if to say, *through there, turn left*. The stairs were darker than the pub's main room and twisted twice before Kate opened a door into a small room, brilliantly lit by the sun streaming through the south-facing window. Everything was in silhouette and her eyes took time to adjust.

Sitting in front of the window, facing her, she could see the outline of a portly man with horn-rimmed glasses and a round face. He stood up and smiled. He was the only person in the room and Kate guessed, correctly, that he must be Ray Kane. Her eyes were acclimatising and she could see he was wearing a dark suit, with a bright multi-coloured bow tie. He held out his hand and simply said, 'I'm Ray Kane.'

'I'm Kathab, but please call me Kate.' She turned, saying, 'This is a colleague of mine, Roya Talfah.'

He gestured for them to sit opposite him. 'Before we begin, can I suggest we order our lunch immediately and get our drinks? Fortunately, few of the tourists know about this room, but in half an hour the office workers will arrive and there will be a queue at the bar.'

While ordering, Kate looked around. The room was small, perhaps capable of seating no more than twenty to thirty people. The panelled walls were covered with memorabilia, including an annex with glass walls in which sat two dummies dressed as Sherlock Holmes and, she assumed, Dr Watson.

Ironic, most tourists don't know this room exists.

Kate took some time explaining the history of the war game, how it had been designed by James at Bracknell Staff College and its security feature, the chess key. She outlined how it had been bought by Iraq, how she had been part of the Iraqi team that had worked with ICL and how

MoD had agreed to allow Iraq to add its own features. She emphasised how the chess position would unlock the game, how James had promised to give it to her on his departure from Baghdad but was unable to do so because of his wife's death. She avoided telling him of the veiled threats to her own family and hoped he wouldn't ask too many questions.

Ray Kane hadn't said a word. He had listened intently, nodding from time to time as Kate paused with her story, occasionally saying, 'Fascinating.'

'Presumably, the chess position is used in some way to kick start a sequence of random numbers that encode the game's data?' he asked when she had finished.

Kate looked blank. She had no idea how it worked, but managed, 'Yes, I think so.'

'You see,' he continued, 'there are countless legal chess positions – more than there are atoms in the universe. If James has found a way of generating several numbers from a position, then an algorithm could create an infinite series of random numbers that would be impossible to decipher.' He stopped and saw he had left his two listeners behind. 'For example, a simple method to generate random numbers is to kick start a sequence from a clock.' He looked at his watch. 'It's 1223. If you start with the first two numbers as 12 and 23, then the next random number could be 35, then 58, then 93.' He paused. Again there was no light from the girls. 'All I'm doing is adding the last two numbers together to create the next. A simple algorithm such as that would, of course, be broken easily by a skilled decoder, but using a chess position to start is brilliant.' He stopped; there was stunned silence. Kate broke the impasse.

'Speaking of decoding, can you break the code?'

'I'll try, of course. What is it?'

She handed Ray a piece of paper. Printed on it were the words: WHITE CLOAKS UNLUCKY LATVIAN.

He looked at it and frowned. 'To describe a chess position needs four or five pieces of data, White's name, Black's name, the number of moves played, when and, possibly, where. When James gave you the puzzle, did he give you any further clues?'

Kate thought back. 'He once said some words can have several meanings.'

'Anything specific?'

'Something about Spain, I think.'

A light came over Ray's face. He smiled. 'It's a game of Capablanca's.'

'How do you know?' It was Roya who had asked the question. Up to now, she had hardly spoken.

'Because the Spanish for white is *blanca* and a cloak is *capa*, or cape in English.' He looked pleased with himself, continuing. 'The game is probably a Ruy Lopez opening, sometimes called the Spanish Opening. Capablanca was a Cuban, Spanish speaking and world champion from 1921 to 1927. Many believe he was the greatest player of all time. I'm puzzled though,' he paused for a moment, 'because he didn't play king pawn openings very often, at least not in his later period. I suspect the game must be one of his earlier ones.'

'But what do unlucky and Latvian mean?' Again it was Roya asking the question. She seemed to be paying unusual attention.

Ray answered, speaking his thoughts. 'There weren't many Latvian players around during Capablanca's career. The only one I can think of was Petrov. I am not even sure they played each other. I would have to check that. At home I have a book with all of Capa's games. There isn't a Latvian variation in the Spanish Opening either... ' He stopped. The girls left him to his own thoughts. Kate was getting a sinking feeling. Perhaps even this most knowledgeable chess addict was not going to break the puzzle. He stroked his chin, looking past them into the ether, lost in a world dominated by bits of wood on an eight by eight board. Then, suddenly, his face lit up.

'I know. The game is Capablanca versus Edward Lasker, New York 1915. The word Latvian refers to the Riga variation of the Spanish Opening, so named because it was first played in a correspondence match between Berlin and Riga in 1906. The New York game is famous for two reasons. Firstly, Capablanca found a refutation to the variation that has stood the test of time ever since. The variation is never played anymore at the highest level. Secondly, he arrived at the board with only two minutes left to play his first fifteen moves, because he had slept in late.' Ray was beaming and Kate couldn't help thinking that he resembled a wise owl with his large, circular-framed spectacles.

Roya seemed to be enjoying the analysis and pushed him further. 'What about unlucky?'

'Well, Capablanca rarely blundered, and certainly not in that game. I think unlucky simply refers to the number of moves played by Capablanca – thirteen.'

Kate and Roya were impressed. Ray Kane had deciphered in fifteen minutes the puzzle that had defied General Tufiq's men for fifteen days and, unknown to them, GCHQ's best brains too.

'Can you show us the position?' ventured Kate.

Ray took out of his pocket a travelling magnetic chess set. He placed it carefully on the table in front of them and slowly began to explain the moves. Kate noticed the first four or five moves were the same as the position James had shown her in the sand at Ur. Her mind briefly wandered back to that wonderful weekend.

Stop it, concentrate, you must remember this game.

She marvelled at how easy chess players seem to be able to remember games.

Here is a man showing us a game played over sixty years ago.

Finally he said, 'There, that's the position. Capablanca has just played 13 NxQ ch.'

'Will you write the position down for us, please?' asked Kate. She thought her quest was over.

'I'll keep that!' Roya's hand had practically snatched the position from Ray before he had finished writing it down. His face dropped. He looked confused and surprised. Kate shrugged her shoulders and smiled – a sad, little smile. She held her hand out and thanked him. Roya was already out of the door.

'Are you alright?' he asked, stunned at Roya's behaviour.

'Don't worry about it. She's got what she wants. James was right. He said you were good and would be able to decode the puzzle. If you ever see him again please tell him we met and that I will always remember him. Goodbye.' Her eyes welling up at the thought of never seeing James again, she turned and began to leave. Ray's analysis of the puzzle had been so absorbing that she noticed, for the first time, the room had filled with lunchtime drinkers. The grandmaster remained to finish his bottle of Chateau Neuf du Pape.

CHAPTER 26

The frostiness and nastiness had returned, worse than ever. Roya never spoke as they returned to the embassy. Triumphant, she made great play as she announced that she was about to contact General Tufiq immediately and give him the chess position.

Kate shrugged her shoulders and went to her room. She felt alone and unwanted. She hadn't met James, nor did she have the chess key. However, she knew the position and felt certain she could reproduce it. Tomorrow morning they would be on the first flight back to Iraq. There was no way out. Her mind raced as she drowned in despondency.

God, if only I could escape. Go back to Cambridge, disappear and never be seen again. Why did I have to fall in love with James? Why wasn't he at home yesterday? Why did I go to Kewstoke in the first place? Why did I take him to Samarra? It all began there. I should never have volunteered to take him to Ur. Why? Why? Why?

She had vowed to forget him and treat all men with disdain. But deep inside her, his flame glowed; she knew it always would. There had been no one like him before and there never would be again. She undressed, had a long hot bath and climbed under the duvet. Her hands and feet felt cold. She shivered as she thought about her family's safety being at stake for Nastia Game. Drawing her legs up close to her body in order to get warm, she decided not to go down for dinner.

I don't want to see Roya again.

Slowly she sank into a deep sleep, and dreamt of being with James in Babylon.

***

The red phone rang in Admiral Johnson's outer office, situated in the Metropole Building in Northumberland Avenue. His Personal Staff Officer glanced at his watch. It was 1705 hours, *time we were knocking off*. However, the red phone indicated the call was being scrambled and, almost certainly, was urgent.

'Admiral Johnson's office, Major Lewis speaking.'

'Deputy Commissioner Weston here, Special Branch. I'd like to speak to Brian. Is he in?'

'Yes, sir.' The PSO knew the voice of the second-in-command of Scotland Yard's Special Branch, although he had never met him. He pressed the intercom, and announced, 'Mr Weston for you, sir.'

'OK, put him on,' replied the Admiral.

'Brian, it's Peter here. It's about those two Iraqi women who you asked me to have tailed.'

'Oh, yes?'

'Not much happened until a couple of hours ago. They went out to dinner the night they arrived with the Iraqi Air Attaché and his wife. As you expected they drove to Weston-super-Mare on Monday, spent an hour in Kewstoke and came back here. They went shopping that afternoon and bought odds and ends. They had tea in Fortnum's, staying in their embassy that night. Today, they met chess master Ray Kane for lunch in, of all places, your local – *The Sherlock Holmes*.'

'No, really?' exclaimed the Admiral.

'The three of them had what my man called an intense discussion. Kane ended up showing them a game of chess on his travelling set, and then it looked as if he wrote the game out for them. They left shortly afterwards. My man tells me the hefty one snatched the paper with the game, and the slimmer one didn't look too happy.'

'That is interesting,' replied the Admiral. 'The slim one is al Jised. She's working for us. The bruiser is Talfah, a niece of Saddam Hussein's wife. We suspect she's working for the Iraqi Secret Service.'

'Well, she may be working for someone else too.'

'Really?'

'Yes. They went directly back to the embassy when they left *The Sherlock Holmes*. However, after about half an hour, Talfah left the embassy on her own. It was the first time they had been apart since arriving. She walked round the corner and made a telephone call from a public box.'

'Interesting, why didn't she do it from her embassy?'

'Exactly. She then walked up to the Albert Hall, found a seat in front of the hall and waited for about twenty minutes. A guy came along and she handed him a piece of paper. They were adjacent to a bus stop and my man joined the bus queue to see if he could overhear their conversation.'

'Did he hear anything?' asked the Admiral.

'Something about it being useless without a password. The hefty one replied, "If she knows it, I'll get it." They broke up and my tail decided to follow him rather than her. And you'll never guess what.'

'Let me guess. He went back to Grosvenor Square.'

'Correct. We've looked him up in our mug shots. He is Major Keith Richardson, a USAF officer posing as a CIA operative; or, maybe, it's the other way around?'

'It confirms a hunch I've been having for some time. Richardson was an Air Attaché in the American compound in Baghdad only a few weeks ago. He tried to con information out of one of our chaps when he was over there on a computer project. Thanks for that, Peter. Tell your man he did well. The two Iraqi women are returning to Baghdad in the morning. I think you can call off the tail.'

'OK, Brian. Glad to have been of help.'

***

233

Kate awoke with a start. Someone was climbing into bed with her. Not fully awake, she thought for a moment it must be James. She pulled the duvet back for him. Then, remembering where she was, she panicked and tried to stop the intruder. The room was dark, but she noticed the backlit digital clock showed 9.30 pm. A hand came across her mouth to prevent her from crying out. She couldn't see her attacker, but could smell him. He stank of drink: beer or whisky – she wouldn't have known the difference. She struggled, but the interloper was much stronger. She was being pinned down on her back. His knees were already pressing her elbows into the mattress as his free hand groped her breasts. Her legs were free and although she tried to use them to wriggle sideways and escape, the weight of her trespasser's body was too much. Squatting over her, the impostor's free hand grabbed her throat and squeezed.

Breathing became difficult; she felt she was passing out. The more she struggled, the worse it got. Life was draining out of her; she stopped kicking her legs – she was weakening fast. To her relief the pressure on her throat eased, but then a worse sensation, the assailant began bouncing up and down on her, crushing her ribs. In an instant the hand covering her mouth was removed. She instinctively tried to cry out, but air rushed into her deflated lungs and no sound came. A gag was rammed into her mouth, and what seemed like a piece of sticky tape secured it. She could barely breathe through her nose. She had started to become used to the dark; she could see the outline of her aggressor. He was wearing a loose-fitting dark shirt, his face masked by a scarf. Breathing was difficult; she felt faint. His knees had moved further apart so that they were now pressing down near her wrists. She thought her arms might break. One of his hands was prying her vagina. She tried to cross her legs to prevent entry, but it was useless. Strangely his hand didn't feel rough. Ironically, for a fraction of a second, she thought of Sally.

He was pushing his groin into her face, taunting her, while his fingers crudely tried to masturbate her. He continued to bounce up and down, seemingly enjoying the power he had over her. Then, suddenly he ripped the tape off her lips, rammed his fingers in her mouth and pulled out the gag. What felt like a small stiff snake was pushed in. It tasted vile, and she instinctively puked. He ignored her coughing and retching. He pushed the snake in further, and violently slapped her across the face. It felt as if he had broken her nose; the pain was excruciating. It dawned on her that it was his penis in her mouth. She felt blood coming down her nose. She tried to shout for help, but only a muted sound emerged.

'Suck me off, you stupid, fucking bitch,' he said. He pushed harder, the snake expanded.

Everything went black; there was no sound, no feeling. Time stopped; there was only the smell of his breath and the taste of her own vomit. She passed out.

When she came round, it was one o'clock. Her first thought was that she must have dreamt being raped. The room was empty, the door closed, the building silent. She staggered out of bed, switched on the light. Instantly she knew that it hadn't been a dream. She was aching all over. She examined herself in the mirror. Horror. Her face was painful, her nose covered in blood and swollen. Her arms were bruised, her ribs hurt like hell. Worst of all, however, her vagina had been ripped and was splattered with congealed blood. She felt dirty and instinctively decided she must have a bath. No matter how much she scrubbed herself with the sponge, she couldn't get the dirty feeling to go away. She felt guilty that she had been abused. She couldn't stop crying.

What did I do wrong to be treated this way?

It didn't occur to her to wonder who did the deed. Somehow it didn't matter. Far more important was preventing anyone finding out.

How can I hide the blood stains on the sheet and the pillowcase?

She remained in the bath for ages, sobbing. More than anything in the world she wanted James to be with her.

He would console me. He would forgive me for what I have done.

The bath began to go cold. She added more hot water. It was already two o'clock.

The car is coming to take us to Heathrow at 4.30 am. There is no point going back to bed.

Looking in the mirror she realised what a mess she was. She was sobbing uncontrollably. Her heart was heaving, banging her ribs, pumping the spurting tears from her eyes that were running down her cheeks. She applied liberal amounts of makeup and talcum powder to disguise the bruises, wrapped her hijab around her face, threw her jupeh over herself and stripped the bed. Descending the stairs she found the duty night receptionist asleep in the foyer. She woke him and asked where the laundry room was. He was surprised to find someone awake.

'Why Miss al Jised,' he said, 'it's in the basement. What's the matter?'

'I thought I'd strip the bed and save the chambermaid a job.'

He asked no further questions and showed her the way to the cellar. She saw the dustbins, opened one and peered inside. She moved the rubbish to one side and pushed her sheet and pillowcase underneath, covering them over to conceal them.

She returned and packed her bags. The task momentarily took her mind off the torturous experience. Then she sat on the bed weeping but scheming.

If it's the last thing I ever do, I'll find out who did this to me and kill him.

She knew it couldn't have been Yassir; he would have been at home with his wife.

No, it could only have been Amer Rashid.

All sorts of ideas crept into her mind. She had unlimited access to poisons at work. She would do her research and select one that would leave no trace on her victim. She would ensure that death was agonising and slow. The only problems were when and how.

When he comes back to Iraq, my time will come. I will have my revenge. He'll wish he was never born.

The idea then grew that, perhaps, it would be better if she could denounce him in some way as a traitor. Using her contacts with the British, she could engineer his disgrace and downfall. Saddam would have him executed publicly.

Yes, that would be even more satisfying.

She smiled to herself, and began plotting a scheme.

***

Kate waited in the foyer, her bags packed. Roya appeared at the last minute. There was a look of disdain on her face. They never spoke to each other as the embassy car sped them to Heathrow. They booked in. They could have been separate passengers. The aircraft was only half full. They sat with an empty seat between them, Roya reading, Kate in a dream world. She ached all over and longed to tell someone of her ordeal.

Anyone else, yes; but not her. She would only gloat all the more.

Twenty minutes into the flight the stewardesses came round offering breakfast. The seat belt signs were still switched on owing to turbulence over northern France.

'Continental or Full-English?'

Both indicated continental. Kate didn't feel like anything, but felt it would take her mind off other things.

'Tea or coffee?' Both asked for coffee.

As the stewardess began to pour hot coffee into Roya's cup, the aircraft dipped suddenly and violently. Steaming coffee fell onto her lap.

Her reaction was instant and furious. 'You stupid, fucking bitch.'

The stewardess backed off, apologising profusely and pressed an overhead button. It had been a pure accident.

The senior steward arrived promptly. 'If you will come with me, I'll clean your dress in the galley. I can only apologise. Perhaps, you would like an upgrade to first class for the rest of the journey?'

Roya disappeared, never to return. Kate was happy to be on her own. But something nagged at the back of her mind. It was the way Roya had said, 'you stupid, fucking bitch.'

I must be imagining things. It couldn't have been her last night. Could it?

CHAPTER 27

Kate couldn't stand the thought of sharing the chauffeured car into Baghdad. She avoided Roya at the baggage carousel and took a taxi home. Her train of thought kept criss-crossing this and that way. From her undergraduate days, she remembered some lectures in marine biology on the sexual lives of fish. The sea bream could be born female and after three years become male or, even, vice-versa. She briefly wondered if it had happened to Talfah, but dismissed the idea as utter nonsense.

She must be a hermaphrodite and never had an operation. It would explain a lot. In the university officers' corps, she shunned the boys and was very friendly with a girl who, it was rumoured, had unorthodox sexual tendencies. If I'm going to get revenge, I'm going to have to create some convincing evidence. She's in Tufiq's books, a Ba'athist, and distantly related to Saddam. I'm going to have to make myself indispensable. Whatever it takes, from now on, it's me or her.

Kate felt her inner confidence growing. She was going to be in charge of researching and producing chemical weapons that would have the capability of destroying masses. Only she would know where they were stored. It would be her bargaining counter.

Armageddon or Roya Talfah.

She went straight to her apartment. There were the usual domestic chores to complete and she busied herself washing, cleaning and shopping. She prepared her evening meal. She was surprised no one rang. She had expected Tufiq to be demanding her presence.

Perhaps he is satisfied with getting the position from Talfah.

The next morning she arrived at her office promptly, as always. Her secretary smiled, welcoming her back, adding, 'You have a visitor waiting in your office, an air force officer, Lieutenant Colonel Tumbrah.'

'Have you given him some coffee?'

'No.'

'Then please bring us some in, he's an old friend.'

She entered. 'Azi, this is an unexpected pleasure. How are you?'

'Fine, Kathab. What about you?'

'I've been better, but you don't want to hear my problems.' They embraced, exchanging the customary kisses. 'I see congratulations are in order.' Azi looked puzzled. 'Your promotion, well done.'

'It's partially due to the war game. That's what I've come to see you about.'

The coffee arrived and while Kate poured, she asked, 'How can I be of help?'

Azi sipped his coffee. 'Let me explain. As I understand from General Tufiq, you couldn't contact James when you were in England on Monday?' He paused.

Kate said nothing, allowing Azi to continue.

'However, the next day you found a chess master who was able to solve the chess riddle?'

'Yes, Ray Kane. He worked it out in fifteen minutes. Tufiq's men couldn't do it in fifteen days.' She laughed. 'Roya Talfah took the position and was supposed to transmit it to Tufiq that afternoon.'

'She did. Yesterday morning General Tufiq came out to the College and expected me to be able to get into the encrypted data files of Nastia Game. Unfortunately, there was a problem.'

'What? The position is wrong?' asked Kate, somewhat taken aback.

'No, I don't think so,' reassured Azi. 'It's just that we need James' password as well.'

'I don't follow.'

'You may remember that you have to have a password to play the game. However, when you log into the game, unless you have the right password then the software will not give you the opportunity to access the data. At Reading, only James and Hamish could do that.'

Kate sat silently, slowly nodding. She was beginning to remember something James had said, *'You'll need my password.'*

Azi continued. 'Tufiq was furious when he realised we could not get into the programs. He began ranting and raving, threatening to have you and Roya shot for incompetence. Poor old Brigadier Murthah had a hell of a job calming him down. In the end, he managed to convince Tufiq that there must be a simple explanation and that you would probably be able to resolve the situation. I've come to warn you; hoping you might be able to help.'

Kate sat in a daze. The thought of Tufiq having Roya shot made her smile, prompting Azi to ask, 'What are you smiling at?'

Kate came out of her trance. 'Oh, it's the idea of seeing Roya Talfah shot.'

Azi grinned. 'Yes, she is a pain in the ass.'

'You only know half of it. However, getting back to the game, is there a log of when James last made alterations to the data?'

'Yes, I expect so.' Azi didn't sound too convincing.

'Haven't you looked?' Kate couldn't believe she needed to ask the question.

'No, what good would they be? The log doesn't reveal the passwords.'

'No, but it does print out, as asterisks, the number of alphanumerics used. That might be a big clue.'

It was Azi's turn to become pensive. Kate finished her coffee. She could see Azi was realising he may have missed a trick or two. It was also dawning on Kate that she was becoming even more indispensable.

Revenge will be sweet.

'I'll tell you what,' began Kate. 'Ring Brigadier Murthah and tell him we're on our way back to the College. Tell him I think I may be able to help, although I can't guarantee it. However, neither Talfah nor Tufiq are to be there when we try to work out the password.'

Brigadier Murthah greeted Kate, whom he had never met, at the front steps of the College. He was charming. 'Your father is an old friend. How is he keeping? I am sorry you were unable to come to dinner last week with Squadron Leader Douglas. He was a good man. What happened was a tragedy. I hope he will recover from his loss. I gather you went to England for the funeral but were too late?'

'I'm afraid so.' They shook hands and Kate saw the eyes of a tired man. Probably of a similar age to her father, but lacking the spark of life that keeps men young. They made small talk as Azi led the three of them to the main computer complex.

While Azi was asking one of the Omanis to get the log archives, Brigadier Murthah asked Kate questions about Cambridge. 'My wife was there last year. She would love to meet you. Would you like to come over to our place some evening for a curry?' Kate accepted gladly.

'I had hoped to get the password for the game when in England, but James had taken his son away for a holiday to Scotland. However, I am hoping I can recover the situation for you.' The Brigadier mumbled something about hoping so too.

Azi returned to the computer suite with a roll of paper. 'This is the log from a week last Monday, the last day James was here. I remember that day well, we talked about ideas for improving the game as well as some of its weaknesses.' He rolled the log out in front of them. It showed the sequence of James logging on.

MONDAY – 17 JUL 78, 0814
LOGIN PASSWORD ***********
CHANGES TO DATA? (Y/N) N
ENTRY ACCEPTED

Kate counted the asterisks. 'There!' she exclaimed. 'His password has eleven alphanumerics.'

'But can that help us?' asked Brigadier Murthah.

'I'm not sure,' replied Kate, 'but it might.' She sounded excited and turned to Azi. 'Have you got a pen?'

'Yes.'

'Good. Write out, AVA GARDNER. How many letters?'

'Ten.'

'OK, try, GREGORY PECK. How many?'

'Eleven.'

'That's it, then. His password is GREGORY PECK. He said it would make me laugh.'

'But,' asked Azi, looking mystified, 'how did you know what to try?'

'Do you remember the first day we turned up at ICL Dataskil in Reading? James said I looked like Ava Gardner, as in the film *On The Beach*. I later did some research and pulled his leg that he wasn't that unlike the hero of the film, Gregory Peck. We often laughed about it.'

The Brigadier chipped in. 'A wonderful film. It had a big impact on people's opinions about nuclear weapons.'

Kate nodded, ignoring the remark. She was too excited. 'Log in using that password.' Azi obeyed.

THURSDAY – 27 JUL 78, 1047
LOGIN PASSWORD ******* ****
ILLEGAL PASSWORD
ENTRY DENIED

All three looked blankly at the message. All three were deflated.

'That can't be right,' asserted Kate. 'Hang on; it didn't like you putting in the space between Gregory and Peck. Look, there is a space between the asterisks.'

Azi tried again, typing in GREGORYPECK.

242

```
THURSDAY – 27 JUL 78, 1048
LOGIN PASSWORD **********
ILLEGAL PASSWORD
ENTRY DENIED
```

'James and I only briefly discussed passwords when he was giving me the word puzzle. I'm sure we're on the right track,' explained Kate.

Both men were looking at her, hoping she would, somehow, be given divine inspiration. They were mentally willing her on, not daring to say anything that might disturb her concentration.

After a little while, she added, 'I know, let's go back to Ava Gardner. Azi, try AVA-GARDNER.'

```
THURSDAY – 27 JUL 78, 1052
LOGIN PASSWORD **********
CHANGES TO DATA? (Y/N)
```

'Bingo!' cried Kate, pleased with herself. The delight on both Azi and Ahmed's faces was something else.

'Come on,' encouraged the Brigadier, 'hit Y.'

Azi did as ordered, and pulled out from a drawer a small chess set with the key position already set up. Kate peered at the board and recognised it at once as that given to them by Ray Kane. The console, meanwhile, had printed out five questions to which Azi gave the answers.

```
WHAT IS ON H1? – K
WHAT IS ON D8? – N
WHERE IS kb? – H2
WHERE IS KB? – A4
WHAT IS ON D5? – <RET>

DO YOU WISH TO CHANGE THIS POSITION (Y/N)? –
```

Azi looked at the Brigadier, who nodded. Azi hit 'Y'.

THE DATA FILE IS NOW READY TO ACCEPT CHANGES.

'Brilliant!' remarked the Brigadier. 'I can't thank you enough, Kathab. I think we should all go out for a celebratory lunch, don't you?'

'Sounds good to me,' replied Azi. 'I'll quickly change the position, so no one can enter the files and then order up your staff car.'

***

Over the next few weeks Kate settled back to working in her laboratories. On 1st August she was officially appointed head of all research, development and storage of Iraq's weapons of mass destruction. She had become, de facto, one of the most powerful women in Iraq. Regular meetings were held with the military to provide reports on progress. General Tufiq, as Head of Military Intelligence, was invariably chairman. He began to treat her more as an equal; not someone he could bully as previously. Supplies of raw materials to make the weapons were always going to be a thorn in the flesh. Tufiq accepted that Kate would have to make contact with Peter Stacey to ease the provision of chemicals from Britain and agreed to give her odd snippets of information to exchange. The Revolutionary Command Council, chaired by Saddam Hussein, effectively ran Iraq; it believed Western Governments would be happy to close their eyes to the development of chemical weapons as long as they were supplied with cheap oil. Kate learned that it wasn't only Britain involved in the deception. Germany, Japan and the United States were also major suppliers. It was on her first meeting with Peter Stacey, in early September 1978, that he dropped two bombshells into her lap.

'Do you remember Ben Green at Reading?' he asked.

'Yes, why?'

'Apparently he's vanished. I've been asked to enquire what you and Azi Tumbrah thought of him,' Peter continued.

'Azi never liked him, but then Azi is more anti-Semitic than me.'

'You both thought he was Jewish?'

'Yes. In private, Azi called him "The Zionist".'

'What was his job at Reading?' asked Peter.

'Hamish gave him the simulation of the tank battles to program. From what I could see, he did it very well. He appeared to be on top of the complex tactics involved.'

'I'm not privy to the details, but I think the feeling back home is that he was planted into the programming team by Mossad; probably to get details of your weapon sites,' replied Peter.

'Then they'll be disappointed because nothing highly classified was entered into the game until we got back to Baghdad.'

'The second piece of intelligence I have for you is, undoubtedly, more important. Do you know Roya Talfah has connections with the Americans?' he asked.

Kate's jaw dropped.

Peter continued. 'After seeing Ray Kane, you returned to your embassy.' He paused, and Kate nodded. 'About half an hour later, Talfah left on her own, made a phone call from a public call box. Twenty, or so, minutes later she met someone from the American embassy. She gave him something, we don't know what.'

Kate was livid and fumed, 'I do – the chess position. Have you any proof?'

Peter sensed her anger and decided not to mention that the American had been in Baghdad recently. 'No, unfortunately not. No photographs were taken, but we thought you would be interested just the same.'

'Yes, definitely. It sounds to me that it was Talfah who must have made the attempts at the Staff College to break into Nastia Game using Richards' and Hamilton's passwords. Somehow she must have been given them by the Americans.'

'If you are right then the Americans are responsible for their disappearance and the death of Mrs Douglas,' remarked Peter, 'but remember we have no proof.'

'For you maybe, but for me it's all I need.'

I've got her!

CHAPTER 28

Kate found her new job demanding. Apart from regular contact with Tufiq and sitting on various working committees, she managed a staff of over 200 in her R&D department. There were twenty research teams, typically consisting of eight to ten graduate scientists developing new products, each backed up with lab technicians and administrators. She held a weekly meeting with the leaders of her teams to ensure each knew what was going on elsewhere within the labs and to give guidance on strategy coming from the working committees. Progress was monitored at monthly team meetings where she offered ideas and encouragement. Her knowledge of chemical and biological weapons, counter measures and defensive clothing built up rapidly. Her expertise on the subject soon became unique, certainly within Iraq and, probably, anywhere worldwide outside America and Britain.

Although the strategic purpose of research within her department was the same for all the teams, the span of their weapons development was wide ranging. At one extreme were the *heavy* teams, researching biological products that by their nature were virtually uncontrollable if released into a population, such as anthrax, gas gangrene, botulinium toxin and ricin. At the other end of the scale, the *light* teams were researching novel ideas, such as exciton and enditon, toxins that affected the chemicals naturally released by the brain to tell the body to speed up or slow down.

The Ba'ath Party controlled Iraq through various councils. The most important, the Revolutionary Command Council, had eight permanent members, with Saddam Hussein as its chairman. It was equivalent to the British Cabinet. Members included the foreign minister elect, Tariq Aziz; the vice-chairman, Izzat Ibrahim; the Minister of Defence, Hashim Ahmad; the Head of the Army, Ali Hassan; and the Head of the Civil Service, Sahib al-Majid. Reporting to the Command Council were various subcommittees and working groups. The peripheral boards tended to be composed of two- and three-star generals, or their equivalent civilians. Kate sat on two: the National Security and Intelligence Committee, headed by two-star General Tufiq, and the Military Procurement Committee, headed by Major General Ahmed. Their role was to flesh out the policies from above and make recommendations to the higher council for their implementation. It meant that Kate regularly attended meetings to give presentations on the way forward. She began rubbing shoulders with the most powerful men in Iraq.

Kate had been astonished to find the biological weapons produced before she took over her new job were stored in a warehouse in the suburbs of Baghdad. At her first meeting with the National Security Committee, she pleaded that storage policy should be radically changed. She pointed out that even a small leakage in the current depot could release enough toxins to destroy the entire population of Baghdad. She was given carte blanche to implement whatever steps she felt necessary. The first materials she buried in the Empty Quarter southwest of Ar Ramadi were 200 gallons of anthrax spores, enough to kill a million people.

She used the method James had explained to her in the sands at Ur to hide the deadly materials. She had played through the chess game he had shown her many times and memorised it. She knew it by heart. The location of the anthrax was duly coded so the records were indecipherable. Cheap immigrant labourers were used to bury the weapons, *just in case there is an accident*. The excuse was accepted without a quibble. It took several weeks to hide the most dangerous poisons; the workers having no idea what they were handling. Kate was the only person in Iraq who knew how to find the toxic materials.

The research being undertaken into exciton and enditon fascinated her. When the body begins to get excited, such as when someone is playing a game, or even having sex, the blood pressure rises, the heart rate increases, the nerve endings become sensitive. The brain is releasing hormones that enhance the experience. However, at some point the brain decides, for safety reasons, that enough is enough. It then releases a retarding chemical that lowers the heart rate, reduces the blood pressure and normalises sensitivity. At her first meeting with the team undertaking this research, the leader explained what they were attempting to do with exciton and enditon.

'A person injected with exciton is unable to stop getting excited. In other words their heart rate and blood pressure just go through the roof until they die from a heart attack or similar complication. We have not experimented on humans, but all the evidence with mice and stray dogs is convincing. The lethal amount required for a human will depend on the individual's size and gender. Enditon is the exact opposite. Someone exposed to enditon will become lethargic. In extremis he won't want to do anything; neither eat nor even defend himself. We believe a small dose would lead to death. Our main line of research is currently looking at ways of administering the two toxins: sprays, powders and so on.'

'What evidence would there be left in the body if, say, someone had been given exciton?' asked Kate. There was an ulterior motive for her question.

The team leader breathed in deeply, before replying cautiously. 'We're not sure, but if the right quantity was administered, then the chances of a post-mortem discovering anything would be remote as the cause of death would look natural. After all, people have heart attacks every day. Someone having sex could literally die on the job!'

He, and the rest of his team in attendance, laughed. So did Kate. Only she knew, however, that was exactly what she had in mind. She authorised research to begin on humans. 'Try it out on some of the Kurds in Abu Ghraib jail.'

The work of other teams worried her, however. She was appalled at the photos she was shown on the effects of CPCs. Chlorostridium Perfingenicmercuric Contaminants had been developed that would enter the nasal cavities and cause the muscles in the face to bloat, the skin to split, and disintegrate. Having given it the name gangrennex, her predecessor had authorised it to be trialled on humans. Exposure to the droplets for about a second resulted in the most horrific death of all – a stinging sensation as the skin melted. Pictures of corpses without a face made her stomach turn. She momentarily closed her eyes, but knew she must show no emotion in front of the team. They seemed to see nothing wrong with their product.

Perhaps, they have hardened their feelings over the years, but I couldn't do this; not even to Talfah. I'll make sure this weapon never gets used.

Ironically, one day it would save her life.

Kate had been in her new job for just over two months. October had arrived. The Camp David Peace Accord had been signed by Israel and Egypt. Rumour had it that Saddam in one of his periodic rages had called President Sadat 'a Jewish bastard' and vowed to wipe him off the face of the earth. He attempted to whip up Arab support for his anti-peace views, but as usual most of the Middle East states prevaricated and did nothing.

Autumn was bringing cooler air to Baghdad; her plan for Talfah was firming in her mind. She had forgotten Nastia Game. The memory of James had faded but was not totally extinguished; nor would it ever be. One morning after returning to her office from a meeting with one of her research teams, her secretary met her with a puzzled frown.

'What's the matter?' enquired Kate.

'The British Air Attaché, Wing Commander Platini, has been on the phone this morning. He wants you to ring him back.'

'OK. Get him on the phone. I'll take it in my office.'

'Hello, Gerry. This is a surprise. How can I help you?' asked Kate when she was patched through. Her guard was down. The last time she had spoken to him over the phone, she had chosen to be formal.

'Kathab, I'm wondering if we can meet. I have something to tell you that can't be said over the phone.' Gerry sounded distant.

Kate wondered why. Her first thoughts were that Sally must have confessed about their brief frisson, but quickly dismissed the idea.

He doesn't sound cross, just very sad.

'When and where do you want to meet?' asked an intrigued Kate.

'Is there any chance of you coming over to my place this evening? Sally would love to see you again and we could have supper together.'

'Well as it happens, I was wondering what I was going to have this evening. I'd love to come. What time?'

'Say, seven-thirty?'

'Fine, I'll be there.' At which, they said their farewells and put the phones down.

Kate arrived promptly. She was greeted by her hosts as a long lost friend. They sat down to some warm canapés, washed down with orange juice. Small talk predominated. Gerry explained that they were leaving Baghdad at the end of the month. He had been posted to the MoD in London and was looking forward to his new job. Sally was pleased as they could move back to their family home near Grantham from where Gerry would be able to commute daily. 'It will mean long days, but that's far better than living apart from Monday to Friday in some awful flat in London,' remarked Gerry.

At one point Sally said, 'Kate, I know it's a long shot, but if you ever come to England, we want you to come and stay with us, don't we, Gerry? We have plenty of room.' He nodded. 'It's easy to find us. In case you don't remember when I told you before, our house is in a village, a few miles south of Grantham, called Colsterworth. It's just off the A1. The cottage is called The Old Post Office.'

Kate promised that she would look them up if she ever did visit England. Despite the bonhomie, Kate could feel a tension in the room. It was as if they wanted to get something off their chests, but didn't know how.

They sat down for supper. Conversation went embarrassingly quiet. Halfway through, Gerry, who was looking dejected, finally plucked up courage.

'Kate, I'm afraid we've got some bad news. There was never going to be an easy way of saying what I've got to tell you.' He stopped, unable to go any further. The sorrow in his eyes told Kate something was wrong, so she put her knife and fork down and looked at him expectantly.

It was Sally who continued. 'The English newspapers arrive at the embassy several days late. I think you should see what was in *The Times* three days ago.' She handed Kate a neatly folded cutting.

IRA AMBUSH BRITISH SERVICEMEN
TWO OFFICERS KILLED IN N IRELAND
By Our N Ireland Correspondent

The Ministry of Defence have named the two officers killed in an ambush in County Armagh, two days ago as Major Bill Norvic (R Signals), 29, a married man and a father of two from Northampton, and Squadron Leader James Douglas RAF, 37, a widower from Fort Halstead in Kent. The officers were believed to be conducting trials with a prototype handheld communications device.

The IRA has issued a denial of any involvement in the ambush, but a splinter group, calling itself the Independent IRA, has claimed responsibility. Their statement said that the two officers were challenged a mile inside the Irish border, refused to surrender and were shot in the ensuing battle. Their bodies were then buried in a lake to the east of Castleblaney.

The MoD has demanded the immediate return of the bodies, stating that the last known position of the two officers indicated they were 'well within the N Ireland border'.

'The bastards,' muttered Kate. She felt her eyes welling up and scrambled to find her handkerchief. The flame that had glowed faintly inside her was suddenly blown out. She felt its tiny column of smoke drifting up her throat. The warmth from the hope it had provided was now gone forever. Her hands and toes felt like ice. Her stomach turned. Sally and Gerry were looking at her, their faces full of grief.

She felt obliged to say something. 'I...' she began, but stopped to wipe her tears. 'I had always hoped somehow, you know...' and faltered. Sally put her arm around her. Kate looked into Sally's eyes. 'I'm OK, honest.' She wiped her face and blew her nose. They all sat silently, their meal going cold.

It seemed ages before Kate asked, 'There won't even be a funeral?'

'No, I suppose not,' answered Gerry.

'What will happen to poor Stuart? First his mum and now his dad.'

'I would imagine that the RAF Benevolent Fund will pay for his education at a boarding school. He'll probably stay with his grandparents during holidays.'

'But they are not getting any younger.'

Gerry shrugged his shoulders and whispered, 'I don't know... ' His voice tailed away. They sat at the table picking at what was left of their food. Sally cleared up, and served coffee. Little was said.

Eventually, Kate felt it was time to go. 'I want to thank you for the kindness and understanding you have shown toward me. I am glad you invited me around here this evening. It would have been awful to have heard the news some other way. I don't expect I shall ever get to England, but if I do, then I will take you up on your offer.' She smiled, they hugged each other and Kate left thinking she would never see them again.

She drove back to her apartment, through the near deserted streets of Baghdad. Tears flowed uncontrollably down her cheeks, the flood gates had opened. Her world had collapsed with the news of James' death. Although she had always known their brief affair could lead nowhere and would probably create more problems than it would solve, there had always been a flicker of hope. Now that was gone forever, dashed on the rocks of life. Without hope, there was nothing; only revenge on Talfah. Once she had achieved that goal, she would leave Iraq, go away somewhere, anywhere that would allow her to forget those wonderful two weeks that began in Samarra and ended in Ur.

She slept badly. She felt wretched going to work and was surprised when her secretary informed her that Azi had already been ringing for her. 'Did he say what he wanted?'

'No. Only would you ring him back?'

She entered her office, while her secretary patched her through; uncertain of what he could want. It had been almost two months since she had decoded the password for him.

'Yes, Azi, how can I help you?' she asked.

'You remember we broke into the war game and found out how to change the data files?' he enquired, the shared credit for the achievement not going unnoticed by Kate.

'Yes?' She wondered what was coming next.

'Well, did you know there is a further ring of protection on the programs themselves?'

'I'm sorry. I don't follow you,' she replied.

'For the last couple of months I've been busy getting to grips with the data files. Updating and enhancing them has been no problem. However, last week I decided I should try to incorporate some subroutines to simulate the effect of weather and logistics consumption. No matter what I try, I can't get past a series of questions that seem to be protecting the programs. I suspect there is a second inner chess position we didn't know about.' He paused in anticipation.

'I'm afraid that I can't help you. It's news to me. I don't remember James mentioning anything like that.'

'I was hoping you might know what to do. I haven't had the courage to tell Tufiq yet.'

'Then don't. He'll never know, surely?'

'The trouble is that before James left, James and I had discussed the weaknesses of Nastia Game with Brigadier Murthah. It was he who asked me to think about enhancing the software.'

'Have you explained the problem to him?' asked Kate.

'Yes and it was the Brigadier who suggested you might be able to help. He thinks very highly of you. He told me you went to his residence last month for a curry supper and talked a fair bit about the game. He thought perhaps you might be able to get in touch with James and get the second position from him.'

The suggestion of contacting James, made in all innocence, made Kate feel worse than she already was. Her stomach went empty, her mind momentarily blank. She rested her head on her elbow, struggling to find the right words. 'I am afraid that will be impossible, Azi. James was killed last week in Northern Ireland by the IRA.'

There was silence at the other end. Kate wondered if they had been cut off. She waited a while, then asked, 'Azi, are you still there?'

'Yes, I'm here. Who told you he was dead?'

'I went to see the Platinis last night. They showed me a cutting from *The Times* with the news. The British suspect his body, along with another officer, was buried in a bog.'

'But that's terrible.' Azi paused, then added, 'I am sorry, Kathab, really sorry. I know you and he were fond of each other. I liked him too. Brigadier Murthah will be upset when I tell him.'

'No. Please don't do that. I was going to ring him myself this morning. I think it might be better if the news came from me, don't you?'

'Yes, you're probably right.'

Kate pressed the bell for her secretary to come into her office. 'I want you to get hold of Brigadier Murthah, person to person. You will get his personal staff officer when you ring him, but I don't want to speak to her. Patch me through as soon as you know it's the Brigadier on the line.'

'Very good.'

Kate waited in her office. Knowing that the Brigadier was going to be terribly upset, she wondered how best to tell him.

'Brigadier, it's Kathab al Jised here.'

'Hello Kathab.' He sounded pleased to hear from her. 'To what do I owe the pleasure?'

'Wing Commander Platini rang me yesterday afternoon. He invited me to his house last night for supper. His purpose was to give me some terrible news. I am sorry to have to tell you that Squadron Leader Douglas was killed in Northern Ireland last week by the IRA.'

There was a deafening silence at the other end. Kate, yet again, wondered if the line had been cut. Finally a weak voice replied, 'You must be mistaken?'

'I wish I was. The Platinis showed me a report on an IRA ambush from *The Times*. Apparently he and another officer were trialling some sort of communications device. The IRA claimed they caught them inside the Eire border and shot them.'

The silence on the other end of the phone suggested the Brigadier was stunned, but Kate thought she heard a faint click.

'I don't know what to say.' His tone was one of utter despair. 'After what happened to his wife and daughter, now this. It's unbelievable. You must be devastated.' It wasn't a question, and Kate didn't answer. He was right, she was devastated. Her red eyes were welling up again. After what seemed an interminable time, the Brigadier continued. 'Kathab, there is nothing I can say that will ease your pain. Time will slowly lessen the numbness, but you and I will never forget him. He was a fine fellow. Changing tack, you know I retire at the end of the year. I have got a month's leave saved up and am going in four weeks time. I would like you to come to my farewell dining-out night at the College as my personal guest. Dacksi, my wife, will be there and she would love to see you again. Will you come?'

'I'd be delighted.' An idea flashed through her mind: *This might be the chance I've been waiting for.*

Kate had made it routine practice to show her face each day by walking around her patch. The researchers appreciated her showing interest in their work and she soon got to know their first names. By her asking searching questions, they quickly realised that their boss had a first-class brain. She understood the frustrations of research work, including the need to keep accurate and up-to-date notes. She had stressed from the beginning that she would not tolerate sloppy paperwork. They knew that Kate had to account to the military council for all the money they spent, but deep down they knew she was on their side. She was a scientist not a bureaucrat.

That afternoon she decided to seek out the team leader researching exciton and enditon. 'Just thought I'd pop in and see how things are going,' she said.

'Very well,' he replied. 'There were two Kurds awaiting execution. We tried exciton on one and enditon on the other. With one we put five grains of exciton, in powdered form, into his drinking water while he was exercising in the gym. It dissolves instantly and is tasteless. With the other prisoner we sprayed enditon into his cell while he was asleep. The results were interesting.'

'What happened?'

'The Kurd in the gym went berserk. He began running on the treadmill, getting faster and faster. He wouldn't slow down or stop. We believe that at the end he was running as fast as an Olympic 400 metres runner; the difference being that he had already run over 1,500 metres.'

'You said at the end.'

'He collapsed suddenly and was dead in seconds.'

'So, five grains,' Kate paused, calculating. 'That's about a third of a gram?' She looked at her team leader for confirmation.

He nodded.

'...is enough to be fatal?'

He nodded again.

'My concern,' continued Kate, 'is how are we going to use the stuff? After all, if we put it into air burst shells and exploded them over an advancing army...' She stopped, trying to imagine the consequences.

'Quite,' answered her team leader. 'They would get hyped up and become fearless. It's possible that they would not receive a fatal dose. Goodness knows what could happen.'

'I see exciton as a tool for individual assassinations,' said Kate thoughtfully.

'I think you're right,' he agreed. 'However, enditon is a different matter,' he added. 'The Kurd in the cell is wasting away. He refuses to do anything except lie on his bunk. He hardly drinks anything and eats even less. So far, it has been seven days. He complains of headaches, stiff joints and feeling nauseous. Another week and he will be dead. Used in air burst shells it could be very effective, depending on the dosage received by the individual. However, it could take weeks, months, or even years if only small quantities were ingested.'

'I'd like you to write up a report on your findings with enditon,' said Kate. 'I will present it to the next meeting of the military council. In the meantime I would be grateful if you could give me half a gram of exciton. I will do some research myself.'

CHAPTER 29

Kate had no clear idea of how she would use the exciton; only on whom she would use it. Her job kept her so busy that planning the assassination of Roya Talfah, with all its risks and possible repercussions, had to wait.

The time will come, she told herself, *and then I will act.*

A few days before Brigadier Murthah's dining-out night, she met Peter Stacey, with General Tufiq's approval, to try and ease the purchase of materials including sulphuric acid, sodium and mercury. It was her first opportunity to disclose the location of the anthrax spores she had hidden in the desert, near An Nukhayb. They met at the *Mansour Milia Hotel,* had a drink, and walked into the hotel's gardens. 'This is our list of wants,' she said, 'but more importantly, this is the location of 200 gallons of anthrax spores.'

He looked at the first piece of paper; it was a list of chemicals. He recognised their names, realising they were essentially basic inorganic materials necessary to make more complex chemicals. The second paper simply read, 42.00 degrees E, 32.00 degrees N. He looked at Kate, but said nothing.

She felt obliged to explain. 'The spores are in a powdered form, suitable for using in air burst shells. They are contained in glass jars, inside stainless steel drums and buried in the sand at a depth of about five to six feet. I don't care how you get rid of them, either in situ or by taking them away. The site is about a mile north of the Karbala road, approximately fifty miles from the Saudi border. Porton Down may have developed a new sterilant for anthrax, I don't know. We are researching new ideas all the time, but this is our latest decontaminant.' She handed him a third slip of paper.

It read: Sodium Peroxide 30%, Chlorine Dioxide 50%, Butyl hydroperoxide 20%.

Again Peter did not speak. Again Kate explained, 'That mixture will destroy the spores, but it takes several hours. It's no use blowing the pile up; the spores are incredibly resilient. An incinerator has to be at one thousand degrees centigrade to be effective. The problem is that anthrax spores protect themselves by creating a type of shell and then lie dormant until disturbed. It is one of the theories behind the myth of Egyptian mummies taking revenge when their graves were opened.'

'I didn't know that!' exclaimed Peter. He then asked, 'How many people know the exact location of the anthrax?'

'Only me.'

He raised an eyebrow, as if asking, *how's that?*

'Trust me, I have an infallible system. Our records show the location as somewhere else. However, I have a key that uses the false location to give me the actual position.'

'Do you mind telling me how it works?'

'It was an idea of Squadron Leader Douglas.' I transpose a chess position on to a map of the area where I intend to bury the weapons. I then choose a square where the weapons will be recorded as being buried; say *a4*, and record its Lat/Long. If there is a chess piece on that square, then the weapons will actually be buried on the square where that piece was prior to arriving at *a4*, say *d1*. I am the only one who knows the chess position.'

'Sounds complicated.'

'I thought so at first, but once you have memorised the position it's easy.'

'What if there isn't a piece on the square you choose?'

'I intend to use such squares for burying less harmful weapons.'

'Such as?'

'Ah,' she smiled. 'I have to have some secrets, don't I?'

'Point taken. Obviously, I don't know what my bosses will do with this information, but thank you. I am sure the site will be cleaned somehow. I will ensure that the delivery of your chemicals goes smoothly. Is there anything you want to ask me about? You know Sally and Gerry have returned to the UK? They left last week.'

'Yes, I knew they were leaving. I saw them a month ago. They gave me the news that James was killed in Northern Ireland.'

'That was tragic, coming so soon after his wife's accident. I am sorry. I know you were fond of him. He was a great guy.'

Kate felt her eyes welling up, her fingers and toes going cold. She knew it was time to leave. She turned away to hide her emotions. 'We'll keep in touch,' she said, and left.

Peter left worried by what he had just seen. He felt his report to his masters in MI6 should include a comment that Kate might not be totally stable. Perhaps pressure of work, coupled with emotional disturbances, could lead to her cracking up, he thought.

***

Shortly after returning to her office, the phone rang. It was Brigadier Murthah. 'Kathab, I must be quick. Roya is out of the office and I don't want her to overhear our conversation. I have been rattling my brains all week about what to give her as a farewell gift. She has been my PA for over eighteen months, and although there have been times when I could have happily wrung her neck, she has been most efficient. I know you went shopping in London together and thought you might have some ideas as to what sort of things she might like. Have you any ideas?'

'I'm not sure. Let me think for a minute or two, and I'll ring you back. Is that OK?'

'Yes, but don't be long, I'm expecting her back in the next half hour, or so.'

Kate didn't have to think for long, ringing him back five minutes later. 'Brigadier, when we went shopping in London, Roya tried to buy a perfume called Arpege. We couldn't find it anywhere. It didn't surprise me, as I have only ever been able to get it in France. I know she likes it, but you have left it too late to get some sent to you before you leave. However, I have a spare bottle, unopened, and still in its box. If I bring it up to you, you could tell her that you had bought it especially for her and had had it sent from France. She would appreciate that even more.'

'Wonderful, Kathab. Will you bring it around to my house? Or shall I arrange for someone to come and pick it up?'

'I'll bring it to your place tomorrow evening, if that's OK?'

'In that case, you must stay for some supper. Dacksi will be delighted to see you again. I'll pay you for the perfume, of course.'

'That's alright, it will be my pleasure. See you tomorrow then, about seven o'clock.'

You're dead, Talfah!

***

British Embassy, Baghdad
Mon 27 Nov 78
Ref, Bgd/Int/241/5
To: Head of Middle East Sect
MI6 London
Dear Harry,
Ref, Agent Kathab al Jised (241/5)
Met KAJ this am. She continues to produce quality info. Three points:
200 gallons of anthrax spores have been buried at a depth of 6 feet at Lat 42.00E Long 32.00 N. KAJ thinks you should remove it.

Iraqi's best decontaminant, Sodium Peroxide 30%, Chlorine Dioxide 50%, Butyl Hydroperoxide 20%. KAJ suggests Porton may have quicker acting mix, theirs takes 2 hrs.

Am concerned about stability of KAJ – clearly upset re death of Sqn Ldr Douglas. Could impede her motivation to work for us. Ideas?

Let me know if you want help to remove danger.
Yours aye
Peter S

A Stanley knife, rubber gloves, clear super glue, some cotton wool buds, a small bottle of white spirit, an unopened bottle of scent, a small confectioner's funnel normally used for piping icing sugar and five grains of exciton; not much, but coupled with patience, under a good light with a magnifying glass, make a fatal combination. It took Kate about an hour to complete her task. After carefully unpicking the cellophane wrapping around the box with the sharp blade, dissolving the glue with the cotton buds dipped in white spirit, the rest proved uncannily easy; unscrewing the atomiser top from the bottle, using the funnel to allow the grains to enter the perfume, replacing the top, putting the bottle back into the box, and finally sticking the cellophane back in place. No one could have guessed that the box had been interfered with. The exciton had dissolved as her researcher had said: colourless, odourless and tasteless. It would be deadly. Kate had even bought gift wrapping paper. She parcelled the box as well as any professional in a French *parfumerie*, tying the bow with large loops.

That will do nicely.

***

'Roya has agreed to come to work on Friday morning to help me clear my office. It will be the last time I will see her, as Dacksi and I are leaving for India the following day,' said Brigadier Murthah to Kate as she arrived the following evening. 'This gift will be a big surprise for her.'

'Let it be our secret,' replied Kate.

There's irony in your words, old man. Her big surprise will be a fatal shock. You won't see her again, at least not alive.

'I hope you don't mind, but when I knew you were coming this evening, I took the liberty of asking a friend of mine to come for supper as well. I believe you met him in London, Brigadier Amer Rashid?'

At that moment, the door bell rang. Dacksi answered it and Kate heard her saying, 'Come in.'

The introductions were friendly and warm. Conversation at table was largely about the Murthahs' plans for retirement in India. Kate sat opposite Amer, noting his hands were large, hairy and strong. He was pleasant, witty and mentally sharp. Although older than Kate, she found him attractive. The evening passed incredibly quickly.

As they left, Amer asked, 'Would you like to sit with me at Ahmed's dining-out? I am sure I can persuade the mess manager to arrange the seating.'

'Yes, that would be nice. Thank you, I shall look forward to seeing you on Thursday evening.'

***

MI6 HQ, London
Thu 30 Nov 78
To: British Embassy, Baghdad
FAO, Peter Stacey
Ref, Agent Kathab al Jised (241/5)
Your 27 inst. Will arrange meeting between Porton, SAS, and selves. Re KAJ, watch situation closely, advise whether to come in, leave, or eliminate.
Yours aye
Harry P

***

Kate arrived at the College for the dining-out night, punctual as usual. The reception area was already heaving with bodies, but Amer Rashid was waiting at the front door and greeted her with a friendly smile. 'You look the bee's knees,' he said, grinning from ear to ear. It was a new expression for Kate; she hoped it was complimentary. As they entered the anteroom for pre-dinner drinks, Brigadier Murthah and Dacksi were welcoming the queue of guests.

'We'll try to catch up with you later,' Ahmed said to them. He winked at Kate, nodding as if to say, *You look a fine couple.*

They moved nearer to the centre of the room. 'I'm glad you asked me to accompany you this evening,' she said to her consort. 'I would have been on my own, otherwise. I hardly know anyone here.'

'That's not quite true,' Amer replied. 'I have arranged for us to be with the Tumbrahs, Azi and his wife. 'I got to know Azi a little when you and he were at Reading. He used to come to the embassy and receive instructions from time to time.' They chatted together for only a few minutes before Azi and his wife, Sawsan, arrived. Conversation changed, preventing Kate from getting further background on her companion.

The dining-out went well. Ahmed's speech was both witty and interesting as he regaled stories from his thirty-five year career, including his tours in India and Saudi Arabia. Kate looked around the dining room and spotted Roya on the top table, next to Tufiq. She wondered what they saw in each other.

There's no accounting for tastes, but my revenge is coming. Make the most of what time you've got left Talfah. Tonight might be your last.

CHAPTER 30

Kate had planned to take a few days off work to visit her parents. She hadn't seen them since taking James to Samarra. She drove alone in her Datsun. Memories of the last trip flooded back. So much had occurred since she had fallen in love with James and had an affair with him – the only man who would ever mean anything. As a result, she had, perhaps stupidly, become a double agent. Then James' wife had been mysteriously, even conveniently, murdered. She had travelled to London and found someone to solve the chess puzzle. She had been raped. She had poisoned her assailant. James had been killed by the IRA. She had been promoted to a new job and become one of the most powerful women in Iraq. Yet she longed to turn the clock back.

Oh, to be a boring housewife for James – an impossible dream. I would give anything to re-live last July. At least then, there was hope. Now there is none.

The greatest fear of all is having no hope.

She tried to focus on the positive: her work was interesting and challenging. It allowed her to meet the most influential people in Iraq. The secret chess key, drawn in the sand at Ur, allowed her to be Iraq's conscience on what could and would be used for chemical and biological weapons. She had made a hit with Amer. He had asked her out next week. She had accepted.

I must accept my lot and make the most of it. You know you are good, just be more confident when dealing with the Tufiqs of this world. She glanced at her watch. *With a bit of luck, Talfah could be dead by now. Good riddance.*

***

As always her parents were delighted to see her; their welcome was as warm as ever. It felt good to be with her family again, although her sisters weren't there. Hind was at university and Lina out with friends. The three sat down for tea in the sun-lounge. Ala had prepared small patisseries made of almond paste and honey – a favourite of Kate's when she was a little girl. It was her mother's way of saying, *we love having you home.* As usual, Qassim wanted to know what Kate had done since her last visit. It wasn't going to be easy to tell him. She decided to bite the bullet.

'Do you remember James?' she ventured hesitatingly.

Ala beamed, giving away her feelings. 'Of course, how is he?' she asked enthusiastically.

'I am afraid he's dead. He was killed whilst on a military operation in Northern Ireland about six weeks ago.' Kate replied.

Ala's face dropped. Her smile disappeared. Her eyes welled up. She sighed, 'Oh no,' and began to sob, fumbling for her handkerchief. Kate moved from her chair, putting her arm around her mother's shoulder to give comfort.

Qassim looked mournful. 'He was a good man. I am sure his family will miss him very much.'

'I'm afraid that's only half of it. About ten days after being here with us, his wife and baby daughter were killed in a car accident. It meant he had to go back to England in a hurry. I never had a chance to say goodbye.'

'Allah works in strange ways,' mumbled Qassim, looking at the floor.

Kate wondered if there was a sense of relief in his voice.

Conversation had dried up. Each sat in silence alone with their thoughts. Slowly Ala, who had been affected badly by the news, began to recover. Her answer was to make herself busy. She gathered up the tea cups and took them to the kitchen. Kate and her father were left alone.

'Did you get to Babylon and Ur with him?' The question was loaded, and Kate knew her doubts of a few minutes previously were well founded. *He can't even say his name.*

The tone was as a father would ask his daughter anywhere in the world when he suspected there may have been an improper liaison.

There was no way her answer was going to be the whole truth. In the Islamic world inappropriate relationships, especially with someone from another faith, were better kept secret. She didn't want to hurt her father's feelings. She replied breezily, 'Yes, we got to see the sites. We were with a party of French and East German advisers; the French are helping us to build a nuclear reactor at Osirak, and the Germans are teaching our pilots to fly Migs at Al Kut.'

Qassim seemed happy not to delve deeper. *He probably knows what went on. He forgets I'm nearer thirty than twenty,* she thought.

'How are you getting on at work?' was his next question.

Kate was now on firmer ground. It was a good excuse to introduce the forthcoming Ba'ath party revolution into their conversation. 'What do you think of Saddam Hussein?' she asked.

Her father answered instantly. 'Not much. Why?'

'You know he's plotting to overthrow President Bakr?'

'It's no big secret,' the old man replied. Kate hadn't thought of her dad as an old man before, but the question seemed to age him by twenty years.

'Once in power, he intends to get Arabstan back from the Iranians. He's planning the war now, even as we speak,' she said.

'It will be the ruination of Iraq. Millions will die on both sides. The Persians won't lie down and give him Kazistan on a plate.' Kate noted her father had used the Iranian name for the disputed province.

'Father,' Kate began hesitatingly, 'have you ever thought of leaving Iraq if things were to go badly wrong?'

'What sort of things?'

'Well, Saddam is ruthless. When he gets in to power there will be a purge. Anyone considered remotely dangerous will disappear; especially President Bakr's friends.'

He never replied. She wondered if he had even heard the question. 'Father? Did you hear me?'

'Yes, I heard you; I was thinking. Did you know Lina has been offered a place at Cairo University to study medicine, beginning next September?'

'No, that's fantastic. Cairo University has one of the best faculties of medicine in the Middle East, if not in the world. Why didn't you tell me sooner?' asked Kate.

'She only had confirmation of the offer yesterday. She will be able to live with your mother's youngest sister, Aunty Raghad.'

Qassim continued. 'With Hind graduating from Mosul University in the summer, and if anything were dire enough to make us leave, that would be the time to go.'

Kate was relieved to hear her father being flexible. Her family's safety was all that mattered. 'So, you will give serious consideration to leaving Iraq, if things go haywire?'

'Yes, although I will have to begin preparing soon. We couldn't just drop everything, pickup sticks and get in the car.' He paused, before continuing. 'We would have to transfer monies. Perhaps The Royal Jordanian Bank would be the easiest. I've had a small deposit account there for years. I would need to sell this house, if we were to have a reasonable standard of living. Would you be in a position to tell us when the revolution is likely to take place? Or, when there will be a war with Iran?'

She replied encouragingly. 'When Saddam decides to have his coup will be a well-guarded secret and I won't hear about it any sooner than you. However, the build up to the Iran war is another matter as I will be heavily involved with the preparation of weapons. Of course, I'll let you know. I think it would be a good idea that as soon as he takes power from President Bakr, you should begin preparing to leave. The war will follow within a year, you can bet on it.'

'If we were to go to Egypt, would you come with us? Surely, your safety would also be compromised?' The concern in her father's voice moved her.

'There will be no need to worry about me. I am making myself indispensable at work. If things were to go badly awry, I have an insurance policy to get out quickly.'

'What exactly is the nature of your new job, then?'

'Well, Dad, I'm in charge of all research and development of our chemical and biological weapons. It means I sit on two committees that report directly to the Revolutionary Command Council. Anything to do with Home Security or the Military and I know what's going on.' She continued to give her father a sanitised summary, leaving out details such as anthrax and gangrennex. He listened with interest, realising that his eldest daughter was someone special, but unaware that she was a double agent playing a Nastia Game.

The extended weekend passed all too quickly. Kate travelled back to her apartment on Tuesday afternoon, arriving around four o'clock. She was surprised to find among her waiting correspondence a hand-delivered note from Azi. She had no idea how he knew her address and read the note:

Dear Kathab,

Came around to see you on Sunday, but you weren't in. Assume you are out shopping! Can you give me a ring as soon as you get in? My number is 214675.

Yours ever,

Azi

She rang the number. Azi's wife, Sawsan, picked up the phone. They chatted, agreeing that Brigadier Murthah's dining-out had been pleasant and that they must get together sometime soon.

'Azi has left me a note to ring him, is he in?'

'Yes, I'll get him.'

He came to the phone, apologised for leaving the note, and then said, 'I don't want to tell you over the phone, but I've got some bad news for you. Can I meet you in half an hour? Say, somewhere central, in front of the Armenian Church, perhaps?'

Situated on the corner of Port Said Street and Nidhal Street, the Armenian Church was a well-known landmark.

'OK,' replied Kate, puzzled that Azi would not say anything else.

She drove into town and parked her car in Sheik Omar Street. It was only a few hundred yards from the church. Azi was already waiting.

After greeting each other, Azi proposed they walk towards the river.

'I'm sorry about the cloak and dagger stuff, but the news is about Roya Talfah. Bearing in mind her relationship to Saddam, I thought we should be careful,' said Azi.

'What are you talking about?' asked Kate, trying to hide the fact that she knew what was coming.

'She was drowned on Saturday. I thought you'd want to know straight away and not find out at work by accident,' he replied.

Kate stopped abruptly in her tracks. 'Drowned?' she exclaimed in disbelief.

Don't tell me all my plotting was for nothing.

'Yes,' replied Azi. 'I still can't get over it.'

'How did it happen?'

'You probably know she used to keep herself very fit and went to the gym at the College every day.'

'I didn't know she went that regularly.' Kate was getting interested in what was coming next.

'Well, the swimming pool is adjacent to the gym, separated by the changing rooms. On Saturdays there is only one Corporal Physical Training Instructor on duty; he has to watch the gym and the pool. Last Saturday, the Corporal, who was on duty for the afternoon and evening shift, saw Roya at four o'clock in the side-gym, where the weights and training equipment are kept. He hadn't seen her arrive, but noticed that she was going at the treadmill hammer and tongs. He didn't think too much about it. There were some youngsters playing five-a-side soccer in the main gym and he joined them. He regularly left the game and patrolled the site. At five o'clock he saw Roya swimming up and down the pool. He described her as "thrashing water everywhere". She had a reputation among the PT staff for being one of those swimmers who think they own the place; everyone else has to get out of her way. As she was the only one in the pool, he let her get on with it. He returned to supervise the youngsters, mostly, children of the College's staff. At six o'clock he again looked in the pool; it was empty. He assumed Roya had gone home. He coached some of the officers' wives at badminton until it was time to close the whole complex at seven o'clock. He checked the changing rooms and locked up; handing the keys in to the guard room at exactly 1915 hours. Roya was found the following morning at the bottom of the pool by the cleaners who open up at half past six.'

'How awful, but how on earth did she drown if she was such a strong swimmer?'

'A post-mortem was held that afternoon. Apparently, she had a heart attack in the pool and drowned. Had there been a pool attendant on duty, he could, perhaps, have saved her.'

No, he couldn't.

'Poor old Brigadier Murthah will be upset when he finds out.'

'Yes, I wrote to him yesterday. He had left for India before all this happened.'

'Well, I'm glad you let me know. Drowning must be a terrible way to go.' Kate was lying through her teeth, convincingly. She continued. 'Oh, by the way, how did you know where I lived?'

'We shared a taxi when we came back from Reading. Don't you remember?'

'Of course.'

They shook hands and departed in different directions. Azi didn't notice Kate skipping joyously back to her car.

Revenge is sweet!

CHAPTER 31

The New Year had hardly begun when news arrived on 16th January 1979 that the Shah of Persia had fled Iran, ostensibly for health reasons. He would never return. A fortnight later Ayatollah Khomeini returned from exile in France to a tumultuous welcome by massive crowds. Within a further six weeks, a referendum overwhelmingly accepted the setting up of an Islamic State.

The repercussions for Iraq were to be enormous. Kate's workload increased dramatically. The Revolutionary Council was meeting daily and bringing out new directives. Kate's two working committees would then have to resolve the problems of implementing the policies. Frequently, it would be after midnight when she would get back to her apartment. There was very little time for socialising with Amer who was paying her a lot of attention: asking to take her out to dinner and the theatre.

Her unique position vis-a-vis Iraq's programme of developing chemical and biological weapons meant that occasionally she would accompany General Tufiq to attend Revolutionary Council meetings. She quickly concluded that Lieutenant General Ali Hassan al Majid, the Head of the Army, was a hothead. It was clear at the council's meeting on 18th February that Khomeini would become the leader of Iran. This prompted the General to urge Saddam to bomb Tehran with 'whatever we've got'. Ali turned to Tufiq, looking for support. Tufiq, in turn, turned to Kate. Saddam, no fool, could see a potential clique ganging up on him.

'Well, al Jised,' asked Saddam, 'what do you think?' Kate had not expected to be asked. At her first council meeting, she had not spoken a word and no one had spoken to her. She was surprised that the great man had remembered her name, presumably from meeting her and James when he had opened the refurbishment of the Caliph's Palace in Samarra.

'I fear, sir, we have neither the capability to successfully bomb Tehran at this time, nor, more importantly, are we in possession of the right weapons.'

'Rubbish,' interrupted the three-star general. 'We have two hundred gallons of anthrax. We could use that.'

She was not going to argue with Ali Hassan who, for his use of cyanide and nitric acid when bombing Kurd villages, had been nick-named Chemical Ali. She wanted to say something about the possible international consequences, but chose to keep eye contact with Saddam, who got the message.

He thought for a few seconds, and then addressed the council. 'When we allowed Khomeini to live here, before he buggered off to France, I offered to assassinate him for the Shah. The idiot wouldn't let me. He didn't want Khomeini to become a martyr. It was against my better judgement.' He turned to look his general straight in the eye and continued. 'Bombing Kurdish villages with acid, or whatever, is one thing, but Tehran is something altogether different.' He looked back at Kate. 'Al Jised, have we anything that could get rid of Khomeini without being too obvious?'

'You mean a poison?' she asked hesitatingly. *I got away with poisoning Roya Talfah; I must be careful what I say.*

'Yes.' He answered in a way that implied, *what else could I have meant?*

Kate replied, 'Khomeini is an old man. We have a substance that we are still testing called enditon. It slows down all the body functions until they stop. A small quantity could take weeks, but eventually the recipient dies of something akin to old age. He would become lethargic, stop eating and so on. It leaves no trace in the body and can be administered in several ways.'

'Excellent,' exclaimed Saddam. 'I want you, Tufiq, to plan the assassination. You have one month to come up with something concrete.'

Tufiq looked at Kate, his eyes saying, *now look what you've done.*

However, Saddam wasn't finished. 'I visited the Air Force Staff College some six months ago to watch their war game. Al Jised, here, helped develop it in England.' He stopped and nodded towards her. The others turned to look at her. Kate felt her cheeks blushing with all the attention. 'As you all know, the game simulates attacking Iran. Some of the games have lasted months. From the regular reports I am getting, important lessons are being learned, one of which is that we have insufficient weapons, both conventional and chemical, for outright victory. When we go to war with Iran, I would dearly love to bomb Tehran out of existence. However, we will not be ready for war for at least a year, possibly two. Consequently, I want the provision of munitions to have top priority over everything else in the coming months. Since both of you are here this afternoon, you can give me a brief resume on the state of our weapon stocks. Al Jised you start on chemical and biologicals, and then you, General Tufiq, can report on the conventional weapons.'

It was a fast ball for both of them, and they looked blankly at each other for a second or two.

Kate cleared her throat, wishing she had been on stage second. 'I have been in charge of chemical and biological weapons research, development and storage for about six months. The first three months or so were spent largely taking over the inventory, getting to know my team and finding somewhere safe to store our stocks, mostly anthrax and gas gangrene.' She stopped and looked at Saddam. 'Do you want me to be blunt, sir?'

'Yes, of course.'

'Well, frankly I am appalled at the low level of our stocks. Our inventory consists mainly of anthrax and gas gangrene, which are about the most useless CB weapons for a war with Iran.'

Ali couldn't resist interrupting her. 'And what gives you the right to say that?' he demanded crossly.

She looked at Saddam, her stomach all of aflutter. Chemical Ali was a cousin of Saddam. She was afraid she had overstepped the line.

However, their supreme leader smiled at her, turned to Ali Hassan, and said quietly, 'I'd be interested to hear her views. Please, continue.'

'To answer General Al Majid's question first. When we go to war with Iran, the whole world will be watching. You can bet your bottom dinar the Iranians will make sure their armies are accompanied by international journalists.' She noticed Saddam nodding. 'When they report worldwide that we have used anthrax and gas gangrene, or even our own more potent gangrennex, as weapons, the UN will vilify us. They leave too much evidence of their use. Anthrax is particularly dirty. It can take hundreds of years to clear. If we used it in Arabstan, for instance, we would be destroying our own territory.' She paused. She hoped Saddam agreed with her; otherwise she could be rapidly out of a job and into a coffin.

Ali Hassan stared at her, and sneeringly asked, 'And what do you suggest? Surely, we must have CB weapons?'

Kate had been expecting the question and launched in, without looking at her leader for support. 'We must produce the types of weapon that leave little or no evidence of their use. I am talking of mustard gas, sarin and ricin. Perhaps, best of all, a new nerve gas my team are developing based on VX. Even old-fashioned cyanide is, to a greater or lesser extent, better than anthrax. The new generation of weapons is biodegradable. Journalists might suspect we have used such agents, but they would have a job proving it.'

The entire council were silent and thoughtful. They were deferring to Saddam Hussein to react. He looked at Kate, and asked, 'What problems are we going to have getting sufficient quantities of these weapons?'

'Firstly, sir, raw materials will have to be imported. Thanks to General Tufiq we are able to get some from the British.' She thought she should try and get some brownie points for her boss when the opportunity arose. She noticed Tufiq sit up straighter in his chair. 'However, I fear we will also need to persuade the Americans and the Germans to supply us as well.'

Saddam nodded again, clearly accepting the points she was making.

She decided it was time to attack. 'The biggest problem is not researching how to make these substances, but their full scale production. We are woefully short of the type of chemical factories necessary to make the quantities we are going to need. For example, I believe we are talking about hundreds, or even thousands, of gallons of sarin, ricin and so on.' It was time to stop.

Saddam looked at her thoughtfully. His eyes narrowed; it was difficult to read his mind. He turned to his senior civil servant, whose responsibilities included international trade. 'Who do we get to build a chemical plant in a hurry?' he asked.

Sahib al-Majid was small in stature, but had a huge cranium. He was renowned for diplomacy and his profound analytical brain. He thought only briefly before answering. 'The Germans would be our best bet; failing them the Japanese. Both badly need our oil, especially if we offer it at ten per cent below OPEC prices.'

'Timescale?'

'Two years minimum, possibly three.'

'You'd better get them both to build one. Tell them whoever completes first will get oil at fifteen per cent below OPEC prices for five years afterwards.' There was a mischievous smile on his face. Saddam turned to Kate. 'Thank you for your assessment. You will have your chemical factories up and running within eighteen months.' He turned to Tufiq. 'Now General, what about our conventional weapons?'

'The picture is broadly the same. As you correctly mentioned earlier, the games being played at the College are showing that we have insufficient munitions. I found it hard to believe at first, but I am convinced the simulations are accurate. If we were to attack today, our stocks would be exhausted within ten weeks.'

Discussion followed. Kate was not involved. She had had her day. She spent the rest of the meeting watching the various factions vying each other for position. Above all, remaining totally in control was

Saddam. She began to see why he had reached the most powerful position in Iraq.

We need a strong leader like him to keep Iraq together, she thought.

The day after her attending the Revolutionary Council meeting, Tufiq was expecting Kate to drop everything and help him come up with a plan to assassinate Khomeini.

'I can provide you with enditon,' she protested, 'but it is your job to plan the execution.'

He was not satisfied seeing the documents from previous experiments and arranged for human guinea pigs to be found from Abu Ghraib jail.

'I must see its effects at first hand,' he demanded.

His experiment hindered the directing of her research teams. It was the academic challenges of her job that excited her most. She resented having to waste time attending Tufiq's gruesome experiment. Somehow, he had found two old men in jail. 'Similar ages to Khomeini,' Tufiq had remarked. One was given a few drops of the drug orally; the second had it sprayed into his cell whilst he was asleep. Kate was surprised how quickly the first died. Within twenty-four hours he was gone. His body functions simply stopped. To all extents he had died of old age. The other guinea pig took longer. He stopped eating and drinking, his movements slowed down, he became incontinent. A week later his respiratory system stopped. Tufiq kept the experiment secret, insisting that full post-mortems be carried out by an unsuspecting pathologist. He was delighted when the autopsies revealed nothing except death by natural causes.

'Excellent,' he had remarked to Kate. 'How much enditon have we got?'

'Only small quantities; we have no production facilities and make it to order in the laboratory. We could make a few fluid ounces fairly quickly.'

'Mmm,' he pondered. 'How are we going to get near enough to Khomeini to administer the enditon?'

'I'm sorry, sir, but that is your speciality, not mine. It won't be easy. After all Kennedy couldn't kill Castro, even with an exploding cigar.' It was a jocular remark, but didn't go down well with the General.

Kate found herself embroiled in her work, to the exclusion of all else. However, Brigadier Amer Rashid didn't lose his romantic interest. Kate found it flattering that he would take her out to dinner whenever she could find time, typically once a month. She liked him. His approach was old fashioned, strictly correct. He was good company; conversation never dried up although she found her mind was rarely far away from her research.

One of her teams had produced a nerve gas based on VX, originally developed at Porton Down, but subsequently mass produced in America. Her team called it vexun. One drop on the skin was quickly absorbed and almost instantly prevented the transmission of nerve signals. The consequent loss of muscle control affected breathing, as the lungs cannot work, and speech, as the jaw cannot move. Total paralysis was swift and death within minutes was inevitable. As a nerve agent it was excellent. Unfortunately, there were problems. In the process of its synthesis, secondary salts were created that could not be eliminated by distillation. Blockages kept forming on the pipes. It would remain a major problem for her team for some time.

A second research team worked to further develop an existing nerve gas, sarin. Its effects on humans were similar to vexun, but less swift. It caused disruption between the nerve cells, creating spasms and nausea. Death wasn't always certain. Production from the constituent chemicals, a mix of diesel fuel and several alcohols, was relatively simple. They named the poison zarin. However, it degraded rapidly even when stored in a vacuum. It was perfect as a weapon as within forty-eight hours all traces of its use had vanished. Kate and her team tried various methods of storage, but to no avail. It was whilst dining with Amer one evening and discussing mutual problems that a solution availed itself.

'Why not keep the chemicals separate in the warhead?' Amer had asked.

'What do you mean?'

'I can't see any reason why the warhead shouldn't have two, or three, thin glass compartments. When the aerial bombs are fired at the enemy, the glass phials would shatter, the chemicals would be reacting together en route and the explosion would scatter pure zarin.'

'Could that be done?' she asked, marvelling at the simplicity of the idea.

Why didn't I think of that?

***

Kate's life was hectic. Typically, she awoke at 5.30 am, listened to the news headlines on the overseas BBC programme while having breakfast and was in the office before seven o'clock. She would discuss research problems with her teams in the mornings, grab a half-hour lunch if she was lucky, attend meetings in the afternoons, and clear up endless administration that frequently didn't finish until late at night. Only Friday was free. It was a toss-up between seeing Amer or a quick trip to Samarra to see her parents and sisters.

Her only break from the busy routine was the odd meeting with Peter Stacey to procure raw materials for research. She was amazed that the excuse she used, the chemicals were needed for a new water purification plant, never seemed to wear thin. She wondered why. She had little to give in return as information from Tufiq had all but dried up. He was, presumably, too preoccupied trying to plot the assassination of Khomeini.

Trips abroad to conferences ceased; work was too hectic. She allowed her Heads of Teams to go whenever time allowed. It increased her popularity with her staff, but little else. Few new ideas ever came back.

Kate didn't always accompany Tufiq to meetings of the Revolutionary Council. The need-to-know principle was strictly enforced. Consequently, she was out of touch with many developments. However, she was asked to attend the meeting held a week after Mrs Thatcher's election as Prime Minister in May 1979. As before, she took her place with other attendees who, like herself, were only officially *in attendance*. They sat along one side of the room; the main players being seated around a large rectangular table with Saddam at its head. There were several items on the agenda that impinged on her area of responsibility.

Item 8 – Progress on Khomeini. General Tufiq outlined that one of his agents had infiltrated Khomeini's staff and was analysing the best way to use enditon. This surprised Kate. She had heard nothing from Tufiq on the matter since her joke about Castro's cigar, almost three months previously.

Item 12 – Progress on Falluja Chemical Plants. Sahib al-Majid briefly summarised progress on the building of the two new chemical factories. The Japanese and the Germans were falling over themselves to complete first, he said. Although only two months since the initial agreement to proceed was given, both sites, to be called Falluja 1 and Falluja 2, were cleared and foundations were being laid. He praised Saddam's idea to build the two factories within sight of each other. 'It keeps them on their toes.' Kate noticed the great man smiling to himself. He turned and looked at her, said nothing, but gave her a wink.

Maybe, he was right. I will have factories up and running within eighteen months.

The meeting wore on, many items irrelevant to Kate. However, on turning over the page of the minute sheet, she saw Item 28 and panicked. She was expected to give a resume of latest developments in her work.

Item 28 – Progress on new nerve agents. She thought quickly. She began by outlining the advantages of vexun and how it would kill within minutes. However, her team was struggling to overcome its production problems. She felt sure they would be overcome presently. Secretly, she hoped no one would ask how presently. No one did. She moved on to zarin, its ease of production, its speed to biodegrade, but its problem of storage. She outlined Amer's idea of warheads with glass phials, but let the Council believe it was her brainwave.

'Excellent,' said Saddam, 'you have done well.' He turned to Major-General Ahmed. 'This is your cup of tea, General. Start designing the glass internals for the war heads.'

Item 36 – Any other business. Nothing of interest to Kate was mentioned until at the end when Saddam mentioned Margaret Thatcher. 'Our ambassador in London was called to the British Foreign Office yesterday to explain how the German company Hoechst had won a contract to build Falluja 2. Apparently, a British subsidiary of Hoechst, called Uhde, is to build sections of Falluja 2, which let the cat out of the bag. The good news is that Mrs Thatcher's Department of Trade are not objecting; their Export Credit Guarantee scheme is backing Uhde.' He chuckled; his cohorts did likewise.

***

Several months passed; little happened to disturb Kate's routine. At one of her regular dinner dates with Amer, he had mentioned that some of his staff had been given the task of designing easily shattered glass phials to be inserted inside the warheads of aerial bombs and mortars. Their design brief hadn't revealed the purpose, but Amer had put two and two together. Kate apologised, explaining how the opportunity had arisen to bring the idea up at the Revolutionary Council meeting. He told her that the prototypes were proceeding well. 'It will be a fine arrow to our bow.'

Kate knew Amer had got the metaphor wrong, but didn't try to correct him. *He's a good man; he'd make a fine husband.*

***

The second week of July came, and Kate felt low. She knew why. It was the anniversary of her trip with James to Babylon and Ur. She tried to bury her personal feelings by throwing everything into her work. She couldn't get James out of her mind, until she heard the news at breakfast.

16th July 1979 – Earlier today Baghdad Radio announced the resignation of the Iraqi President, Ahmed Hassan Bakr, due to poor health. He has been President for eleven years. His successor is to be his cousin, Saddam Hussein al-Tikriti.

Yes!! Now we will show the Iranians and the world we can't be shoved around.

Driving to work, she could feel a buzz in the streets. *I hope they don't expect too much, too soon.*

CHAPTER 32

The summer months of 1979 saw big changes to the way the Iraqi state was run. On 22nd July, Saddam called a meeting of Ba'ath Party leaders. In a speech lasting several hours, he claimed to have found conspirators. He read out the names of some sixty-eight members of the party, fifth columnists, who had been plotting to kill him. They were asked to leave the room and were immediately arrested. None were ever seen again. That was only the beginning. Rumours abounded of hundreds of killings and the imprisonment of Saddam's political opponents across the country.

Fortunately, Kate's father wasn't one of them. He had taken his daughter's advice and admitted to Kate that he was secretly stashing away deposits into a Jordanian bank. Arrangements had been made for Lina to start her medical studies at Cairo University in September and Hind had decided to accompany her sister. She had been accepted on a Master of Arts course in the History of Ancient Egyptian Art. She wanted to become a teacher afterwards and planned to do a second year to become qualified.

'When will the war with Iran start?' her father had asked on one of her visits home.

'Don't worry, Dad. I'll give you plenty of warning.'

Attending occasional meetings of the supreme council allowed Kate to see Saddam in action. She became ever more impressed as she realised that there was much more to him than a gangster wanting to wage war on Iran. Rather, she saw him as a social revolutionary and moderniser.

He was passionate about having a Western-style legal system. Iraq became the only Middle Eastern country that was not ruled by Sharia Law. Consequently, women were given added freedoms and he appointed several females to his government at high level in the fields of finance, medicine and education. He was a breath of fresh air, as long as you didn't get in his way.

He was conscious that three quarters of Iraq's population were not Sunni. He made great efforts to introduce social programmes that were unpopular with conservative traditionalists. His patience was to be sorely tried on many occasions; his leadership style being take the carrot or the bullet. Nevertheless, his 'Compulsory Free Education' campaign was to produce the highest rate of literacy in the Persian Gulf. Electricity was made available to all but the most remote villages in the north. Free hospitalisation to everyone was to earn him an award from UNESCO.

He introduced subsidies to farmers to allow them to mechanise agriculture on a large scale. Peasant farmers were allowed to purchase their own land. Co-operatives were set up. There was an air of euphoria in the country as the economy grew rapidly. His popularity increased when he nationalised several foreign oil companies. Posters and murals of him appeared everywhere: schools, airports, shops.

Nevertheless, Kate was only too aware that there was a hidden price. She was sometimes asked to attend meetings at the Department of General Intelligence, the most notorious and feared arm of the state security apparatus. Their use of torture was legendary. Kate's input was to provide truth serums that were being developed by one of her research teams. Assassination by poison was, fortunately for her, not their style; the gun and the bomb were favoured.

The other problem with Saddam was his ego. She noticed he began making references to the Abbasid period, when Baghdad was the pivot of political and economic power in the Arab world. He reputedly confided to some close friends that he was the re-incarnation of Nebuchadnezzar, ruler of Mesopotamia for seventy years.

Kate's relationship with Amer was slowly growing warmer. He dated her whenever he could; he seemed to have more time than her. Nevertheless, it came as a surprise when one evening in late August, he asked her to marry him. There had been no intimacy. Indeed, their contact amounted to little more than gentle hugs when kissing farewells. She didn't know what to say. She liked him. She liked being with him, but she didn't love him. With James there had been passion, excitement, even danger. But with Amer it was steady, sober and staid. However, she was conscious that she would be thirty next birthday. She was aware that she had been staring blankly at Amer for some time after his unexpected proposal.

'I'm sorry,' she said. 'Do you mind repeating that?'

'I asked you to marry me,' he answered with a broad smile on his face.

'But we hardly know each other.' It was a feeble excuse. She was floundering on how she could get out of her dilemma without hurting his feelings.

'I feel I've known you all my life,' he replied. It was a line straight out of a movie; Kate didn't know which.

'Look, I'll tell you what,' she said, getting what she thought at the time was a brilliant idea. 'Why don't you come up to Samarra next weekend and meet my parents?' She was hoping the invitation would put him off.

'Excellent,' he replied with evident enthusiasm.

Oh my God, what have I done?

***

With Tufiq's approval, a few days later she arranged a meeting with Peter Stacey. Research was bounding ahead and raw materials were becoming scarce. She handed him a list, but Peter never looked at it.

'From now on, you will get all you ask through the usual trade channels. You will not need to come to me.'

'Why is that?' asked Kate.

'It's something to do with our Department of Trade backing a British Company to help the Germans build Falluja 2. The new Trade Minister, Paul Channon, has refused to block any trade with your government. Apparently, Mrs Thatcher has made it very clear in cabinet that she intends to support Saddam's regime as opposed to Khomeini's. It's ironic because I warned my masters what is going on with your research into CB weapons. At the highest level, we advised caution as we know full well what you will use Falluja to produce. However, if the chemical plant is not seen to be a legitimate civilian operation then the Export Credit Guarantees cannot finance the project. So, there you are, that's politics for you. From now on, Kate, you can have as much chlorine and caustic soda as you want.' He laughed a hollow laugh.

She smiled. *It'll make my life easier if I can get anything I want. Tufiq will be pleased too...* Her thoughts tailed away.

'There's just one problem with that,' she replied.

'Go on.'

'Bringing you a list of requirements allows me to arrange to see you in full view of Tufiq. If I have some other information I want to give you, I can always use it as an excuse. Arranging to meet you secretly is far more complicated and can easily go wrong. If you don't mind, I'd prefer to keep our current arrangement.'

She's sharp as a pin, I'll give her that.

'OK, we'll leave it as it is.'

Kate then asked, 'Did you make a decision about the hidden anthrax?'

'The reply I received was that we are leaving it where you have hidden it. Apparently, moving so much anthrax would be tricky, especially as we would have to do it covertly. Destroying it, I was told, would be too dangerous. Furthermore, after our last meeting, I described to London, as best as I could, the method you are using to hide the chemicals. They were impressed. They believe you have hit on an infallible method of disguising the location of the weapons. They are happy for you to continue the practice. However, there was a word of caution in their reply.'

'Really, what?'

'You will have to be on your guard at all times.'

'Why?'

'As long as no one knows what you are doing, you'll be safe. But suppose your enemies get wind of your hiding method. You are the only person who can decode the records. However, if you were eliminated the weapons would remain hidden for all time. Iraq could never find them and your enemies would be safe from the scourge. To put it bluntly, you have become indispensable.'

'I hadn't thought of it in those terms.' She was lying through her teeth. She knew she had become the most important woman in Iraq. It just hadn't occurred to her that the Iranians would put her on their hit list if they found out about her scheme.

'I have been authorised to give you this.' He handed her a sheet of paper.

She looked at it and instantly realised its importance.

Peter continued. 'I understand it's a mixture that will destroy anthrax spores in minutes instead of hours. Perhaps you will be able to produce it in Falluja and save lives rather than destroy them.' There was an air of sarcasm in his voice and Kate detected it.

'Your country hasn't been invaded since 1066,' she countered. 'You are not facing an enemy threatening to wipe out your very existence and impose their medieval Sharia law. If you were facing such a threat from an army that outnumbers you by three to one, then you might understand why we have got to have defensive chemical weapons. We're going to need all the mustard gas we can get.' She stopped, she was cross and she wondered if she had gone too far.

'You're quite right, Kate. I'm sorry if I upset you. I guess it's that very argument that is behind Mrs Thatcher's decision. On another tack, I am recalled to London next month on promotion. I am to become our number-two at our Middle East desk. My successor is an Oxford man, but he can't help that, Mike Noble. When you want to contact him nothing changes; everything we discussed that night with James remains extant. Have you got anything to tell me?'

'Yes. General Tufiq has been instructed to assassinate Khomeini.'

'Really, how?'

'We're planning to poison him. I don't have any more details.' Kate thought she shouldn't mention her role in the affair and especially not reveal the existence of enditon.

'I don't think you will succeed. There are always a minimum of twelve protection officers around him. He has a team that tastes all his food and above all else he has at least two doppelgangers.'

'Two what?' Kate asked with a puzzled look.

'Doppelgangers, lookalikes, if you prefer. Actors made up to look and talk like him. They're so good they often take his place at rallies and no one knows.'

'In that case, how do you know?'

'We have recorded his speeches and had a computer analyse his voice patterns. A human can't tell the differences, but so far there have been three different people involved. I wish you luck with your quest, but you have only got a thirty-three per cent chance of getting the real Khomeini.'

'That's useful information. I'll report that back.'

They shook hands, Peter wishing her 'The best of British' and they departed.

It was on her way home that an important penny dropped.

The British know what I am doing. If they were to become our enemy, instead of our allies against the Iranians, what then?

***

From: British Embassy, Baghdad
Sun 2 Sep 79
Ref, Bgd/Int/241/5
To: Hd of Middle East Sect, MI6 London
Dear Harry
Ref, Agent Kathab al Jised (241/5)
Met KAJ this am. Informed her decision to leave anthrax alone – no probs. Gave her anti spores formula – no probs. She was tetchy when

criticised use of CBs. Warned her she is target if enemy realise her importance. She seemed surprised. Warned me Iraqi plot to ass Khomeini by poison. Told her about doppelgangers Assessment: believe her motivation still good, but in longer term? Still unsure. May have to be taken out at some future date.

Yours aye

Peter S

***

When Kate, the next weekend, introduced Amer to her father as Brigadier, she saw her dad's chest expand, and his height increase by several inches. Their warm handshake told her that Amer had her dad's approval even though he had only met him for less than a minute. By contrast, her mother was rather shy, neither knowing what to call him nor how to treat him.

'You never told us you were bringing a Brigadier home,' she mildly rebuked, when they were alone in the kitchen preparing dinner.

'Mum, he's just a man friend. Be your normal self.'

But Kate's words fell on deaf ears. Ala was excited, already imagining her eldest daughter marrying a brigadier.

The two men were alone in Qassim's library while dinner was cooking. Qassim was proudly showing Amer his collection of ancient scripts, when Amer chose to say, 'Sir, I want to ask you for Kathab's hand in marriage.'

The older man put his scripts down, looked Amer in the eye and asked, 'Does Kathab know?'

'Yes, I have made my intentions clear.'

'What did she say?'

'She invited me here for the weekend.'

'Then,' and thinking his daughter must have accepted, 'you have my blessing. I hope you will be as happy together as Ala and I. However, I must warn you that Kathab will not be able to give you any heirs. When

290

she was young she had to have an operation to remove an internal cyst. It was successful but left her sterile. Only Ala, Kathab and I know.'

'Sir, that doesn't worry me. As you know, I am a widower and have a son from my previous marriage. He lives with my mother. I am now almost forty-five. The thought of starting again with babies horrifies me.'

'Excellent,' replied Kate's dad. 'Please call me Qassim from now on.'

And at dinner, Qassim couldn't hide his pleasure, announcing to Ala proudly, 'Kathab and Amer are getting married.'

Kate dropped her spoon and Ala began to cry. She stood up and hugged her daughter. 'We're so proud of you,' she sobbed.

Oh my God, how do I get out of this?

'You must get married before your sisters go to Cairo next month,' said Qassim.

Kate was lost for words. All she could do was smile – an embarrassed smile. She was trapped. Like an animal in a snare, she could either struggle to get out and harm herself (and in this case, her parents too) or stay quiet and accept the inevitable. Her mind was racing nineteen to the dozen. She decided there were worse things in life than having a kind, quiet man as a husband. She would be thirty next month on 3rd October. She knew there would be few opportunities again. She'd had her fling with James and now he was dead. She should make the most of a bad job. She began consoling herself that it probably wouldn't be that bad anyway.

And so, a week later they were married in Samarra. Only very close relatives attended, including Amer's nine-year-old son. Ironically, he reminded Kate of Stuart. It didn't make their first night any more successful; her mind being elsewhere.

CHAPTER 33

Kate and Amer settled into their new home on the northern outskirts of Baghdad. It was convenient for Kate to go to work, less so for Amer – his job being in the city centre. Their busy lives meant that they only saw each other late in the evenings and at weekends. Kate had no regrets marrying Amer and was delighted that his son had not shown any resentment towards her. Their marriage was more akin to a brother and sister relationship than a passionate affair. This suited both of them. They never argued; they discussed disagreements sensibly and always came to equable solutions. She had told him that she worked for Tufiq as a double agent; he approved. She led Amer to believe it was simply a way of getting around embargos of chemicals, necessary for research. She warned him not to answer the phone unless it rang more than four times, explaining it was a signal that a meeting had to be arranged. He believed the signalling system was innocent and above board. Kate had decided it was better if her husband didn't know she was swapping state secrets occasionally. They enjoyed each other's company; knowing that their partner was their best friend. However, outside their cosy existence the world was moving apace.

***

At Kate's next meeting of the Revolutionary Council, in mid-September 1979, Tufiq outlined his plan to use enditon on Khomeini. Because he had a team who tasted all his food, a spray had to be used. A volunteer had agreed to get close to him at one of his many rallies. Tufiq proudly declared that his staff, meaning Kate's team, had tested the product successfully on elderly prisoners. He forecast Khomeini would be dead within two weeks. No one would ever know. Saddam, having sat quietly listening, turned and looked at Kate.

'Any comments?' he asked.

'Two things worry me. Firstly, the spray may spread if there is a wind and kill others in the vicinity. Even if used indoors, those nearby will be at risk, including the user of the spray. Secondly, when I was with one of the British Intelligence officers earlier this month,' she paused briefly and quickly added, 'with General Tufiq's agreement, Khomeini's name cropped up. The British have been recording his speeches and analysing his voices with a computer. There are at least three different Khomeinis.'

There was total silence. A pin could have been heard to drop.

'Are you telling me that old bugger has doppelgangers?' asked Saddam.

'Yes, sir,' replied Kate.

He turned, asking Tufiq, 'Did you know this?'

The General shuffled on his chair, looked uncomfortable and replied, 'Yes. Al Jised told me, but we've a thirty-three per cent chance of hitting the real Khomeini.' Kate felt Saddam wasn't convinced, but he never flinched.

'We'll go ahead. However, General, I want you to scour your officer corps. Find four men resembling me. You, Omar, I want you to find the best makeup artist, the best speech therapist and, if necessary, the best plastic surgeon. I believe Churchill had doppelgangers in the Second World War. So shall I. We'll show that old bugger Khomeini a trick or two.'

***

Kate and Amer had been married barely two months when the news on Baghdad Radio, Amer's choice at breakfast, announced, 'Militant

Islamists, mostly supporters who want Ayatollah Khomeini to become President of Iran, today stormed the United States Embassy in Tehran. They have taken seventy hostages. Their demands for the release of the prisoners are not known. A spokesman for US President Carter in Washington has demanded their immediate release. The UN Secretary General, Kurt Waldheim, has described the action as an outrage, and threatened sanctions against Iran.'

'That will play to our advantage,' said Amer.

'How come?' asked Kate.

'The Americans will cut off their supply of weapons and aircraft spares, and trade with us instead.'

***

3rd December 1979

The news on Baghdad Radio: 'It has been announced in Tehran that Ayatollah Khomeini has been appointed the Supreme Leader of Iran's Revolutionary Council. In a speech accepting his appointment, he has vowed to remove Saddam Hussein from power and restore Sharia Law in Iraq. He is quoted as saying that "Iraq will soon belong to the dustbin of history".'

'Saddam's not going to like that one little bit, even though he knew it was going to happen,' said Kate.

'The trouble is that we are not going to be in a position to go to war with them for at least another year. A shame really, because I suspect their armed forces are anti-Ayatollah as much as we are and pro-Western in outlook. They may even have welcomed us,' Amer replied.

Two weeks later, the attempt to assassinate Ayatollah Khomeini was implemented successfully. The problem was that statistics won. A doppelganger fell mysteriously ill after giving a speech in a hall in the northern city of Tabriz. Five others attending the rally also became ill and eventually died several weeks later. Tehran Radio announced that a viral infection called Legionnaires Disease was the cause. Apparently, it had emanated from the hall's air conditioning units that had not been maintained correctly. The manager of the complex was executed for failure of duty. The names of four of the dead were made public; the fifth dead man was unknown. The radio announced, 'Ayatollah Khomeini is in hospital and is making a full recovery. He is expected to leave hospital tomorrow.'

Several days went by. The phone rang in the office. 'Kathab,' she recognised Tufiq's voice immediately. Kate had never known him call her by her first name before.

He obviously wants something.

'I want you to meet your British contact and find out if we hit the real Khomeini. Despite Tehran Radio claiming he recovered, we know the Khomeini we sprayed is dead. Unfortunately, our agent died a true martyr.'

And so, Kate met her new contact, Mike Noble, for the first time on 21st December 1979. He was more distant than Peter. She excused his manner. After all, she had spent some time with Peter and got to know him reasonably well. *We were both Cambridge University alumni.*

However, Mike Noble, for whatever reason, gave her the impression that he saw her as someway inferior. She decided she didn't like him. She tried to break the ice with comments about Oxford and Cambridge rivalry, but this didn't work. 'Why do you want to see me?' he asked coldly. He seemed to be thinking that their information flow would always be one way.

'I have a favour to ask,' she began. 'Do you know whether we killed the real Khomeini?'

'I was expecting you to ask us that.' He laughed in a condescending manner. 'Fraid you missed the bull's eye; only got an outer.'

'How can you be so sure?' Kate asked, annoyed at his cocky arrogance.

'Computer analysis, old girl. Yesterday, the real Khomeini definitely sat in their parliament. Luckily for you they believe their own story about Legionnaires Disease, what?'

Being called an old girl was the final straw. Kate exploded. 'Look you public school, Oxford-educated prat, with your worthless degree in PPE, get one thing straight. I'm putting my neck on the line. I know the location of enough anthrax to destroy half of Europe and will be supplying your side with information when we go to war with Iran that will be invaluable. Make no mistake, if you don't give me total support, and I mean one hundred per cent co-operation, then your boss Peter Stacey will get to know about it quicker than shit can fly off a blanket. Right?' She knew she'd confused her metaphor, *but what the hell?* The look on his face was worth it.

He gulped, looked sheepishly at his shoes, and nodded. A woman had never spoken to him like that before. Indeed, Kate had never spoken to a man like that before.

They parted without saying farewell.

***

From: British Embassy, Baghdad
21 Dec 79
To: Hd of Middle East Sect
MI6 London
Dear Harry
Ref Agent Kathab al Jised (241/5)
Met KAJ for first time this am. A very tetchy young woman. Wanted to know if Iraqis successful assassinating Khomeini. Became aggressive when said no. Wonder if she is worth keeping on books.
Yours etc
Mike

***

From: MI6 London

22 Dec 79

To: British Embassy, Baghdad

FAO, Mike Noble

Ref, Agent Kathab al Jised (241/5)

Harry P been promoted upstairs. Am now Hd of desk. Patience! KAJ can be temperamental (she once gave me a bollocking!). Potentially excellent source of material (our only agent with ears in Iraq's Rev Council). Handle her with kid gloves and she will respond.

Good Luck

Peter Stacey

***

25th December 1979

Baghdad Radio reported: 'The Soviet Union has invaded Afghanistan.'

'Shh, listen,' Amer said to Kate over breakfast. The radio continued with the story that the Afghan government had requested help from the Soviets to quell uprisings by Taliban guerrillas in the north-east of the country.

'I fear the Soviets don't know what they've let themselves in for,' remarked Amer when the bulletin finished. 'They have created for themselves a Vietnam. They will come to regret it in years to come. However, the Iranians will now have to keep an eye on the giant bear on their northern border. It will consume some of their resources – all good news for us.'

The New Year came. It saw Kate and Amer busier than ever. Kate's teams continued to research their weapons; seeking more efficient methods of production in readiness for the two chemical factories being built. The target was to commission both toward the end of the year.

However, ever since her bust-up with Noble, she had begun to analyse her own personality. Her reaction that day had surprised her, *so unusual for me to be so intolerant.* She was changing. She could feel herself hardening; becoming less caring about others. The business of dealing with weapons of mass destruction on a daily basis was dampening her natural philanthropic disposition. Her social conscience was being replaced by a lack of concern. The job mattered, nothing else. Her brooding malevolence wasn't deliberate, it seemed outside her control. Rubbing shoulders with some of the most evil men in Iraq was affecting her. She spent long hours in the evenings, particularly when Amer was away, worrying about why she no longer cared about the possible long-term consequences to humanity of her work. Her sisters had both settled well at Cairo University. She corresponded with them regularly. Her parents were still in Samarra and covertly Qassim was still moving his nest eggs to Jordan. Her marriage to Amer was ticking along nicely. There was nothing for her to be worried about, but she worried nevertheless.

I must keep a sense of proportion. I don't want to become like Ali Hassan, or Tufiq.

Her introspection was, however, self-denial. She couldn't bring herself to accept that there was already blood on her hands. At the back of her head, Roya Talfah was haunting her.

That winter, relations between Iraq and Iran deteriorated. There were constant incidents on the Shatt al-Arab waterway such as Iranian militia firing on Iraqi patrols. Iranian gun boats were regularly impeding ships bound for Iraq in the Persian Gulf. Kurds, with arms supplied by the Iranians, were attacking isolated Iraqi police posts in the north. Chemical Ali's response was to bomb Kurd villages with what few supplies of mustard gas and cyanide were available. In one attack up to 3,000 people were killed. Ali was satisfied, Kate horrified. Fortunately, Kate was able to prevent him demanding the use of anthrax or gangrennex. However, she knew her promises of manna tomorrow, *when we get the Fallujas on line,* would not keep him off her back for ever.

On 2nd April 1980, whilst visiting Baghdad University an attempt was made to assassinate deputy Prime Minister, Tariq Aziz. A group of radicals, members of the banned Shia party, the DAWA, threw a grenade at him. Five students were killed while Tariq escaped relatively unharmed. DAWA's stated purpose was the creation of an Islamic State in Iraq. Saddam reacted by declaring anyone found to be a member of DAWA, whose head quarters were in Tehran, would be executed.

***

21st April 1980

Tehran Radio announced that an attempt by United States marines to liberate the American hostages had backfired. The operation, code named Eagle Claw, collapsed when helicopters carrying marines crashed whilst refuelling. Eight Americans were reported dead. US President Jimmy Carter admitted the failure to a press conference in Washington. 'Tens of thousands of Iranians have flooded onto the streets of Tehran shouting the praise of Ayatollah Khomeini and demanding the public execution of the American hostages.'

'Trust the Yanks to make a cock-up. Khomeini's popularity will go sky high. All they've done is to add fuel to the fire,' groaned Amer.

***

6th May 1980

Baghdad Radio announced: 'A siege of the Iranian Embassy in London by six Iraqi nationalists wanting independence for Arabstan ended yesterday when a team of specialist British forces, known as the Special Air Service, or SAS, stormed the building. Five of the Iraqis were shot dead in cold blood. A statement by the Iraqi Foreign Minister, Tariq

Aziz, denies any Iraqi Government involvement and condemns the callous treatment of those shot.'

'I only hope that we didn't have anything to do with it,' remarked Kate. 'Otherwise the assistance we're getting from Mrs Thatcher's government might stop.'

'I hope so too. Unfortunately, you can never tell with the Bloody PISS. They're a law unto themselves,' replied Amer.

***

By June 1980, diplomatic relations between Iraq and Iran had been severed. Cross-border clashes increased. There were regular reports of Iranians making forays by night across the Shatt al-Arab waterway to blow up easy targets such as water towers, telephone lines and so on. The war had effectively begun.

Amer had day-to-day responsibility for munitions procurement. Trips were made to Soviet Russia to discuss Iraq's specific requirements. Consequently, he was frequently away for long periods of time, sometimes up to a month. Stocks of arms of all types were being procured. New sites had to be found and built for storage and maintenance. Four new Maintenance Units were rapidly built west of Baghdad, carefully camouflaged and well away from centres of population. Between October 1979 and April 1980 Iraq had increased its weapons stocks by 200 per cent. Amer's brief was to increase the stocks by a further 300 per cent by September 1980. One day with Kate, he confided the significance of his deadline. 'By September we will have sufficient munitions for two and a half years of war. Don't be surprised if the balloon doesn't go up then.'

She decided to warn her father, as any loving daughter would.

Kate was asked to attend the meeting of the Revolutionary Council on 16th July. Tufiq had asked to see her an hour before their assembly. 'This will be the crunch. I suspect Saddam will give us two months to prepare for war. What is the situation with our chemical and biological weapons?' he asked.

'Not good. We have got nothing in sufficient quantities. Until the Falluja sites are up and running, it's going to stay that way. I believe the Germans expect to hand over Falluja 2 at the end of August and the Japs a month later. We will not be able to produce weapons in the quantities we want for at least a further year. I have been getting the raw materials and stockpiling them, but training engineers and technicians takes time.'

'Can we not purchase the weapons we want directly?' Tufiq asked.

'Only the Americans have what we want. Until President Carter is booted out then I can't see them being very helpful. Can you?'

'The latest plays of Nastia Game are suggesting we can win Arabstan in less than six months with a following wind. We have sufficient conventional weapons to last much longer than this, so, hopefully, everything will be OK.'

'I seem to remember Squadron Leader Douglas thinking the war would get bogged down, like the First World War. It could drag on for years.'

'Let's hope he was wrong. If it does, then we're going to need all the chemicals you can produce to defend ourselves,' commented Tufiq somewhat mournfully.

CHAPTER 34

The meeting was, as Tufiq suspected, the crunch. Saddam was clearly frustrated with Iran's interference with his shipping in the Persian Gulf, the cross-border incidents and the claim by Ayatollah Khomeini that the Shatt al-Arab waterway was Iranian territory. Khomeini did not accept the Algiers Accord, made in 1975 with the Shah, which set the centre of the waterway as the boundary. Above all, the attempt on Tariq Aziz's life irked Saddam. 'All our troops are to be put on five days' notice,' he declared. 'I don't want to do anything in the next two months unless I have to, but by mid-September we must be ready to roll.'

The usual topics came up on the agenda, including Kate summarising the parlous state of CB weapons. 'We won't need them,' interrupted the great man. 'Arabstan will be ours within six weeks. Its population is largely Sunni. They will see us as liberators and welcome us with open arms. We will have total control of the Shatt al-Arab waterway. We will fortify Arabstan's eastern boundary and we will have a deep sea port for all time.'

For much of the rest of the meeting, Kate had no input. She observed, however, that the generals were in high spirits. They believed that the revolution in Iran had destabilised the country. Most of the Shah's Army had been disbanded. Officer purges had been particularly brutal. The Ayatollah had alienated Western governments, especially the Americans, and so a shortage of spare parts was crippling their military. The Iranian defences along the Shatt al-Arab, it was thought, would be minimal.

On 20th July 1980, Kate arranged, with Tufiq's approval, to meet her British contact, Mike Noble, for only the second time. She had used the reason, 'we desperately need growth cultures to further research into vexun.' She needn't have bothered with an excuse; Tufiq had his mind elsewhere preparing for war.

Noble was a changed man. He apologised for giving her the wrong impression at their first meeting and asked, 'How can I be of help?'

She smiled.

That's better. Amazing what taking a tough line can achieve with Hooray Henrys.

She gave him an ambitious list, half expecting him not to bother looking. However, unlike her final meeting with Peter Stacey, he examined it carefully, line by line.

'What's this?' he asked, pointing to the last item. 'Five hundred tons of talcum powder to be odourless, medium grey, and 3 to 4 microns in diameter. It is to be labelled mercuric silicate kyanite. Surely not?'

'It's the most important item,' Kate replied. 'I need it to be able to dilute our more dangerous substances.'

'I don't follow you,' he queried.

'Look. The real reason I've asked to see you today is to let you know that we are going to war in the middle of September. I don't know the exact date, but it's definitely on. Furthermore, our two production sites at Falluja will be completed soon afterwards. By the middle of next year we will be producing our own CB weapons in large quantities. If Ali Hassan wants to use chemicals on the Iranians then I will need a harmless filler substance to reduce their effects. Whatever happens, I will not allow anthrax, gas gangrene, or gangrennex to be used.'

'But, surely, they will eventually cotton on to what you have done?'

'I will try to prevent that from happening for as long as I can, but if it does, then I shall have to escape. You will have to bring me in, as promised.'

'I will report this immediately. You will get these substances as soon as possible.'

They parted on better terms than previously.

⁎

From: British Embassy, Baghdad
21 Jul 80
Ref, Bgd/Int/241/5
To: Hd of Middle East Sect, MI6 London
Dear Peter
Ref, Agent Kathab al Jised (241/5)
Met KAJ yesterday. You were right, she is potentially valuable source. Two points,
War definitely will start mid-Sep (exact date uncertain)
KAJ needs talc as filler to dilute weapons. Believe she has conscience and won't allow worst Bs to be used whatever circumstances.
Yours Mike

⁎

From: MI6, London
22 Jul 80
To: British Embassy, Baghdad
FAO, Mike Noble
Ref, Agent Kathab al Jised (241/5)
Told you kid gloves would work! Date of war noted. Our DOAE at West Byfleet forecasts stalemate by Christmas. Will make sure she gets her talcum powder!
Yours aye
Peter S

⁎

On 17th September 1980, Saddam declared that both sides of the Shatt al-Arab waterway were Iraqi territory. Five days later a full scale invasion was launched. The primary objectives were to secure the waterway and annex Arabstan. Secondary aims were to regain disputed lands around Mehran and Dars-e-Shirin. Politically, Saddam wanted to overthrow Khomeini and establish Iraq as the major player in the Middle East.

The Iranians appeared to be taken by surprise and Iraqi advances were initially rapid. A three-pronged attack was used. In the north, the Iranian border town of Dars-e-Shirin was seized on the first day. Troops then advanced a further fifteen miles into the foothills of the Zagros Mountains, stopped and dug in. A lesson had been learned from Nastia Game, don't advance; simply prevent any Iranian counteroffensive from Kermanshah.

In the centre, a similar ploy was put into effect. Troops advanced towards Mehran, stopped short and blocked any possible counter advances from the town. Both of these attacks were swiftly and efficiently carried out with few casualties. They allowed the main thrust to be made in the south.

The third prong was into Arabstan, where two-thirds of the population were Sunni. The Iraqis had always believed the province should have been a part of Iraq when the Ottoman Empire was carved up after World War One. Eight of the Iraqi Army's twelve divisions were deployed. Three divisions advanced towards the three main centres of population in the northern sector, Susangerd, Dezful and Ahwaz. However, they met heavy resistance and progress halted. In the southern sector three divisions were ferried across the Shatt al-Arab intending to capture Khorram Shar; then use it as a base to seize Abadan. Unfortunately, the lessons from Nastia Game did not appear to have been learned. The armoured Iraqis found fighting in the built-up areas to be a death trap. Their training for such conditions had been either skimpy or ignored. Using only rifles, grenades and hand-made bombs, the Iranians were able to employ ambush tactics in the narrow streets filled with obstacles. Losses were high. It took two weeks and 5,000 Iraqis died securing the town.

The fighting hadn't all been one way, however. The Iranian Navy, the least affected of the three forces by Khomeini's revolutionary purges, bombarded the Iraqi port of Al-Faw, knocking out two major oil refineries. They were to blockade the port for the rest of the war, trapping inside thirty-three Iraqi ships. This meant that future Iraqi supplies had to be channelled through other friendly Gulf States, such as Kuwait, Saudi Arabia and Bahrain.

Late September 1980 had seen the Falluja 2 plant finished and handed over to the Iraqis by the Germans; Falluja 1 was only three weeks behind. However, it put pressure on Kate. She was to have overall day-to-day responsibility for both plants and be directly responsible to Sahib al-Majid for their efficiency. She had been given the job of selecting the senior staff to run the two plants. Each had to have a managing director. She chose engineers rather than accountants, her reasoning being that when it came to matters of State security, money would not be a problem. She had appointed both in June, giving them carte blanche to make decisions on how they would run and organise their plants. Falluja 1 was to produce biological weapons such as ricin and botulinium toxin while Falluja 2 would concentrate on chemical weapons such as mustard gas and zarin. Recruiting engineers, technicians, accountants and administrators had been rapid throughout the autumn. Training courses had commenced by the time the war was getting bogged down in the rainy season. Kate had every reason to believe the plants would be fully operative by March 1981.

***

5th November 1980

Baghdad Radio was making its usual daily claims of huge gains in the war with Iran. Kate knew the truth. Amer, working long hours in the Iraqi War Office, had told her of the problems facing their troops. She had remarked at the breakfast table, about the only time they could ever talk to each other, that she remembered Squadron Leader Douglas warning Azi that being unable to simulate the weather was a major weakness of Nastia Game. 'He forecast then that a stalemate would ensue,' she had said.

'I fear he was right,' agreed Amer mournfully.

The next item on the news made them both sit up. 'The new President of the United States is to be the former Governor of California, Ronald Reagan. He carried forty-four of the fifty-one states against his opponent, the outgoing President Jimmy Carter. He has vowed to lower taxes and increase spending on the military. He will be inaugurated in January to become the fortieth President.

'That's interesting,' said Kate. 'It might mean we will be able to get chemicals from America in future.'

***

Having finally taken Khorram Shar, the Iraqi Army stopped for almost a month, deciding to use the time to train troops in hand-to-hand combat. It was, therefore, November when they began the siege of Abadan. Abadan is an island, the Shatt to the west, the Gulf to the south, the Bahamsheer River to the east and the Karun River to the north. The heavy rain had started. The rivers were swollen, the roads quagmires, the marshes became lakes. The Iraqis could only get across the Karun River in disjointed spurts and met fanatical resistance. What had been planned to take weeks was taking months. Casualties were unexpectedly high and the consumption of munitions greater than forecast. Furthermore, the Iranians were reinforcing rapidly. They set up forward command centres on the higher ground in Dezful and Ahvez, whilst the Iraqis had to waste resources building flood control banks and all-weather roads to hold their positions in the lower plains.

By early December, with Abadan still under Iranian control, the war was in a stalemate. The weather precluded any further fighting. The pause was allowing Iran to reorganise its Army and Air Force. Under the common threat from Iraq, the revolutionary Islamists and the old guard traditionalists agreed to bury the hatchet. Although the United States had cut off supplying Iran with spares, Israel saw Iraq as the greater threat. Spares for Iran's American equipment began to arrive on Israeli ships in exchange for oil. The Iran-Contra affair had begun.

***

19th January 1981

Baghdad radio announced: 'Today President Ronald Reagan is being inaugurated as the fortieth President of the United States. Government sources are saying that this will be the start of a new relationship with America. It is being hinted that full diplomatic relations will soon be resumed.'

***

20th January 1981

After the usual propaganda about the expected resumption of battles to 'finally liberate Arabstan', Baghdad radio threw in a brief note at the end of the news bulletin. 'After prolonged discussions over several months in Algeria, it has been announced that the Iranian Government is to release the seventy American hostages that have been held in Tehran for a total of 444 days.'

'That's interesting,' remarked Amer.

'Why?' asked Kate.

'Because the Americans must have given something in return and I'll bet it is spares and ammunition for the Iranian Air Force. They're two-faced. Don't ever trust the Yanks, Kate. Whatever chemicals they offer you, there'll be a sting in the tail.'

***

The next meeting of the Revolutionary Council that Kate attended was held a week after President Reagan's inauguration. Considering the state of the war, Saddam was in a good mood. He told the meeting that the Americans had been in touch and expressed an interest in restoring full diplomatic relations after a break that had lasted thirteen years. 'They are, today, removing us from their list of so-called terrorist countries and have promised to give us satellite intelligence. We will be able to see what the Iranians are up to from outer space. Even as I speak, twelve American intelligence advisers are on their way to give us aid and train our staff.'

A ripple of applause went around the table. Kate politely followed the others, but Amer's words were ringing in her ears. 'Don't ever trust the Yanks.'

CHAPTER 35

Owing to the atrocious weather, the lines drawn between the opposing forces in November 1980 remained largely static throughout the winter. Small skirmishes and occasional firing of shells and missiles did occur, but casualties were not great on either side. The Soviets, who had initially stopped supplying Saddam when the war started, resumed supplies. They had realised the reputation of their equipments' performance was at stake. Meanwhile, Egypt had sold the Iraqis $2 billion worth of their Soviet-manufactured equipment to satisfy Iraqi consumption.

The lengthy lull in the fighting allowed the Iranians to reorganise their Army despite much mistrust remaining between the Army hierarchy, the militia and the ayatollahs. The Iranian Army moved in force to Kazistan, but the mullahs positioned their militia behind the troops. It was a ploy to prevent desertion in the ranks. A counter-attack was planned around Dezful, but unknown to the Iranians, Iraq was alerted to the preparations by the American spy satellites. The result, on 28th January 1981, was a massacre. The Iraqis were able to feign a withdrawal from the advancing Iranians, box them in to a killing zone that was little better than a sea of mud and their artillery did the rest. Some 10,000 Iranians were either killed or injured. They fled the battle field leaving some one hundred tanks bogged down behind them. Fortunately for them, the Iraqis couldn't pursue because of the terrible condition of the terrain. Ayatollah Khomeini's reaction was to dismiss his president, Badi-Sadr.

The war during the summer remained relatively quiet as the Iranians continued to sort out their differences. When the power struggle was finally resolved, the Army and militia began joint operations; their tactics and planning improved.

Nevertheless, the Iraqis gradually wore down resistance and captured Abadan. To their surprise the local Sunnis showed no enthusiasm to help. It seemed nationalism was stronger than sectarianism; a sporadic guerrilla street war ensued.

Kate's father had sold his house. He and Ala had moved to Cairo. Kate was sorry to see them depart, but Amer was sympathetic to their move. He supported them by using his contacts in the military to get them the necessary visas. Kate promised to visit them at least every year, but knew that with the war and the Falluja plants becoming productive, it was a hollow promise.

Amer had told Kate that the Americans were now working closely with the Army and Air Force planners. The dozen initial advisers had mushroomed. He estimated there may be as many as one hundred in Baghdad. 'Fortunately, I do not come into contact with them,' he said. Kate noted his antipathy towards them, but didn't ask why. She suspected her husband was anti-Semitic and considered any friends of Israel to be enemies of Iraq. His attitude made her feel uncomfortable as she was indifferent to Jews. She had met many at Cambridge and had always found them to be courteous and friendly. However, her understanding of her husband's point of view was to undergo a dramatic change.

***

7th June 1981

There was only one topic on Baghdad Radio at breakfast. The announcer was animated. 'This morning Israeli F-15 American bombers attacked and destroyed the nuclear reactor at Osirak. The Satanist Israeli Prime Minister, Menachem Begin, personally ordered the cowardly raid. The seventy megawatt uranium powered reactor was nearing completion. It

311

was due to go on-line and produce electricity in three months' time. The reactor was being built with the help of the French Government. It is reported that at least seventy-five people have been killed, including several French technicians. The French Government has issued an international condemnation of the attack.'

'Saddam is not going to like this,' said Amer. 'You can't trust the Yanks. I bet they planned the attack. It would be their aircraft and their missiles that were used. It was the same in the 1973 war – they were on both sides.'

Kate had never seen him so livid.

***

Two days later Kate found herself attending a meeting of the Revolutionary Council. She had never seen Saddam like it before. He was raging about the bloody Zionists. He told the assembled members that he was bringing forward a plan that he had had on the drawing board for over a year. He was contracting a Canadian ballistics consultant, Gerard Bull, to build two super guns, each having a 1,000 mm calibre. They would be capable of firing 1,000 lb bombs over a distance of 650 miles. 'We are calling this *Project Babylon,* as, like the tower, we are reaching for the sky,' he said. He was visibly swelling with pride as he told the surprised audience.

He must have an incredible number of secret groups working for him, Kate thought. *It's obvious none of his generals knew about this, judging from their reactions.*

Saddam continued. 'These super guns will be positioned to destroy Tel Aviv and Tehran. The world will sit up and see they cannot ignore us. Bull tells me the guns will be able to put a small satellite into space.'

Saddam allowed the meeting to descend into a rowdy, excitable free-for-all. Everyone was vying to congratulate their leader. It was Tufiq who iced the cake when he announced that waiting outside he had four potential doppelgangers. 'Bring them in,' Saddam boomed, 'but they'd better be as handsome as me, Tufiq, or you're for the chop!' Everyone laughed, even Tufiq, although Kate thought she saw a tiny hint of fear in his eyes.

When Kate saw the four men, she smiled to herself. Tufiq had done well. They all looked like the great man himself.

***

As the biological weapons began to come off the production lines, Kate had to spend more and more of her time planning where to bury them. It was the one aspect of her job that she couldn't delegate. She insisted on going alone to the chosen sites with only the itinerant workers and an NCO driver.

She was sitting in her office, poring over a map of an area west of Tikrit, when her phone rang. Her secretary buzzed through. 'It's Lieutenant Colonel Azi Tumbrah for you.'

'Hello, Azi. How are you?' she asked enthusiastically. She hadn't spoken to him since their meeting outside the Armenian Church, two and a half years previously. They exchanged pleasantries, commenting on how time flies and catching up with news.

Azi hadn't realised Kate had got married. His reaction was positive. 'I'm delighted for you, Kate, I really am. Amer is a good man. He will look after you.'

It doesn't work that way, Azi. I look after him, she thought. *Any woman will tell you that.*

Conversation continued for several minutes, before Azi said, 'The reason I'm ringing is to let you know that I've been ordered to give the chess key of Nastia Game to the American advisers who are swarming all over this place. It's Tufiq's orders. I thought you'd want to know.'

'Why do the Yanks want the key?' asked Kate.

'I don't know. I've persuaded Tufiq that I only give them an early copy of the data base so that they don't know all our secrets.' He paused. 'You know that we now have the sites where you have chosen to hide our CBs on the system?'

Not the actual sites, you don't!

'Yes, I knew Tufiq was putting the locations on the game's files. As long as the Yanks don't know everything then I guess it will be OK. I do wonder what their interest is, however. I vaguely remember James telling me that it would be impossible to work out the encryption algorithms even if the key was in the public domain. Although now I think about it, it may have been Ray Kane who told me. I can't remember. I'm sorry, but thanks for letting me know. Perhaps the Americans think they can work backwards from the chess key. Amer and I must get you and Sawsan to come over for dinner one evening.'

Amer's words echoed in her ears: *The bloody Yanks, you can never trust them.*

***

Two days later she arranged to meet Mike Noble and gave him a list of requirements. He took it and asked, 'Did you get your talcum powder?'

'Yes, thanks. It's safely stored away. However, the reason I wanted to see you as soon as possible was not to give you that list. Your men in London will want to know that the Americans have got the chess key to Nastia Game. I assume Peter Stacey briefed you on my involvement?'

'Yes, he did. Do you know how they got it and why?'

'Not exactly, but it must have been in exchange for something they are giving us. This could be critical. If the Yanks can, in some way, work backwards and crack the algorithms that encode the data and software then, who knows?' She left the sentence hanging.

'Don't worry; I'll report it back straight away. I'll make sure you get your wish-list. Is there anything else?'

'Yes,' she hesitated, unsure whether she should divulge such a secret to him. 'Saddam has found a Canadian, Gerard Bull, to build him two large guns. They are to have a 1,000 mm calibre and be able to fire 1,000 lb shells up to 650 miles. They will be aimed at Tel Aviv and Tehran.'

'I would have thought it would be impossible to build such a gun.'

'I would have thought so too, but Saddam seemed confident when he announced it at the last Council meeting.'

'Do you know any other details, such as where they are to be positioned?'

'No, that's all I know.'

'OK. We'll try to keep in touch.'

They left. Noble's opinion of Kate's usefulness had rocketed.

***

From: British Embassy, Baghdad
18 Jun 81
Ref, Bgd/Int/241/5
To: Hd Middle East Sect, MI6 London
Dear Peter
Ref, Agent Kathab al Jised (241/5)
Met KAJ earlier.

1. She is certain Americans have acquired chess key to Nastia Game. Believes Americans given diluted data base info. Thinks in exchange for satellite info on Iranian positions.

2. Saddam is employing a Canadian, Gerard Bull, to build 2 guns capable of firing 1,000 lb shells 650 miles. Targets: Tel Aviv and Tehran.

A good girl this!
Yours Mike

***

From: MI6, London
18 Jun 81
To: British Embassy, Baghdad
FAO, Mike Noble
Ref, Agent Kathab al Jised (241/5)

Possible Nastia Game compromise and big guns (I don't believe it!) reported to Hd Military Intelligence Committee.

Told you she was good. Next meeting give her my regards. Ask her to get more info on guns – esp. where sited.

Yours Peter

CHAPTER 36

The news of the Americans getting the key to Nastia Game reached the desk of Rear Admiral Johnson on Friday, 19th June. He immediately called for impact statements from the various groups using the chess-key system for computer security in MoD. However, although he had given them three weeks to respond, few replies had been received when on Tuesday, 30th June, the following announcements were made in *The Times*:

Senior Appointments in the Services

Rear Admiral B J Johnson to be CinC Nav Home, in the rank of Vice-Admiral, with effect Tuesday, 1 September 1981.

Brigadier I A Morrison to be Chairman Military Intelligence Committee, in the rank of Major General, with effect Monday, 24 August 1981.

Group Captain J O'Rourke to be Deputy Chairman MIC, in the rank of Air Commodore, with effect Monday, 24 August 1981.

Handovers in the military rarely last longer than one week; even for senior officers. Most posts have a comprehensive standing brief that describes the job, the necessary contacts, and its procedures in some detail. Both Brian Johnson and Ian Morrison had known of their respective promotions several months before the announcements were made public. John O'Rourke's appointment was made much later. Consequently, Brian and Ian had agreed to combine the two handovers into one. The first two days were largely taken up with one-hour presentations given by security and intelligence specialists from other Government Departments such as the Foreign Office, the Home Office and the Metropolitan Police. Much of the emphasis in the briefings was given to the threat from the IRA.

One of the briefings given on the second morning was by the Government's Senior Scientific Officer, a civilian of three-star status. In his team, supporting him, were various specialists including a computer security expert, Dr Richard Kelly.

'Have you come to any conclusions about the significance of the Americans getting the chess key? I am thinking of the possible breach of security in projects such as Ptolemy,' asked Major General Morrison.

'The latest thinking is that our systems will remain secure, sir,' replied Dr Kelly. 'Shall I explain why?'

'Yes, please do,' replied the General.

'The secret of achieving unbreakable codes is random numbers. The German Enigma machine in the Second World War had 10^5 possible starting positions. By comparison, the most authoritative estimate of the number of chess positions, known as the Shannon Number, is 10^{120}. Bearing in mind that there are only 10^{81} atoms in the universe, then you can see what a clever trick it was to kick start randomising from a chess position.' He paused to see if his audience were taking it in. All three senior officers nodded; although he suspected the Air Commodore was already lost.

He continued, largely for the RAF man's benefit. 'Putting it another way, the most powerful computer, a multi-processor Cray, would take from now until doomsday to guess all the possibilities and would still only be half way there.' He stopped again. The airman looked happier. 'The second part of the process to encrypt data is the algorithm. The Dataskil Algorithm, as my team call it, uses the three fundamental elements of evaluating a chess position: material, space and time.' Dr

Kelly paused for a moment. He could see he was leaving all three officers behind.

There were three blank faces in front of him. 'Let me explain. The easiest element to evaluate is material. White may be a pawn up, for example. If the other two elements were even then it is highly likely that White is winning.' There was a glimmer of understanding. 'Space is the second element. A player can sacrifice material to gain an overwhelming space advantage. A player might sacrifice his queen to mate his opponent a few moves later. He wins even though he has much less material.' There was light in their eyes. 'Finally, time. A player can lose even if he has the advantage of material and space. Skilled players often complicate the position and swindle their opponents by getting them into desperate time trouble.'

'All very interesting, Dr Kelly, but what has this got to do with the question?' asked the General.

'I'm coming to that, sir. The algorithm designed at Dataskil was, to put it simply, brilliant. If they'd put a copyright on it, they'd have made a fortune. It used the material in the chess position to calculate the first random number. Do you want me to explain how?' There was a shaking of heads. 'It then calculated the second random number by evaluating the spaces on the board controlled by White. The algorithm would then kick in and begin calculating a sequence of random numbers by a complex set of rules involving addition and multiplication.'

They seemed to be keeping up. 'Now for the clever bit; while producing the numbers, the computer is simultaneously playing the original chess position forward. Whenever a piece is captured, it recalculates the material and space on the board. Two new random numbers are created to begin a new sequence using the algorithm. Sometimes this occurs every few micro-seconds, but, depending on the position, it may not happen for several minutes. Put another way, the random numbers are being randomised depending on the initial chess position. The guys who designed the system should get MBEs for their efforts.'

'I'm afraid they're all dead,' remarked the Admiral mournfully. No one in the room noticed General Morrison's right eyebrow rise, ever so slightly, as he looked at the Admiral.

'I'm sorry, sir. I didn't know that.'

'Look. I'm a simple *Brown-Job*.' The General laughed at his own joke. He continued, looking at Dr Kelly. 'On my right is a *Fish-head* and on my left, a *Crab*. We are simple soldiers. Am I right in thinking that without the starting position, no computer in the world can break the codes?'

'Yes.'

'But the Americans have the starting position?' queried the General.

'What they've got won't help them to break into any of our systems. It will only allow them to understand how they work, nothing else. They will probably copy the method from now on to secure their own computer systems. A locksmith knows how a lock works, but he can't open the door without the key. In this case there are an infinite number of combinations to stop him picking it.'

Admiral Johnson thought, *I think I've heard that argument once before.*

The three officers took a short lunch-break together. Everything was proceeding as expected, although Ian Morrison had noticed the Admiral was rather quiet. 'What's on your mind, Brian?' he asked.

'Now that the Americans know how the chess code works, I was thinking about all that trouble we went to three years ago. Ironical really, the system was impregnable all along. Mrs Douglas and her daughter died for nothing.'

'You never really got over that episode, did you?' asked Ian. He turned to his successor. 'John, remind me to fill you in on the history of the chess codes some time.'

The Admiral remained silent for several minutes, thinking of Emma's and Jennifer's murder, the movement of James, his son and in-laws to Fort Halstead, and the subsequent debacle at Castleblaney. Then he said, 'Ian, if you don't mind, I'll take tomorrow off. I have a job I must do on my own.'

He went into his office and spoke to his PSO. 'Lewis, get me the outer office of John Nott, will you? Urgently, that's a dear chap.'

By 1400 hours, Admiral Johnson was sitting in the Minister of Defence's outer office on the 7th floor of the MoD Main Building. He had never been inside the Minister's office before and he was apprehensive. John Nott had a reputation for having a short fuse and being anti-Royal Navy. He had met him briefly once before at a dining-in night held on *HMS Victory*; he hadn't taken to him. It was no secret amongst Royal Navy senior officers that the Minister had inaugurated an inquiry into the Navy's future having decided already what the outcome should be.

Arriving a few minutes early, the Personal Private Secretary had given Admiral Johnson the 'Release of Information from the Agency Protection Department (APD)' form that needed to be signed. Admiral Johnson had carefully filled in the details, as he knew them, of the person on whom he sought the facts. As he waited to be called in, he wondered how much the Minister might ask about why he wanted the information. Indeed, he wondered how much he should tell him.

A large panelled door opposite him opened and John Nott entered the outer office. Looking incredibly dapper, he strode towards the Admiral, arm outstretched. 'Brian, nice to meet you again,' he said smiling. 'What can I do for you?'

'I need you to sign this form, sir. It will allow me to access information on someone who has been protected under the APS, the Agency Protection Scheme, for several years.'

'Why? What's he done?' asked the Minister.

'He's not done anything, sir. He had to be protected when the CIA murdered his mother and sister and the IRA killed his father.'

'So what's changed?'

'We believe the Americans have got what they were after from another source. He could now be in danger.' Admiral Johnson was lying, trying to give away as little as possible.

At that moment, the PPS's phone rang. He picked it up, listened for a few seconds and turned to his boss. 'It's the PM's outer office for you, sir. They say she sounds angry.'

Nott's face reddened. He took the form, scribbled his signature on the bottom and handed it back to the Admiral saying, 'I must go.' He turned and disappeared into his office, banging the door behind him.

The Main Building has seven floors above ground floor and three below. It was into the bowels that Admiral Johnson went next, to find the APD. After descending to the basement in the lift, he had to walk down stairs to the lower basement and along what seemed miles of dimly lit, dark green corridors. The APD was little more than a registry. After scrutinisation of his pass and form by, what he guessed, was an elderly spinster who had been there since WW2, he was ushered to a hard chair and a small table.

Without saying a word, she took the form and disappeared into a back room, coming back minutes later with a purple folder, which she handed to the Admiral.

'Can I take notes?' he asked.

She looked at his release form. 'No,' she replied. 'You only have authorisation to inspect the file, not to take it away.'

'I don't want to take it away. I only want to copy some of its information.' The Admiral could feel his blood pressure rising.

These bloody civil servants, they think they own the place.

'If you were to copy the file or parts of it, then that would be the same as taking it away.'

The Admiral sighed. He knew she was right, of course. He just wished she wasn't so damned condescending and showed him some respect. He knew he should have checked what the form allowed him to do.

The file cover simply had a file number and nothing else. He was surprised, as MoD files always carried a title on the front cover as well as a file number.

He opened the slim volume. On the left inside cover was a photo. He recognised the face instantly. Opposite was a page with various data fields. Some had been filled, many had not. He glanced down the sheet. He concentrated on what he must remember, skipping over the unnecessary.

Surname, MacKinnon

Address, Glenfinnan, Badachro, nr Gairloch, Wester Ross

Telephone, None

No telephone; I can't check to see if he'll be there.

He was amazed at the amount of space for personal data: National Insurance No, National Health No, Bank Details, Education History, Copy of Birth Certificate, Distinguishing Features, Height, Weight, Next of Kin, and so on. Many of the fields were blank. He repeated the address to himself several times. Rising, he smiled at the old girl, who had not taken her eyes off him for the whole time he had handled the file, thanked her, and left.

He was back in his office before three o'clock. 'Lewis, get me on the first flight tomorrow morning to Inverness and back on the last. I'll need at least eight hours on the ground. If the flight back doesn't give me sufficient time, then book me back on the overnight sleeper. Get me a hire car for the day too.' He didn't know exactly where Badachro was, but he knew the location of Gairloch. As a young Lieutenant he had been commanding officer of a minesweeper and sailed the waters off north-west Scotland frequently. He had refuelled his ship at the NATO refuelling depot in Loch Ewe, a dozen road miles north of Gairloch, many times.

***

The aircraft arrived at Inverness shortly before 10.15 am. Thirty-five minutes later, he was driving out of Inverness on the A9 for the Muir of Ord. After Strathpeffer, it was mostly a single track road. He passed Loch Maree, marvelling at its beauty. He then kept an eye out for the turn to Badachro. He'd studied the map the previous evening. He'd kept his foot down, but it was almost 1330 hours when he turned into Badachro. He was feeling hungry and saw a pub: *The Badachro Inn*. A board outside declared: 'Food served 1200 – 1400, 1900 – 2100'. He entered. It was a long narrow room. There was a long bar on the left, some tables scattered randomly on the right, behind which were several large windows overlooking a beautiful bay. In the far corner, several customers, who looked like yachties, were drinking pints and eating fish and chips. The smell filled his nostrils. *Fantastic,* he thought. There was no one to serve him at the bar. He saw a bell and rang it. A woman appeared from the door behind the bar and the Admiral could see into the kitchen behind.

'Yes?' she enquired. The barmaid was a thirty-something, peroxide blonde. Her hair needed a wash; her cover-all too. Admiral Johnson formed the impression that he must have disturbed her.

'Can I have a pint of bitter, please? Am I too late for some food?'

'No. What do you want?'

He hadn't the heart to ask for a menu and took a chance. 'The fish and chips smell great.'

She proffered a reluctant smile, pulled him the pint and disappeared into her kitchen.

He sat in the middle of the room looking out at the small bay. He thought, *it's a world away from Whitehall. Some day when I retire, I'll sail my yacht up here.*

He finished his meal in contemplative silence and when paying his bill asked the barmaid, 'Do you know which house is Glenfinnan?'

'Aye,' she replied.

He paused, waiting for an answer to his question, but none came. She handed him his change. His monosyllabic hostess was clearly not prepared to give anything away.

'Would you mind telling me where Glenfinnan is?' he asked, in as polite a fashion as he could muster.

'At the end of the village, turn right. It's the second or third on the right.'

He thanked her and left. The yachties were on their third or fourth pints.

He found the house easily, parked and walked down a steep path through a densely wooded garden. He knocked on the first door he came to. A dog barked, and after a few moments a young teenage boy opened the door.

CHAPTER 37

On 2nd September 1981, the Iranian Army came to life. At several points along the front line in the northern region of Arabstan, near Dezful and Susangerd, they struck, pushing back the Iraqi positions. However, the attacks were decoys. As Iraq moved reserve troops north to boost their defences, five crack infantry regiments supported by artillery and tanks crossed the Bahamsheer River to relieve Abadan.

After three days of heavy fighting, the Iraqis had to withdraw and fell back across the Karun River to Khorram Shar. The Iranians were welcomed in Abadan by the locals and claimed total victory on 13th September. The world was shocked, but the Ayatollahs were worried by their success. They were suspicious that the Army's boosted morale might kick-start a coup. The Iranians, knowing that Kuwait was supporting Iraq with money and refined petroleum products, as well as being the main supply route for other goods, attacked Kuwaiti oil facilities. It was a warning to all the Gulf States to keep out of the war.

America, alarmed by the attacks on Kuwait, moved forces to the region. A rapid reaction force was set up on the island of Diego Garcia in the Indian Ocean – to prepare for any contingency. Their intelligence satellites were put on twenty-four hour watch. As the second winter of the war approached, the entrenched Iraqi and Iranian troops further improved their defences whilst each country replenished stocks of munitions. There was little activity on the ground. In the air, however, things were different.

Iran exported most of its oil from the refineries on Khark Island. Consequently, the island's air defence systems, surface-to-air missiles and air defence interceptors based on the island, were comprehensive; even more so than those surrounding Tehran. During the week beginning 28th September, seventeen Iraqi Mig-23 aircraft, at the edge of their operational range, were shot down as they attacked the island's oil refineries. By mid-November, the total of Iraqi losses had mounted to eighty-five aircraft. The Iranian air force was quickly learning to co-ordinate its resources. On 17th November, Saddam called off the attacks on Khark's refineries. Iran's oil exports had hardly been affected.

***

With the ground war in stalemate for the winter, the rejuvenated Iranian Air Force began daring sorties. Each day two Phantoms, having been refuelled over international waters in the Gulf, would probe the Iraqi air defences. Flying at 200 feet, they would push and prod further into Iraq, trying to find a safe corridor to Baghdad. By early December the Phantoms were flying over the Iraqi capital, frequently as low as sixty feet. They became known to the locals as the 'High Noon Cowboys', because they regularly appeared at midday; although it may have had some reference to Fred Zinnemann's famous film. Such was their speed and altitude that SAMs were ineffective. Often the SAM would miss the Phantom and instead hit a high-rise building. People would stand in the street, defying the air raid warning sirens, to watch the impertinent display.

On 20th December, at exactly 1200 hours, two Phantoms appeared in the blue sky over Baghdad. Flying lower than ever, observers estimated as low as thirty feet, they each dropped two 500 lb bombs on the Headquarters of the Iraqi Army building in the downtown area. Having successfully released their load, they circled over the burning building, performed victory rolls and disappeared south. Twenty-six people were killed. One of the casualties was Brigadier Amer Rashid. Kate had been married for just two years and three months.

The loss of her husband, and best friend, was a devastating blow. From simply liking him, when they married, she had slowly grown to love him. He had been a kind, gentle and caring man. She had become fond of returning to their apartment at the end of the day, cooking a meal together, sitting down afterwards and swapping stories. They had been open and honest about what each was doing for the war effort. He had confided that attacks by the Iranian Air Force on oil and gas facilities at Mosul and Kirkuk had put a stop to Iraqi oil production. Worse still, the Kurds, encouraged by the Iranians, had severed the oil pipeline into Turkey through which they usually exported thirty-five million barrels of oil annually.

'Without generous loans from Saudi Arabia, Kuwait and Abu Dhabi we would be on our knees,' he had said one evening. 'Do you remember how many US dollars you could buy with one dinar when you went to London?'

'We were getting three dollars to the dinar,' she had replied.

'Well today you would only get one-third of a dollar.'

'I didn't realise things were that bad,' she answered.

'We owe Kuwait five billion dollars, that's fifteen billion dinars. How will we ever be able to pay it back? I don't know.'

Such knowledge was dangerous; she had to keep it to herself. No mention of Iraq's problems had ever been brought up at the Revolutionary Council meetings that she had attended. By comparison, her news for Amer had usually been favourable. Both the Falluja plants were operating at full capacity. The two managers she had appointed were up to the task. CB weapons were being made at a satisfactory rate. Although the production of vexun was still giving difficulties, stocks of mustard gas, ricin and sarin were building up. She was confident that by the spring of 1982 Iraq could stop any Iranian advances with their chemical weapons.

***

Her reaction to the loss of Amer affected her, as it had when James had returned to England. She threw herself ever more into her work. She had been almost alone at Amer's funeral, Amer's son and mother being too distraught to attend. Kate's family were in Cairo. Only Azi and Sawsan were at her side when the coffin was lowered into the ground. The eye witnesses' reports about the Phantoms' victory rolls over the Baghdad sky after the attack firmed her resolve. She would help Iraq win this war come hell or high water.

I'll find a way to solve the problems with producing vexun. We'll make it in quantities that will destroy the Farsis once and for all.

When there is no one to return home to at the end of the day, there is no point in returning. Parkinson's Law applied: the more she did, the more there was to do. There were days when she would put in eighteen hours, go back to her apartment, fall into bed without eating and be back in the office by 0630 hours. She began to lose weight, but she didn't notice. Her appetite simply disappeared. She hardly ever felt hungry.

Even Tufiq noticed. She was accompanying him to the meeting of the Revolutionary Council on 5th January 1982 when he commented. 'I'm worried for you, Kathab. You need to take some time off work. Build up your strength. Come back refreshed.'

Saddam looked drawn. Kate knew what was going on, but suspected most of the others attending the meeting did not. However, despite his appearance, he was upbeat. He declared that France had agreed to sell thirty Super Etendard fighter bombers. They would turn the tide as they would be equipped with Exocet anti-ship missiles and have a range sufficient to attack Iranian tankers in the Gulf and at Khark Island. Twenty pilots were already on their way to Brest to train on the aircraft. France had also promised to send technicians to Iraq to help maintain the aircraft. Some fifty Mirage F1 interceptors had also been purchased that would match the Iranian Phantoms.

Chemical Ali asked, 'What are we going to do with the Kurds who blew up our pipeline?'

'What do you suggest?' replied Saddam.

'Intelligence reports tell me the majority of the perpetrators come from the Barzani clan. They hang around in Shirwan. I think we should destroy the lot of them.'

'How?'

'With vexun.'

Saddam looked at Kate. 'Well?'

'How big is Shirwan?' she asked.

'A population of no more than five thousand,' replied the Head of the Army.

'In that case, may I suggest we use mustard gas? Stocks of vexun have not yet reached the state where we can afford to waste it on the Kurds. I believe I have almost solved the production problem. I have designed a ceramic condenser, internally coated with Teflon. I have persuaded the resident liaison Japanese engineer at Falluja 1 to build a prototype. I am confident it will be successful. I'll then get the Japanese to manufacture the condensers for us. They are the world leaders in this technology. By May, we should have sufficient quantities of vexun coming off the production line to use against the Iranians.'

And so, two weeks later, some 3,500 Kurds perished when their village was bombed by planes dropping one hundred tons of mustard gas. The bombs, designed to explode 200 feet above the ground, released droplets of liquid that caused itching, inflammation, blisters, tissue degeneration, infection and finally death. Men, women and children perished. Some took ten days to die. Only a handful survived.

Kate knew little about the massacre. She had managed to get a visa to Egypt via Jordan and had stayed with her parents for two weeks. Ala had gasped when she saw the state of her eldest daughter. Two weeks of cosseting and sleeping put her back on her feet. 'Please, don't go back,' she had pleaded with her daughter.

'I've got to go, Mum,' she replied. 'The Iraqi Army will be overwhelmed unless our chemical weapons are produced in the right quantities.' She promised her mother that she would look after herself better.

***

2nd April 1982

The BBC World Service (Kate had gone back to listening to her preferred radio programme) announced that Argentina had invaded the Falkland Islands. *I wonder if it will affect our supplies from the British.*

***

On 20th April the Iranians began their spring offensive across a wide front, but principally in the centre. Code named 'Undeniable Victory', the push was designed to cut the communication lines between the northern and southern Iraqi Armies. The operation was to change the pattern and tempo of the war. In places, the Iraqis were outnumbered by four to one. A new tactic was employed by their adversaries: mass human wave attacks. So-called volunteers, some as young as twelve years of age, usually tied together in groups of twenty – so that they couldn't easily turn around and run away – were pushed forward ahead of the regular Army. Each youngster had been promised by Ayatollah Khomeini that death would guarantee entry to heaven. They had been given a yellow plastic key to open the door to paradise and a passport, signed by Khomeini, stating that the bearer had died a heroic martyr. As many as 20,000 would perish at a time as the Iraqis used mortar shells filled with mustard gas or zarin to defend their positions. The problem, however, was that the Iraqi front line didn't have sufficient logistics to sustain the shock waves. Supplies couldn't be transported quickly enough to the front line from Kate's repositories. The Iraqis found themselves falling back.

Nine days later, the Iranians took the initiative again. Operation 'Holy City' focussed on Khorram Shar. Three thrusts, mostly attacking at night, saw the town fall on 9th May. In less than three weeks Iran had regained some 300 square miles of their former territory. The borders were almost the same as they had been before the outbreak of hostilities.

21st May 1982

The World Service announced British troops had landed on the East Falklands. *I'd forgotten they had a war too.* Kate's policy of hiding the CBs efficiently had not won her any friends with the Army hierarchy. She had worked non-stop to provide what was wanted, but Tufiq was ranting that they must in future be stored 'where we want them, not in some God-forsaken hole in the desert'. Consequently, it was agreed that only the most dangerous biologicals would remain buried: anthrax, botulinium toxin, gas gangrene, gangrennex and ricin. Vexun had begun to come off the production line satisfactorily, although weight for weight it took twenty times longer than zarin to make. The Teflon coated condenser prototype had been a success. Despite its complex 'S' tubes, with each bend having a drain tap that had to be opened and closed manually, they worked well. The condensers had been manufactured in Japan by a subsidiary company of Honda who were using ceramic-coated Teflon technology to line barrels and pistons in their grand prix motorbikes. To future generations of industrial chemists the condensers would be known as 'Jised tubes'; few would know of their macabre origin.

***

14th June 1982

'The Argentine Forces have today surrendered to the British Forces on the Falkland Islands. Mrs Thatcher has appeared on television and praised her Army, Navy and Air Force for undertaking such a difficult task so professionally.'
Why the hell can't we do that?

That same day Kate attended a Revolutionary Council meeting. She was shocked to see Saddam. He looked dreadful; as if he hadn't slept for a week. The old optimism was gone, he was drained. He announced that he had asked the Swiss Embassy to contact the Iranians and tell them he was willing to stop the war and withdraw to the 1979 borders. He emphasised it wasn't surrender; merely an acceptance of the obvious, neither side could win the war. Kate was furious; she could see several others were too. However, none dared argue the case for continuing the struggle.

Ayatollah Khomeini's response to the peace proposal was, as Kate suspected it would be, 'bugger off'. He knew he had the upper hand and nothing short of unconditional surrender was going to satisfy his lust for power. It was time for the Iranians to push for all-out victory. On 13th July 1982, Operation 'Ramadan' began. Iranian forces launched a three-pronged drive directed to cut off Basra. Taken by surprise at the ferocity of the attacks, the Iraqis withdrew, but large numbers of Iranians were to perish. In just two days the Iranians advanced ten miles inside Iraq before they were stopped. However, it had cost them an estimated 10,000 killed and 20,000 injured. Defending their own territory, the Iraqi Army had shown great resolve to hang on until reserve forces could arrive.

On 21st July, the Iranians made another push, but were let down by the poor co-ordination between their Army and their Air Force. They only advanced a further two miles over a ten mile front, mostly mosquito-infested swamp. On 28th July, a further major assault was made. Using their mass-wave technique, some 18,000 teenagers lost their lives to Kate's vexun. The July offensive had cost at least 33,000 lives. Although now entrenched inside Iraq, not far from Basra, the land occupied was a strategically worthless marsh.

With the Iranian advances in the south, rumour began to spread throughout Iraq. The population became restless. Saddam's popularity began to wane. On 23rd August, an assassin shot him whilst he was making a visit to Dezful, a Shia town thirty-five miles north-west of Baghdad. Unknown to all present, it was one of Saddam's doppelgangers who died. Saddam blamed the DAWA and fierce reprisals took place.

Some 180 men were taken into the desert, never to return. Kate heard of the assassination attempt on the radio. Much play was made of the public announcement. She wondered, however, if the whole affair hadn't been orchestrated by Saddam to whip up Sunni support.

On 30th September, the Iranians made another move. Bogged down in the south, they made an attempt to capture Baghdad. They chose to attack the town of Mandali, just eighty miles due east of the capital. However, the area was well defended and, although fierce fighting continued until 10th October, the Iranians lacked sufficient armour and air power to break through. Both sides incurred heavy losses that didn't seem to affect the Iranians politically, but Saddam knew it was hurting his side as he was becoming economically strapped. His regime was in danger; he was hearing reports of a swell of opinion wanting to bring back former President Bakr with whom Ayatollah Khomeini would be more amenable to negotiate a cease fire.

Kate had been asked to attend the Revolutionary Council on the same day that Iran was beginning its drive towards Baghdad. As the meeting wore on, she wondered why Tufiq had asked her to attend. Any Other Business came and went. She hadn't said a word. As she rose to leave, after most of the main players had left, Tufiq took hold of her arm and whispered, 'Please wait. Saddam wants to talk with us.'

Only Saddam, Tufiq, Kate and Tariq Aziz remained in the underground bunker.

The great man looked at Kate and gestured for her to sit near him. He had powerful eyes, hypnotic, magnetic, cruel and dark; the type that can look through you and see what's at the back of your head.

'Al Jised,' he began, in his deep, guttural voice. 'You are loyal to our cause, are you not?'

'Of course.'

'Do you want to see Iraq run by Farsis with their medieval Sharia Law?'

'No, never.'

'Do you know that ex-President Bakr plans an internal coup and then to surrender to Khomeini?'

'It must not happen.'

'Good. General Tufiq and I have agreed he must go – permanently. We want your help. This is the most important thing you may ever do. Only the four of us in this room will ever know.'

'What do you want me to do?'

'Kill Bakr.'

The words were spoken slowly, deliberately, coldly and without any emotion. His voice sounded inhuman. The three of them stared icily at Kate. Researching and developing weapons of mass destruction was one thing, but using them at first hand was something else. She was trapped. She was committing herself to becoming one of them. She would be joining their club, something she had vowed not to do. Her conscience was telling her to back out, but how? She sat frozen, looking into the face of the male Medusa.

Bewitched, she asked, 'How?'

'Tomorrow he is coming to meet myself and Tariq. We are to give him a presentation on the state of the war. We want you and General Tufiq to give five-minute, no longer, briefings on the state of our chemical and conventional weapons. I will ask you midway through the presentation to pour and hand out the coffee. As you will be the only female there, he will not suspect anything unusual; he's a bit of an old traditionalist. You are to slip a few drops of enditon into his cup.'

Kate found herself calm, even relaxed at the idea. It was as if someone inside her was saying, *it will be an honour to serve the State*. Not sure where the voice was coming from, she found herself saying, 'He will die of old age within a week.'

***

4th October 1982

Baghdad radio announced the death, after a short illness, of former President Bakr. There was now more blood on Kate's hands. As she listened to the news, she shuddered. It had dawned on her what she had done. *I'll end up in hell for this. At least Roya Talfah had violated me; this man had done me no harm. I will never be able to look my father in the eye again.*

***

With the ground war apparently in stalemate for the forthcoming winter, the Iraqis began a new phase of attrition, *The Tanker War*. The French Etendards, equipped with Exocet missiles, had sufficient range to attack the Iranian tankers and refineries on Khark Island. The problem for the Iraqi pilots was one of identification. Neutral merchant ships were being attacked as well as Iranian. Lloyd's of London became alarmed and urged Prime Minister Thatcher 'to use her influence'. Whereas Saddam took note of the request, seeking sophisticated equipment to help identify neutrals and instructing his aircrew to restrict attacks to the oil installations, Khomeini sought revenge. Iranian aircraft began attacking tankers, any tankers, in both Kuwaiti and Saudi waters.

Then, on 2nd November 1982, against all odds, Iran launched another massive offensive. It attacked Fakkeh, a border town, some thirty miles from Al Amara, which lies on the main road between Baghdad and Basra. Tanks and artillery hit the town at night, minimising the effects of Iraqi air power in the area. Fakkeh fell and the Iranians had won a further 240 square miles of territory. To prevent Iranian advances towards Al Amara, Iraq's last reserves were called up. They dug into well-defended positions on the high ground and wisely spent the rest of the year boosting their positions, creating a semi-circle around the city. When the operation to conquer Al Amara began, on 6th February 1983, Tehran radio was claiming that the fall of Al Amara would cut Iraq in two and be 'the final military operation that would determine the outcome of the war'. Six divisions were used, but they had to cross marshes. Superior Iraqi air power, especially the new American Hughes defender helicopters, acquired a few months previously, won the day by spraying vexun. Iran had won one hundred square miles of land, but had not scored the major breakthrough. It was becoming clear to neutral observers that the war could not be won nor lost by military means, but only by the political or economic collapse of one side.

In the early summer of 1983 there was little movement over the entire front. Iran probed but couldn't advance. Iraqi soldiers were better defenders than attackers. However, the Iranians were plotting a new ploy. On 22nd July a Kurd militia, backed by the Iranian Army, overran the north-eastern town of Haj Omran. It gave the Iraqi Army an excuse to use chemical weapons for the first time in an offensive role, as opposed to a defensive role, against the Iranians. One hundred tons of mustard gas were dropped, 16,000 were reported to have died. As the remaining population and troops fled east, up into the mountains, the Iraqis relentlessly pursued their foe, dropping gas shells ahead of them. Unfortunately for those fleeing, mustard gas is heavier than air and the deadly clouds fell back towards them. Few escaped.

On 5th November 1983, the United States Security Council made an unprecedented announcement. 'The US will do whatever is necessary to prevent Iraq losing the war with Iran.' To confirm the statement, its chairman, Donald Rumsfeld, met Saddam Hussein in Baghdad on 19th December to assure him of American support. He backed up his words with a loan of $5 billion, given through Italian Banks to purchase 'whatever it takes'. Heeding the advice of his American advisers, that winter Saddam spent millions of dollars constructing extensive fortifications that would channel future Iranian attacks into prepared killing zones. 'Fort Iraq' was being built.

The pressure to produce CB weapons at the Falluja plants was relieved after the Rumsfeld visit. The Americans began giving Iraq unlimited amounts of precursors, such as thio-di-glycol for mustard gas, glycol-phosphoric-sulphide for VX, even unlimited ricin and anthrax. Kate calculated that Iraq had enough CB weapons to kill the entire population of the planet. Hiding them was becoming her major task.

So it was alarming when in February 1984 a new phase of the war began. Saddam decided to attack Iranian cities with conventional missiles and rockets. Kate realised it would only be a matter of time before he asked her for chemical weapons. These she could dilute with talcum powder without raising too much suspicion. But what would happen when he decided to use biological weapons? Total War had begun.

CHAPTER 38

The attacks on Iranian towns were both ineffective and counterproductive. They simply created retaliatory bombing on Iraqi cities. Innocent civilians were the victims. As Nastia Game had predicted six years previously, the Iranian incursions were more effective than Iraq's. Despite a priority effort to convert the older Badger aircraft to tankers, the modifications had taken longer than expected. Consequently, the Iraqi bombers' radius of combat was still limited. Not only had they to fly high to conserve fuel with less payloads, but to get to Tehran they had to traverse the Zagros Mountains at an altitude where they were easily seen by ground-based defence systems. By comparison, Iranian aircraft could fly low, sweeping over the Iraqi marshes to Baghdad at 200 feet, well below radar cover.

Saddam increased the Super Etendard attacks on Iranian tankers, hoping to cut off Iranian fuel exports. He hoped the countries affected by the loss of Iranian oil would side with him. However, when a Greek tanker, the *Antagoni*, and a Liberian ship, the *St Paul*, were sunk because of faulty identification – both within the space of two months – these attacks also became counterproductive. The flow of Iranian oil slowed down, but, so too, did the flow from the Gulf States that were aiding Iraq. Iran stepped up attacking neutral tankers, particularly those entering or leaving Kuwait.

American intelligence reports were suggesting a gigantic build-up of half a million Iranian troops, preparing to attack Basra. Iraq faced the possibility that by autumn it might cease to exist. At a Revolutionary Council meeting, on 14th April, Kate was placed in an impossible dilemma. Chemical Ali had decided that millions of photographs showing the effect of gangrennex on prisoners should be printed and dropped over the Iranian positions as well as Tehran. 'We'll frighten the buggers and show them the potency of our biological weapons,' he declared.

Saddam agreed and looked at Kate. 'Have we suitable photos?' he asked.

'Not really,' she replied. It was the wrong reply. It would lead to one of the worst incidents of her life.

Saddam turned to Tufiq. 'Get half a dozen Iranian prisoners, subject them to gangrennex and take the photos.' He next looked at Sahib al-Majid, the Head of the Civil Service. 'Arrange for the printing of three million copies.' To Hashim Ahmed, the Head of the Army, 'I want them distributed by air within the week.' They were orders: clear-cut, precise. No one would dare argue. No one dared ask what the possible consequences might be.

Kate was shocked that prisoners of war would be murdered in such a vile way. She tried to bide for time, lying. 'All our supplies of gangrennex are safely buried in the desert. It will take several days to retrieve them.'

'You've got twenty-four hours. Tufiq will give you as many men as necessary.' There was no further dissent. It was tantamount to *do it, or be shot.*

Six prisoners were rounded up, stripped naked, locked in a room and photos taken every five seconds as they were sprayed with gangrennex. Their cries of agony, as they died, their skin literally dissolving from their bodies was horrific. Fortunately for them their misery lasted less than a minute. She turned away, violently sick. The images were to live with her for the rest of her life. For weeks afterwards, she would wake up regularly in sweats in the middle of the night as the pictures flashed in front of her. Even Tufiq was disgusted. He whispered to Kate, 'This is not why I became a soldier.' It was to affect him so badly that he shot himself two days later.

Everyone who saw the photographs was affected; the series of shots showing the rapid deterioration of a face to a bloody skeleton with no eyes, nose or mouth in less than a minute were almost impossible to look at. Kate couldn't believe Saddam would go through with the plan, but he did. What effect the dropping of the leaflets had on the Iranians she never found out; the planned invasion, however, never materialised. She vowed that never again would she uncover the hiding places where she had stored anthrax, gangrennex or the other biological killers. *Even if they kill me.*

The scheme may have deterred an Iranian invasion, but the reaction from the international community had not been predicted. The Iranians were quick to show the foreign journalists what a rotten regime they were dealing with. The condemnation was worldwide. The UN met in general session, unanimously condemning Iraq. For the first time, Saddam found himself on the back-foot. Although few newspapers showed the worst photographs, there were lurid descriptions to accompany the less frightening shots. Words such as grotesque, despicable, diabolical, callous, brutal, inhuman, beastly, satanic and pestilent were used freely. A few days after the UN disapproval, a photograph of Kate, taken whilst she was a student at Cambridge, was shown in several British tabloids under the caption, *Dr Germ*. Three popular dailies accused her of being the mastermind behind Iraq's CB weapons.

In London Peter Stacey saw the articles and was alarmed. He realised the danger that Kate was now in. He immediately demanded a meeting that very evening with the three editors of the newspapers concerned. Editors of daily tabloids are not accustomed to being called to MI6 Headquarters at short notice. They tried to wriggle from the meeting, but the threat of D-notices soon had them to heel. They would not reveal their source. Peter hadn't expected them to. However, by then, with the contacts available to him, he had already found out. A freelance journalist, with a middle-eastern name, but carrying a Libyan passport had written the article. The photo of Kate had come from Cambridge University archives. Peter Stacey named the Libyan to the three editors and dared them to deny his responsibility. None did. They looked sheepish when a livid Stacey swore at them, 'You have just endangered the best British undercover officer we have in Iraq. If we have to bring her in from the cold, then it could cost millions of innocent lives. Tomorrow you will print an apology to Doctor al Jised, stating that the article had no basis of truth whatsoever. Understood?'

All three, in unison, agreed. Unknown to them, the Libyan had already been arrested by Special Branch officers on passport irregularities. Reporting restrictions were enforced when he appeared the following day at Uxbridge magistrate's court and was remanded for trial. An application for bail was refused.

***

From: MI6, London
5 May 84
To: British Embassy, Baghdad
FAO Mike Noble
Ref, Agent Kathab al Jised (241/5)
Am secure faxing you copies of articles that appeared in British press yesterday. They are self explanatory. Retractions today in papers but believe damage done. KAJ could become target for Iranian subversives. Offer to bring her in. She will get new ID & pension of Principal Scientific Officer, or a job with us. She must make the decision, not you. Do not try and force the issue; she can still be invaluable in Iraq if she stays.
Yours aye
Peter S

***

That evening Kate had not been long at home when the phone rang: one, two, three, four she counted. Then it stopped. She had grown used to not answering before the fifth or sixth ring. This was the first time it had stopped exactly after four rings.

Can it really be almost six years ago since I was with James and Peter Stacey?

341

She wondered whether to ignore the call. Perhaps they would go away and leave her alone. She was depressed. Tufiq's suicide had knocked the stuffing out of her. She had never liked the man, but had grown slowly to respect him. He had held firm beliefs and stuck to them, even unto death. Looking back on their relationship, she began to realise that he had always seen CB weapons purely as a defensive measure, never as an offensive one. The moral distinction might be dubious, but it was one with which she agreed. The treatment of the prisoners sprayed with gangrennex had brought Saddam and his cousin, Ali Hassan, down to the level of the Nazis. *The trouble is we're now all tarred with the same brush.* After a short while, she rang through to the Chinese takeaway, made an order, and said she would pick it up in fifteen minutes.

'Velly good, Miss al Jised.' They knew her as a regular.

Mike Noble was waiting for his chicken fried rice. They nodded, picked up and paid for their dishes. They sat next to each other in the nearby park eating their meals with a plastic fork. As best as he could, Mike explained what had happened and the danger she was now in. He offered to initiate her escape to England.

She sat shaking her head. 'No, I must stay for as long as possible to the end of the war. There is still a lot I can do. The Americans are sending us biological weapons by the boat load. A recent consignment contained 200 gallons of Botulinium Toxin. Do you know what that means?' she asked.

'A lot of poison?' Mike replied hesitantly. His answer indicated to Kate that he hadn't a clue of its consequences.

'It's enough bloody poison to wipe out Europe's population several times over. If I wasn't here to hide it for all time, using James Douglas' chess system, God only knows what might happen.' She stopped to catch her breath. Then the pressure caught up. She held her head in her hands and began weeping quietly.

Mike, remembering Peter's warning, gently took hold of her hand. After what seemed ages, he said, 'It's very brave of you to stay. We all appreciate it in MI6. When you feel the time is right then you only have to let us know. Now, on another tack, this will be our last meeting. I have been posted to Riyadh next month. Brian McCormack takes over from me. I'm afraid you're getting another PPE man from Oxford.' He smiled. Kate saw the funny side and smiled back. They sat talking for some time, Kate filling Mike in on what she knew of Saddam's intentions for the war. They finished their takeaways, shook hands and departed.

The following day, Lieutenant General Ali Youseff, now Head of Internal Security, called for her. He showed her copies of the articles in the British press. She read them carefully, trying not to show that she knew of their existence. When finished, Ali announced, 'I don't know where or how they got hold of that rubbish, but I am going to put you under twenty-four hour protection. We can't have you being blown up by these bloody Farsis, can we?' He was smiling at her. She was both relieved and worried; relieved that she was considered sufficiently valuable to warrant a twenty-four hour guard, but worried that it might impede her movements should she need to contact Brian McCormack in the future.

***

From: British Embassy, Baghdad
6 May 84
To: Hd of Middle East Sect, MI6 London
Dear Peter
Ref Agent Kathab al-Jised (241/5)
Met KAJ yesterday evening. She has decided to stay for time being. Upset about newspaper reports, but admits gangrennex photos genuine. Tells me she has transferred production of most Falluja 1 bio weapons to chemical. Tells me US has recently given (sic) them 80 galls Anthrax, 200 galls Botulinium Toxin, and 50 galls Aflatoxin. Assures me all is safely being buried and will never get used – 'they will have to kill me first' – Wants another 500 tons talc to dilute zarin.

Although I have not met her often over past 4 ½ years, I have seen her

age. She is a wonderful woman, but stress is taking its toll. I worry she
may crack if ever tortured for her knowledge of location of CBs. I will brief
McCormack when he arrives for handover.

    Yours etc

    Mike N

***

The governments that had supplied Iraq with aid began to withdraw their support. The first to condemn Saddam's regime was Germany. They cut off their supplies of chemicals and withdrew their support engineers from Falluja 2. Simultaneously, they closed their embassy. Others followed, but the British and Americans remained silent in their condemnation, at least publicly. As reports of the world's reaction flooded in, Saddam moved rapidly.

His Foreign Minister was despatched to the UN to declare, 'The photos are clever fakes. We made ceramic skeletons, used plastic and wax to create the illusion of real people, just like Madame Tussauds' models. Our aim was to deter the massive invasion of sovereign Iraqi territory by the half million Iranian soldiers currently planning to attack Basra.' Saddam's ploy worked. Most of the uncommitted nations, not wanting to indirectly support Khomeini, believed Tariq Aziz's explanation. The affair remained secret to the Iraqi public. Few ever heard of the temporary international upheaval.

In late May, Donald Rumsfeld made a second visit to Iraq, assuring Saddam of continued American support. A further $5 billion of aid was promised to allow Iraq to buy non-military hardware such as tank transporters, computers, ambulances and medicines.

The French had no scruples. Exocet missiles, being consumed at an alarming rate, were being donated freely. The attacks, by the Super Etendards, on Iranian tankers near Khark Island intensified to the point that Iranian exports were, at last, being reduced. Khomeini's solution was to block the Straits of Hormuz – a move that had immediate impact on the rest of the world. The Soviet Union and America agreed to act jointly. It was the first example of mutual co-operation since the end of World War 2. Ships of any nation were allowed to fly either the Soviet or the American flag. If attacked by Iranian forces, then the attack would be considered to be an attack on either Russia or America. A declaration to this effect was promulgated in the UN on 1st June. Khomeini backed off, but not before American intent was tested. On 6th June, the USS Vincennes shot down two Iranian Phantoms that had approached too close. The waving of Soviet/American flags effectively kept the Gulf open for the rest of the war.

Meanwhile, on the ground little was happening. The leaflets ploy seemed to have knocked the stuffing out of the planned invasion. Saddam continued to build his defence bunkers in the southern sector. In the north the Kurds continued to annoy, and the Syrians had to be watched. They could not be trusted. Saddam knew they were freely supporting Khomeini. The Syrians had cut off his oil pipe line to the Mediterranean two years previously and although the Saudis had immediately agreed to help him build a new one through their territory to the Red Sea, it was one year away from completion. Saddam was in a tough situation, caught between a rock and a hard place. He could not stop the war without losing power, but to continue he needed unlimited support from the other Gulf States. The success of Tariq Aziz's explanation at the UN had to be capitalised upon. He decided that Tariq should declare to the world, at the UN, that Iraq was offering to end the war, but were being spurned. Iraq was willing to accept peace. Saddam offered his excuse for going to war originally as 'the prevention of the Islamic Revolution'. He pointed out that the friends of Iran were the rogue states: Libya, Syria, North Korea, and China. Iraq's offer of peace won the diplomatic battle, but the economic battle was hopelessly lost. Only Saddam and his nearest advisers knew that they owed $100 billion to America, Britain, France, Germany, Japan, Saudi Arabia and Kuwait.

CHAPTER 39

September 1984 saw Kate managing to see her family for only the second time since they had moved to Egypt. Her youngest sister, Lina, had graduated successfully from her course and had begun her year in the largest Cairo hospital as a junior house doctor. She had decided she wanted to specialise in neurology. Having always seen her eldest sister as a role model, she had applied to go to England the following year to study at Addenbrooke's Hospital in Cambridge. Kate's reason for visiting Egypt, however, was to attend the wedding of her other sister, Hind. She had qualified as a teacher after her MA degree. She had met Adom Nasser, a fellow teacher at her school in a town on the Mediterranean coast, El Hamman. After the wedding, Kate stayed with her parents for a further week before, sadly, returning to Iraq.

As the winter of 1984 began, Saddam realised there was little he could do to regain lost ground. His Army was well dug in, but lacked the drive and the manpower to unsettle the Iranians who had reinforced their positions with vast numbers of infantry. His only hope of resolving the stalemate was to increase the use of air power against oil tankers and attack Iranian cities. He was encouraged to take the initiative by polls in America forecasting President Reagan would be re-elected for a second term. Reagan had been Saddam's ally and Saddam saw no reason why their special relationship shouldn't continue for a further four years. In the event, in November Reagan won forty-nine of the fifty-one States against his Democratic rival, Walter Mondale, the biggest margin of all time.

The tanker war became ever more confusing. As more Iranian tankers began to be hit by the ever improving Iraqi pilots in their Super Etendards, Khomeini decided to mine the international waters across the Straits of Hormuz. The act created uproar in the UN. A Security Council Resolution, number 418, was passed unanimously on 28th October condemning Iran. British and American minesweepers were despatched to the Gulf to begin clearing operations.

Encouraged by what he thought was unlimited support from the Americans, in January 1985 Saddam began a phase of the war that was to be labelled by the world's press as the *War of the Cities*. Iraqi technicians had been working for several years to convert former TU-16 Badger bombers to tanker aircraft. The major difficulties had been the design of the probe, the co-ordination of the pumps, and pilot training. Having overcome the problems, a squadron of ten aircraft went operational on 1st January. For the first time it allowed Iraqi bombers to strategically attack Tehran with full loads and fly the last 200 miles under ground-radar. In retaliation, Iran fired SS-1 Scud missiles, supplied by North Korea, at Baghdad. Attacks then escalated. Iraq began attacking civilian trains and aircraft. In March, an Iran Air Boeing 737 airliner was strafed at Shiraz International airport killing seventy civilians and wounding many others. In the first four months of this phase of the war, sixty-five cities were attacked in 236 sorties. By May, Saddam, having become sufficiently confident that he could do what he liked, began arming his aircraft with chemical weapons, mostly zarin. Unbeknown to everyone except Kate, the zarin was diluted with harmless talcum powder, considerably reducing its potency. International antipathy towards the Khomeini regime was such that there were few repercussions. When, finally, the UN did condemn Iraq for using chemicals against civilian targets, the war would be almost over – another three years away.

***

12th March 1985

The BBC World Service made an announcement that no one could have foreseen as the most significant political change of the 20th century: 'The death has been announced of Konstantin Chernenko, the General Secretary of the Soviet Communist Party. He has been replaced by Mikhail Gorbachev, aged fifty-four. He is the first person born after the 1917 Revolution to have been appointed leader of the Communist Party. Sources close to Downing Street are suggesting that Gorbachev is seen as a reformer and believe he will herald a new phase in the relationship with the West.' Kate heard the news and, like millions of others, thought no more of it.

***

During this period, Kate had surreptitiously met Brian McCormack several times, on each occasion warning him of developments in the war. The move towards attacking civilian targets with chemicals had raised his eyebrows until Kate had told him she was diluting the weapons. 'As long as people remain indoors for twenty-four hours, they should be OK,' she assured him. She revealed that the Americans were using their Airborne Early Warning Aircraft, or AWACS, to help guide Iraqi pilots to their targets. Brian seemed to be unaware of the scale of help they were now receiving from the US. 'We received another load of anthrax last week. Would you believe it? I am spending half my time hiding the bloody stuff.'

'The work you are doing to contain the biologicals is not going unnoticed. Peter Stacey keeps a watchful eye on what is going on. However, the Yanks are a law unto themselves. A rogue part of their complex administration, the National Security Council, or NSC, is, we believe, secretly selling arms to Iran in exchange for the release of hostages in the Lebanon. We think President Reagan doesn't know about it – yet.'

'What hostages in the Lebanon?' asked Kate. 'I didn't know there were any hostages.'

'I'm afraid hostages have been getting taken regularly by groups such as DAWA and Hezbollah, ever since the release of the sixty-seven Americans in January 1981. There are at least thirty in the Lebanon, six of whom are American. The head of the NSC, Robert McFarlane, is using one of his henchmen, a Colonel Oliver North, to handle the deals with the Iranians. He uses the Israelis to broker the deals. Ironically, the Israelis think the package is above board and has been sanctioned by the President.'

'Saddam will be furious, although he is aware that the Israelis are selling some American equipment to Iran.'

'Yes, it has been going on for years, but this arrangement is sinister. Much of the stuff exported up to now has been rejected stock of poor quality and been sold at hellish mark-up prices. The new NSC stock is pukka. I suspect Peter is somehow currently orchestrating a leak. When it gets out, all hell will break loose. On another tack, does General Youseff know you still meet me covertly?' asked Brian.

'Yes, I had to give him a full briefing on how I came to meet you and your predecessors when General Tufiq died. Why?'

'It's just that you might wish to inform Youssef what is going on between the NSC and the Iranians. A snippet like that will help your standing with him.'

As they departed, Amer's words rang in her ears: *Never ever trust the bloody Yanks.*

***

The two targeted approach, the oil tankers and the cities, had given Iraq the initiative. The lull in the ground fighting allowed Ali Hassan to partake in his favourite pastime, hunting Kurds. Several of his own regiments were withdrawn from the front line and, without Saddam being aware, moved to the north-east. There, he exacted revenge on the

Kurds, in what amounted to ethnic cleansing. The campaign, which continued until 1987, was codenamed *The Anfal* executions. Bombing villages with vexun and mustard gas and then torching the buildings killed roughly 100,000 people. The world either didn't know or didn't care.

***

Kate, knowing that she could be a target for an Iranian gunman, was worried. If she was going to be shot by a lone sniper from half a mile away, then there would be little she could do. However, it seemed far more likely that an assassin would attempt to get as close as possible and fire the fatal shot at point-blank range. On one of her regular visits to Falluja 1, the resident Japanese engineer, Haruki Tai, who had helped design the al Jised tubes, noticed Kate's two guards. Haruki never seemed to have any problems at the plant. Kate used to think Falluja 1 was like her Nissan car, *it never goes wrong.* She wasn't sure whether this was because Haruki, being a talented engineer, foresaw problems and prevented them, or whether it was simply owing to the excellence of Japanese technology. By contrast, Falluja 2 frequently seemed to have a production problem. The resident German engineer, Hans Stenner, usually blamed the snag on a faulty component that had been subcontracted to the 'bloody British'.

Haruki had asked Kate why she needed guards. She replied that the Iraqi Government was worried about her safety.

'What are you doing to protect yourself?' he queried.

'What do you mean? I have these escorts twenty-four hours a day.'

'In Japan, ladies carry CS gas aerosols to offer protection from muggers.'

'I'm not sure an aerosol would protect me from a gunman.'

'I wasn't thinking of CS gas,' he replied.

'What, then?' she asked.

'Something that would blind him instantly and kill him in less than half a minute – gangrennex.'

'Wouldn't there be problems with the viscosity of gangrennex in the nozzle of the spray?' asked Kate. 'And what about the range and spread of the droplets?'

'Those are problems that we shall have to overcome. If you wish, I will begin designing a prototype.'

And so, each week Kate visited Falluja 1 to discuss progress with Haruki and help with the design. Various experimental models were made, frequently being sent to Japan for modifications beyond the facilities available in Iraq. After three months, the design was firming. An aerosol tube had been made of ceramic, internally coated with Teflon. Measuring five inches in length by less than ¾ inch in diameter; it was about the size of a thick ballpoint pen. A carbon fibre coat added strength, necessary because of the high pressure inside the tube. The push-button at the top, identical to that on a common pen, caused an apparent nib to protrude by a ½ inch. The ballpoint was, in reality, a ¼ inch diameter barrel. The pen's clip was the gun's trigger which fired the gangrennex away from the bottom of the pen when pressed. A jet was shot eight feet before it funnelled out into a spray. The device was invisible to a metal detector and weighed less than three ounces.

'This mini-barrel is the clever bit,' Haruki proudly told Kate. 'It had to have a very smooth internal bore so that the fluids would remain as a jet before they began to spread. Only Teflon would do the trick. Coating the inside of a tube that narrow is a first. I have also experimented with different propellants, at various pressures. Helium at 100 lbs per square inch, about three times the pressure in your car tyres, shoots the fluid out at 60 mph. It, therefore, takes less than one-tenth of a second to travel to its target – eight feet away. I think we are ready to make a production run of fifty guns. When you have them, I suggest you practice pressing the button and the trigger rapidly until you can guarantee hitting your assailant in the eyes every time.'

Kate was in awe at the beauty of the miniature feat of engineering in her hands.

Haruki continued. 'Your potential assassin will have about one-fifth of a second to react to your using the spray. After that he will be in such agony, as the gangrennex burns his eyes and face, that he will be unable to use his gun. Look carefully at him. If he manages to get off his one and only shot, his hands will already be moving towards his face for protection. Therefore, if he is right handed, his shot will be marginally to your right, and vice-versa. Consequently, you should also practice diving the other way after firing yourself. My last suggestion is that we should paint the carbon fibre sheaf to make the aerosol appear to be a simple ballpoint pen.'

***

The significance of the city bombings was to spur Iranian determination to smash through and conquer Basra. Operation 'Badr' began using conventional means, as opposed to mass-wave attacks. The road between Baghdad and Basra was breached – briefly. Saddam's response was to use chemicals on southern Iraqi soil for the first time. Kate, having been made aware of the dire consequences if the Iranians could hold their positions, supervised the releasing of stocks of tabun, vexun and cyanide. The all-out Iraqi assault pushed the Iranians back and the status quo on the ground resumed.

The rest of that year was a continuation of the air war. Iraq, with its limited number of home-made tanker aircraft, could fly to areas deep inside Iran previously unattainable, but only in small numbers. Raids against industrial targets such as factories making bulldozers, boilers, construction equipment and chemicals were successfully undertaken. The Iranian air force was suffering from a lack of spares and was becoming impotent in intercepting the Iraqi attacks. AWACS patrolling the skies and US warships patrolling the Gulf were using their sophisticated radars to warn Iraqi pilots of Iranian interceptors approaching them. The Iranian leaders were realising that the war was slowly turning against them. The accurate attacks on their oil tankers were strangling their exports. Rafsanjani, the Iranian politburo leader, without informing Khomeini, approached the Egyptian leader, President Mubarak, to hint that Iran was prepared to negotiate a treaty, asking him to intervene.

Saddam knew he was getting the upper hand. His *Total War* was winning.

CHAPTER 40

The complete mobilisation of all available Iranian troops reached its peak in September 1986. US satellite intelligence confirmed that at least 650,000 troops were beginning to arrive near the southern front, apparently preparing to attack Basra. Half a million of those being assembled were Pasdaran and Basij militia; men of all ages between twelve and seventy. Their training varied from forty days to none. All leave passes for the regular Iranian Army had been cancelled. All hospitals in Iran were put on high alert. The final offensive was expected imminently. Rafsanjani was quoted as saying that 'the fall of Basra will be tantamount to Saddam Hussein's death'. The timing of the operation was designed to coincide with the winter, so that the heavy rains would hinder Iraqi armour and air superiority.

The desperate manoeuvre was most probably triggered by the success of the Iraqi air war squeezing Iranian exports and the knowledge that the new Iraqi oil pipe line through Saudi Arabia was up and running. Compounding their precarious position, however, was the lack of aircraft spares for their Phantoms and Tomcats. Seven tons of US-made arms and spares had arrived in July from Israel after a trip through Spain and Yugoslavia. Since then, there had been nothing. Iran was pushing for the release of Lebanon hostages in exchange for more missiles, hoping their release would bring some relief to their dire position. The lid blew off the pot when, on 3rd November, the Lebanese magazine *Ash-Shiraa* exposed the scandal of the illegal National Security Council weapons for hostages deals that by-passed US Congress legislation.

The article cited the recently appointed head of the NSC, Admiral John Poindexter, as masterminding a new plan to sell arms to Iran. Instead of using Israel, the sale was through an arms dealer who was a close relative of Rafsanjani. The proceeds of the sale were to go via Swiss bank accounts to the Contra guerrillas fighting the left-wing government in Nicaragua. Oliver North was still the intermediary. The plan had gone into effect in February, but by September, only one hostage had been released and two small shipments made.

Seeking to confuse the Iraqis, the Iranian Government immediately confirmed the *Ash-Shiraa* story. President Reagan had no alternative but to go on TV on 13th November and admit the sale. Facing mounting pressure from Congress, the President set up a commission to investigate the matter. Some months later the Tower Commission would criticise the President for not properly supervising his subordinates.

Saddam's response to the scandal was unprintable. 'There is a war to finish,' he announced to his Council on 15th November. 'Youseff hinted to me at the beginning of the year that I mustn't trust the Yankees. He was right.' He stopped and smiled at his Head of Intelligence. Few noticed Youseff glance a smile at Kate, as if to say thank you.

'We will finish this war,' he continued, 'with an escalation of the air war and the completion of a plan I dreamt up some years ago to strengthen our defences around Basra.'

Firstly, the Iraqi Air Force hit the Iranian supply lines and their defence industry complex near Isfahan where a string of ammunition factories had been built by Swedish firms. They were badly damaged and resulted in postponing the final push by almost two months.

Secondly, and more spectacularly, Saddam's engineers completed building an artificial barrier using local dykes and the Jasmin River to create a lake. Known as the *Fish Lake*, it measured twenty-three miles in length, by one mile wide. Electrodes were placed in the water. On either side of the lake, minefields stretched for a further ten miles. Behind them were a series of trenches. Behind them barbed wire and concrete bunker command posts. The forty-mile long barrier became known as *Saddam's Wall*.

The American satellites could see the massive build-up to the east. The CIA Director, William Casey, was alarmed. He immediately informed the Iraqis and personally took charge of arranging a fleet of twenty-three Hercules aircraft to supply ammunition, vehicles and self-propelled artillery guns to Basra from Diego Garcia. They flew around the clock for a week from 28th December 1986 to 3rd January 1987.

The *Mother of All Battles, Operation Karbala-5*, began on the morning of 9th January when the Basij militia attacked the Iraqi defences with a human-wave assault south of the *Fish Lake*. The weather on the previous three days had been thick fog, which allowed the Iranians to assemble their troops without interruption. They overran the Iraqi positions by virtue of their sheer numbers, then crossed the lake in wooden boats, some little bigger than five-man canoes. From there they made a further desperate charge, but met stiffer resistance from Iraqi Republican guards. The Iranian casualties on the first day were fifty per cent greater than on day one of the Battle of the Somme. Some 30,000 Iranians perished. Nevertheless, by 10th January, two of the defensive lines had been taken and the Iranians were digging-in just seven miles from Basra. They then began to shell Basra with their North Korean rockets and artillery. The city was in a state of panic. The population fell from two million to 100,000 in two weeks. The road to Baghdad was blocked by refugees fleeing north while Iraqi Army reserves and supplies tried to head south.

On 14th January, the Iranians had cut through the third line of trenches. A week later they were within five miles of Basra, now under continuous heavy bombardment. The situation was so desperate that Saddam or one of his doppelgangers, no one ever found out, made a rare visit to the front line. His generals demanded to be given carte blanche to conduct operations without political interference. He conceded to their request, unknowingly learning, at last, a lesson from Nastia Game. The Iraqis now had their backs to the walls; only their superior air power could save them.

Iranian positions were attacked day and night by the Hughes helicopters, spraying chemical weapons. The recently acquired Mig-29 night fighters, with sophisticated electronic counter-measures, were used to strafe the Iranian positions with cannon and rockets during the long hours of darkness. During the day, the process was continued by the Su-17s and the Mig-23s. Iranian supply routes were also bombed with conventional and chemical weapons twenty-four hours a day. Tehran, Isfahan and Qom were bombed relentlessly to try and divide the population. The Iranian Air Force, desperate for spares, was hopelessly outnumbered and could do nothing to prevent the slaughter. It had fewer than fifty serviceable combat aircraft to Iraq's five hundred.

By the fourth week of the offensive the Iranians were running out of steam; their forces were spent. A total of 95,000 Pasdaran and Basij militia were dead. A counter-attack by the Republican guards on 8th February pushed the Iranians back to their starting positions a month previously. Although Iran boasted the operation had been a success and would be followed up with more attacks later in the year, nothing materialised. Operation Karbala-5 was, in reality, the last major 'final offensive'. Future offensive moves were to be limited in the north where they would support Kurdish guerrillas, still a thorn in Saddam's flesh.

Seemingly satisfied with having regained the *ante-bellum* boundaries, the Iraqis spent the rest of the summer building up their air force, and creating five new super airfields. The hardened air shelters, or HASs, were built by Yugoslavs with reinforced concrete walls a yard thick. Each airfield had fifty HASs that were much wider than those seen in Europe and could shelter very large aircraft, such as the Mig-25s. The bases, costing over $1 billion each, had two runways in excess of 12,000 feet and covered an area of twenty square miles. Even the taxiways could be used for take-off and landing.

Iran's time was up. Iraq's massive reconstruction and rearming continued through 1987. Huge deliveries of tanks, aircraft and military equipment arrived daily from the USSR on the Moscow-Baghdad air bridge. Soviet advisers helped to alter and enhance the Army's tactics from the defensive to the offensive. Perhaps, better late than never, Saddam had realised the chain of command needed to be changed to give field commanders more responsibility. Large-scale exercises were conducted to sharpen Iraq's offensive capability.

On 20th July, the Security Council of the United Nations passed Resolution 598 calling for an end to the fighting and a return to pre-war boundaries. Neither side took any notice. Iraq could see victory in its sight; Khomeini wouldn't accept the poisoned chalice.

At daybreak on 17th April 1988, the Iraqis initiated *Operation Ramadan*. Massive artillery barrages and helicopter attacks were directed at the Faw peninsula. The Iraqis were sufficiently confident to mount a commando type raid behind the Iranian lines blowing up bridges and cutting off Iranian supply and escape routes. The Iraqi advance continued unabated throughout the night and by the following afternoon the Iraqis were marching into Al Faw to cheering crowds.

That evening, another blow was to befall the Iranians. In the Persian Gulf, some sixty miles east of Bahrain in international waters, the US Navy frigate, the *USS Samuel Roberts* was escorting several tankers to Kuwait. It was suddenly hit by an Iranian mine, blowing a twenty-five feet hole in the hull and injuring ten sailors. The turbines were blown off their mountings and the engine room flooded. An Iranian frigate, the *Sabalan*, was about twenty miles away and had been monitoring the event. It closed in to attack, but turned away when it realised the stricken ship was not an easy target. In Washington there was a unanimous demand for a swift response. Admiral William Crowe, Chairman of the Joint Chiefs of Staff, persuaded Reagan to inaugurate *Operation Praying Mantis*. Three Iranian oil platforms would be destroyed.

The following morning, the US Navy struck, bombarding the platforms after giving the Iranians warnings to evacuate. Some stayed to fight; they died. Marine demolition parties boarded the rigs and finished the job. The small Iranian Navy undertook what were, in effect, suicide missions, attacking US Naval vessels. The sea battle lasted most of the day, at the end of which, six Iranian gunboats and two frigates had been sunk. There were no American casualties other than a reconnaissance helicopter, crashing due to a mechanical fault.

The ground war was lost, the air war was over and the Navy decimated. The Iranian Parliament led by Rafsanjani was in a state of shock as a result of the direct intervention of the US. It gave Khomeini an ultimatum: accept the terms of UN Resolution 598. 'We can't fight the Yankees and the Iraqis,' he urged. Khomeini remained unmoved. During May, Saddam's troops completed liberating those areas of southern Iraq that had been under Iranian control. The Americans stepped up pressure on Iran by heavily jamming Iranian fighters' airborne radars, effectively blinding them to Iraqi Air Force intrusions.

Fearful of an Iraqi push in the autumn, and on the verge of total defeat, the last Iranian soldiers occupying Iraqi soil in the north were withdrawn. Iran's top politicians and clergy met in Tehran on 14th July 1988 and gave Khomeini his final ultimatum: accept Resolution 598. Khomeini, however, wanted one final shot at Saddam Hussein. On 15th July, a single Phantom F-4E, crewed by the best two pilots Iran had, was assigned to bomb the presidential palace in Tikrit where Saddam was believed to be in residence. The early morning take off went well. The 200 feet ingress was flawless; the target successfully overflown. However, the bombs hit the gardens in front of the building. Saddam was unharmed. It was the last deep strike mission the Iranian Air Force flew before Resolution 598 was officially accepted by Iran on 18th July 1988.

Although some skirmishes did occur for several weeks, on 8th August the UN Security Council unanimously approved the details of 598. The truce was to start at 0630 hours on 20th August by which time a UN peacekeeping force, UNIIMOG, would be in place. Saddam declared a three-day public holiday starting on 9th August. On 21st August, a parade was held in Baghdad in honour of his victorious troops. A fly-past of over 200 planes coincided with the march through the streets. A public investiture was held in front of the presidential palace. At the end of the medal awarding ceremony, the highest honour of all, Hero of Iraq, was conferred on sixteen heroes. The first to receive the award, *for her unstinting services to arms production,* was Kate. She was the only female ever to receive the honour.

***

After the *victory at all costs* war, came the day of reckoning. A previously healthy and expanding economy lay in ruins. Some 250,000 Iraqis were dead, though the casualties on the Iranian side were at least five times greater. Iraq's war debt was over $120 billion, most owed to UAE, Saudi Arabia and Kuwait. For Saddam, hoping to become the leader of a pan-Arab coalition, it was highly embarrassing. Faced with the enormous task of rebuilding the broken infrastructure of his country, he went cap in hand to his neighbours for post-war reconstruction.

Saddam used the argument that the struggle with Iran had been fought for the benefit of all the Sunni dominated Arab States. Therefore, a large share of the Iraqi debt should be written off. In particular, he argued, he had saved Kuwait from Iranian domination and his accumulated debt with them, some $50 billion, should be forgotten. The Kuwaitis refused.

His second ploy was to attempt to raise oil prices by getting the other oil-exporting countries to cut production. Kuwait, again, refused. Instead, at meetings of OPEC, the Kuwaitis proposed the exact opposite: to increase production and, effectively, reduce its cost. As Iraq needed to sell oil at high prices to pay its debts, the tensions between the two neighbours rose. The Kuwaiti oil reserves were roughly the same as the Iraqis. Each had about 20% of the world's known reserves. Kuwait's population, however, was less than 10% of Iraq's. It made Kuwait a very rich neighbour per head of capita.

Historically, Kuwait had been a part of Mesopotamia. Iraqi nationalists maintained that it was, therefore, part of Iraq. The country had only come into existence as a result of the 'British Imperialists' in 1920. The borders between the two countries had always been open to dispute. And it was in northern Kuwait where most of the oil fields were situated.

For years Saddam had argued that the Kuwaitis were slant-drilling and taking oil from beneath Iraq territory. He had complained many times publicly at meetings of the Arab Council, but had done nothing.

Now things were different and in an attempt to get the Kuwaitis to stop thieving his oil, troops were moved to the border in November 1988. The deployment of forces merely served to deteriorate relations, although the Kuwaitis did stop slant-drilling.

That same month, George Herbert Walker Bush was winning the Presidency of the US, defeating his rival Michael Dukakis. The Reagan administration was about to end. It had been generous in its support for Saddam, having given him almost $40 billion to fight Iran; mostly on credit. At the height of the war, Iraq had been the biggest recipient of US assistance in the world. Saddam had no reason to believe the special relationship with America would change. After all, Bush had been Reagan's Vice-President for the past eight years. What Saddam didn't know was that much of the aid had been given to keep him from forming too strong an alliance with the Soviets. What George Herbert Bush knew was that the Soviet Star was receding over the horizon. Within eighteen months there would only be one super power and there would be no need to subsidise Saddam any more.

***

16th February 1989

The BBC announced: 'The Soviet Union today completed its withdrawal from Afghanistan. At the height of their occupancy, there were over 100,000 soldiers in Afghanistan supporting the Kamal regime. It is believed that over 15,000 Russian troops were killed in the ten years that they have been fighting the Taliban. The pull-out began a year ago as a result of President Gorbachev introducing perestroika, the restructuring of the Soviet economy.'

Amer was right. Afghanistan did turn out to be the Soviet's Vietnam. Can it really be almost ten years ago when he sat here with me? God, I am feeling old this morning.

September 1989 would have been Kate's 10th wedding anniversary and on 3rd October she would be forty. The war had not only taken a toll on the infrastructure of the country, but on the individuals living in it. Kate, owing to her privileged position, had been luckier than most. She had neither suffered too much from food shortages nor interruptions to services such as electricity and water. However, postal services were exceedingly erratic; phone lines were almost constantly down. So it was no surprise when on Wednesday, 1st March, she received a letter from Egypt postmarked 14th January. She recognised Hind's handwriting immediately. Upon opening the letter, she read that her father had died three days previously from cancer. He had been a heavy smoker in his youth, although had reduced his consumption over the years. When diagnosed with lung cancer in December, it had been too late. He had also, by then, secondaries in the brain. Hind had tried to ring Kate continuously for several days but had had to give up. All lines from Jordan to Iraq were down, she had been told. By contrast, Hind had not had a problem getting through to Lina who had been able to fly out from England for the funeral.

God, I wish I was living in England too. Life would be much simpler. Why did James have to be killed? I would have made him a good wife.

It dawned on her that she hadn't thought of James in that way for a long time.

I must be thankful for meeting Amer. Pull yourself together and get on with life.

Kate resolved to go and see her mother at once. She tried to contact her family by phone, but couldn't get through. She rang Ali Youseff. If anyone could arrange for her to leave Iraq quickly, he could. He immediately arranged a visa and booked a flight to Amman for her later that day. By 11 am the next morning, she was knocking on her Aunt Raghad's door. She was staggered when it was opened by Lina. 'What are you doing here?' Kate asked in astonishment.

Lina said nothing, her eyes flooded and she opened her arms to hug a puzzled Kate. 'We buried Mum yesterday,' she choked. 'We tried to contact you all last week when it looked as if Mum was going to die. We couldn't get through. The Iraq embassy here in Cairo wasn't helpful. We even tried threatening them, saying that you were a member of the Revolutionary Council. They just shrugged their shoulders.'

Kate was devastated, a deep feeling of guilt descended over her. 'It's entirely my fault,' she moaned to her sisters and aunt. 'It was me who persuaded Mum and Dad to move to Cairo. They should have stayed in Samarra. The town has been relatively untouched by the fighting.' It was an emotional reaction to the double blow of losing both her parents, but hardly a logical one.

'You're not to blame,' assured Aunt Raghad. 'My sister was heart-broken when Qassim died. They had been happily married for forty-three years. They had a good marriage. They wouldn't want to see you distraught like this.'

Kate stayed with her sisters for a week, gradually recovering from the shock and by catching up on each other's news, slowly realising that no one held her to blame. Lina was now a junior registrar in neurology at a hospital in Leeds. She was enjoying life and had several boyfriends in tow. Hind was expecting a baby. The thought of Kate becoming an aunt made her realise time was passing her by.

'Why don't you come back to England with me and why do you always have that pen strapped to the inside of your sleeve?' Lina had asked one afternoon.

'First, I would need another visa to go to England and I wouldn't get one. I was lucky to get this ten-day visa to come to Egypt. Second, this…' she paused to show her sister the tube attached to her loose-fitting sleeve by a Velcro strap, 'is a disguised pepper spray.'

'But, why do you carry it?' persisted Lina.

'My work has made me a potential assassination target for the Iranians. We must have killed nigh on a million of them with our chemical weapons.'

'But, would a pepper spray stop an assassin?'

Kate smiled at her youngest sister. 'It's a very special sort of pepper,' she replied. 'I can hit someone between the eyes with the jet in less than a quarter of a second.'

'Why won't Saddam let you leave now the war is over?' Lina always had been too inquisitive for her own good.

'For a start, we're still fighting the Kurds in the north and I have a horrible feeling we may soon be fighting the Kuwaitis in the south. But, for God's sake don't tell anyone I said so. My problem is that I have become indispensable. I am the only person who knows where the biological weapons are stored.'

'Haven't you got records of their locations, then?'

God, she's persistent!

'Yes, but I am the only one who can understand them. If I go, they would remain hidden for all time.'

'But, that's good, isn't it?'

'For the human race, yes; for me, no.'

CHAPTER 41

4th June 1989

Listening to the BBC World Service that morning, Kate was elated to hear the news. 'The death was announced in Tehran yesterday of Ayatollah Khomeini, Supreme Ruler of Iran. He had been in hospital for almost two weeks following a heart attack. He was aged eighty-six. His successor has not yet been announced.'

I'll bet Saddam is pleased. I wonder what they'll do with his doppelgangers.

In Iraq things were slowly getting back to normal. Kate found more time to supervise her research staff. She was no longer a regular attendee at meetings of the Revolutionary Council. Chemical Ali was happy as long as she could supply him with sufficient chemical weapons to chase the Kurds. Saddam was trying hard to have loans cancelled whilst at the same time rebuild his torn country. There was no unemployment as roads were repaired, canals restored, power stations rebuilt and power cables buried underground. The universities were beginning to train teachers and doctors again; schools and hospitals were refurbished. The problem was that the activities were being financed by international credits; more debts were accruing.

In an attempt to get world sympathy for his efforts at reconstructing his tattered country, Saddam Hussein encouraged the international press to send journalists to Iraq. He hoped they would favourably comment on his post-war building and development efforts. In so doing, they might influence the International Monetary Fund to help finance, by grants rather than loans, his humanitarian steps at improving Iraqi standards of living. As journalists arrived, they were allocated a minder – officially an interpreter, but in reality a member of the BPISS.

One of the reporters who arrived in late August was Farzad Bazoft, a freelance journalist working for *The Onlooker*, a left of centre Sunday paper, printed in London. Bazoft had been born in Iran, thirty-one years previously, but had settled in the United Kingdom in the mid-80s. He held a British passport. On 19th September 1989 he heard a rumour that there had been a mysterious explosion at a military complex ten miles north of Baghdad. Whereas other Western reporters were forbidden to approach the site, somehow Bazoft slipped his minder and persuaded a nurse from the Red Cross, Denise Parr, whom he had befriended, to drive him to the complex at Al Muthanna.

The next day, while waiting for his flight back to London, he was arrested at Baghdad airport. In his luggage was a thirty-six frame roll of film and some soil samples taken from near the Army base. Eighteen of the frames, when developed, showed the Al Muthanna camp. He was held in custody awaiting trial at the Abu Ghraib prison. His accomplice, Denise Parr, was kept under house arrest awaiting trial for espionage.

***

The supply of chemicals from the West, virtually unlimited during the Iranian war, was drying up rapidly. On 2nd October, Kate met General Youseff. 'We cannot go on producing chemical weapons at the rate General Hassan al Majid is using them in the north,' she said. 'Germany has cut us off completely and the supply from Britain and America is down to a trickle.'

'If I remember rightly, you told me you had a special arrangement with the British,' remarked Youseff.

'We have not needed to use that arrangement for four or five years. During the war supplies were so plentiful,' replied Kate.

'What about biologicals? There must be plenty of those. After all we never used any on the Iranians. Perhaps, I can persuade Hassan to use them instead.'

Kate shivered. 'No! Don't encourage him. He once wanted to bomb Tehran with anthrax spores. Can you imagine? Every country in the civilised world would have turned on us, crying "Weapons of Mass Destruction". It would have led to a war, Iraq versus The Rest; or, worse still, the Americans nuking Baghdad.'

'Nonsense,' retorted the senior General. 'The Americans gave us most of our anthrax. Why would they do that if they didn't expect us to use it?'

'Because...' and here Kate slowed down, wondering if she should contradict the second most important man in the Army, '...because, if they think we are about to use anthrax or botulinium, it will give them an excuse to invade us for our oil. My husband used to say, "Never ever trust the Yanks". I believe someday he will be proved right.'

'Very well, I'll talk to Ali. I think he has more or less quelled the Kurds' revolt, so consumption should slow down. There will be no more wars until late next year, when we'll only need conventional weapons anyway.'

'Are you talking about Kuwait?' asked Kate.

'I couldn't possibly tell you that, now, could I? There is another thing I want to discuss with you, however. Do you know you have been getting followed recently?'

'No, by whom?'

'An Iranian with a British passport, called Farzad Bazoft.'

'I've never heard of him.'

'No, I didn't expect you to. He has taken a dozen photos of you entering both your apartment and Al Muthanna.'

'What the hell for?' asked Kate.

'We believe he works for Mossad. He is currently being interrogated at Abu Ghraib. We are expecting a full confession from him shortly. He will then go on trial with his accomplice, a Red Cross nurse called Denise Parr. I am afraid I shall have to reinstate your 24/7 bodyguards. I suspect he could have been eyeing out the land prior to an attempt on your life. He claims he was trying to get a scoop, I believe that's what it's called, on a follow-up over those articles some years ago when the British press called you Dr Germ.'

'Well, I'm glad you caught him when you did. On the matter of getting chemicals, if you agree, I will make contact with the British and try to resurrect our relationship. I could argue that it would reduce our likelihood of ever having to resort to anthrax.'

'OK, go ahead.'

***

On 18th October, Kate openly met Brian McCormack in the foyer of the *Sheraton Hotel*. It was their first meeting for four and a half years. After exchanging pleasantries, Kate explained her purpose was to resurrect the old arrangement of exchanging chemicals for information.

'I'm afraid that will be a decision taken by our Department of Trade and Industry. It's nothing to do with my side of the house,' was Brian's initial response to Kate's request.

'The problem I've got is Ali Hassan. He's using up our spare stocks fighting the Kurds. It won't be long before he'll be demanding to use biologicals such as anthrax and botulinium toxins. The only way I can prevent that happening is to keep him happy with chemicals. I'm not asking for the more esoteric stuff, but simple precursors for mustard gas would make a hell of a difference.'

'I thought you told me that the biologicals are safely hidden and your side will never be able to find them.'

'That's true. However, I have a feeling that Hassan intercepted some of the American anthrax spores several years ago. The delivery notes didn't add up. At the time, I put it down to a clerical error; now I'm not so sure.'

'How much went missing?' asked Brian.

'Fifty gallons.'

'That's a lot.'

Kate wasn't sure whether Brian was stating a fact or asking a question, and answered, 'Enough to kill a million people or more.'

'If Chemical Ali has got the anthrax, do you think he'll use it?'

'He's mad enough! What's worse, he'll use it without realising the long-term consequences and probably won't tell Saddam until it's too late.'

'Have you brought me a wish list?'

'Yes. Now I have two snippets for you. Firstly, General Youseff let it slip when he was agreeing for me to meet you that we are intending to invade Kuwait next year.'

'Do you know when?'

'No, but when I do, I'll let you know as soon as possible.' She paused for a moment, and then smiling, added, 'Providing you get me those chemicals, of course.'

Smiling, Brian replied, 'It goes without saying. There is a new minister in the DTI, Nicholas Ridley. He's more radical than his predecessor, Lord Young. I don't think we should have too many problems getting him to reverse their supply policies with you. Anything else?'

'Have you heard of someone called Farzad Bazoft?'

'No, why?'

'He's supposed to be a freelance reporter working for *The Onlooker* and has a British passport, even though he was born in Iran.'

'Go on.'

'He's been arrested and is in Abu Ghraib gaol, pending spying charges.'

'I'm amazed I haven't heard of his arrest. I shall look into it when I get back to the embassy.'

***

On 1st November, Bazoft appeared in front of TV cameras, looking slightly the worse for wear. He confessed to being an Israeli agent. Signals had flashed from the British Embassy in Baghdad to London the same evening that Kate had informed Brian McCormack of his arrest. MI6 had wasted no time in raising the stakes to Prime Ministerial level. The same day that Bazoft was confessing to the world, Saddam Hussein received a personal letter from Margaret Thatcher pleading for mercy. Saddam replied, assuring her he would get a fair trial.

Whether the pending trial of Bazoft had any influence, or not, is a matter of pure speculation, but by mid-November 1989, supplies of basic chemicals from Britain were back to their pre-1980 levels. Youseff was pleased with Kate's efforts. Ali was happy to be using mustard gas. Kate was glad no one was going to use the biological weapons; her lie about the missing anthrax had worked.

***

At the MI6 HQ in London the news of Bazoft's admission that he was an Israeli agent had hit Peter Stacey's desk. He knew the full history of Nastia Game and its chess protection system, now widespread in many top secret government computers. He knew of the murder of James Douglas' wife and daughter, and the subsequent tragedy in Northern Ireland. The two senior military officers involved in what had become known, internally, as the *Douglas Affair* had both retired. Admiral Johnson had retired to continue his passion for sailing and was living in Devon while General Morrison had acquired several acres on the Cheshire–Flintshire border to pursue his love of horse riding. The two officers had led Peter to believe that the accident in Weston-super-Mare had been the work of the CIA trying to get the secret of the chess key. Stacey also knew that the Americans had acquired the key by supplying the Iraqis with information during the war with Iran.

But now he was having second thoughts. Could it have been the Israelis, after all, who were after the chess secret? Why? What had changed? Was there a link between what had happened almost twelve years ago in Weston-super-Mare and Bazoft being exposed? Was it possible that the CIA and Mossad were working together?

He arranged to meet Air Vice-Marshal O'Rourke, now Head of Military Intelligence. He ordered Mike Noble, from the Riyadh desk, to attend. On Friday, 17th November, Peter chaired the meeting. He outlined the history of the chess key, the subsequent death of Mrs Douglas, the sad death of Squadron Leader Douglas some months later, the theory that the CIA had been responsible for what had occurred in Weston, and that Israel were behind Bazoft attempting to get photos of Al Muthanna and al Jised. He outlined his worries that, perhaps after all, 'we could have got it wrong'.

O'Rourke spoke first. 'I'm sorry, old boy, but I feel I'm not going to be much use. It was all before my time. I vaguely remember General Morrison mentioning this business to me when I took over the deputy post from him, but I know very little more than what you have just summarised. However, I will stay and offer my opinions, if you wish?'

'I would be most grateful if you did,' replied Peter.

Like most meetings when there isn't a clear cut agenda, the meeting dragged on. As lunchtime approached, no conclusions had been reached on who had been responsible for the early skulduggery. However, all three present agreed that there was a strong likelihood that the Israelis were now actively seeking to find where Iraq kept their CB weapons. They had discovered al Jised might be the key and they could be planning to kidnap her to extract the locations, prior to destroying the weapons.

'The trouble is,' sighed the Air Vice-Marshal, 'the wretched stuff is safer staying where it is – buried in the sands. If the Israelis were to bomb the sites, all they would achieve is the release of the spores into the atmosphere. It could be an environmental disaster.'

'Exactly,' exclaimed Peter, 'that is why al Jised's safety is paramount. The Iranians would like to assassinate her. The Israelis would like to kidnap her. Chemical Ali will have no hesitation in torturing her if she blocks him from using biologicals. The Americans would like to know how she hid the weapons. Mike, I want you to go to Baghdad and stress on Brian McCormack how vital it is that we don't let her slip out of our sights.'

***

On 10th March 1990, following a one-day trial behind closed doors, Bazoft was sentenced to death. Denise Parr was given a fifteen-year prison sentence. Bazoft was hanged at 0630 hours on 15th March. A month later, following a plea for clemency by Margaret Thatcher, Parr was released and deported from Iraq. The story of the affair had been suppressed in the West. Once Parr was free, however, the press had a field day triggering outrage in Europe and America. The attempt to generate Western sympathy towards Saddam's regeneration projects by using the press had backfired badly. Instead it had contributed to the international isolation of his regime.

CHAPTER 42

Saddam's plans for restructuring Iraq were in turmoil as a result of the Bazoft affair and Kuwait's intransigence over oil production. The movement of troops to the border in late 1989 had been a hollow threat. Now, he began to think again. How would other countries react if he were to claim Kuwait as the 19th Province of Iraq? He began to create his case for invasion. There was the dispute over his financial debt, every barrel of oil sold for $1 less decreased his income by $1 billion per year. Kuwait, by increasing its oil production by 40% since the end of the Iranian war, was throttling him. Moreover, although he could not prove it, they had begun slant-drilling again.

He knew historical claims based on Kuwait being originally a part of Mesopotamia would carry no weight with the international community. Kuwait, when part of the Ottoman Empire, had been within the Province of Basra. The British had split Iraq and Kuwait into two separate emirates in 1920 when Britain was given the mandates to run the two countries by the League of Nations. Iraq had never accepted Kuwait's independence, or its borders; largely because of the deliberate constriction of Iraq's access to the Persian Gulf. Saddam was in a corner and could only see the way forward by lashing out. America and Britain had ceased exporting dual-use technology and he saw this as yet another conspiracy to weaken his position. He was becoming paranoid. The fact that the Kuwaitis were seemingly unafraid of his threats on the border suggested that they had secretly been given tacit assurances by the Americans. The admission by Bazoft that he was an Israeli agent convinced him that Israel was preparing to attack his chemical and biological weapons' production factories.

On Monday, 3rd June 1990, Kate was asked to attend a Revolutionary Council meeting. Saddam put forward a paper for discussion: *The Case for the Accession of Kuwait.* The hawks argued that Iraq had historical and moral rights. The family that had ruled Kuwait for generations, the al Sabahs, were extremely unpopular. Women had no rights whatsoever; Palestinian migrant workers were treated as dirt. The Emir himself had insulted Iraqi women, calling them prostitutes because they didn't wear head coverings. Kate was surprised to hear that Nastia Game had been used to simulate different ways of attacking Kuwait. General Ali Hassan bragged, 'We will be in Kuwait City in less than thirty-six hours. Casualties will be minimal. Most of the Kuwaiti Army will flee to Saudi. We will be welcomed with open arms by the populace.' Inwardly, Kate groaned, she'd heard it all before.

The doves, including Youseff, offered caution. 'The annexation of Kuwait will be easy,' he said. 'Rather, it will be the fallout that will be the problem. We must get reassurances from the international community that they will not get involved with what amounts to our border dispute.'

Kate got the impression that Saddam was listening to Youseff's arguments. She was not asked to give a resume on the state of CB weapons. Presumably, Saddam was convinced they would not be required. At the conclusion, he declared, 'I will ask the new American ambassador to meet Tariq and me next month. If we believe, as a result of the meeting, that the Americans will take no action, then we will strike fast. I want the Army to be put on a week's alert from the middle of July.

Kate met Brian McCormack two days later. She informed him that Saddam was seeking a meeting with the American ambassador to find out if the Yankees had made any secret defensive treaties with the Kuwaitis. 'If he gets the green light, then I believe we will attack within a week. Our Army's simulations suggest Kuwait City will fall within two days.'

'I will keep a close watch on April Glaspie's movements. When she meets Saddam, then if what you say is correct, sparks will fly a few days later. I do know that she is in Washington at the moment. I wonder if she is getting instructions on how to handle the situation. My worry is that Iraq could be falling into a trap.'

'What do you mean?' asked Kate.

'Do you remember when James Douglas' wife and daughter were killed in a road accident?'

'Yes, of course. Why?'

'It was before my time. I was still at university. However, I understand that our analysts now believe their deaths were the result of a joint operation between the CIA and Mossad. Previously, we thought only the Americans were involved trying to get hold of the chess key. Now the thinking is that the Israelis wanted to find the locations of your nuclear, biological and chemical weapons, so that they could destroy them.'

'Well, they succeeded when they destroyed Osirak. So you're saying the Israelis wanted Nastia Game for the information on the game's files,' remarked Kate.

'Yes, I suppose so,' replied Brian. He continued. 'We believe the version of Nastia Game you gave the Americans at the beginning of the Iranian war was largely sterile. The Israelis have changed tack. We think the reason Bazoft had photos of you is that Mossad were, and probably still are, planning to kidnap you to try and get the CB locations. They are afraid that Saddam intends to use his Babylon Guns to fire biological weapons at Tel Aviv. Satellite images are suggesting the guns are almost complete.'

'I'd forgotten about those guns. It must be six or seven years ago since that project started.'

'Actually, it's longer than that. Saddam has had great difficulty getting the barrels made. Initially the West Germans were contracted to build them in sections. For some reason, they fell out with your engineers. The Romanians then won the contract, but their steel wasn't up to standards. The latest country to get involved is India.'

Brian paused, looking at Kate. *She must be a dozen years older than me,* he thought, *but she's still a handsome woman. I wonder if she really did have an affair with Squadron Leader Douglas.*

His thoughts triggered him to continuing. 'I have been asked by Mike Noble to remind you that the offer to bring you back to England still holds. You will be given a completely new identity, a pension, and will be free to live wherever you wish. With your qualifications, you will be able to get a job easily.' He was encouraging her as best he could.

'It's a very tempting offer. Let me think about it. I could easily see myself settling into life again in Cambridge. Let's see what happens after the Kuwait business, shall we?'

'Cambridge might not be the safest place for you to go.'

'Why?'

'There are bound to be people there who will remember you from when you did your PhD. Jonathon Gleeson would be about the only one who could be trusted not to give you away. However, I can recommend Oxford.' He laughed.

She laughed as well and nodded. 'Yes, you're right. Perhaps, Bath might be better. I remember it as a lovely city.' She began to dream of the pleasant weekend she'd had with James' family and shopping in Bath with Emma. She came out of her brief trance. 'You never told me why Iraq could be falling into a trap.'

'Several things, unrelated in themselves but all to do with the Americans. Firstly, their part in the *Douglas Affair*. Secondly, the Iran-Contra business: supplying Iran with weapons through Israel. Thirdly, Iraq has the fourth largest Army in the world after the Chinese, the Soviets and the Americans. Bush believes that if he can cripple you, then it will help stabilise the Middle East. He will push this notion with the Saudis and the Egyptians and get them to join a coalition to liberate Kuwait. Fourthly, Bush is an ex-CIA Director; he's a cunning bastard. I believe he will encourage Saddam to invade Kuwait. He will use the invasion as an excuse to come after Iraq. He will be showing everyone that the US is the world's only super-power. He will then set up an Iraqi puppet government and pinch your oil. Don't forget his oil wells in Texas are almost dry.'

'How do we stop him?'

'Don't invade Kuwait.'

***

On Wednesday, 25th July, the American ambassador, April Glaspie, met Saddam and Tariq Aziz. She was the first woman, from any country, to have been appointed as an ambassador to Iraq. A fluent Arabic speaker, having previously worked in the embassies in Egypt and Syria, she had been given specific instructions from President George Herbert Bush 'to broaden cultural and commercial contacts' with Iraq. After the usual pleasantries had been exchanged, she began. 'My Government know that you have deployed massive numbers of troops on your southern borders. It is none of our business, but it is seen as a threat by your neighbour Kuwait. My President has, therefore, instructed me to ask, "What are your intentions? Why are your troops so close to Kuwait?"'

Saddam was formal in his reply. 'Firstly, let me offer my warmest greetings to your President and offer him my sincerest congratulations on his recent appointment to the most powerful office in the world. Secondly, allow me to reassure him that my troops are positioned purely as an exercise. As we speak, the Egyptian President, my good friend, Hosni Mubarak, is setting up a meeting between myself and the Kuwaiti Emir, al Sabah. It will take place next week in Jeddah.'

April replied, 'That is good news, sir. I will relay it back to President Bush immediately. We hope you will be able to solve this problem peacefully and quickly. Secretary of State, James Baker, has asked me to emphasise to you that the United States has no opinion on Arab–Arab conflicts. The Kuwait issue is, therefore, not associated with America.'

The meeting ended soon afterwards and a day later Saddam Hussein received a cable from Bush thanking him for his 'warm wishes'. The trap had been set.

***

Kate attended a Revolutionary Council meeting on Friday, 27th July. Saddam was hyped up. He clearly believed that April Glaspie's remarks that, 'America would not take a stand on Arab–Arab border disputes' and 'had no intention of starting an economic war with Iraq' were a diplomatic green light.

He declared, 'On 2nd August 1990 at 0200 hours we invade Kuwait. By 1900 hours on 3rd August, I expect my old friend, Hussein Ali, to be the new governor of the 19th Province.' There was a stunned silence for a few moments, then a round of applause. Several round the table, including Tariq Aziz and Chemical Ali stood up.

When the excitement had subsided, Kate was taken by surprise.

It was General Youseff, looking sombre and grave who spoke. 'Sir, my intelligence officers in Riyadh, Bahrain and Kuwait City are all telling me the same thing.'

'What?' snapped Saddam.

Kate got the instant distinct impression, *Saddam doesn't like Ali Youseff.*

'Firstly, America is co-ordinating with Saudi Arabia, the UAE and Kuwait in a conspiracy. By reducing the price of oil, they know it will badly affect our military industries and scientific research. Secondly, they are setting up the Israelis with new long-range ground attack aircraft to strike our most important factories. There is a grand conspiracy afoot.'

'Are you telling me that the Saudis and other Arab States will gang up with the Yankees to liberate Kuwait as an excuse to attack us?'

'Yes, sir. They will liberate Kuwait to get cheap oil. The Americans don't care how they do it. You can't trust the Yankees,' stressed Ali Youseff.

'Rubbish! The trouble with you Ali is that you see conspiracies everywhere. They're terrified of having another Vietnam.' Saddam laughed and looked around the room. It was a signal for everyone else to laugh too. Kate forced herself to smile, but felt ashamed at seeing her boss humiliated.

The words of Amer echoed in her ears: *Never ever trust the Yanks.* She never saw Ali again. The following day, his deputy Brigadier Wafiq al Samarra, was made a Major General and had taken on the role as Head of Military Intelligence.

On 2nd August, the invasion began. Four Armoured Divisions of the Republican Guard swept into northern Kuwait. Iraqi Army Special Forces were deployed in helicopters and fast coastal gun boats to attack behind the Kuwaiti lines. Commandos seized airports and blew up lines of communication. Air superiority was total. The Iraqi squadrons of Mig-23s and Mirage F1s ruled the skies. As predicted, by 1900 hours on the second day of the war, it was all over.

The propaganda war, the diplomatic battle, Operations *Desert Shield* and *Desert Storm* were about to begin.

CHAPTER 43

Within forty-eight hours of Iraq's successful invasion of Kuwait, both the United States and Britain had started to deploy troops and aircraft to Saudi Arabia. Simultaneously, efforts began to be made to urge other countries to send forces as well. To justify American troops going half way around the world to fight for a rich oil sheik, Bush covertly began a propaganda war at home. Wealthy supporters formed an organisation calling itself 'Citizens for a Free Kuwait'. It hired America's biggest PR firm, Hill and Knowlton for $1 million per month to produce material designed to sway public support. Most of the fees were paid by the now exiled Kuwaiti Emir. Phoney TV news bulletins were prepared to be shown on prime time television. A book, *The Rape of Kuwait*, was prepared. A quarter of a million copies were made and distributed to American troops. Worst of all was the renowned 'incubator babies case'. A girl, purporting to be a Kuwaiti nurse, gave evidence to Congress that she had seen Iraqi soldiers taking babies out of incubators in the Kuwait City hospital and leaving them to die whilst the incubators were taken back to Iraq. She turned out to be the fifteen-year-old daughter of the Kuwait ambassador to the US and hadn't been in Kuwait City for many years. Although the story was disproved three weeks later, it was too late. President George Herbert Bush's image of being a 'wimp' had been replaced as a 'hawk'; Saddam was now public enemy number one in America.

By contrast Saddam's efforts at propaganda were disastrous. He resorted to old-fashioned German WW2 tactics made infamous by Lord Haw-Haw: radio transmissions aimed at the forces building up in Saudi

Arabia and the dropping of leaflets. He opened a new radio station, 'The Mother of all Battles Radio'. The themes pumped out had two purposes: firstly, to bolster Iraq's own forces and any Arab listeners and, secondly, to paint the Americans as immoral cowards. The radio announcers were quickly nick-named 'Baghdad Betty' and 'Iraqi Jack'. Whereas the choice of music was excellent, much better than that offered locally, the propaganda content was absurd. The producers of the programmes clearly didn't understand the target audience. They had a jaundiced perception of life in America, its culture and traditions. The broadcasts' credibility rapidly deteriorated as they claimed most American soldiers were Jews, addicted to wine and loose women. They would spread AIDS throughout the Middle East. The leaflets fared no better. Written in English, the grammar was appalling, the spelling littered with mistakes, information dated and facts frequently incorrect. A leaflet titled 'Liberty Weeps' showed the Statue of Liberty, but called it the 'Liberty Stadium'. Instead of lowering morale amongst the coalition forces, the propaganda fuelled their belief that the Iraqis were little better than a bunch of backward dagos.

Iraq's image was further damaged internationally when Saddam refused to let foreign nationals leave his country. He was seen on TV with a young boy, Stuart Lockwood, ruffling his hair – one of 2,500 human shields. 'They are our guests,' he said, 'and their presence is to prevent the scourge of war; they shouldn't be here for long.'

The Arab nations made great efforts diplomatically to settle the dispute peacefully. Egyptian President Mubarak encouraged the UN Secretary General, Perez de Cuellar, and Soviet President Gorbachev to use their influence with Tariq Aziz. The problem was that the overwhelming desire for an Arab solution allowed Saddam to forestall a response. He knew the Arab League was divided: Jordan, the PLO and Yemen broadly supported him. Meanwhile Desert Shield had a momentum of its own. Bush stood back, happy for diplomacy to run its course. His only condition was that any diplomatic settlement must not reward Saddam in any way for his aggression.

By November 1990, it was becoming obvious, even to the frustrated Egyptian leader, that Saddam was intransigent. His problem was that he did not understand the influential decline of the Soviet Union, thinking they would step in and prevent the on-coming American action. He had also considerably underestimated his ability to amass popular support from the Arab nations. He could not believe that they would sooner support the Americans than himself.

The UN Security Council had passed various resolutions after the invasion condemning Iraq and reaffirming Kuwait's sovereignty. They imposed sanctions. However, on 29th November, the UN passed Resolution 678, explicitly authorising the use of force to remove Iraq's troops from Kuwait. The news of the resolution hit Saddam's desk that evening. It had been a terrible day, for earlier he had been informed that Margaret Thatcher had been replaced as British Prime Minister by John Major. Losing Reagan had been bad enough, but losing Mrs Thatcher was rubbing salt into his wounds. When, the following afternoon, he was told that President Mubarak had announced he would be sending 30,000 troops to help with the forthcoming Operation Desert Storm, Saddam knew he was bleeding to death. He would have to resort to desperate measures to survive. He called an emergency meeting of his Council for Saturday, 1st December and Kate was called to the special meeting. Surprisingly, Saddam seemed upbeat.

Can he really believe he can get away with the invasion? thought Kate. She was soon to see why there was still optimism in the camp.

'The UN has given us until 15th January to begin the withdrawal of our troops,' Saddam declared. 'I want you, Tariq, to keep up the pretence of seeking a peaceful, negotiated settlement. Go to the UN, Cairo or Moscow as often as it takes. We'll drag the process out as long as possible.'

Tariq looked tired, but nodded affirmatively. However, he replied authoritatively. 'Mr President, we must give up the human shield hostages. Mr Gorbachev has stressed that he will not receive me until the last one has left Iraq.'

Poor old Tariq, he must be suffering from jet lag with all his toing and froing.

Saddam agreed. 'Begin to release them next week.' He then turned to Kate. 'Al Jised, what is the state of our CB weapons?'

It was an easy question. She had come prepared. 'We are up to stock. General Hassan has recently replenished his shells and mortars, 150,000 of each. There is plenty of zarin and mustard gas for the sprayer helicopters.'

Saddam looked at Ali Hassan, clearly expecting him to nod or disagree. The Head of the Army stared through Kate. 'I think,' he said deliberately, 'I think, the President and I have decided the time has come to use biologicals. How long will it take you to release the botulinium toxins and anthrax?'

Kate could see what was in their minds. *They're planning to drench Kuwait and the US forces with anthrax.* She shuddered at the thought. She wondered if anyone had noticed her instinctive reflex.

'How much do you want?' she asked. Her mind was racing. For ten years she had prevented the use of biological weapons, but now Armageddon had come.

'Twelve hundred gallons of anthrax will do for a start,' replied Chemical Ali. 'I plan to use a force of sixty Hughes helicopters, each carrying twenty gallons.'

'I have stored anthrax in batches of ten five-gallon drums. Each cache is typically two metres under the ground. Give me a team of a dozen men, with a mechanical digger, and we could give you what you want in about two to three weeks,' said Kate.

'Why so long?' he asked.

'The locations are not adjacent. It may take us many hours to go from one site to the next, sometimes many days.'

'We were thinking of putting botulinium toxin in the warheads of Scud missiles to fire at Israel.' It was Saddam who spoke, looking at Kate. He was sounding out her opinion.

'It would not be very effective because of the heat from the rocket's engines. By the time the scuds exploded over Israel, the botulinium would be all but destroyed. Zarin would be much better. But why target Israel?' Her question to her leader had been instinctive. She knew at once she shouldn't have asked. Both Saddam's and Ali Hassan's faces went black. They never replied. There was a deathly silence in the room.

Kate thought of the answer almost immediately. *They want Israel to attack us, effectively supporting the Yanks. Then they hope the other Arab States will join us and Saudi Arabia will tell the Americans to bugger off! Very clever.*

After what seemed ages, Saddam spoke. 'I think we can leave the excavation of the anthrax up to about two weeks before we need it. Don't you, Ali?'

'Yes. We will tell you when we want it, al Jised,' said Ali Hassan.

***

Two days later, Kate managed to meet Brian McCormack. She outlined Saddam's plans to use anthrax on Kuwait City and the advancing coalition forces as they chased the Iraqis out of the occupied territory. 'We never used biologicals once against the Iranians,' she said, 'but this time I am afraid I will be unable to stop their use.'

'I thought your hiding method was infallible,' he remarked.

'It is, but when push comes to shove and they realise what I have done, then my time will be up. I've heard of some of the treatments that the BPISS get up to with women. Frankly, it fills me with horror.'

She looks fragile today. I suspect when they stick electrodes on her breasts she might break. 'How long have you got before they demand you release the anthrax?' he asked.

'I don't know. Soon? When will the war begin?'

'It will begin with a bombing campaign. Ground forces will not move until General Schwarzkopf is satisfied that he has knocked the stuffing out of the Republican Guards. The air war could take two or three weeks.

That gives you to the beginning of February to get out, or stay. What is it going to be?' Brian realised his question had not been put to Kate as gently as it should have been, but her answer surprised him. In an instant she had changed. In front of him was a hardened virago, her steely eyes blazing fiercely at being asked such a question.

'I will stay for as long as possible. When and if I am ready to get out, I will contact you.'

'There's one big snag,' he paused, wondering how much he should give away.

'What?'

'A day or two before 15th January, all the coalition embassies will pull out. Even the Swiss intend to leave, so there will be no one left in Baghdad to spring you.'

She looked blankly at him, her eyes ever more piercing. Then, as quickly as the anger had appeared, she changed. She looked feminine again. He thought he saw the beginning of her eyes welling up. She blinked and said coldly, 'Then this might be our last meeting. Give my regards to Mike and Peter when you see them.' She offered her hand. He shook it, took it to his lips and gently kissed it.

'It's been nice knowing you all,' she said. She turned and walked away.

What a peculiar mix she is, from a beautiful butterfly to a stinging wasp in seconds and then back again. I can't leave it like this, he thought. *There has to be something we can do.*

***

From: British Embassy, Baghdad
3 Dec 90
To: Hd of Middle East Sect, MI6 London
Copy, Riyadh (Attn, M Noble)
Dear Peter
Ref, Agent Al Jised (241/5)
Met KAJ this pm. She informed me Saddam intends to use anthrax

385

and botulinium toxin on Kuwait City and any coalition troops who follow retreating Iraqis. 60 helicopters, each carrying 20 galls of bios, will fly at heights of 10–20 feet, below radar detection, to carry out the attack. Other points covered:

Human shields will be released next week.

Tariq Aziz will continue hoax negotiations with Gorbachev.

Scud attacks on Israel start soon. Designed to bring Israel into conflict. Scuds may carry zarin (She will attempt talc dilution.)

Main worry is KAJ, she looks fragile. Believe if subject to torture she will reveal locations of hidden bios. She seems determined to hang-in as long as possible. Have warned her we pull out on 13/14th Jan. Urge you to consider getting her out by force. Kidnap, if necessary. Otherwise, consequences could be too terrible to contemplate.

Yours aye

Brian McC.

***

From: MI6, London

4 Dec 90

To, British Embassy, Baghdad

FAO: Brian McCormack

Ref, Agent Al-Jised (241/5)

Copy, Riyadh (M Noble)

Dear Brian

All points taken on board. Am arranging meeting with Chf of Mil. Intelligence re feasibility springing KAJ after 15 Jan. May be possible using SAS squad. Try to avoid this by seeing her before you leave Iraq.

Yours ever

Peter S.

***

On 10th December the exodus of the human shield hostages began. Iraq Air ferried the passengers to Amman under the supervision of the Soviet ambassador and his staff. Within four days of the airlift starting, all the 'guests' had been evacuated. Tariq flew to Moscow on 15th December, the first of four trips he would make in the next month.

By 12th December, the first Scud attacks on Tel Aviv had begun. A mixture of conventional explosives and zarin, unknowingly diluted with talcum powder, were used. Thanks to Kate having warned Brian that this phase in the war was imminent, little damage was inflicted. The Israelis had been forewarned to stay indoors. Despite the rocket attacks, Israel remained outside the conflict. President Bush had stressed they must not retaliate. He was sufficiently savvy to realise the raison d'etre behind Saddam's efforts to get Israel into the war. He explained to Prime Minister Yitzhak Shamir that his own Special Forces and the British SAS were combing the western Iraq desert for the Scud launchers that could not be seen from the air because they hid beneath bridges and camouflage netting during the day. Despite their policy of massive retaliation, ever since the State's foundation in 1947, Shamir's Government kept their peace.

***

Whereas MI6 is part of the Foreign Office, the Chief of the Military Intelligence Staff is beholden to the Minister of Defence. Like all Government Departments they understand that information is power. Although politicians strenuously deny it and even attempt to change some of the archaic working practices, the unwritten rule is to keep your cards close to your chest. Formal meetings between the Military men and their civilian counterparts, MI5 and Special Branch, both Home Office, and MI6, Foreign Office, are always recorded precisely and correctly. Everyone is courteous; everyone smiles. But secrets are secrets to be kept secrets.

John O'Rourke was, therefore, surprised when he received a phone call from Peter Stacey, recently promoted to the Head of MI6, asking for an informal chat over a spot of lunch. They agreed the RAF Club in Piccadilly was convenient.

'How can I be of help?' asked the Air Vice-Marshal.

'It's about our old friend, Nastia Game,' replied Peter.

O'Rourke chuckled. 'Ah, that old chestnut. Believe it, or not, I played it as a student when on No 63 Advanced Staff Course at Bracknell in 1973. It was a paper exercise in those days. If you ask me it should have stayed on paper; much less trouble all-round, what?'

Peter didn't respond immediately, but thought, *Where do they get these guys from?*

'Did you ever know Squadron Leader Douglas who wrote the original programs?' asked Peter.

'No. He was an education officer; basket weavers we call them. General Morrison told me his wife was killed and at our meeting last year you thought both the CIA and Mossad were responsible. I know he was the brains behind the use of a chess position to create a secure encryption method for software, now common in MoD, and was later killed in Northern Ireland. Why?'

'Just to recap, you will also remember that Douglas and ICL set the game up at the Military College in Baghdad. One of the Iraqi liaison officers on the project was a woman called al Jised. She became, shall we say, friendly with Douglas. Possibly as a consequence, she became a double agent. The best we've ever had.'

'Yes, I remember all this. She was the infamous Dr Germ, wasn't she? But what has it to do with me?' asked the airman.

'Allow me to finish.' Peter's fuse was beginning to heat. He now out-ranked the two-star RAF officer and wasn't going to put up with any bullshit.

'Dr Germ was an unfortunate term, as she single-handedly prevented Iraq from using biological weapons. She systematically hid them in the desert and doctored the records so that no one will be able to find them. During the eight years of war with Iran, Iraq never used biologicals once, even though we believe they have sufficient quantities to kill everything on the planet.' An observer listening to Peter's reply would have detected a degree of assertive animation in his voice.

'Yes, but what has this got to do with me?' repeated the disinterested Air Marshal.

'Three days ago, al Jised met our man in Baghdad. She told us that Saddam has hatched a plot to bomb Kuwait City and the coalition forces with anthrax. Sixty helicopters will attack at heights well below radar cover and spray twelve hundred gallons of spores. They've only ever sprayed mustard gas and zarin up to now. This is something different.'

'But you just told me that no one will be able to find the bloody germs.' The AVM struck Peter as a most impatient sort of fellow.

'True. However, our worry is that when Saddam discovers that al Jised has been deceiving him by encoding the files, he will torture her to get the truth. When she breaks, as she surely will,' he paused, 'who wouldn't with electrodes attached to your genitalia and nipples, then we will also be facing the probability of them using botulinium toxin and gas gangrene, as well as anthrax.'

'Why can't you sneak her out of Iraq before all this blows up?'

'She has a misplaced sense of loyalty, and won't come – at least, not until the eleventh hour by which time we will have vacated the Baghdad embassy where I have only one operative. The Iraqis are not letting anyone into the country. They've closed the borders. Furthermore, she has a set of guards giving her 24/7 protection. Also, as I told you last year, we still believe the Israelis are after her. They want to find the biologicals and destroy them.'

'So you want us to kill her?'

'No! I want you to get her out; if necessary, by force.'

'Using the SAS?'

'Yes. I know you've got several teams in Iraq under cover already.'

'Their work is vital. Diverting them to bring in a spy may be seen as secondary.'

'Finding Scud launchers are nowhere near as important as saving the planet. I don't want to have to take this to the PM, but if I have to, then I will.' Peter's intense stare made the AVM feel uncomfortable.

'Look,' he replied. 'I'll tell you what. Tomorrow morning I have to give an intelligence briefing to Lieutenant General Peter de la Billiere, our Commander-in-Chief. It's at 1000 hours in MoD Main Building. Come with me and put your case to him. He's the only one who can make this decision. I have a feeling, however, he will agree with me. It will be easier to shoot her, cheaper too.'

The callous bastard; no idea of team work.

Peter Stacey spent the rest of the day preparing what he was going to say to convince the British Commander-in-Chief why Kate should be sprung. He need not have worried, as in the event, he found the General much more receptive to his arguments.

'She sounds to be a most accomplished young woman,' de la Billiere declared after silently listening to Peter Stacey's case.

Peter smiled, thinking to himself, *Ah, the difference between a public school pongo and a grammar school crab.*

'It'll be a good exercise for some of our chaps to bring her back. You'll have to give us the details of where she lives and forewarn her so that she co-operates. I don't want her shooting one of my men in a blind panic when they burst into her apartment. We'll need to know a bit about her guards too. They'll have to be put away first. Can you do that?'

'No problem, sir. We'll get on to it right away. How do we contact you from now on?'

'What's your man in Riyadh called?'

'Mike Noble.'

'Fine. I'll tell my PSO to expect a call from him when you want us to react.'

***

During the last weeks of 1990, various peace proposals were floated between the allies and Iraq. The US insisted that Iraq must make an unconditional withdrawal. However, Saddam demanded that any withdrawal must be reflected by Israel leaving the West Bank, the Gaza Strip and the Golan Heights. No deal could be struck.

Friday, 11th January 1991, had been Kate's day off work. She had spent the day catching up with house chores. That evening the phone rang four times and stopped. She looked out of her living room window, situated on the third floor of her apartment block. Across the street in a black Mercedes were her two minders. In the dark, she could see the glow of a cigarette, one of them was smoking. Her guards undertook eight-hour shifts and always kept a discreet distance from her. She had slipped out without their knowing before; down the back stairs, into the alley where the trash bins and stray cats lived, across some waste ground and away. She rang the Chinese takeaway and placed her order. Brian McCormack was waiting when she arrived.

'We haven't much time,' he said, gently leading her outside. 'Tomorrow we are leaving Baghdad. All our embassy staff will be gone. Our business is being handled by the Jordanians. Have you been asked to start recovering the anthrax yet?'

'No, why?'

'Tomorrow the US Congress will approve "Operation Desert Storm". You can expect the first phase, the bombing, to begin on the Tuesday. Do you want us to help you to escape to England when everything goes sour? You must tell me now. If you say no then I'm afraid you're on your own. Ali Hassan will torture you until you tell him your method of concealing the biological weapons. He will then kill you. Everything you've done for the past twelve years will have been for nothing.' McCormack was speaking quickly and urgently, looking around all the time to see if they were being observed. He sounded out of breath.

'What do I have to do?'

'We have some SAS, Special Air Service, soldiers working undercover in Baghdad. They operate in small teams of three. Their job is to surreptitiously gather information such as the exact location of targets and so on. Each evening from the 15th onwards, between 2100 and 2130 hours, they will watch your apartment. When you are ready to escape then that evening you are to put a plant pot, or something similar, on the windowsill of your living room overlooking the road.'

'You do know there will be guards watching outside. The night shift comes on at 2200 hours. They're always sitting in a black Mercedes across the road.'

'Yes, we know about the guards. They will have to be quietly killed. I would imagine the SAS will strike around 2330 hours. By then the night shift guards should be getting bored and dozy. The SAS troops will rush in to your apartment, kicking the door down. You are to pretend to struggle with them; don't be afraid to shout and scream. They will knock you out with a fast-acting tranquiliser and carry you away. I've been told that you can take a small holdall, if you wish. Have it ready by the door of your flat. The plan is to make it look as if you have been kidnapped by the Israeli Mossad. Inside your apartment they may let off the odd shot and will shout loudly in Hebrew. Hopefully, the commotion will create an odd witness or two who will say they saw an Israeli badge on the troops' battledresses. The guns will be the type used by the Israelis. Within a few hours, if all goes well, you should be in Riyadh with Mike Noble. I wish you good luck. May Allah be with you. Perhaps, someday we'll meet in London.' He turned, still looking around nervously, and left Kate to retrieve her foo-yung and sneak back into her apartment.

CHAPTER 44

On 12th January 1991, the US Congress authorised the use of force to expel Iraq from Kuwait. It was a close-run vote, despite George Herbert Bush's propaganda efforts. The margins in both the Senate and the House of Representatives were the closest since the 1812 War of Independence. Other parliaments, however, began to follow suit. The Iraqi occupation of Kuwait was about to end.

At 0230 hours Baghdad time, on 17th January, 'Desert Storm' began. Apache helicopters destroyed Iraqi radar sites near the Iraqi-Saudi border. By 0245 hours, F-111 bombers were hitting Iraqi airfields in western Iraq. At 0300 hours Baghdad was under attack from Tomahawk Cruise missiles. Other coalition aircraft were striking government buildings, TV stations and electricity generating plants. 'The Mother of all Battles' had begun. The first priority for the coalition was the destruction of the Iraqi Air Force; the second was the command and communication facilities. By the end of the first week, the Iraqi Air Force had had enough and began fleeing to Iran. At least 200 aircraft, mostly air defenders, made it safely to Iranian bases. The aircraft were never returned, the pilots were to remain 'guests' of the Iranians for several years.

By the second week, the air campaign took a different slant. High altitude mass bombing, using the B-52s from Diego Garcia, began attacking troop positions. Although the Iraqi troops were well dug-in, 1,000 lb bombs falling from 20,000 feet can penetrate a long way and be especially effective when their accuracy is assured using laser technology.

So successful was this phase of Desert Storm that it altered future thinking on the deployment of troops. No longer would entire divisions dig in to face the enemy; rather they would be dispersed much more widely.

On 31st January, Kate received the call she had been dreading. She met with General Wafiq al Samarra and General Ali Hassan. 'The time has come to prepare to use biologicals,' Ali declared. 'I have authorised ten teams to be allocated to the task. Each team will have a Lieutenant and a SNCO, plus ten men. I want you to brief the officers this afternoon. Explain how you have recorded the locations, tell them where to go, what precautions they must take, what to expect and so on. Any questions?'

They mustn't start digging until tomorrow. How do I slow them down?

'No, I don't think so. The briefing may take several hours. Do they know how to use a sextant and a theodolite? They will require a clock and a radio to get the Greenwich Mean Time signal. Do they know how to take bearings? Each team will need its own equipment. I only have my own. There aren't many features in the desert to help pinpoint one's position, so they will have to be accurate with their latitude and longitude calculations. The teams will have to be careful with their mechanical diggers. If they rupture the stainless steel cylinders, they'll be goners.' Kate was trying to make it sound as difficult as she could to train the officers. She hoped Chemical Ali would swallow her story.

'They are all engineers and should be quick to pick up the necessary techniques,' he growled. 'I want them ready to move to their first site and begin digging in the morning. How many anthrax sites are there altogether?'

'We have about two thousand gallons, spread over forty, or so, locations,' lied Kate. She knew there was much more.

'I want twelve hundred gallons as soon as possible. Get the records of the nearest co-located sites and bring them to your briefing this afternoon. I will attend the start of the session to emphasise to the officers the importance of their task.'

'A lot of the sites are in the desert, west of Ar Ramadi, south of the Damascus road.'

'Excellent, then that is where we will concentrate our efforts.'

***

Kate spent much of the rest of the morning preparing her briefing. She retrieved from a secure safe in the underground bunker below the Defence Buildings the files and records. Towards lunchtime, she began worrying. She decided to visit her research labs for what would be the last time. She reasoned that if the SAS were unable to rescue her that evening, perhaps because of the curfew after dark, then there was no way she could tolerate torture in Abu Ghraib. She thought exciton might be the answer, take plenty and go for a jog. Then, she considered enditon, but rejected it as too slow as it might take days. In the end, there was only one simple, effective solution – sodium cyanide. Swigged down with alcohol, it would be quick, even if excruciatingly painful for the twenty seconds, or so, before she would become unconscious. She would be dead by the time her body would be found. She carefully filled a phial and slipped it into her pocket.

The afternoon training session was a success. The enthusiasm of the young men reminded her of when she had enjoyed being a lieutenant with Azi at Reading, thirteen years previously. *Ah, the innocence of youth,* she thought. *They believe their politicians and leaders are always right and that their intentions are for the betterment of the populace. Why have I become so cynical? Was it the tragic loss of James? He was the only man who could make me feel a real woman. Or was it the loss of my kind and caring Amer?*

She thought about the loss of her parents; missing her father's and mother's funerals because of a war that achieved bugger all. *What have I achieved in life? Nothing.*

There was little to show for ten years of hard work at university; just a widow beginning to go grey with breasts that hadn't been excited by a man for years.

She looked at her audience. Young men prepared to die. *For what?*

She wanted to tell them, 'leave here, desert, go and find a woman who can make you happy'. Instead, they hung on her every word as she explained how she had buried the anthrax spores, the need to be exact with their Lat/Long calculations and, above all else, not to break the canisters. She lay it on thick that when they had garnered their crop, the twelve hundred gallons would suffice to make Kuwait a no-go area for fifty years. They seemed to think this was acceptable.

Thank Allah, it will never happen.

She arrived home that evening, exhausted from teaching the lieutenants. It was barely after six o'clock. She had been to her local supermarket and chatted up the manager, a man she had got to know well over the years. He kept a small range of wines under the counter for special customers. Kate was special. She asked for a bottle of his strongest wine.

'This Spanish Rioja is fifteen per cent,' he assured her. 'You'll sleep all night,' he laughed.

Under the circumstances, it wasn't the best joke she had ever heard. Her usual tipple was white wine, but desperate times necessitate desperate measures. She collected what would be, one way or other, her last Chinese takeaway.

She unpacked her meal, poured a glass of the Rioja and flopped out in an easy chair. She didn't feel particularly hungry but ate anyway. The wine, rather too dry for her palate, improved as she began the second glass. While pouring the third glass, there was an explosion outside. She went to her window, criss-crossed with strong sticky tape to help prevent it shattering. She put the bottle down on the windowsill and peered out. A mile away, a building was on fire. Below in the street was the obligatory parked Mercedes. So far the coalition forces had only targeted the non-civilian buildings well away from the crowded suburbs, but this bomb was as close to her living accommodation as she had seen so far. She drew the curtains and sat down. She put her feet up and closed her eyes.

There was suddenly an enormous crash. She woke with a start. In front of her stood a giant in light coloured camouflage battle dress. He wore sun glasses and a black and white *keffiyeh* that covered his head, neck and shoulders. Behind him was a similarly dressed man-mountain. Both pointed mini UZI submachine guns at her; she recognised the distinctive Israeli-manufactured guns from her training in the university officer corps. She was terrified and instinctively screamed.

The Israelis have found me, she thought.

The giant hit her across the face with the back of his hand. It hurt. She instinctively reached to protect herself, grasping to find her gangrennex spray strapped inside her sleeve. However, being dozy from the wine-induced sleep, she was slow.

He had already grabbed her arm and asked in a heavy regional accent, that she thought could be Scottish, 'Are you Ava?' She had been dreaming of Reading and James calling her Ava only seconds previously, or so it seemed. She was coming round rapidly; the slap had woken her up. She realised they couldn't be Israelis as they wouldn't have known her code name.

'Yes,' she gasped.

Within a second, he had produced a syringe from nowhere and stabbed her in the thigh. She felt the sting and yelled. Then she felt she was glowing all over. Then she felt heady. Then, nothing.

***

At 0550 hours on 1st February, the next day, the two guards assigned to protect Kate for the morning shift arrived outside her apartment. Inside the black Mercedes were two of their colleagues, both shot through the head from close range. They knew what to do and rushed up the stairs to Kate's apartment. The door had been kicked in, several bullet holes adorned the walls and some furniture had been overturned. It appeared as if she had not gone without a struggle. They picked up Kate's phone to ring their boss, but the line was dead. They knew all hell was about to break loose. One began knocking on Kate's neighbours' doors while the other returned to their own Mercedes to use its radio to get help.

Within an hour of the discovery of Kate missing, activity around her apartment resembled flies swarming on a carcass. Major Hamid al Hayani had arrived within ten minutes of receiving the radio message from the morning shift. He knew this was not the type of kidnap, now so frequent, that could be swept under the carpet with a shrug of the shoulders. Accordingly, he had elevated the news up the line. However, even with his twenty-five years of experience in the military police, he had not expected two of the most senior Army officers to descend on this middle-class suburb of northern Baghdad so quickly.

General Wafiq al Samarra, his boss, asked, 'What do you know so far?'

'Well, sir, the old couple who live on the floor below al Jised and have known her for ten years saw her coming home from work at about six o'clock last night. She had been shopping because she carried a bag of groceries. They went to bed at about ten o'clock and the old boy says he was woken by what he thought were two shots outside. Puzzled, he went to the window, but couldn't see anything unusual. Thinking he had dreamt it, he began to get back into bed when he heard an enormous crash on the landing above. There was a scream, some shouting and two more shots were fired. His wife was awake by this time. She also heard the commotion above them in al Jised's flat. He went to his front door, opened it slightly and saw two men in camouflage, wearing black and white *keffiyehs*, coming down the stairs. One had al Jised slumped over his shoulder. The old boy thought she was either dead or unconscious. The second man was carrying a small bag and saw the old boy. He fired at him. The bullet hit the wall, inches away from his door frame. I have extracted it. I can't be certain, but it looks like a nineteen millimetre.'

'Did he say what time this happened?' asked the General.

'Yes, he looked at his clock. It was exactly 2334 hours.'

His boss looked at the other general, who the Major knew was Ali Hassan.

It was General Ali Hassan who asked, 'What else did the old boy say? You mentioned he heard shouting. Did he know what language was used? Did he see anything unusual about their dress? Did he see them get away? Why didn't he contact the police straight away?'

'He says he tried to use the telephone in the hall of the apartment block, but the lines were dead. He is in his mid-eighties and is too scared to go out at night. He did say, however, that he had never heard the language before,' replied the Major.

'It wasn't English?'

'No, he says he knows a little English. He thinks the soldier who shot at him may have had a small flag on his uniform. At the top of his shoulder – here.' The Major pointed to his left shoulder.

'What was the flag?' asked Chemical Ali.

'He doesn't know, only that it was blue and white. It all happened so quickly.'

'Israel?' asked General al Samarra.

'Or the UN,' replied Ali Hassan. 'However, it's all too damn convenient. Al Jised going missing today – the very day we are supposed to be getting anthrax from her so-called safety stashes. I have an uneasy feeling about this.'

Major al Hayani, having stood next to the two generals, listening to their conversation, thought he had better add his last snippet of information. 'Apparently, their get-away car was a white Nissan.'

'That's not much bloody good; just about every car in Iraq is a white Nissan,' grumbled General Hassan.

***

By mid-afternoon that Friday, all the Iraqi teams designated to dig for the hidden weapons had reported back that they could not find anything. Each junior officer, scared of being accused of incompetence, swore to their commanding officer they had checked and re-checked their readings. By 1500 hours Gen Ali Hassan, Head of the Army and the second most important man in Iraq, knew he had been tricked by 'that bloody tart, al Jised'. He rang his colleague, al Samarra. 'You're the intelligence supremo, sort this bloody mess out.'

General al Samarra replied calmly, 'Calm down, Ali. What do we know about al Jised? Who knows her best?'

'About ten or twelve years ago she worked on a project with Brigadier Azi Tumbrah. He probably knows her better than anyone else in the military. He's now Commandant of the Military College. He might be able to help you.'

Within an hour Azi was sitting in General Wafiq's office. He explained how he had worked with Kate; how he found it hard to believe she would have hidden the weapons deliberately and explained her role in the chess key algorithm.

'Do you think she could have hidden the weapons using some sort of chess key?' asked the General.

'I wouldn't have thought so. I don't think she knew much about chess.'

'Mmm...' pondered the General. 'Unfortunately, it's the only thing we have got to go on. I will call Professor Fakhri from the university to see if he can decode al Jised's records. We can't afford to lose this one, Azi.'

By 1730 hours, the mathematics professor was sitting drinking coffee with the General. He listened to the story: al Jised's role in storing the weapons and her incidental part in the chess key to Nastia Game. 'Have you got the records here so that I can see them?' he asked.

'Yes, of course.' Wafiq passed a thick file marked Top Secret.

The Professor looked at the first four or five records for several minutes, comparing them. He was puzzled by the occasional dots scattered in the information fields. 'Have you noticed these dots?' he asked the General.

General al Samarra examined the records himself. 'I assume they are typing errors. Perhaps she used an old typewriter?'

'I think not,' replied Dr Fakhri positively. 'There must be a link. Some of the records have as many as seven or eight dots, others only three or four. They appear to be random, but I am not so sure. There is no link between the dot and any particular letter or number. I am guessing and need more time to investigate, but I suspect the dots will tell us how to alter the Lat/Long positions to give us the exact location where the weapons are hidden.'

'I don't want to rush you, Professor, but we haven't got time. Is there nothing we can be doing in the meantime?'

'I will take the first twenty of these records away and get my best mathematicians to begin analysing them at once. Meanwhile, all I can suggest is that you go back to the Lat/Long positions and begin spreading out. Dig another hole exactly one kilometre north, one east, one west, and so on.'

'Why one kilometre? Why exactly north and south?'

'Because, if she has linked the burials to a chess board system, the squares will be aligned in that manner. A one kilometre square is as good a place as any to start.'

CHAPTER 45

As the two Iraqi generals were beginning to realise they had a problem on their hands, some 650 miles south of Baghdad, in Riyadh, Kate was waking from her drug-induced sleep. She found herself in a king-sized bed in a room large enough to include a coffee table and several easy chairs. It was decorated tastefully in soft pastel colours; the curtains and carpet were suitably matched. A nurse, in uniform, sat in one of the chairs casually reading a magazine. She must have heard Kate stirring, for she turned, smiled and greeted her in English.

'Hello, Kate. How do you feel?'

'Feeling groggy,' she replied. 'Where am I?'

'In the British Embassy in Riyadh. You have been asleep since you arrived at eight o'clock this morning. It's now four o'clock in the afternoon. Mike Noble told me to ring him as soon as you woke up.'

She picked up a phone on the table. 'Hello, Mike, this is Sharon. Kate has just woken up… OK, I'll tell her.' She put the phone down. 'Mike is on his way up.'

Kate began to notice her surroundings. She saw she was wearing a pink, off the shoulder, nightgown. She touched it – pure satin, and looked at Sharon.

'It's OK. It was me who undressed you. Your clothes are in the laundry and should be ready for you to wear again soon. I'm afraid your journey on the floor of the helicopter got them a tad dirty. The ballpoint pen that was in the cuff of your dress is in your bedside cabinet, along with your holdall.'

There was a knock on the door. Mike Noble entered. 'Hello, Kate, it's good to see you again. How do you feel?'

'A bit woozy.'

'I'm sorry if the journey here wasn't too comfortable.'

'I don't remember anything since last night.'

'Perhaps, it's just as well. If I may suggest, take your time to come round. Have a shower and then come down for dinner. Tomorrow you have a long day.'

'Why? What's going to happen?'

'You're due to catch the eleven o'clock VC10 flight to RAF Brize Norton. I told you I would get you to Oxford.' He laughed at his own joke. Kate wasn't sure what he was on about. 'You remember Peter Stacey? He'll meet you there and take you to London.'

Kate nodded. She felt as if she could sleep for another eight hours.

***

That Friday night, two RAF Tornado GR1A recce aircraft of XIII Squadron took off from their base in Dhahran, Saudi Arabia. Their role was to look for Scud launchers known to be operating under the cover of darkness from the desert, west of Ar Ramadi. The aircraft, fitted with infrared sensors and digital video recorders allowed the navigator, seated in the rear seat, to see clear images in real-time. Flying at low level and working as a pair, the Flight became mystified when they began to see what appeared to be random holes in the desert, each about ten feet deep. They ignored the first hole, were puzzled when they saw an identical hole about ten miles further on and were intrigued when they came across a third hole. During their two hour patrol, they sighted a total of seven holes.

By 0300 hours on the Saturday morning, a team of RAF intelligence analysts, as they liked to call themselves, but who are in reality photographic interpreters, were examining the evidence from the recce flight and plotting the location of the holes on a large scale map. In charge of the team, Warrant Officer Dicky Briggs was baffled. The holes seemed meaningless. Nothing had been put in them, so the Iraqis must have been looking for something already buried. But what? He wrote a short report on the holes and put it in his out-tray for Squadron Leader Alec Hammond, his boss. He could sort out the enigma when he came on duty at seven o'clock. *After all, that's what he's paid for.*

By the time Alec Hammond had finished examining the evidence of the mysterious holes, ten Iraqi teams were already sweltering in the desert, under camouflage netting. Most were finishing digging their second hole of the day, the first exactly one kilometre north of yesterday's effort. Now their second effort was one kilometre due east. None had found anything and they began preparing to head one kilometre south. The instructions given to the lieutenants in charge had been clear, up to a point. If when they arrived at the site for their next dig and it was obvious nothing could have been buried there – perhaps it was a building or a road, then they should move on a further kilometre. No one had told them in which direction.

The first team leader to have found himself in this dilemma, Lieutenant Hadir, had decided that as his second location for the morning was a well-defined track, he would move his team one kilometre north. He didn't know its significance, but he was about to dig a hole exactly two kilometres north and one kilometre east from his first square of the previous day. After half an hour of toil and sweat, one of his troops shouted, 'Sir, come and look.' The first cache of anthrax had been uncovered.

Sqn Ldr Hammond hadn't understood the meaning of the seven holes any more than his Warrant Officer, but he had decided it had better be referred up the chain of command. He had faxed the images to *INT HQ* in Riyadh. The senior British Intelligence officer, Brigadier Harry Gledhill, had been about to give his morning briefing to General de la Billiere when the photos arrived. He had glanced at them, shrugged and put them at the bottom of his briefing notes. At the finish of his briefing, the General had asked, 'OK, Harry, is there anything else before you go?'

'Just one thing, sir. It's probably insignificant, but XIII Squadron took some pictures last night of holes in the desert. It looks as if the Iraqis were digging for treasure.' He laughed, thinking it might be funny.

'Let's have a peep.'

The Brigadier showed the General the images. A bell rang in de la Billiere's head. *What was it Stacey told me a few weeks ago? Something about burying biological weapons in the desert and that female agent we sprung from Baghdad two days ago.* He sat upright, as the penny dropped. *They're getting the anthrax ready.*

'Harry, get Mike Noble in here at once.'

'Do we need MI6 in on this?' asked the befuddled Brigadier.

'Yes, we bloody do! Hurry, man.'

He turned to his PSO. 'Get me General Schwarzkopf immediately.'

Minutes later. 'Norman, Peter here. We've a problem.'

'Tell me about it!'

Peter de la Billiere's career in the Army had been unorthodox. He had spent much of his time with the SAS. As such, he was not prone to panic. However, the prospect that the Iraqis had somehow blown the cover of al Jised's method of hiding biological weapons filled him with horror. He knew the nuclear, biological and chemical protective clothing that would be worn by the allied forces was well proven. Nevertheless, it could easily be ripped, or perhaps not be fitted correctly. In which case, the troops may as well be wearing swimming costumes. He outlined his theory to his senior colleague, *Stormin Norman.*

'I believe the eradication of these teams takes top priority, Norman, even over finding Scud launchers. We don't know how many teams the Iraqis have got out there looking for the anthrax. We think there may be seven, but it could be more. Perhaps, you can get one of your satellites on the job?'

'Consider it done. I'll get back to you when I know more.'

It was almost lunchtime when Mike Noble found himself in Peter de la Billiere's presence. The General asked, 'Is that Iraqi agent we rescued still with you?'

'I'm afraid al Jised's plane has left. Do you want me to get it to turn back?'

'There's little point,' replied the General, 'but I would like you to tell me all you know about how she hid the biological weapons.'

***

At about the same time, Gen Wafiq al Samarra heard Lieutenant Hadir's team had hit the jackpot and were bringing the treasure back to their base. He rung Professor Fakhri immediately and excitedly told him the first stash had been uncovered and was being brought in at that very instant.

'Funnily enough,' the Professor replied, 'I was on my way over to see you. We think we have deciphered al Jised's code. Before I come, however, tell me how many squares Hadir's team was away from their initial starting point.'

'Two squares north and one square east,' the General replied.

'That confirms it – a knight move. She used a chess code and I think I know how. I'll be with you in about half an hour.'

Forty minutes later, the Professor was sitting drinking tea with the General. 'Chess squares are numbered using an alphabetic, from *a* to *h*, followed by a number, from *1* to *8*. My staff and I decided there was no pattern with the dots on the records, except one. The first dot was always after an alphabetic and the second dot always after a number. The problem we had initially was that sometimes the letter used was not between *a* and *h*. For example, it could be a *p*. We decided she had a simple code, a *p* for a *b*, and so on. Have you the record for the team that has found the first stash?'

'Yes, it's here.'

The Professor only needed a cursory glance to see what he wanted. 'The dots tell us the square was *e4*. Lieutenant Hadir found the anthrax at a point two kilometres north and one kilometre east. That would be equivalent to the square *f6*. You told me yesterday that al Jised knew little about chess. I believe she is using a system whereby the square recorded has a chess piece on it, but the weapons are buried at the square where the piece was previously. I wouldn't mind betting that she used the same chess position for all the locations. Check your records. See if there are any others where the dots indicate e4. If they do, then tell your teams to dig two kilometres north and one kilometre east.'

'What about the records that don't have e4 as the start square?' asked the General. He was already flicking frantically through the records on his desk.

'That's where I can't be of much help. You see I have no idea what the position was that she used. There is no way of guessing. It is believed there are 10^{120} possible positions on a chess board. That's more than all the atoms in the visible universe. What I do suggest, however, is that your teams should fan out logically. For example, if the dot codes indicate the starting square is on the a file, then there is no point digging to the west as they would then be off the imaginary board. Similarly, if the code indicates the starting square is on the first rank, don't dig to the south. Sooner or later you'll hit lucky. I have drawn up some patterns to help you dig fewer holes. However, in the worst case you may have to dig for the location between twenty-five and thirty-five times before hitting lucky. Then you can repeat the process we've just been through. However, there could be an even bigger problem facing us,' cautioned the Professor.

'What?' asked an already exasperated General.

'From what you have told me about al Jised, she is a highly intelligent young woman. She probably began to realise, after hiding the weapons many times, that a pattern was emerging. She could then have done several things to make our task harder.'

'What could she have done?'

'Firstly, alter the scale of the board – make the squares five or ten kilometres in size. Secondly, she could have changed the position. In that case we are pissing into the wind, we'll never find the biological weapons.'

'Let's hope you're wrong. Our very existence depends on finding these weapons.'

Analysis of the early records showed three further sites recorded as being at e4. They were spread all over Iraq. By the time General al Samarra was ordering his ten teams to new locations to begin excavating, it was 1300 hours. The teams didn't know it, but their digging had been watched from space for almost an hour.

**

It was 1345 hours by the time Mike Noble had given a detailed description of how the biological weapons had been kept hidden from the Iraqi hierarchy for so long. Peter de la Billiere had no doubt what had to be done. He rang General Schwarzkopf for the second time. Stormin Norman knew the answer before he had heard the question.

'The satellite has been watching nine teams digging holes this morning. A further team may have found something. Their hole was abandoned, but we picked them up heading back to Baghdad with what looked like five-gallon oil drums. The other nine teams continued to dig in a regular pattern of one kilometre squares. However, about fifty minutes ago they stopped and are moving to new locations. They are still on the move and seem to be spreading out in all directions,' said the American General.

'Then they must be stopped at all costs,' insisted General de la Billiere. 'Norman, this is not about winning the war with Iraq, we'll do that easily. It's about winning the Middle East for future generations. Whatever happens, Ali Hassan mustn't get his hands on any more anthrax. It looks as if one of his teams may have just found fifty gallons and MI6 believe he already has a further fifty gallons.'

'Where the hell did he get all this bloody stuff from?' enquired the senior US Commander.

'I hate to say it, Norman, but we believe most of it came from the CIA several years ago.'

'Goddamn it, I might have known Langley would be at the bottom of this mess. OK, Peter, I'll get ten F-111s to take the teams out within the hour. I'll fax over where the hits took place, and perhaps you can get XIII Squadron to do a recce to make sure everything has been destroyed.'

'Not so fast, Norman. If we take the teams out singly en route, so to speak, the Iraqis may get further teams tomorrow. Can I suggest the take-outs all occur at the same time?'

'OK, Peter. This is your party.'

The satellite watching the ten Iraqi teams from space communicated their positions in real time to the individual F-111s allocated for the attack. Sophisticated terrain following software chose each aircraft's course so that the strikes all occurred simultaneously.

It was several hours later before Gen Wafiq al Samarra was passed the bad news. It was minutes after that when Chemical Ali blew his top to his Personal Staff Officer. 'Get me the Head of the Mukhabaret. Now!'

CHAPTER 46

By the time the VC10 was arriving at RAF Brize Norton, Ali Hassan was briefing the Head of the Iraqi Security Services, Bureau Director Rafi Dahham. Although Ali was superior to Rafi in the Iraqi hierarchy, he had to be careful. Rafi, like himself, was a distant cousin of Saddam. Ali explained that he believed al Jised had betrayed the motherland and that she had been liberated to England. Rafi, who had been fully briefed on Kate's departure by Major al Hayani, looked at the Head of the Army and asked, 'What makes you think it was the British who sprung her and not the Israelis?'

Ali tossed a file across his desk. 'That!' He could not hide his frustration as he spat the word out. 'Read it. She has been cavorting with British agents for over twelve years. She was the mistress of one of them.'

'Yes, I know all that. But it was all done above board. It began when Tufiq encouraged her to get the chess key secret so we could manipulate Nastia Game. Then, Youseff controlled her while she procured chemicals that we couldn't get from anywhere else. Finally, al Samarra has been watching her like a hawk. I agree we failed to realise how cunning she was when hiding the biologicals, but that's our fault. She conned us. Even if you're right, Ali, and I'm inclined to think you are, there's not much we can do. The British will give her a new identity. There are over fifty million people living in the UK; finding a needle in a haystack would be child's play.'

'I don't agree. There are three leads we should follow up to find her, then extract the chess secrets from her and finally eliminate her. Firstly, she has a sister living in Britain who is a doctor. She must be traceable. Al Jised is bound to seek her out, sooner rather than later. Secondly, there are the Platinis. He was the Air Attaché during the period when she was probably recruited by MI6. Tufiq mentions in the file that he suspected she may have been familiar with Platini's wife. It is highly likely al Jised will make contact with her. There can't be that many Platinis in England. Thirdly, Brigadier Tumbrah, who was her colleague when she worked in Reading helping to convert Nastia Game, mentions in that file that she was forever going back to Cambridge at weekends to see friends. Need I say more?'

'Our big problem is going to be smuggling an operative into Britain who can pass for a Caucasian. Anyone looking Arabic, even with a valid Jordanian or Egyptian passport, will be checked out thoroughly and watched. Ever since the cockup with Sallam Hassan killing Abdul Razak and that wretched Iranian Embassy affair, MI5 have been on their toes. I have a light-skinned Azerbaijani who could pass off as a southern European; his mother was Italian. However, he will need to improve his English if he is to find his way around. It may take four or five months to have him ready. I am inclined to send him into Italy and let him stay there for a few weeks. From there he can travel overland to England. Security checks at sea ports are much more relaxed than at airports. We have a sleeper in London who can supply him with the necessary hardware. Are you happy with that idea?'

'Yes. Put it into action.'

***

Peter Stacey greeted Kate as a long-lost friend. 'Do you realise it's over eleven years since we last met?' he asked, as he accompanied her through the waiting lounge to a chauffeur-driven Jaguar. 'You gave me a bollocking over your need to have chemical weapons. I never forgot it. I deserved it, of course. You were quite right. So much has happened since. We have plenty of catching up to do. I believe you were married soon after I left.'

'Yes, Amer was a good man, but he was killed in a bombing raid a few years later. I don't seem to have much luck with men.' There was weariness in her voice and Peter could see a big difference in her. The years of pressure had taken their toll. He was too much of a gentleman to mention it. She had kept her slim figure, her deportment was still like a ballet dancer's, there was even a slight hint of fire behind the eyes, but not like it used to be.

I'll bet she could still give me a bollocking if she had a mind to, he thought.

The idea produced an involuntary smile, as he said, 'You're looking well. I'm taking you to our town house in Twickenham this evening. My wife, Jenny, is preparing supper. I thought you would prefer to be with us, among familiar faces, at least for the weekend. I will outline the itinerary for the next few weeks as we go along.'

He explained that a varied program had been drawn up, starting on Monday. There would be sessions with different specialists setting up her new identity and periods when she would be asked about the biological and chemical stocks as well as the overall situation in Iraq. There would be cultural outings, shopping expeditions and visits to look for an apartment of her own. 'It will all take time and may drag on for three or four weeks. The production of documents such as a passport, a driving licence, bank accounts, education certificates and so on have to be done carefully. Even choosing an anglicised name will need thought.' He grinned as he said, 'You will know it is coming to an end when they begin asking about your hobbies and interests.'

It was early evening by the time they arrived at Peter's town house. 'We usually go to the country for the weekends, but Jenny and I agreed leaving you alone would not be the most hospitable start to your coming to England. Our two children are away at boarding school so the house will be quiet.'

As they entered the terraced pre-war house, a smartly dressed, well-coiffured woman about the same age as Kate came towards them from the kitchen at the rear of the house. Kate instantly felt distinctly uncomfortable. Jenny was so spruce whereas Kate in her crumpled outfit that she had been wearing since the evening of her escape felt decidedly scruffy. 'I don't think you ever met Jenny when we were in Baghdad.'

They hadn't met and it was Jenny who remarked, 'I've heard a lot about you.'

'Not all bad, I hope,' smiled Kate.

'Oh no, far from it. Peter has often told me how valuable you have been. It really is nice to meet you after all these years. Let me show you to your room. After such a long journey, you must want to take a shower and change. Dinner will be ready in about twenty minutes.'

'I'm afraid I have nothing to change into,' replied Kate.

'Oh, don't worry. Even though tomorrow is Sunday, there are a lot of shops open. We'll go to Richmond and get you some new outfits.'

In the shower, Kate wondered how Jenny expected her to purchase new clothes when she had no money.

Conversation over dinner was purely social, if somewhat one sided. Kate was still suffering from the rigours of her escape and jet lag; she did much of the listening, made excuses and retired to bed as soon as she could.

Sunday, 3rd February, proved to be an enjoyable day. At breakfast Peter explained that Kate had been allocated a generous kitting-out allowance with which to buy essentials such as clothes and personal items. 'The first thing we must get you today is some warm clothing,' Jenny declared. 'English winters can last until April.'

'Yes, I remember frosts at Cambridge as late as May,' Kate replied.

Kate was surprised to see the shopping centre of Richmond so busy. Jenny turned out to be a great help when decisions had to be made as to the choice of colour, material and style. Peter was little more than a porter. The boot of his car was practically full of goods by the time the three of them took a late lunch in a pub just off Twickenham Green. Kate was beginning to recover from the ordeal of the previous seventy-two hours. She was starting to look forward to her new life in Britain.

On Monday, Peter took her to her new home for the month – a hotel in Russell Square. He explained that the hotel bill had been paid in advance. A furnished apartment would be found to her liking over the next few weeks. After depositing her belongings in her en suite bedroom, she accompanied him the short distance to a building in Theobald's Road where the acclimatisation process would be carried out over the following weeks.

Peter introduced Kate to Milly Forster. 'Milly is to be your companion until you are fully settled in. She will be your *fidus Achates* and is on call day or night if you have a problem.'

About Kate's age, Milly was short in stature, rather rotund, with short, grey hair. She had a friendly face with a grin that emphasised her dimples. Kate felt comfortable with her immediately. 'I am sure we will get to know each other very well over the next few weeks,' she said as they shook hands. Peter left and Milly explained that various specialists would visit most days to arrange Kate's new curriculum vitae. 'Unless you object, I will be in attendance with you all the time.'

The first specialist appeared shortly afterwards. 'My job is to help you find a new identity,' he said. 'Have you decided on your new names?' he asked.

'No, but I would like to keep the anglicised version of my Iraqi name, Kate.'

'Fine,' he replied. 'We'll put you down as Kathryn. What about your surname?'

'It's al Jised,' she replied without thinking.

He looked at her over the top of his glasses, as if to say *don't be daft*. He said nothing for a moment, and then suggested, 'What about Jackson? There's an actress called Kate Jackson in *Charlie's Angels*.'

Kate hadn't a clue who he was talking about, but nodded approval.

'Do you want a middle name?'

'My mother was called Ala.'

'Mmm, I'm not sure it sounds quite right. What about Helena? It's similar.'

414

And so, Kathryn Helena Jackson came into being. She was the only daughter of a doctor from East Anglia who had gone to the Yemen. There he had met a local girl and married her. Kate's new date of birth, 2nd January 1950, made her a few months younger than she really was; this both amused and pleased her. Being born in Aden, where she spent her early years, explained her ability to speak Arabic. Her family had returned to Norwich when she was eleven. After secondary school she had obtained a BSc in Botany at Nottingham University, chosen not so much for the excellence of its department, but because Kate remembered James had studied there. Afterwards, she had completed a four-year PhD at Cambridge University. 'You can use Jonathon Gleeson as a referee, should you ever need one,' the specialist said. 'I have now enough information to get you a National Insurance Number, a National Health Number, a driving licence, and a passport. I assume you can drive?' he asked.

Kate nodded.

He looked at Milly. 'I assume I use the usual home address?'

Milly replied, 'Yes, of course.' She turned to Kate and explained that when she had her own apartment in a month's time, she would have to notify the authorities herself of her change of address.

That afternoon, Milly accompanied Kate to a hair stylist. They had tea at Fortnum and Mason's. Afterwards, they visited Foyles book shop. Milly bought Kate a book, *Heritage of Britain,* a potted history of the British Isles. 'This is your homework,' she laughed. 'Tomorrow afternoon I thought we should visit the British Museum as it's just around the corner from your hotel.' They left each other outside Kate's hotel and agreed to meet the following morning in the office.

The second morning, Tuesday, saw a different specialist arrive. He was a rather dishy young man, with a heavy pin-striped suit, blue shirt with a white collar, and a bright red tie. 'I'm your banking man,' he said. He scarcely looked at Kate.

Perhaps I'm too old for him; what a shame. Fifteen years ago it would have been different!

'Have you any money of your own?' He asked the question in a manner that gave Kate the impression he was expecting a negative answer.

'Yes,' she replied.

'I'm afraid if it's in an Iraqi bank, we'll not be able to get it out.'

'Apart from my current account in Iraq, I have two deposit accounts. When my parents died I inherited a third of their estate. That money is on deposit with the Anglo-Egyptian Bank in Cairo. When the war with Iran began, I started to transfer small sums monthly to the Royal Jordanian Bank in Amman. I have brought both pass-books with me to England.'

'Excellent,' he replied, looking at her properly for the first time. 'We should be able to transfer those deposits to England fairly easily. In the meantime, I want to set you up with a current account here in London so that we can begin paying you your monthly pension, and a lump sum. Your account will be with the Government Agents, Cox and Kings Branch of Lloyds. Now, would you mind filling in these forms?'

The next three mornings were different. Kate was quizzed about her role in Iraq, the nature of her research laboratories and the approximate amounts of chemical and biological weapons she had hidden in the desert. She described how she had hidden them. She listed the members of the Revolutionary Council and what she knew about them. Her inquisitors seemed more interested in Chemical Ali than Saddam. They wanted to know about how Ali had subdued the Kurds, how often and where the chemicals had been used against them, as well as the type of chemicals. She mentioned the gangrennex pens and said she had brought a couple of samples with her to England to show the scientists at Porton Down.

One of the men, who Kate assumed was the senior of the two, looked at Milly and said, 'Perhaps next week you could arrange to bring Kate to Salisbury for the day.'

The afternoons were a pleasant break from the morning inquisitions. Milly took Kate on cultural visits. The Houses of Parliament, the Victoria and Albert Museum and the Tower of London completed her first week, or so she thought.

'Tomorrow, I'll pick you up at the hotel at nine o'clock,' Milly said, taking Kate by surprise. 'I have booked us into a hotel in Norwich on Saturday evening. We will look where you went to school. Then, on Sunday we will return here via Nottingham University.'

The second week of the induction was not dissimilar to the first. By Wednesday, Kate had been given the necessary documents for living in a modern society: driving licence, bank debit card, passport, even the death certificates of her imaginary parents.

The day-out on the train to Salisbury went well. The gangrennex spray intrigued the scientists at Porton Down who asked her to return as soon as she had completed her assimilation period. 'You can have a job here any time.'

Other visits that week included Runnymede, Windsor Castle, Wembley and Lords. 'You must get to know a little about soccer and cricket,' Milly declared. On the second Friday, Kate was offered a temporary job within the department as an interpreter. 'Your office will be on the top floor of this building.' She accepted.

'In that case,' commented Milly, 'I think we should look for a flat for you this weekend. Do you want to live in the middle of the city, or would you prefer somewhere a bit quieter and commute?'

Kate chose the second option and by Sunday afternoon she and Milly were negotiating a six-month lease on a furnished apartment in Hertford. 'So convenient for trains to King's Cross and an easy walk to the office,' Milly had declared.

During the third week, Kate met the security specialist. 'You do realise that it is possible there is a price on your head?' he asked.

Kate looked blank.

'It is highly likely that Saddam will send someone after you. We tried to make your escape look like an Israeli kidnap, but we can't be sure it fooled the Iraqi Intelligence Service. We will be watching all our ports of entry for anyone suspicious, of course, but there is no guarantee. However, there are one or two things you can do to help yourself.'

'Such as what?' Kate asked.

'Is there anyone in this country you are planning to visit?'

'I have a sister in Leeds, a family who I knew in Baghdad living near Grantham and some old friends from my time in Cambridge.'

'You mustn't go near them, at least not for a year. After that time, it is reasonable to assume the coast will be clear. The Iraqi Intelligence Service probably knows about them and could be watching and waiting for you to pitch up.'

The warning made sense, but it frightened Kate. For the first time since arriving in England, she felt alone again.

CHAPTER 47

The final two weeks of Kate's time with Milly was effectively a crash course in British history and traditions. Their visits covered the major periods: for the Romans they went to Bath, for the Norman Conquest to Battle, for the Tudors to Hampton Court, and for the Regency years to the Brighton Pavilion. By the end of their time together she and Milly had become firm friends.

From the news broadcasts, Kate learned that Saddam Hussein was withdrawing his troops from Kuwait. She wondered if his threat to bomb the Americans with anthrax had materialised. No mention was made of biological weapons on the BBC; only that his troops were setting fire to Kuwaiti oil fields as they retreated. The TV news also showed 'The Highway of Death', the devastation caused by Americans bombing the fleeing Iraqis.

The two sides are as bad as each other. More pointless deaths, more pain for Iraqi mothers.

The needless war sickened her. President Bush's declaration of a cease-fire, with the claim that Kuwait was liberated, seemed to epitomise *the arrogance of ignorance.* Kate knew how the al Sabah family gave Kuwaiti women no freedom, treating them in a medieval fashion. By comparison with Saddam's liberal approach to women's rights, Kuwait was still in the middle ages.

Milly helped Kate move into her apartment in Hertford and Kate soon became an invisible commuter on the 0750 hours train to King's Cross. Her work was routine and boring, mostly translating Arabic documents of little importance. Occasionally, she was called to interpret for the Metropolitan Police when they wished to question an Arab suspect who claimed to be unable to speak English. The human contact involved, even though most of those she met could be described as lowlife, was more challenging. However, she itched for something better. She began looking for jobs as a lecturer in the universities, but the requirement for botanists seemed limited. She thought about the offer from Porton Down, but decided that it should be the last resort.

There would probably be as much politics at Porton as there was at Al Muthanna.

As the weeks turned into months, Kate began to feel lonely. Her mind turned to her sister in Leeds. She had not seen any suspicious characters following her. She felt safe and began to think that she couldn't do any harm by making contact. Accordingly, she decided to take a few days off work, hire a car and drive to Leeds. On Wednesday, 1st May, having packed an overnight bag, she left Hertford after breakfast. Three hours later, she was parking outside the Leeds General Infirmary. She entered through the main entrance and followed the signs for Neurology. She went to the reception desk. A young lady looked up from her paperwork, and asked, 'Can I help you?'

'Yes. I am looking for my sister, Dr Lina al Jised, she's a consultant neurologist.'

A puzzled look appeared on the receptionist's face. 'She left last September after getting married.'

Kate felt faint. The colour must have drained from her face, as the young girl asked, 'Are you alright?'

'I have been away in the Middle East and lost contact with my sister. Postal and telephone services are notoriously bad out there. Do you know where she is now?'

'She married a New Zealand doctor who was here on a two-year exchange programme. He was a consultant psychiatrist. They went back to New Zealand shortly after the wedding. If you go to the Human Resources department, they will probably have their address.'

The HR department was unhelpful. 'If you write to your sister at our neurology department, we will send it on to her. We are not allowed to give away personal information.'

I'm sure Peter will get her address for me.

'Thank you for your help.'

She returned to her car feeling deflated.

What now? I might as well go back to Hertford.

She drove south down the A1, her mind a blank. Newark came and went, then Grantham. No bells rang in her head, but soon afterwards she saw a sign pointing to the right: *Colsterworth 1 mile.*

That's where the Platinis live. I wonder if Sally is home.

Automatically, she drove into the right-hand filter lane, took care crossing the northbound dual carriageway and entered the village. *The Old Post Office* was easy to find on the High Street. She parked in the drive and rang the bell.

Sally opened the door looking annoyed, as if she had been interrupted from doing something, and asked, 'Yes?' She clearly didn't recognise Kate.

'Sally, it's me, Kate.'

Sally's face dropped, registering surprise. Then she beamed, opened her arms, hugged Kate, and simply said, 'Kate!' They remained in the doorway, holding each other, for a considerable time before Sally said, 'What a wonderful surprise, do come in.'

The reunion was warm and animated. Sally couldn't stop asking questions, often not giving Kate time to answer. They sat drinking tea in the rear garden under the shade of an old apple tree. For Kate the setting was idyllic: warm, quiet and peaceful. Being with an old friend was a real delight. The catching up of news had taken over an hour when Sally said, 'I was busy preparing a meal for this evening when you arrived. We are having one of Gerry's wing commanders and his wife to dinner – Phil and Jean Watson. Gerry is a group captain now at Cranwell, in charge of Initial Officer Training.'

'In that case, I'd better go. I don't want to hold you up,' replied Kate.

'No way! You mentioned earlier that you had planned to stay in Leeds tonight. I insist you stay here instead. Gerry would never forgive me if he knew I had let you go. He will be home from work in another hour. The Watsons are a lovely couple. You will enjoy their company. We will have a great time. Go and bring your bag in from your car and I will show you to your bedroom.'

And so, three hours later, after a shower, a long chat with Gerry and a large glass of sherry, Kate found herself dining with the Platinis and the Watsons. Gerry had introduced her to the Watsons as Kate Jackson, but it was difficult to explain to them how they knew each other.

'What did you do in Baghdad?' Phil had asked early on.

'I was the specialist interpreter. My mother was Yemeni, so I speak fluent Arabic.' Kate's reply seemed to satisfy and no one probed her background any further until the subject of hobbies and interests came up later in conversation.

It was Phil who asked Kate, 'Do you play chess?'

Kate looked blank and frowned. Gerry, realising the possible sensitivity of the question hurriedly intervened and explained to Kate, 'Phil is a former RAF chess champion.'

Without thinking through the ramifications of her question, Kate asked, 'Did you ever know James Douglas?'

'Yes, of course. He was a good friend of mine. How did you know him?'

She gulped, realising she had dug herself into a hole with her casual question. Gerry's face was saying, *you got yourself into this.*

'He came to Baghdad when Gerry and I were there. He worked on a computer project with ICL. We met him then, didn't we, Gerry?' She lied convincingly.

Gerry nodded, not saying a word. There was silence for a while as they continued eating.

Then Phil, who had clearly been trying hard to remember something from the distant past, threw a fast ball. 'I know who you are, you're Queen Soraya.' Everyone stopped eating and instantly stared at Phil.

'Pardon?' queried Kate.

'You went to RAF Kinloss with James and another bloke from the Iraqi Air Force to see how we use the Nimrods. I remember Tony Horner, who was OC Ops Wing there at the time, describing how you mesmerised some of the boys in the bar that evening after dinner. His description of you was right too, you do resemble Queen Soraya.'

There was a deadly silence. Gerry looked highly embarrassed. Kate blushed and didn't know how to respond. Jean eyed Kate suspiciously as if she was a villain. Sally inwardly sighed knowing they would have to come clean about Kate's past.

It was Gerry who grasped the nettle. 'Phil, what I'm about to say must go no further as it's officially top secret. Kate was in the Iraqi Air Force and helped with ICL's development of Nastia Game at Reading. When James and the ICL team came to Baghdad to install the game, we recruited her to keep us informed of Iraq's programme of research into biological and chemical weapons. It's thanks to her that no biological weapons were ever used in the Iran–Iraq war. However, as a result of the Kuwait business it had become too dangerous for her to stay in Iraq. She was recently brought in from the cold and now has a completely new identity. Do you both understand the significance of what I have just said?'

Phil and Jean, who had been in the RAF herself, both nodded gravely.

Gerry accepted their assurances and thought he would change the subject by simply adding, 'What happened to James when he returned to the UK was a tragedy.'

However, Phil didn't take the hint to move on, remarking innocently, 'I know he was supposed to have been killed in Northern Ireland, but I'm not so sure.'

Gerry, Sally and Kate put their knives and forks down on their plates for the second time in as many minutes, looking to Phil for an explanation. Jean, on the other hand, continued to eat her beef wellington. She'd heard this theory before.

'About seven years ago, I played an unusual variation of the Spanish Opening in the RAF championships against a Corporal Mackenzie. I had played it many times before, but no one had ever known how to refute it, until him. Afterwards, I asked how he knew the refutation and he told me he had met it a year previously in a tournament in Oban.'

Gerry interrupted, for Kate's benefit, 'That's a small town in the north-west of Scotland.' Kate nodded, and looked at Phil to continue.

'I am convinced the man who showed Corporal Mackenzie how to refute the variation was James Douglas.'

'Why?' asked Kate excitedly.

'Two reasons. Firstly, it had been James who had shown the variation to me many years previously and I've never known anyone else play it. Secondly, Mackenzie is an RAF policeman, trained to observe. The description he gave of his opponent was uncanny. He said he was left-handed, had a scar on his left forefinger and, for me the clincher, he wrote his moves down using the German notation. The only problem was he called himself MacKinnon.'

'Surely, all this could be a coincidence,' remarked Gerry.

'Possibly, but I have been playing chess competitively since I was ten years old. MacKinnon was described as five feet ten inches, weighing twelve stone, with blue eyes and brown hair. Just like James Douglas,' answered Phil.

'Was it the Riga variation?' asked Kate, intrigued by Phil's tale.

'Yes, how did you know?' asked a surprised Phil.

'It's a long, long story,' replied Kate, thinking about her meeting with Ray Kane. She looked at Sally and knew she was thinking the same thing.

If there's any chance MacKinnon could be James, then I must find out.

It was Sally who asked, 'Would there be any way we could find out if MacKinnon is James Douglas?'

Phil thought briefly and then replied, 'I could contact Corporal Mackenzie. He's now in the Police Flight at RAF Lossiemouth. He's bound to have some contacts with the Northern Constabulary. I'll try and contact him tomorrow, if you like, and let you know.'

After the Watsons had left and as Kate was preparing to go upstairs, having helped clear the table, Sally said, 'Now, tomorrow we are going to

Nottingham for a girl's day out. Gerry has promised me a new dress for the summer ball next month and I want you to help me choose it.'

Overhearing this, Gerry laughed. 'If it saves me the hassle of being dragged around the shops, then tomorrow evening I'll treat you both to a Chinese meal in Grantham.'

The pair had a successful day in the shops. Sally took Kate to see the statue of Robin Hood in front of Nottingham Castle after their light lunch in *The Trip to Jerusalem Inn*. They returned home via Belvoir Castle, its hilltop setting commanding stunning views over the surrounding countryside.

The Chinese restaurant was a treat. It made Kate's former Baghdad takeaway look very drab, but revived memories that made her feel melancholic until Gerry said, 'Oh, by the way, Phil Watson made contact with Corporal Mackenzie. He rang someone he knew in the Northern Constabulary in Gairloch because that's where he thought MacKinnon came from. Believe it or not, Mackenzie's contact knew a Robbie MacKinnon as he sometimes plays golf with him. Mackenzie returned Phil's call and gave him MacKinnon's address. I've written it down for you.' He pulled a crumpled piece of paper from his pocket.

Kate looked at it. It read: *Glenfinnan, Badachro, near Gairloch*. Her face brightened up, her depression vanished. She looked at Sally, grinning from ear to ear.

Sally smiled, a rather sympathetic, sad little smile. 'You're going to go, aren't you?'

'Yes, I must. Don't you see?'

'Yes, I understand. I just hope you won't be disappointed. That's all.'

Gerry tried to bring a touch of reality back into their conversation. 'It's a hell of a long way. You might find MacKinnon is not there. What then?'

Kate wasn't listening. She was planning already. 'Tomorrow, I'll ring work and take next week off. I'll contact the hire car company and extend my lease for another week.' She looked at Gerry and asked, 'How long will it take to drive there?'

He sighed, knowing nothing would stop her. 'It will take the best part of two days. If you leave here after breakfast, you should reach Perth by early evening. The following day will be slower as the roads after Inverness aren't very good.'

The following morning, Friday, 3rd May 1991, Kate made her phone calls and said her farewells to the Platinis. Then she headed up the Great North Road for Scotland.

CHAPTER 48

Gerry was right. It was a long way. Kate had taken Gerry's advice. North of Darlington, she'd left the A1 and taken the A68. 'A more interesting route,' he'd said. What he hadn't said was that it was more tiring. Traffic on the Edinburgh bypass hadn't been too heavy and once past the Forth Road Bridge, the rest had been easy. Nevertheless, when Kate struggled into the centre of Perth around five o'clock, she was exhausted. She saw signs for a hotel, *The County*. She parked, entered, booked a room, had a shower and fell asleep.

The following morning with a blue sky reminiscent of Iraq, the delightful A9 allowed good progress through some of the most beautiful countryside in Scotland. Stopping for a sandwich and a coffee at a roadside pull-in south of Inverness, she took advice from the vendor and stayed on the A9, by-passing the city. At the Tore roundabout she took the A835 for Strathpeffer and then the A832. 'It'll get slow from there on,' he had warned. 'It's mostly single track. You'll do well to get to Gairloch by tea time.' He was right, but for the wrong reason. Kate found herself slowing down to view the scenery after nearly every turn in the road. She re-fuelled at Achnasheen. 'Keep your tank full,' had been his other piece of advice. The climb past Loch Maree, considered by many to be the most beautiful loch in Scotland, was breathtaking. Kate had never seen anything like it. It stirred the romantic spirit within her.

I could live up here. It's safe, so open, so clean and awe-inspiring.

It was late afternoon when she saw the sign for Badachro, but she continued on. She had decided her priority was to find a room for the night in Gairloch. A few miles later, she entered the village and saw *The Old Inn* on her right. She parked at the rear and entered.

The reception desk was unattended. Kate pressed the bell and a young girl appeared from around a corner. She looked no older than seventeen, wore a tee shirt and jeans, her fair hair pulled back in a pony tail. Behind her followed two dogs, a border collie and a spaniel. She gave Kate a warm, genuine smile and asked, 'How can I help you?'

'I'd like a room for one or two nights, please. I'm not sure how long I will be staying.'

'That's OK; we have a room with a double bed and en suite shower. Will that be suitable?'

Kate nodded. The girl asked her to sign the register. The two dogs watched intently. When the girl, carrying Kate's bag, showed her upstairs to her room, the dogs followed.

'I'm Morag, by the way. If there's anything you want, please ask. Will you want dinner this evening?'

Kate replied in the affirmative, but said that she first of all wanted to go back to Badachro to see if she could find an old friend.

'Who will that be?' the girl asked. 'I might know him.'

'His name is Robbie MacKinnon.'

'Oh, he won't be there,' she replied smiling more broadly than ever.

Kate's heart sank.

'He's just across the road playing golf with my father and two of their cronies, Dr Macdonald and George Young, the advocate. That's Robbie's dog, Jed.' She pointed to the collie. 'I keep an eye on you when your master is playing golf, don't I, Jed?' She bent down and ruffled the dog's thick, black, shiny coat. Jed wagged his tail appreciatively. 'Mr MacKinnon taught me maths at school. He'll be back here in about half an hour. They usually have a pint before they go home.'

Kate remembered James had a degree in physics and had trained to be a teacher. *Perhaps it is him.* Her spirits rose.

'In that case,' began Kate, 'I'll take a shower, and change into fresh clothes. It's been a long day.'

'Have you come far?' the girl asked. It wasn't so much a nosey question, but rather an amiable comment to make Kate feel at home.

'Only from Perth,' Kate replied, unsure how much she should tell the teenager, who took the hint.

Still beaming, she turned to leave. 'Well, I'll see you later. If you want me just come and shout.' The spaniel followed her as she began to descend the stairs, but Jed remained looking at Kate through the doorway. He had big, sorrowful eyes and seemed to be saying, *I know you*. Kate knelt down, stroked the back of his head, and said, 'Go on, you follow Morag. I'll see you later.'

Satisfied with the attention, the dog turned and scampered down the stairs, its tail wagging more furiously than ever. *A strange name for a dog*, she thought.

She unpacked, took a long hot shower, sat on the bed and closed her eyes. She woke with a start, forty minutes later. She dressed, choosing to wear a traditional Iraqi style, loose fitting, long-sleeved, ankle-length dress, but with a broad belt that highlighted her slim waist. She back-combed her hair and applied her lipstick and favourite perfume. She looked at herself in the mirror.

Not bad for forty-one, even though I say it myself.

Her heart was in her mouth as she descended the stairs. At the bottom, in the reception area, she stopped and wondered if she could go through with it. She took a deep breath and went through into the bar. She saw Morag serving a customer and then noticed four men sitting around a square table in the window. The two men facing toward her looked up, smiled politely, but then resumed their conversation. The other two men had their backs to her, neither resembled James. One had almost shoulder-length hair, going grey while the other was bald. She froze.

It's been a wasted journey.

She turned to leave the bar. Her heart broken, her eyes began to well.

I shouldn't have been such a bloody fool. Sally said I would be disappointed.

Morag had finished serving the customer and standing behind the bar, shouted loudly across the room, 'Robbie, this is the hen I mentioned who has come from Perth to see you.'

Kate heard a chair scraping on the rough slate floor behind her. She turned to look. She knew at once, it was James with a beard and long hair.

He knew at once too. 'Kate, my God it is you.' He rushed towards her, his arms open wide. He picked her up around the waist and held her aloft like a trophy. As he lifted her into the air, he felt her firm breasts rub across his face. The aroma of her perfume was intoxicating.

That Arpege, I haven't smelled anything like it for thirteen years, he thought. *I've never forgotten it all this time; on her it rouses my sexual drive.*

He lowered her to the ground and holding her tight, kissed her – a long passionate kiss.

She felt her blood rushing through her veins. Her heart was pounding against her ribs. She was glowing all over. He wouldn't let go, she gasped for oxygen. When he stopped, she realised everyone in the bar was watching. He didn't seem to care. He could only stare at her, his wide eyes alight with disbelief.

Moments passed. He took her hand and led her towards his three friends. 'Let me introduce you,' he said. 'This is an old friend, lads. Kate meet Glenn Fraser – Morag's dad and owner of the pub; George Young, one of our legal experts in the village; and, most important of all...' he laughed, 'Dr Jim Macdonald, our local GP.'

She shook hands with them and smiling said, 'I'm Kate Jackson.'

It was Dr Macdonald who offered her his chair and said, 'Let me get you a drink. What would you like?'

'A dry white wine would be nice, thank you.' He left towards the bar.

James' friends were amicable and polite, but they could discern that Kate and Robbie wished to be alone. After a few minutes of listening to Robbie explaining how he had met Kate on an assignment many years previously in Reading, Dr Macdonald excused their presence. 'I am sure you two have much catching up to do and it's time George and I are off. It's been nice meeting you, Kate. I hope we'll get to know each other better over the coming days. I assume you are staying a while?'

Kate smiled, felt herself blushing and looked at Robbie. 'If Robbie wants me to,' she replied.

'Of course I do,' he responded with enthusiasm. 'You can stay as long as you want. I have plenty of spare room.'

Glenn offered, 'If you wish to book out from here, I won't mind. You might as well stay with Robbie in Badachro. It would make sense.'

'But I have used your shower,' protested Kate.

'No matter. A friend of Robbie's is a friend of mine.'

No mention had been made of war games, Iraq, or anything else that could reveal their military connections. Kate suspected James had successfully misled his colleagues over the years about his background. In her brief conversation with them she had been ultra careful not to bring up any topics that might prove to be embarrassing. Fortunately, none of the three had asked any probing questions.

When they had left, James and Kate remained at the table in the bar. They were alone for the first time in nearly thirteen years, except for Jed who had joined them. He lay obediently at Robbie's feet, looking warmly at Kate. James took hold of her hands, bent forward, and whispered, 'Jim Macdonald was right, we have a lot of catching up to do.' His eyes were telling her how exhilarated he was at seeing her again.

'It's going to take weeks to tell you everything that has happened, but first of all, how is Stuart?' she asked.

'Stuart's fine. He's in his third year at Edinburgh University studying medicine. He'll be home for the summer holidays next month. He still remembers us playing roly-poly at Sand Bay. As for you telling me everything, well, we have the rest of our lives. I suspect my tale will take less time than yours.' He chuckled. 'As you can see, it is rather quiet up here; even more so in the winter.'

'The first thing I've got to do is get used to calling you Robbie. At least, I am still Kate,' she laughed.

'God, it's good to hear you laugh again like that, after all these years. I've thought about you every day since I've been living here.'

'I don't believe that,' she exclaimed.

'It's true. Why do you think I call this fellow,' he looked down and gently prodded his dog with his foot, 'Jed?'

'I did think it was an unusual name.'

'Jed is short for JisED.'

There was a short pause while the penny dropped. Kate was unsure whether having a dog named after her surname was a compliment, or not. She looked at Jed. He seemed to smile back, and gave his tail a wag as if saying, *I'm happy with it.* She laughed. They both laughed. It was paradise being together again.

***

Saturday is a working day in Baghdad and that afternoon in General Ali Hassan's office sat Gen Wafiq al Samarra and agent, grade seven, Arif Rashid of the Mukhabaret. 'Arif is fluent in Turkish and Italian as well as Azerbaijani,' explained Wafiq to his distant cousin. 'He has picked up English much quicker than we anticipated and is itching to serve our cause. We have acquired an Italian passport for him. He will travel overland through Turkey and then by boat and train to Bari in south-east Italy. He will stay with his cousins in Milan and then make his way to England. What exactly do you want him to do?'

'The hardest thing will be finding al Jised. The British Secret Service will have given her a new identity. However, she has friends in England and will, sooner or later, make the error of contacting them. It's all in this file.' General Hassan passed over a red file titled, Kathab al Jised – TRAITOR. 'The best place to start will probably be Cambridge. You are to extract from her the chess position she used to hide our biological weapons. Use any method you wish, truth serum, knee-capping, electrodes on her genitalia, whatever it takes. When you have the position, kill her. Don't worry about cleaning up the mess. Just get yourself back to Paris and give the position to our man in the embassy for immediate transmission. Any questions?'

'How long have I got?'

'As long as it takes.'

CHAPTER 49

Having repacked her bags, Kate followed James and Jed back to Badachro. The road was a narrow, twisty single track with passing places. Eventually, after a slight rise and a left-hand bend, the village, mostly a huddle of whitewashed cottages around the edge of a crescent-shaped bay, came into view. In the middle of the bay was a forested island with a rope bridge attaching it to the mainland's rocky shore. The scene was a haven of tranquillity with the sun shining on a twinkling sea and a dozen small yachts, anchored at random, bobbing up and down.

They passed through the village, Kate's car twenty yards behind James'. She wondered, *where is he taking me?*

He took a sharp right, up an even narrower single-track road with grass growing up the middle. He passed several houses and then stopped. Jed jumped out first, then James, who opened a set of double gates. He waved for Kate to enter and they parked their cars side by side.

'Welcome to Glenfinnan,' he said. 'I hope you will be as happy here as I have been. But how on earth did you find me?'

'It's a long story,' she replied.

'In that case, you'd better come in, unpack, and you can tell me as we go down to the pub for a meal. I don't suppose you've got any decent walking shoes with you?'

'I have, actually. Sally said I might need some sturdy shoes up here and she insisted I took hers. Fortunately we're the same size.'

'Sally?'

'You remember her, *G*erry Platini's wife. I have the Platinis to thank for finding you. But that's *only* part of the story. Anyway, why do I need walking shoes?'

'I have a path through the garden that leads down to the shoreline. We can walk along the beach to the Inn. It's a bit shorter than going back around the road.'

They walked down a steep path from their parked cars through a densely wooded, sloping garden. The trees were a mix of pines, silver birches and various acers. There were shrubs such as fuchsia, hebes and rhododendrons that hid the bungalow from their cars; a distance of some thirty yards. Looking at the plants, some of which she had never seen before, reminded Kate how much she had forgotten from her degree in botany. There were irregular areas set aside to grass, surrounded by flowering cherries, bluebells, and late-flowering daffodils. She stopped in amazement to take it all in.

'What's the matter?' he asked.

'I am staggered to see so many varieties in your garden I never thought you would get some of these plants to grow so far north.'

'We have very mild winters. I can't remember when we last had a frost, but come in. There will be plenty of time for you to explore the garden tomorrow.' He seemed to be in a hurry. Kate thought she knew why.

They entered through the kitchen, surprisingly tidy for a man living on his own, and James showed Kate to her bedroom.

They looked at each other smiling and said nothing. Kate knew his intentions. He put his arms around Kate and she closed her eyes as she stretched up to kiss him. His beard initially felt weird, but as her heart began to beat faster, her breathing deeper and her body stiffened, she never noticed it. She had her arms around his neck and was holding him as tight as she could. She felt his hands feeling under her bra; her breasts were bursting. Their panting grew ever deeper as they both gasped for air and fell backwards onto the bed. There was no stopping him. Without saying a word, he had pulled her skirt over her waist and his trousers were down. He pushed her knickers to one side; the frenzied activity was ecstatically rapid. Soon they exploded together and their bodies began to slowly deflate. They lay side by side, holding tightly to each other. Kate was exhausted, but knew she never wanted to be apart from him again. Not a word had been spoken. For thirteen years Kate had dreamt of this moment; now its culmination had lasted but a minute.

They rested, gently winding down from their violent eruption. 'I'm sorry, I didn't mean to hurt you,' James whispered, 'but that's the first time since our last.'

'You didn't hurt me. I understand,' she said, 'but it must have been the quickest quickie of all time.' She laughed. It made him blush.

However, for Kate there had been someone else since their last time together; she thought about Amer and decided she had to tell him. 'Did you know I was briefly married?'

'Yes. Admiral Johnson came up here; it must have been ten years ago. He used to be the Head of Military Intelligence. I don't think you ever met him. He came to tell me that Iraq had given the Americans the chess key and that it would be safe for Stuart and I to return to what he called civilisation. He mentioned you had got married. I was glad for you. You deserved some happiness after all that had happened.'

'Amer was a good man, but I didn't love him. You see I was always in love with you. It was wrong of me, I know, but our weekend at Babylon and Ur changed me forever.'

'We both have guilty consciences. That weekend changed me too. I had to come back when Emma died, but even at her funeral many of my thoughts were of you.' He paused, thinking of Emma, then added, 'God forgive me.'

He turned and drew her ever nearer, whispering, 'I don't want you to leave me again. I want you to stay here with me for ever.'

She clung on to him and kissed him, pressing her face as closely as possible to his. With tears running down her face, she whispered, 'I won't ever leave you, I promise.'

Stretched out on the bed, both in a daze and saying nothing; only looking at the ceiling, it was some time before James broke the silence.

'Before it gets dark, change into something more practical and I'll show you the rest of the garden as we take the path to the shore. Then we can stroll around the bay to the pub and have a bite to eat.'

Dressed in jeans, a sweater and Sally's shoes, they wandered down the steep path to the beach, led by Jed. Kate was yet again in awe at the multitude of bushes, ferns, grasses and trees in the garden that stretched to over an acre. They scrambled over the stones as they rounded the little bay to the centre of the village, a distance of half a mile.

Over their meal Kate explained how she had come to England, been given a new identity and started working for MI6 as an interpreter. She admitted to getting lonely, how she had tried to find her sister in Leeds and visited the Platinis on the return journey. She described meeting the Watsons and how Phil's chess game with Corporal Mackenzie had led her to finding him.

James was intrigued. 'I had no idea Mackenzie was in the RAF police. I guess I was careless,' he remarked. 'However, it's just as well, otherwise we would never have found each other again.'

'Now that you know how I came to find you, how come you weren't killed by the IRA?' asked Kate.

'First of all, Emma's death was not an accident.'

'When I came over for her funeral, I heard a rumour to that effect,' Kate replied.

'Yes, Mrs Norris did tell me you arrived too late on the Monday and missed us by an hour or two. She called you "The Persian Princess" and I can see why although I always thought you were more like...'

'I know, Ava Gardner.'

'Sorry, I got diverted. Emma's death had been cleverly engineered and Admiral Johnson was convinced the Americans had done it to put pressure on me to hand over the secret of the chess key.'

'Do you know that there is a possibility it was the Israelis? They were after the information in the game. Do you remember Ben Gre~ think he was a Mossad agent.'

'I didn't know that. Anyway, I agreed the best th

was to work with the Army at one of their secure bases. We lived at Fort Halstead in Kent in married quarters with my in-laws. However, it was terribly claustrophobic; none of us were happy. When Pat and Bill decided to come up here and bought a croft on the Isle of Skye, Stuart missed them terribly. I decided to resign from the RAF and persuaded Admiral Johnson to bail me out with a new identity. He did so without telling anyone. To arrange my disappearance, I began trialling a communications system in Northern Ireland with an Army officer who had worked undercover inside the IRA, but was about to be exposed. Admiral Johnson planned for the SAS to snatch us when we were in the countryside near the Eire border. A helicopter took us to a safe house in south-west Scotland where we were given new identities, similar to what happened to you. Stuart joined my in-laws, now both dead, for the interim. They were the only ones to know the truth. I decided to live up here where there would be no possibility of anyone recognising me. When anyone asked me about my background I said that my father was from Skye; MacKinnon is a common name there. I said he had been a lighthouse keeper on the Isle of Man. It explained my non-Scottish accent and seemed to satisfy people's curiosity. Stuart loves Badachro; he's big into fishing and sailing. We've a small boat. I took a part-time job teaching maths in the local school and joined the golf and bridge clubs. It's been a good life.'

'Morag told me you taught her maths.'

'She's a bright girl and could have gone to university, but all she ever wanted to do was help her father. Glenn is a widower. They came up here from Glasgow to run *The Old Inn* about six years ago. You probably noticed their accents are harsher than either Dr Macdonald or George Young who are highlanders.'

'She called me a hen. I didn't think that was very flattering.'

'On the contrary, in Glasgow it is a term of endearment. She took to you.'

When they ambled back to the house, his arm around her waist, they ˈlone in the dark. Only Jed, always ten yards ahead, and the stars in the sky kept them company. The only noise was the lapping of the waves on the shore as the tide came in. There were no aeroplanes, no cars, no police sirens and no people. For Kate it was pure bliss.

'It's idyllic here,' she said. 'I can see why you decided not to go back when you had the chance.'

'It's not everyone's cup of tea. I shop weekly in Gairloch, but once a month I go to Inverness for a bulk shop. Afterwards I treat myself to the cinema, if there's anything worth seeing, and an Indian or Chinese meal. Believe it or not, Inverness is as far south as I've been in ten years.'

'I can't say I'm looking forward to going back south,' she replied.

He stopped in his tracks. He looked at her. 'What for?'

'There's the hire car to return for a start. Then, I'll have to hand in my notice, move out of my flat and bring all my stuff up here.'

'Yes. I should have thought of that, but I'm going with you. We'll hire a van from Avis in Hertford for the removals and then we'll be able to return it to their Inverness office.'

The weather remained warm and dry for the next few days and Robbie, as he became more and more frequently called by Kate, took the opportunity to show her the neighbourhood. They took long walks with Jed along the westerly track to Port Henderson and the empty golden beaches beyond. The views towards Skye were incomparable. He took her to the gardens at Inverewe where the botanist in Kate came out. Her knowledge of the trees and shrubs was staggering. There were few she could not identify, even though she had only seen some in books.

They decided to head south for Hertford on Thursday, 9th May. Morag had agreed to have Jed while they were away. 'We've either got two long days driving, or one bloody long day driving. Which will it be?' he asked on the Wednesday evening as he packed a few items to take with him.

They left Badachro before 7 am, and struggled into Hertford at 11.30 pm that night. It wasn't until they were safely in her flat that Kate realised they were going to have to share her single bed. The next day she gave in her week's notice. No one seemed to be surprised. Her boss gave her the impression that he was expecting it; although Kate couldn't see how he could have known of her intentions.

Kate worked out her final week. On Wednesday she was surprised when Peter Stacey appeared in her office unannounced. 'I have come to take you to lunch,' he said. They went around the corner from her building in Theobald's Road and found a French restaurant in Lamb's Conduit Street. They sat in the window. 'When you suddenly extended your holiday last week, we wondered why. I had asked Milly to keep an eye on you and tell me if you did anything unusual because I am still worried that Saddam Hussein will send a hit man to find you. We knew your sister had worked in the Leeds Infirmary, of course, and checked to see if you had tried to contact her.' He paused, pulling out a neat, folded piece of paper from his breast pocket. He handed it to her. 'That's Lina's address, by the way. She lives in Wellington, New Zealand and is a Mrs Gray – an appropriate name for the wife of a consultant psychiatrist, don't you think?' He laughed at his own joke.

As she took the paper, tears of joy came into her eyes. She leant across the table and kissed his cheek. 'I can't thank you enough for this,' she said.

'As I was saying, the sudden week's extension worried Milly and I wondered who else you might have tried to contact. So, I rang Gerry Platini. We hadn't spoken since he left Baghdad all those years ago. He told me you had gone on what he thought might be a wild goose chase to Scotland. Apparently, you wanted to see if James Douglas was still alive. I must admit I was sceptical too, but in my position I can get my hands on information easier than most. However, even I had to get ministerial approval before delving into the dungeons of the MoD. I wish you and James every happiness for the future. I still remember that Sunday evening at the Abu Samba when I recruited you. I knew then that you and he were an item. What happened subsequently was tragic. I only hope everything will work out all right from now on.' Peter lent across the table and held both her hands. She thanked him with tears running down her face.

She left the office for the last time on Friday, 17ᵗʰ May.

Kate and Robbie left Hertford on Saturday morning, spent the night in a cosy hotel in Brough, Cumberland and arrived home late on Sunday afternoon. They collected Jed, had a meal at *The Old Inn*, and retired to bed – exhausted.

Their new life together had begun. Only one thing darkened the horizon for Kate – that worry of Peter's. Was Saddam going to send someone after her?

CHAPTER 50

Kate and James had three weeks together before Stuart came home from university. His vacation was for June only. In early July he had to return to begin medical practice. He was delighted to see Kate. Whenever he could persuade her to accompany him fishing in Badachro Bay he did so. They became bosom pals. Robbie took advantage of the arrangement by disappearing to play golf. Jed usually accompanied Stuart and Kate in the rowing boat. He had learnt how to rest with both paws over the side trailing in the water. Kate began to become an accomplished fisherwoman and their evening meal was often the fresh fish they had caught that day.

Kate found Stuart surprisingly mature. As the time wore on she began to confide with him secrets of her past that she hadn't told Robbie.

'I don't think it's wrong to have secrets providing it isn't likely to hurt Dad,' he said one day. 'I have a steady girlfriend at university, but I wouldn't want her to know everything about me,' he laughed.

'Such as what?' asked Kate.

'When I go away with the university badminton team to play other universities, we usually stay overnight. If there is a hop on, then I will try and pick up a bird for the night. I wouldn't dream of telling her when I get back.'

'Hmm... I'm not sure that's quite the same thing,' replied Kate.

'In a way it is. From what you have told me, the weapons you helped to create are now safely buried away. As far as you and Dad are concerned, does it matter if he doesn't know the details?'

She thought about enditon, exciton, tabun and vexun. She thought about how she had murdered Roya and President Bakr. She thought about watching the six prisoners being killed with gangrennex and the subsequent photographs. She shuddered, but Stuart was right, Robbie didn't need to know. It was over, the past should be buried.

'You know,' she said after a long pause, 'I used to dilute the chemical weapons with talcum powder to make them less potent.'

'There you are then,' he replied instantly, 'your past isn't all bad.'

They continued fishing in silence. Kate was unsure about Stuart's last remark. It had been thoughtless and tactless, typical of a young person. However, he was right. She hadn't been all bad. Nevertheless, there was the black mark of Satan on her, and like it or not, it would always be there. Disclosing everything to Robbie would not remove the stain; she would have to live with it.

'It's likely that there is an agent of Saddam Hussein's trying to find me as we speak. He will kill me if he finds me,' she said suddenly.

Stuart stopped rowing the boat. He looked at her. His face drained. 'Does Dad know?' he asked.

'No, I don't think so.'

'Then you must tell him.'

'Why? There is nothing he can do.'

'You must tell him,' he repeated louder. 'If you don't tell him, then I will.'

'The security services have assured me they will stop anyone suspicious entering the country.'

'It doesn't matter. Our borders are not one hundred per cent secure and you know that. Dad must know, so he can take precautions.'

'Such as?'

'I don't know. Perhaps you could move away from here.'

Kate sighed. It wasn't the answer and she knew it. If an assassin was going to find her, then he would find her. But Stuart was right. Robbie deserved to know. 'I promise I will tell Robbie this evening.'

Over their evening meal, Kate disclosed her fears to Robbie about the potential killer.

'What does he want?' he asked.

'I suspect they are after the chess position you taught me in the sand at Ur. It is the position I used initially to hide the biological weapons in the desert. Without it, their records are meaningless,' she replied.

'You said initially,' he replied thoughtfully. 'Didn't you use the same position all the time?'

'No. When I began hiding the materials, mostly anthrax and botulinium toxin, I used the method you taught me. However, after a while, I began to notice a pattern emerging. I seemed to be using the knight moves frequently, the squares *e4, f6, d5, e3* and so on. After about ten burials, I changed the scale of the chess board. You had suggested one kilometre squares. I decided to make them ten kilometres. The number of dots on the records was altered accordingly.'

'Excellent,' interrupted Robbie.

'Later I bought a beginners book on chess and used positions from the book. From time to time I changed the scale of the squares. Towards the end I didn't care, you were dead, Amer was dead and my mother and father were dead. I destroyed the book and began to simply point a pin on the map with my eyes closed to get a Lat/Long position. Then I dotted some of the letters in the details of the records to make them look the same as the others. I've no idea where any of the later stuff is buried. There is no way the weapons can ever be found again.'

'Wonderful. However, if you saw a pattern appearing, they will have spotted it too. They may come after you for the initial chess position, although changing the positions and scales will be foolproof for the later burials. When you debriefed MI6 about hiding the biological weapons, did you tell them you changed your method of hiding?'

'Yes, of course,' replied Kate. 'Why?'

'It means they know there is no chance of Saddam finding the weapons, other than, possibly, the early toxins.'

The three sat quietly thinking through the consequences of Saddam finding the earlier biological weapons. It was Stuart who asked, 'What are you going to do, Dad?'

'I'll tell Bill Brown, the policeman, to look out for any suspicious strangers coming to Gairloch.'

'Dad, for the next three months the Highlands are full of strangers: Dutch, French, Germans,' protested Stuart.

'But not Arabs,' replied Robbie.

'Saddam is not daft. The assassin won't look Arabic,' commented Kate. 'He will have chosen someone who looks reasonably European.'

'Then the only solution is for us to move,' replied a dejected Robbie.

'If they can trace me here, then they could find out where we have moved to. I have been thinking. The only way they can find me here is through the Platinis and the Watsons. Both know my background and will not reveal the information about Badachro. I'm as safe here as anywhere else. Besides, I have always got my gangrennex spray.'

'What on earth is that?' asked Stuart.

Kate explained that it was the nastiest substance her laboratories produced and how she only allowed tiny quantities to be made. Most was used to make fifty small aerosols that were, in reality, tiny guns disguised to look like harmless ballpoint pens. She went and fetched her handbag and showed them the three samples she had left.

'Each fires a jet of gangrennex up to ten feet in a fifth of a second. The effect is instant. Each droplet is one hundred times stronger than a wasp's sting. Imagine being stung by a thousand wasps simultaneously. Within two seconds the skin begins to melt. The pain is excruciating. The victim's yelling and screaming stops after fifteen seconds by which time their nervous system has stopped functioning. The person dies, usually within forty-five seconds. For years I used to carry one on my person all the time, hidden up my sleeve. I gave two to Porton Down; they were excited at what they saw as a significant development in biological weaponry. I brought five to Britain; these are the last three.'

The two men in her life were speechless.

'So,' said Kate, now fully in control of the situation, 'we remain here, but stay vigilant for any strangers coming up our lane.'

They both nodded, still dumbfounded.

At breakfast the following morning, Kate remarked to Robbie, 'You were restless last night. Didn't you sleep well?'

'No, I was thinking about how we could be prepared if this assassin turns up.'

'And?'

'You should offer to give him the chess position at once, but point out that you will have to draw it for him on a piece of paper. We will place one of your sprays in the pot where we keep the biros and pencils, next to the telephone and pad in the kitchen. Then, if you are in the kitchen, you go to the pad to write the position, grab the aerosol and use it. The second spray we place in the desk, along with the pens and the writing paper we keep in the study. Those are the only two places where you would go to draw the position. The third spray you keep on you at all times; either up your sleeve or in your handbag.'

Kate and Stuart nodded. It seemed a logical use of their defensive resources.

'The other thing that struck me last night was that he can only get here by car.'

Again the other two nodded.

Robbie continued. 'If you were successful with the gangrennex, we would have to get rid of his car as well as his body. I thought of burying him, but we can't bury a car.' He stopped, inviting the others to respond.

Again they nodded; all ears.

'The B-road from Gairloch out to Melvaig after North Erradale runs along the cliff edge, in some places there is no more than three yards between the road and the edge. The only barrier is four horizontal strands of wire attached to wooden posts, spaced every three or four yards. The cliffs are typically 200 feet high with vertical drops into the sea. We could cut the wires and push the car over. With some spare wire we mend the fence, and Bob's your uncle.'

'Pardon?' queried Kate. The expression was new to her. Neither of the men found they could explain its origin.

All three, plus Jed, that morning drove out to Melvaig for a recce.

They all agreed that the road was ideal for their purposes and found the exact position they could use. Stuart had taken an old paint spray; he painted an insignificant arrow on the road to ease finding the spot in future.

'We're going to have to do it in the dark, Dad,' he remarked. He seemed excited at the idea.

On Sunday, 7th July, Stuart returned to Edinburgh to begin his hospital attachment. His 4th year studies would begin in mid-August, so he would not be returning to Badachro until Christmas. On Friday, 19th July, Kate and Robbie went together to Inverness for their monthly stock-up. They rounded the day with a visit to Robbie's regular Chinese restaurant.

Not up to Grantham standards, but better than Baghdad, thought Kate.

'Tomorrow is Captain's Day at the golf club. Would you mind if I played in the competition?' Robbie asked. 'There is a meal afterwards with the prize distribution at seven o'clock. I thought you could come down in the early evening and meet some of the members. Dr Macdonald will be there with his wife, and Glenn with Morag. It is usually a good do.'

'Of course, you must play. I can drop you off in the morning and then come back later.'

'Great.'

The following morning Kate dropped Robbie at the golf club around 11.30 am, agreeing she would return around 5.30 pm. She popped into the Spar shop and bought a few essentials forgotten the previous day. She decided to buy a paper, *The Scotsman.* She drove home, made herself a light lunch, skimmed through the paper and wondered why she had bothered to buy it. Then she took Jed for a walk towards Port Henderson. She turned right up a rough track that led to a nearby beach where several seals were sunbathing on the rocks. It was a favourite spot of Jed's; he liked to search the small bay for suitable items of jetsam to bring back to Kate.

They got back to Glenfinnan around four o'clock. In the lane, Kate saw a red Vauxhall Astra parked near their entrance. It didn't feel right being there.

It must be someone visiting the neighbours.

She went down the path. Jed usually ran ahead and would wait at the back door for it to be opened. He would then charge in and drink from his water bowl, emptying it quicker than Robbie could down his first pint. However, he stopped half way down the path and growled. He turned to Kate. As she looked down at him, his eyes were telling her, *there's someone in the house.*

'Tie that dog up, or I'll shoot it.' A heavily accented Arabic voice shouted.

Kate looked up and saw a man, to all appearances a southern European, standing in the back door that led to her kitchen. She froze for a moment, staring at the 9 mm semi-automatic in his right hand.

'Do it,' he demanded, as he waved the pistol at her. She knelt down, attached Jed's leash to his collar, and tied him to the base of a silver ash. He wined, his eyes asking, *why are you doing this to me?* She stood up. She felt cold; an involuntary shiver ran down her back. She was staring into the eyes of her executioner. She had to play for time.

'You're from Turkey,' she said in Arabic.

'Not a bad guess,' he replied. 'I'm from Naxcivan in Azerbaijan, just across the border.'

'Ah, the area torn between Armenia, the Kurds and the Farsis,' Kate replied.

'You know your history of the region, then?'

'Just a little.'

'Then you'll know why I'm here and working for Ali Hassan. Our enclave has been raped by the Kurds with the co-operation of the Iranians for hundreds of years. Whenever we have regained our own sovereignty, the bloody Christian Armenians have invaded us through our backdoor. In modern times, only Saddam has consistently given us his support. The Turks couldn't give a shit.' He spat on the ground, showing his contempt for them. He waved the newspaper Kate had bought that morning in his left hand, and asked, 'Have you read this?'

Kate was puzzled, and having controlled her nerves to some extent, advanced towards the stranger, who handed her the paper. 'You'd better come inside and read it,' he sneered.

She sat down at the kitchen table, unfolded the paper, and saw an article.

Mysterious Death of RAF Wife – Coroner Returns Open Verdict

Details have emerged of the mysterious death of Mrs Sally Platini, 48, wife of a Senior RAF officer. Mrs Platini was found dead, tied up in a chair on Wednesday, 3rd July, in her home near Grantham, Lincolnshire. There were no signs of a struggle, nor any signs of a break in. Nothing had been stolen. Air Commodore Brian Griffiths, the senior RAF pathologist, in his evidence to the coroner, said that her death was a mystery. The symptoms were similar to a heart attack, but Mrs Platini had been healthy and kept herself fit by daily exercise. He could only postulate as to why her being tied up should have led to her death. When asked what his theory was, the Air Commodore replied that he thought she may have been drugged, but all toxicology tests known had proved negative. 'We are dealing with something very unusual here,' he remarked. The Lincolnshire Police have appealed for witnesses to come forward who might have seen a grey Ford Escort in the village of Colsterworth on the afternoon of her death.

'You bastard, you killed Sally with exciton,' she screamed.

'Yes, taken orally we have found it to be an excellent truth serum. Once the victim starts talking they cannot stop. She even told me you and she had been lovers in Baghdad. You're nothing but a Western whore, al Jised, and you are going to die for it. However, first of all you are going to write down the chess position that you used to hide our biological weapons.' His handgun remained pointed at her chest.

'Why have you taken nearly three weeks to come up here to find me?' she demanded, still trying to play for time.

'Simple,' he smiled. 'To let the fuss die down, return the grey Ford and enjoy the stinking hell hole of London. God, what a place! It's full of homosexuals and prostitutes like you. Someday Allah will destroy it.'

'And if I won't give you the chess position?'

'You have a choice, exciton like your lesbian lover, or I'll start by shooting your dog, then your kneecaps – one by one. Don't think about giving me the wrong position either, it will be easy to return to finish off Squadron Leader Douglas and his son.'

Sally must have told him that Robbie was James.

'I'll give you the correct position, but I want you to swear on the Koran that you will leave here after you have killed me, and not harm the dog. He is, after all, one of Allah's creatures. If you don't swear, then I'll draw the wrong position and you'll have failed. I know what Ali Hassan does to people who fail him. It won't be you who will be returning. You'll be under six feet of earth.'

Arif Rashid contemplated her remarks for a while. He knew the traitor was right. He could not afford to fail. He wanted to kill the dog simply to upset al Jised's lover, but getting the position was all important. *Anyway, after I've shot her, she won't know what I've done to the dog,* he thought.

'I agree,' he said at last.

'Then behind you on that shelf you'll find the Koran. My father gave it to me when I was eight years of age. I want you to swear with your hand on the book that you will leave the dog alone.'

This changed matters. Even Rashid was not going to swear with his hand on the Koran and then break his vow, especially not for a dog. He removed its cover and checked that the book was the Koran. He reluctantly agreed.

'Fine,' she said. She moved towards the telephone pad and the pot of biros.

'Stop,' he ordered. 'Where are you going?'

'I'll use the note pad here,' she pointed, 'to write the position down.'

'No tricks,' he warned.

'You have a gun. All I have is a paper pad and a pen,' she turned slowly towards him, giving a faint smile. His semi-automatic was still in his right hand and pointing at her chest. She turned her back to him.

I must duck to my left when I fire, she thought.

She took the notepad down from the shelf, next to the telephone and placed it on the kitchen work surface. She turned again to check he hadn't moved. He was watching her like a hawk. She turned back to the shelf, reached up for the biro pot, saw the spray and took it in her right hand. She swung around, squeezing the button on the top and the clip simultaneously – a procedure she had practiced dozens of time before, albeit six years previously. Haruki Tai's gun shot out the gangrennex, hitting Arif Rashid in the eyes. His instinctive reaction was to fire at his target as his hands came up to protect his face.

Kate bobbed down to her left, but too slow. The bullet tore through her body somewhere between the top of her breast and her right shoulder. The pain was instant. As she moved her hand to where the bullet had hit her, she could feel the blood spurting from her wound. Her first aid instructor's voice, from her time in the university's military corps, came flooding back, *first of all, stop the bleeding.* She lay on the floor and above her saw the tea cloth folded on the door of the oven. She grabbed it, crumpled it into a rough pad and pressed hard on the wound.

Only then did she remember her assassin. Although he had been screaming in agony for the ten or fifteen seconds since the shots were exchanged, she hadn't heard him. Her own pain had cancelled out all her senses. Still lying on the kitchen floor, Kate looked under the table through its legs. His body, on the other side, was still making involuntary movements, kicking like a dead frog's legs when given an electric stimulus. He had stopped screaming, his face had disappeared. His bloody skeleton stared at the ceiling, the eye sockets empty. The palms of his hands were without skin where he had tried to wipe the gangrennex from his face. His body was stiff due to the reaction of the chlorostridium perfingens on his nervous system.

She stepped over his body and spat on it. 'That's for killing Sally,' she said. She managed to stagger into the bathroom despite shaking with nerves. She bathed her wound as best as she could with Dettol – it stung like hell – but she could only stop the bleeding by pressing a clean towel firmly against it. Despite feeling faint, she knew she had to keep awake else she might bleed to death.

She went into the lounge, opened the address book on the desk, found *golf club* and rang.

'Gairloch Golf Club, Chris speaking,' answered a voice she knew. Chris was the barman.

'Chris, it's Kate Jackson, Robbie's partner. Is Robbie there?'

'Aye, Kate,' he replied, 'he's just come in. He's here with Doc Macdonald.' She heard him say, 'Robbie, it's Kate. She wants you.'

'Hello, love. Are you OK?' Robbie asked.

'No. He's been here. What we feared has happened.' She was crying over the phone.

'Are you alright?' he repeated.

'I've been shot in the shoulder. Please come home at once.' She was feeling weaker. 'Bring Doc Macdonald with you, but whatever you do, don't come in through the kitchen. Come in through the front door.' The pain was getting worse, the blood still seeping through her improvised pad. She never heard Robbie shouting down the phone as she lay back on the sofa and fell unconscious.

As Jim Macdonald's Range Rover sped south towards Badachro, Robbie was unsure how much information he would have to give away to his friend and golf partner. 'It's awfully good of you to come like this, Jim,' he began. 'It seems Kate was cleaning some cupboards. You know what women are like, always tidying things up. To be honest, having lived at Glenfinnan for nigh on thirteen years alone, I suppose it's paradise for a charwoman.'

'I never saw Kate as a charwoman,' laughed his friend, 'more like a Persian princess. Her resemblance to ex-Queen Soraya is uncanny.'

'You're not the first to notice that,' replied Robbie. 'Anyway, while cleaning out a cupboard, she came across an old pistol that I had taken from an IRA prisoner when I was in the Army. I'm afraid it went off and she has shot herself in the shoulder. I've been meaning to get rid for years. Tomorrow I'll go out to the cliffs at Melvaig and throw it into the sea.'

'I didn't know you had been in the Army, Robbie.'

'I did a short service commission of four years in the Staffordshire Regiment. I didn't really like it. Germany was great – cheap booze, but Northern Ireland was the pits. I'd had enough after a year in Belfast and left. I'd be grateful if you could patch Kate up and not mention the gun to Bill Brown.'

'That will depend on how much blood she has lost and the seriousness of her wound. I'll do my best, after all I do owe you one,' the doctor replied as they began to enter Badachro.

'Do you?' asked Robbie.

'Yes, without your extra tuition, Shona would never have got an 'A' grade in her Highers for maths and, therefore, get into Veterinary School. You refused payment, you might remember?'

'Your daughter would have got the grades without my help, Jim. How's she getting on, by the way?'

'She graduates next year; I suspect she will do well.' They went up the single track that Robbie knew so well. 'I see you have visitors, Robbie,' remarked the doctor, nodding towards the red Astra.

Thinking quickly, Robbie lied, 'It's probably someone visiting the neighbours.' *That's the car that has somehow got to disappear.*

They entered through the front door, after having untied Jed from the silver birch. Fortunately, Jim didn't think to ask why Jed had been tied up. Kate lay semi-conscious in the lounge.

'Now, Kate, what have you been doing to yourself?' asked the doctor, as he knelt down beside her. He examined the wound and declared, 'The bullet is still inside. I am going to give you a local anaesthetic, then extract it. It will hurt, I'm afraid. Drop your arm to your side for a moment. Can you lift it up sideways like this?' He motioned to her what he wanted. She couldn't move it at all. 'Mmm. I thought so. You are lucky, young lady. I don't think there will be any permanent damage, but it may take up to six months before your arm regains total mobility.'

Watching, Robbie was surprised how quickly Jim removed the bullet and then stitched up the wound. 'I'm going to be honest with you, Robbie. I would prefer it if Kate went to have an X-ray. However, explaining the gun shot might be embarrassing.'

Kate was coming round, heard the remark and insisted, 'No, I'll be OK, honestly.'

'Well, I estimate from the stains on your towel that you have lost about two pints of blood. You are going to feel weak for quite a few days. You must take it easy, plenty of red meat, red wine and that sort of thing. I want you to keep your arm in a sling for a fortnight, and then I will take the stitches out. In time, you will be as right as nine-pence.'

All three shared a dram of *Islay Mist* before the doctor left.

Kate and Robbie discussed what to do. There was no way Kate could help with the ditching of the Astra; her arm was too painful. It was almost six o'clock on a Saturday evening. 'There's only one solution,' declared Robbie. Without explaining to Kate, he lifted the phone and dialled a number.

'Stuart, it's Dad here, have you got a minute?'

'Hi, Dad. What's up?'

'I need you to come home at once. We've had that visitor we talked about and need to get rid of his car.'

'Is Kate alright?'

'She was shot in the shoulder, but she'll live. Doc Macdonald has been and patched her up, but her arm will be in a sling for several weeks.'

'I'll come of course, but I'm not sure if there is a train to Inverness tonight. I'll ring the station at Waverley and find out. I'll ring you back straight away.'

'Good lad.'

Five minutes later, the phone rang. 'Dad, we're in luck. There's a train at 1920 hours, straight through to Inverness. It arrives at ten past eleven.'

'Listen, Stuart, I'll pick you up. Try and get your head down on the train. We have a long night ahead of us.'

'See you later, Dad. Give my love to Kate.' He hung up.

Robbie then cycled back to the golf club; threw the bike in the back of his hatchback and returned forty minutes later.

Before leaving Badachro at nine o'clock, Robbie insisted Kate went to bed. 'You'll be alright. Jed can keep you company if you don't want to be alone in the bedroom. When you wake up tomorrow, this will be but a bad dream. Stuart and I will have ditched the car with the corpse and his gun. No one will ever know what happened. Doc Macdonald can be trusted.' He kissed her and left.

The train arrived a few minutes early. Robbie asked Stuart if he had eaten. 'No, and I'm starving,' he answered.

'So am I,' replied his dad. 'We'll get a quick Chinese before we leave Inverness and go through what we have to do.'

The road back to Badachro was quiet. They arrived around two o'clock. They struggled to lift the dead Iraqi up the path from the house to his car; his keys had been in his trouser pocket. The gun was placed in the glove compartment; the Iraqi was strapped in the passenger seat. Robbie drove the Astra. Stuart followed in the family car. They found the agreed place, cut the wires of the fence, manoeuvred the car to within inches of the edge of the cliff, tugged and pushed the Iraqi into the driver's seat, opened several of the windows to allow the sea to enter the car more quickly, and pushed the car over the edge. They peered over the cliff, but in the dark could see nothing. They heard an almighty splash. Robbie took out a gardening fork from the boot of his car and carefully raised the turf to remove any trace of the car's tyre tracks. Stuart, meanwhile, repaired the wire fence. No one would ever know.

It was almost four o'clock in the morning as they drove through a deserted Gairloch, when Stuart said, 'There's something worrying me about all this, Dad.'

'What's that, son?'

'The Security Services must have heard about Mrs Platini's murder. They must have realised there was an Iraqi agent involved. Why didn't they do something about it? They should have told you, perhaps giving you and Kate twenty-four hour protection.'

It hadn't occurred to Robbie. He had been too close to the action, too busy worrying about Kate, too concerned about getting rid of the evidence. *My God, he's right. Why didn't they do anything?*

Stuart continued. 'I just can't help wondering if they wanted the Iraqi to succeed, and then arrest him afterwards to get some latter-day glory.'

'But that doesn't make any sense. Why rescue Kate from Iraq in the first place, just to let her be killed now?'

'I don't know, Dad. Unless... '

'Unless what?'

'Unless they rescued her to stop Saddam getting his hands on the weapons of mass destruction.' Stuart paused as they turned up their track to Glenfinnan.

'And?' prompted his father.

'Then they decided they wanted her dead to be able to claim Saddam has got the weapons of mass destruction.'

'Why would they do that?'

'To give them an excuse to complete the invasion of Iraq they suddenly stopped in February.'

'Why would they want to invade Iraq?' asked Robbie.

'That's easy, Dad. To get the oil.'

They tiptoed into the house. Robbie peered into their bedroom. Kate was sound asleep. Jed was lying next to her on the bed. He opened one eye, looked at Robbie and then closed it again.

They poured two whiskies and sat down. Stuart looked at his father. It had been a tiring ten hours. 'Dad, can I make a suggestion?' he said.

'Yes, of course.'

'I think you should do two things. Firstly, write down the whole experience of how you became involved with Kate as a book. Call it *A Nastia Game*. Print several copies. Give two to George Young in a sealed envelope marked, "To be sent to the Editors of *The Scotsman* and *The Sunday Post* in the event of the untimely death of either yourself or Kate". Give a copy to your bank manager and another to Kate's sister in New Zealand. Write a brief summary of the book and send it to MI6, telling them that there are many copies in various locations, but not saying where.'

'And the second thing I should do?'

'Marry Kate.'

Robbie laughed. 'I have been thinking about it,' he replied.

'Stop prevaricating, Dad. Get on with it. Take her to Gretna tomorrow.' Then, looking at his watch, 'No, I mean today.'

On Thursday, 25th July 1991, exactly thirteen years after being raped, the worst day of her life, Kate experienced the happiest. Kathryn Helena Jackson was married by special licence to Robert William MacKinnon.

EPILOGUE

Where are the Weapons of Mass Destruction?

During the summer of 1991, reports began to appear in the British and American press about soldiers suffering from what was labelled *Gulf War Syndrome*. Although its existence is still disputed by the British Government, the symptoms included breathing difficulties, skin infections, gastrointestinal problems and skin cancers: all similar to the effects of exposure to small amounts of anthrax. A US Senator, Donald Riegle from Michigan, decided to investigate the claims of *GWS*. His report would take three years to complete.

By 1992, sanctions and the imposition of no-fly zones were crippling Iraq and its peoples.

In 1993, Kate and Robbie attended Stuart's graduation ceremony at Edinburgh University. In 1994, Stuart completed his one year spell as a junior house doctor successfully. He decided he wanted to specialise in pathology and went to University College Hospital, London, to begin training.

In February 1994, *The Riegle Report* asserted that *GWS* did exist; it was caused by exposure to biological agents and that the agents had been exported to Iraq during the period 1981 to 1988 by the United States. The Report's annex listed over sixty occasions when toxins were exported by the US Department of Commerce.